THE COMPANION PROJECT

CHELSEA CURTO

To the women determined to upend the patriarchy.

And the men who stand by their side and hand them the match, happy to watch it burn.

FOREWORD

Hi friends!

If you're reading this past October 16th, 2022, it's a different version of what was previously published.

THE NEXT PARAGRAPHS CONTAIN A VAGUE SPOILER, SO PLEASE FLIP THROUGH IF YOU DO NOT WISH TO READ IT.

I love Henry and Emma a lot. When it got to the scene of their conflict, which you'll find toward the end of the book, the story went through several changes. What I originally published didn't sit right with me.

While there was no cheating or infidelity involved, and no physical interactions with the opposite sex occurred, some of Henry's comments teetered toward being inappropriate for a man in a relationship to say in a casual conversation with a female who is not his significant other.

I sat on the story for a week, but the longer I thought about it, the more I felt like what transpired would be hard to come back from. It would be hard to trust again. Yeah, it's a romance novel and plot lines are predictable, but I want this to be realistic. Emma is such a strong, dynamic character, and I didn't want to dim her down, brushing off the conflict like it was no big deal.

So, I went back in and edited it.

Chapters 39-41 differ vastly from the first edition of this book.

Chapter 42 is also changed.

Chapter 43 is altered to accommodate the larger changes in previous chapters.

Given that this is a dual POV book, we get in Henry's head a lot. As you read through the story, you see how much he cares for Emma—how much he's *always* cared for Emma. The additions and edits I made for the chapters are important to keeping that adoration intact without murking up the relationship the two of them have built hard to achieve.

Anyway, if you have questions, please send me a DM on social media and I'm happy to clarify! I was torn on including this additional author's note in the story. As someone who strives to have an honest, open branch of communication, I thought it was necessary.

Happy reading!

ONE

HENRY

I HAVE a one-way ticket to hell.

Satan and Hades will shake their heads in disgust when I descend the steps into the fiery Underworld, flames and heat licking my skin, marking my transgressions with permanent, well-deserved burns. They might as well push me headfirst into the waiting pit of lava. I deserve it for what I'm about to do.

"Henry? Did you hear me? You aren't avoiding my question, are you? Kathleen's daughter is so excited you're going to be at the party. We've been trying for years to coordinate you two spending time together."

"That won't be necessary, Mom. I have a date," I say through gritted teeth, pacing the carpeted floor in my large office, wishing the ground would swallow me up and teleport me far away.

The second the words leave my mouth, I regret saying them. The lie I've told my poor, unsuspecting mother slips out too easily, leaving behind a bitter residue. Her relieved sigh dances into my ear, a weight lifting off her aging and generously patient shoulders.

What I really want to do is chuck my brand new iPhone out the tenth-story window and jump out after it. A perfectly logical thing to do in a crisis of this magnitude.

"Finally," she replies, not bothering to mask her excitement. "Why didn't you mention her sooner? I'm so happy to hear things are going well enough with a partner for you to bring her! You're such a good man, Henry. It's time you get serious about your personal life."

It's half praise, half scolding, and I'm slightly offended by her implication that I might be alone forever, as true as it might be.

"I'm happy, too." My throat is constricting, closing up and making it difficult to breathe. I yank on my collar, trying to relieve some of the suffocating tension. "Mom, I have to run. I have a meeting this afternoon, and there's some work I need to finish up."

I'm a terrible liar, and the longer I talk to her, the more obvious it's going to be that I'm the worst son in the history of humanity. I can't have her calling my bluff before I figure out the shitstorm I threw myself into without thinking about the consequences.

"Okay, sweetie. Love you. Call us later this week. I'll send you the email with all the information. What's her name?"

"Will do. Love you, too." I deliberately ignore her parting question and hang up the phone, groaning loudly to my empty office. The four walls offer me no sympathy.

Of course I don't have a date for my parents' 40th anniversary party I've known about for months. That would be too easy. Too simple. Too logical.

I've never introduced a woman to my family. Up until this very moment, I never planned to. I'm content on dying alone; an old, wrinkly bachelor with an extreme disdain for relationships. My parents retired a few years ago—my father from the Massachusetts Supreme Court and my mother as a state representative —and it seems like all of Mom's attention has now been diverted to finding me a life partner. Gone are the days of filibusters and budget presentations, replaced with bi-weekly calls hounding me about my love life.

My purposely non-existent love life, mind you. A girlfriend and committed partnership are the last things I want.

With their questions about attending the party alone and repeated attempts to set me up with the daughter of a family friend, I panicked and said something stupid. So incredibly fucking stupid.

A curt knock interrupts my woeful, self-deprecating thoughts. Noah, one of my best friends, pushes my office door open and stares at me.

"What the hell happened to you? Are you okay?" he asks in lieu of a greeting, assessing my disheveled appearance. I've been running my hands nervously through my hair for the better part of thirty minutes. I can feel how askew it has become, hanging limply off to one side rather than settling into the neat style he's accustomed to seeing. I'm normally calm, cool, collected, and dressed to the nines. A perfect picture of a male in corporate, blood-sucking America.

Right now, however, I'm a complete and total mess on the precipice of a very real, very scary breakdown. It's an odd sensation, and I'm unexpectedly self-conscious *anyone* is seeing me like this. Even my best friend.

Noah and I have a standing lunch date for Wednesday afternoons, and it slipped my mind—again—that the week is halfway over. The forgetfulness happens far too often when I immerse myself in work; the days pass in the blink of an eye, blurring together, and I'm left wondering where all the time has gone and why my best friend is barging into my office like he owns the place.

I've known Noah for two decades. We played club basketball together growing up, becoming fast cohorts as lanky teenagers while we drank yellow Gatorade on the court sidelines. We parted ways after high school; he went to Harvard, and I went to Yale. We never lost touch over the years, both eventually moving back home to the city and picking up where we left off.

A successful, Black entrepreneur, he created a money transfer app a couple of years ago that became the most downloaded app in history for a week straight. After a feature on a national morning show and a commercial airing during the Super Bowl, his name exploded. Forbes Magazine recently named him one of the 40 Under 40 People to Watch in their latest issue.

To me, he's still the goofy, happy-go-lucky dude from when we were younger. Money and wealth haven't changed him. He also puts up with my shit remarkably well, while only tossing in a handful of sarcastic remarks at my expense. That's practically a second job.

"No, I'm not okay," I snarl, walking to my expensive desk chair and collapsing into it. I tilt my head back and stare at the ceiling, willing it to cave in and fall, crushing me in the rubble of decades-old popcorn material. "I'm fucked."

"Like, a good fucked? Or bad fucked?"

"Do you think I'd be this grouchy if it was a good fucked?" I ask flatly, bringing my chin down to give him a withering glare. He snickers, not even trying to hide his obvious amusement, and I throw a vulgar gesture his way.

"Point taken," he concedes, laughing. "You're more subdued and benevolent after you get laid, not a raging asshole who looks like he's about to chuck a stapler at my head."

"I am about to chuck a stapler at your head."

"Do you want to talk about this now or at the restaurant?"

"Restaurant, please." A change of scenery might help defog my brain and give me a clear idea of what to do. Or, at the very least, point me in the general direction of how to not fuck this up.

Spoiler alert: I'm going to fuck this up.

Majorly and epically.

There's no way this ends in anything other than an utter catastrophe. I just hope there aren't too many casualties.

Begrudgingly, I lean over the overpriced chair—that doesn't *really* help to relieve back pain despite boasting that it does—grab my charcoal gray suit jacket, and slip it over my tense shoulders.

"The nice receptionist brought me to your office, so you're going to have to get us out of here," Noah says breezily, stepping aside so I can lead the way down the hall.

"You've been here hundreds of times and you still don't know where my office is? Her name is Lisa, by the way. If you tried to call her that instead of her demeaning title, you might have more success. It's 2022. Why can't we use terms like office administrator instead?"

"Wow. You're trying to give me advice on how to interact with women? Bold move."

I ignore his jab, fastening the top two buttons of my blazer. "What should we get today? Pizza? Sandwiches? Ramen?"

"Ramen sounds amazing," Noah agrees, and we walk out to the main area of the office.

My company is the largest law firm in the city, so it's always bustling with people. You could come in on a Sunday afternoon and there will be someone working, clicking away methodically on their keyboard, trying to meet a deadline. The phone is constantly ringing, and the printer shoots off pages of documents one right after the other, paper littering the floor like confetti in Times Square on New Year's Eve.

If you're here at the right time, you might run into an up-and-coming athlete. Those are my clients. My specialty is Sports Law, focusing on contracts and helping to make sure rookies don't sign away their entire career because someone with no financial experience is giving them stupid advice. I also assure them they don't need four Lamborghinis on a starting salary, no matter what their friends they haven't spoken to in eight years might think.

"Hi, Noah." A feminine voice causes my head to jerk to the left, mimicking a neck spasm.

There's Emma Burns, a fellow attorney, sauntering over in a sleeved black dress, pantyhose, and pointed heels that barely bring her up to my chest. Her petite frame is accompanied by medium-length blonde hair, and the biggest, bluest eyes I've ever seen. They're the hue of ocean water; sparkling deep azure with a hint of faded green that sneaks through in the right lighting.

Noah stops walking and I have no choice but to halt next to him, nearly stumbling at the change in direction.

"Emma," he answers, flashing her a grin. We're going to be here for a minute. "How are you?"

She returns the smile eagerly, a full beam that stretches from ear to ear. The single gesture makes the whole space around us warmer and brighter. Emma is the office sweetheart, and right-fully so. She's smart, thoughtful, caring, and respectful, always jumping in to assist others in a time of crisis. She forms a close bond with everyone she interacts with.

We went to the same high school and never spoke over the course of four years, passing in the hallways like drifting ghosts haunting an abandoned mansion. I edged her out to be valedicto-rian our senior year, and that offense severed any ties of a poten-tial friendship with her down the road. We coexist in the office professionally and amicably, indulging in a rare sarcastic comment when the feeling strikes. And that's it.

There was never a great rift or apocalyptic fight. No one had a falling out. We aren't enemies or rivals. We're just not *friends* and haven't tried to remedy the awkwardness that's followed us to adulthood.

Despite being acquaintances for over a decade and a half, I know scant details about her. There's a small collection of facts I've learned and pieced together, however, forming little snap-shots of enlightenment into figuring out who Emma Burns really is.

I've discovered she's right-handed. She likes to be at work early, often arriving just past 7 a.m. She drinks two coffees a day—one in the morning, then a second midafternoon, after lunch. On Fridays, she brings in her own cup of caffeine, indulging in some concoction that's piled high with whipped cream instead of the communal brew in the break room.

Her favorite colors are purple and pink. She always wears the latter in some form on Wednesdays. Today, the choice is a head-band, and the pastel cotton candy shade is vibrant against her signature blonde. When I asked her about the color choice a year ago, she rolled her eyes and told me I wouldn't get the reference.

An outlandish statement, since it's blatantly obvious I've seen *Mean Girls* like everyone else on this planet. I don't live under a damn rock.

I can't explain why I notice these things about her. They're fairly unimportant observations. In the grand scheme of life, knowing my coworker's coffee order is filed under Things I Shouldn't Care About. But somehow, with her, I do.

It's fucking puzzling.

"I'm great, thank you. How are you?" The authenticity behind the question make me want to melt into a puddle. She's just so nice, probably moonlighting as a theme park princess in her off-time as another outlet for her kindness.

I forget Emma and Noah know each other outside of these brief run-ins. She practices Civil Rights law, and the two have worked together on a few cases in the past. For a split second, I wonder if they've ever been romantically involved, sharing a more intimate relationship that goes beyond casual conversation, spilling over to cozy nights in restaurants and early morning coffee dates, holding hands as they walk down the sidewalk.

I subtly try to observe their body language. Did she lean in closer to hear him speak? Is he smiling brighter now that she's here? Do her eyes sparkle like this all the time or only for certain people?

And what do I have to do to be one of them?

It's also not my place to care, not my place to be emotionally invested in what these two might do after hours, not my place to give a single flying fuck, yet something twinges in my stomach, while my hand flexes with unwarranted vexation.

"A little tired with work stuff, but still awesome. Would you like to join us for lunch?" Noah asks, even though the question is futile. I already know her answer. Emma's eyes go between the two of us in rapid succession, ping-ponging back and forth. She has yet to acknowledge me, and the glance is her first recognition I'm even standing here, taking up space as dutifully as a useless garden gnome.

"I appreciate the offer, but I have a salad in the fridge. You two have fun." She waves, not giving me a second look, and heads for her office on the opposite side from mine.

"I wish I knew why she likes you but couldn't care less about me," I mumble, jabbing the button for the elevator, needing to get out of this building. I'm close to exploding. My chest hurts, and fresh sweat blooms under my shirt, moisture causing the fabric to cling to my skin.

"Because I'm not weird and obnoxious around her," Noah replies brightly. He's enjoying this, reveling in my misery. "I didn't beat her out to be valedictorian. I also don't visit her office specifically to annoy her. Oh! I d—"

"Okay, I get it!" I interrupt, shaking my head and stepping into the blessedly empty elevator. "Thank you for providing the evidence that I'm a colossal jerk. It was more of a philosophical thought."

"God, you lawyers and your Descartes and Machiavellian bullshit."

"I don't think that's right. Descartes was in mathematics. Wrong field, my friend."

Ignoring me, he presses on. "You could try being nice to her. You know, asking how her day is? Making fun of her less? That shouldn't be challenging, even for a man with as little experience getting to know women as yourself."

"I don't make fun of her," I protest. "And trust me, I have no problem getting to know women."

"Banging them in the back of your truck doesn't count, H. Nice try. I seem to recall you making fun of Emma's reading glasses once upon a time. In fact, you called them the 'old librarian kind, and not the hot style.' You said that to her face, man. It's not your business what she wears. Women are free to express themselves without listening to the opinions of men."

I'm sure he's right. He's the expert at understanding women. I, however, prefer physical interaction and fucking over talking and thinking about the unknowable future. At the end of the night after a casual hook-up, the woman and I go our separate ways, parting on cordial terms, a pleased smile on their faces. I set boundaries early and communicate with them up front that I won't be falling in love with them or becoming their Romeo.

That's reserved for other guys. Guys like Noah.

Guys who will buy them flowers and sweep them off their feet. Guys who will remember favorite pizza toppings and colors, anxiously asking when they can meet the family or exchange apartment keys.

Not me. I want nothing to do with that shit.

The doors chime open and we exit onto the lobby floor, my muscles relaxing as we step away from the scene of my crime. We walk two blocks to the best Ramen restaurant in town, the light breeze filtering through the air calming me down, nerves unspooling like thread. On a typical day, my only glimpse of the sunshine is out of my large window when I'm pacing on the phone with a client. I make it to the office just as the sun is rising, and I rarely leave until after sunset.

These brief moments outside the box of gloom and despair become some of the best; a blessed reprieve from the monotony of a desk job. Moments like vitamin D slowly infiltrating my chilled blood. The sound of laughter and happiness. Smells other than whiteout and hours-old coffee beans.

It's cathartic.

Entering the restaurant, we take our usual booth in the back. We give our orders to the waitress and I lean back, grateful for the ice water she delivers seconds later. I gulp half of it down in one sip.

"Are you going to tell me what's going on?" Noah asks. "I haven't seen you this distraught since you were waiting for your bar results. It's freaking me out. This isn't like you. Is everything okay?"

The sincerity causes my lip to twitch. Compassion and loyalty are two of Noah's best qualities.

My finger traces the condensation of the sweaty glass up and down. "My parents' wedding anniversary is in two months. They're throwing a big party for all their friends and the extended family. It's four days of celebration."

"That sounds awesome. Remember the New Year's Eve party of 2018?"

The party? Not so much. I distinctly remember the aftermath, thanks to the alarming amount of tequila I consumed. I woke up under a pile of coats, my head throbbing for days. Noah, the bastard, was as spry as a spring chicken the next morning, telling me I missed out on the karaoke competition and my father attempting to do a keg stand. I've avoided tequila ever since; the smell alone makes me want to bury my head in the dirt.

"Awesome is not quite the adjective I'd use. You know how my parents have been hounding me for years about dating?"

"Yes…"

Every time I talk to my parents, the conversation inevitably circles back to my personal life. It doesn't help that my two siblings are happily married and steadily advancing down the path of life. Houses. Dogs. Children. I'm the lackluster loner rebelling against monogamy, trudging miles behind at a sloth's pace.

I'm 99% certain my mother asked Neil, one of my other best friends, and Noah, to set up an online dating account on my behalf a couple of years back. That got shut down real quick when I found out, appalled by the words they used to describe me. I am many things in life, but *sensitive* and *emotional* I am not.

"I might have mentioned to Mom I have a date for their party."

"Let me guess. You don't have a date," he draws out, not a hint of surprise at my fib.

"Correct. She's been trying to set me up with her friend's daughter for years. The girl thinks she can get me to sleep with her, knock her up, and take a check to the bank. She's only interested in four things: my money, my last name, my dick, and never having to work again in her life."

"You must be fucking fantastic in bed."

"Irrelevant. But for the record, I'm amazing. Five stars on Yelp. That woman doesn't care about me, and I overheard her saying as much to a friend at the last family shindig. So, I lied, and convinced Mom I have a date and to shut down the setup. She was so excited, telling me she can't wait to meet her, and it's about time I settle down. A guest room is probably getting converted into a nursery as we speak."

"I can't believe you lied to your mom, man! That's lame!"

"It slipped out unintentionally. If I could take it back, I would. I was pressured." My shoulders sag, sick over the lie already.

"Have you thought about, you know, *actually* finding someone to date? Someone not trying to extort you, obviously. That seems like the easiest solution."

"I don't have any potential prospects. Almost every woman I've been with in the past has been a one-and-done thing. You know I don't stick around after a night spent with someone."

"Ah, now the playboy needs something serious."

"I'm not a playboy!"

"You're a playboy. You've never had a girlfriend. You don't know how to have a girlfriend."

"That's not true! I dated Sally McCormick in eighth grade."

"And what happened?"

"I dumped her after eleven days when she told me she really liked me and put hearts in my yearbook. I wrote H.A.K.A.S in hers and never spoke to her again."

"See, playboy. And emotionally unavailable, too. Oh, and we can't forget you're someone who responds to confessed attraction by wishing the admirer a kick ass summer. Makes sense."

"Thank you, Dr. Reynolds," I grumble under my breath. "The unsolicited psychoanalysis of my past relationships and personality is always appreciated."

"Relationship. Singular. Barely. There hasn't been another one."

"Can you just tell me what should I do?"

He sits back in his chair and grins, muscular arms crossing over his chest as his eyes twinkle mischievously. "Believe it or not, I might have the answer to your prayers. Before you make any assumptions, let me get all the words out first. Do you remember my friend Jamal?"

"I think so. The football coach?"

"Yeah. He had an event he needed a last-minute date for, and he found out from another friend about this woman who offers her services to dudes who need someone by their side."

"I'm not following."

"She accompanies you to the event in whatever role you want her to play; girlfriend, colleague, scorned lover. Jamal said she was great. The best part is there's no intimacy involved, and it's all totally fake. You give her information about yourself, decide on a backstory, and voilà! A couple in love."

I stare at Noah, bewildered, taking a beat to answer. "I want to make sure I'm understanding this correctly. You're suggesting I pay someone to be my date."

"Precisely."

"To an event I told my mother I'm attending with a girlfriend."

"Mhm."

"Absolutely not."

"Why not?!"

"That's a terrible idea! What if she's a serial killer? Or money hungry? How the hell do you even fake a relationship?"

"From what Jamal told me, you get to know her through emails. She asks you lots of questions; what kind of event it is, basic details about your life. Then you meet in person before the event so it's not totally weird."

"You want me to email someone like we're fucking pen-pals? It's insane," I say, shaking my head.

"Whatever, man. Make fun of it all you want. It's your loss. A no strings attached agreement? It's right up your alley."

I bite my lip, mulling over his words.

It *is* insane.

But could it work?

It's only four days, not a lifetime. And whoever this woman is would go in knowing it was only a business transaction, not some fairytale happily ever after with roses and shit. I pay her. She accompanies me. I never hear from her again.

"You're sure it's legit?"

"Swear on our friendship."

"Fine, I'll take her number," I say before I can second-guess myself. If—and that's a very big if—I go through with this plan, it could potentially solve all my problems. It would get my mom off my back. I wouldn't have to hunt a woman down and jump into something unwillingly. I could write a check, suck it up for four days, then resume my lifestyle, exactly how I like it.

Alone.

Noah fiddles with his phone for a minute, mumbling under his breath while he scrolls. "Ah! Here it is! It's called RB's Companions. I'll text you the website."

An hour later, Noah bids me farewell with a tight hug, part of our standard goodbye. Screw the stigma around men being affectionate with their friends. "You feel better?" he asks, pulling away.

I nod, clasping him on the shoulder. "Yeah. Thanks for your help. I have some things to think about."

"I'll see you later this week for beers with the guys, right?"

"Yup, Friday night. See you then, bud."

After waving goodbye, I slink back to my office, resuming my position in the chair, and putting my head in my hands. I sigh, the heels of my palms pressing firmly into my eyes. I don't hear the knock on my door before it clicks open, too busy wallowing away over my poor life choices to pay attention to anything else.

A throat clearing causes me to look up, blinking away the

spots that have formed in my vision. I'm surprised to find Emma standing in my doorway, fidgeting.

"Hey, Burnsie. To what do I owe the pleasure?" I ask, grinning at her.

She's immune to my charm; it never works on her. Not even a hint of a smile crosses her lips when normally my voice would have a woman dropping to her knees. It's plagued me for years that I can't figure out why she just… doesn't care.

"A new inquiry just came through. Something about a baseball team and the recruit. It got sent to me when it clearly belongs to you." She walks to my desk, thrusting the paper in my direction.

I take it from her, eyes scanning the document. "Thanks for the delivery."

She backpedals toward the door, like she can't evacuate my office fast enough. "Are you okay?"

"Hm?"

"You look terrible. And not like yourself."

"Are you implying that I usually look very *not* terrible?" I wink at her and she rolls her eyes. "I'm fine. I did something stupid, and now I'm dealing with the aftermath. Don't worry, I'll survive."

She nods once; her back turning to me, signaling the end of our conversation. "Good. Have a nice day."

"You too, Emma. It's refreshing to know you'd miss me if I went off the deep end or something. For what it's worth, I'd miss you, too."

The door slams shut, windows shuddering in her wake as she disappears beyond the other side. I grin. That fucking fierceness gets me every time.

It's hard to explain, but the ephemeral moments when Emma gives me a fraction of her time are some of my favorite parts of the day. It's not that way with anyone else.

What the hell does that mean?

TWO

EMMA

TODAY IS GOING to be a good day.

I can feel it.

The first changing leaves of fall cover the sidewalk and crunch under my heels as I sidestep a split in the concrete, narrowly missing stumbling off the curb. The sun's rays are starting to peek out from behind the surrounding buildings, making way for the warmer, brighter parts of Thursday.

It's perfect.

As an attorney, my occupation can be brutal at times: enduring grueling hours and little to no communication with the outside world as I spend all my time behind a computer or with my nose buried in paperwork, heart-wrenching cases constantly flooding my desk. None of the work I do is *fun*, and after a while, it begins to take a toll on even the strongest people.

Out here, under the cloudless sky being roused awake by the morning light, I'm reminded to find the good in every day. Sometimes I have to look hard, searching high and low through all the negativity and pain, but I always discover it; even if it's in the least likely of places.

Sometimes those are the best surprises.

Stopping in front of the glass door to my building, I check my reflection one last time before grabbing the handle and pulling it open.

"Morning, Miss. Emma!" Reginald, the morning security guard, greets me warmly like always, voice carrying over the atrium.

"Hey, Reggie!" I answer, tossing him a smile. "How're you doing?"

"I woke up. There's air in my lungs. The sun is shining. How can I complain?"

"I wish everyone saw the world like you. It would be a better place."

"Anything exciting happening up on ten today?"

"Nothing out of the ordinary! Hopefully everyone stays out of trouble."

"Speaking of trouble, Mr. Dawson is already here. He doesn't seem to be in a particularly good mood, either."

"Still? Thanks for the heads up, Reggie." With a wave, I head for the elevators, hitting the button for the tenth floor and riding up.

I wonder if Henry's attitude is related to the sour mood yesterday. He's typically a ray of sunshine to everyone he encounters. Bubbly and energetic. Loud and boisterous. He had an air of indifference about him after his lunch with Noah, though, when I stupidly ended up in his office. There was a heaviness in his movements, and he seemed worried and anxious. The unusual behavior was off-putting, perplexing, and, as much as I hate to admit it, concerning.

The elevator doors open to the tenth floor and I stand on my toes, peering over cubicles and half-walls, noticing the light on in his corner office. I gnaw on my lip, weighing the pros and cons on if I should approach him again.

No.

I don't need to make popping in to check on him part of my routine. He can figure out his problems by himself.

Turning on my heel, I head for my own office. When I see my

space, I smile. My Columbia Law degree proudly hangs on the wall in a gold frame. It's the first thing your eyes find when you enter the space. The placement was intentional; when I'm frustrated or overwhelmed, plagued by thoughts of professional inadequacy, I look at that single piece of paper and remember *why* I'm doing what I do, swatting away any pesky Imposter Syndrome that lingers around on the tough days. I'm reminded of how hard I worked to get here. The fulfillment I experience whenever I complete another case, success not measured by the numbers on my paycheck but rather the number of people I help. It brings me comfort to know I'm doing good in the world.

My large desk takes up most of the carpeted floor, an oversized, antique monstrosity that was too heavy to move after being abandoned by the previous occupant. A small bookshelf sits in the corner, housing some of my favorite legal books and memoirs, ranging from RBG—may her memory be a blessing—to Bryan Stevenson. All my personal literature is tucked away at home, safe from the prying eyes of my colleagues. They don't need to see the fantasy and romance novels I indulge in during my rare time off, escaping away from reality to a fictional world far better than this one.

I fire up my laptop and gray Mac monitor, scanning the full inbox waiting for me. The number never seems to go down, despite how quickly I answer inquiries; a never-ending cycle of not enough time in the day to accomplish all my tasks. It's impossible to keep up.

The last step in my routine is admiring the view out my window, an expanse of construction, cranes, and newly placed steel greeting me. The moment of peace passes far too quickly as I get to work; off to make a difference, even if it's not noticeable yet.

One day, it will be.

———

"Emma?"

I blink, attention shifting from my monitor to the woman standing in front of me. The warmth and brightness in the room suggest morning has dissipated, leaving behind early afternoon. I rub my eyes, adjusting to the new lighting. I've been so focused on my computer, half the day has passed by.

"Hey, Lisa!"

Lisa is the firm's administrative assistant and one of three other women I work with. We bonded over the lack of female representation within the company one night over wine when I awkwardly asked if she wanted to hang out. We've been fairly close ever since, trading gossip and secrets while giggling over what comically stupid things the men in our office have said and done.

"Sorry. I knocked three times and didn't get an answer." She offers me an apologetic smile.

"I was zoning out as usual. What's up?"

Lisa shifts on her feet, bouncing back and forth on her red heels, purchased on an impromptu shopping trip we embarked on together a few months ago. They look eye-catching on her long, lean legs. I got a matching pair that are slightly higher, and not an article of clothing I can parade around in at work thanks to my short stature. If a man wears new shoes, no one bats an eye. If a woman changes up her look, the questions and unwarranted comments start rolling in.

It's bullshit, honestly.

"Wallace wants to see you."

My spine stiffens and I sit up straight in my chair, a pocket of apprehension settling into the depths of my stomach. "Did he say what it was about?"

"No. If it's any consolation, he didn't seem mad."

"Okay. When is he expecting me?"

"He said whenever it's convenient."

That's code for Right Now. I'm already late.

"Perfect. I'll head in." I stand, hoping my voice conveys a sense of calm and not the terror I'm currently experiencing.

"He asked for Henry, too."

Apprehension morphs into trepidation and fear, covering me in an invisible cloak of nerves. "Lovely," I croak, my throat suddenly dry and scratchy. "Can't wait."

I try to squash the anxiety zipping through me as I stride down the hall, hesitating for a fraction of a second outside Wallace's office. Steeling myself, I knock with confidence. I'm good at my job, dammit, and I have no reason to be afraid.

"Come in."

I open the door, greeted with the sight of Henry sitting in a chair, his ankle resting on the knee of his other leg and wearing a smirk on his face. Guess we're back to carefree and aloof, the rigidity that encompassed him yesterday long gone.

"Emma! Come in! Take a seat!" Wallace motions toward the free chair and I slip into it ungracefully, perching on the edge.

"You wanted to see me, sir?" I ask. I can *feel* Henry's piercing gaze on me, eyes burning my skin as they watch me cross my legs and fold my hands into my lap.

"Indeed. I haven't shared this news with anyone else yet. Richards is planning on retiring next month."

"I'm sorry to hear that," I offer, unsure of how to react to the departure of one of the four partners of our firm.

"I'm not. I won't have to hear about the stupid sailboat he's going to buy anymore." Wallace leans back in his chair and steeples his fingers together. "With him gone, we'll have a partner spot opening up."

The world around me freezes. Henry's posture shifts, both of his feet now firmly planted in a more professional, dignified pose.

"What does that mean exactly, sir?" Henry asks, his low, gravely voice causing me to shiver involuntarily.

He sounds different whenever he's speaking about a serious topic; the tone drops an octave and his inflection becomes stern. Commanding. Like he could demand the attention of a crowded football stadium and they would all listen. I wiggle in my chair at the change.

"It means we're going to be looking for someone to take on his role. You two are my top candidates."

I blink, unsure if I heard him correctly. "Pardon?"

He's considering *me* and *Henry* to replace a man who's been with the firm for 20 years? Partner positions are rare and nonexistent. Offering one to a person with less than a decade of experience is preposterous and unheard of, especially at a firm this size. It never happens.

"The two of you are the best of the best here. You do solid work. You have experience and you're well liked in your respective fields. Over the next few months, a review board and outside personnel will determine who's the best fit. I know you work in different specialties, so they're looking for success rates, feedback from clients, and adaptability to your environment. Among other things."

Holy shit.

"This is such a high honor. Thank you for the opportunity." I manage to get the sentence out without sounding like a complete idiot.

"An unaffiliated, unbiased board is going to select the best candidate. We'll schedule a couple of formal interviews soon. This isn't a competition. We want a good fit, whoever that might be. And please, keep this confidential for the time being. I'm going to make an announcement soon. That's all for today." Wallace turns his attention to his phone, ending our conversation. Resisting the urge to sneak a glance at Henry, I stand, hurrying to the exit.

I'm halfway down the hall before I hear Wallace's door snick closed. I beg my legs to move faster, determined to reach my office without sprinting. Henry, however, has other plans, his long limbs taking half the time to cover the ground I've scurried from, blocking my door and facing me as I reach for the doorknob. My hand grazes his hip as he mercilessly impedes my path.

He peers down at me, a youthful smile that shouldn't belong to a man in his early thirties overtaking his face. His chocolate brown eyes crinkle in the corners, the only indication of his age.

"Not so fast, Emma," he purrs.

Goosebumps erupt on my arms from the poisonous and deadly prose. My body despairingly seeks an antidote for the salacious, sultry way my name sounds tumbling from his treacherous lips, a mix of friendly teasing and heated authoritativeness lacing the words.

"Can I help you with something, Henry?"

The wobble at the end of my question isn't intentional, but my brain is scattered. I feel an overwhelming sense of confusion staring at the man in front of me.

I don't want to scream. I don't want to yell. I want to listen, gnawing on my bottom lip and adjusting my footing as I wonder *what the hell* he has to say.

The thought might plague me until the end of time.

Leaning back against the wood, in no rush to leave, Henry crosses his arms over his chest, taking up far too much of the diminishing free space around us.

He wears business attire extremely well. The navy-blue suit accents his stormy eyes, and I have to look away to avoid being sucked into that cataclysmic gaze. He must tailor the material to hug his every curve, flaunting what I imagine is an obnoxiously perfect physique.

"Looks like we're going up against each other. It feels just like yesterday we were neck and neck for valedictorian, doesn't it? We both recall how that ended."

Yeah, we do. With him on stage giving the keynote speech that should have been mine while I sat in the audience, watching from afar, ambitions foiled by the dark-haired devil in front of me.

"This is my dream job," I say, adding as much conviction behind the statement as possible. "I will do whatever it takes to earn it, and I don't care if your poor, fragile male ego doesn't survive."

Henry hums, trying—and failing—to suppress a smile. "What if I want you to get it, Burnsie?"

Bravely taking a step closer to him, my pointer finger presses into the center of his chest, met with firm muscles hiding deceptively under the soft fabric.

Dang it.

I was right. Obnoxiously perfect.

I try to not let the distraction deter me.

"You're lying."

"Am I?" he asks, tilting his head to the side. His shoulders hunch, shrinking in size, and the height change brings us mere centimeters apart. Our breaths mingle together as one, and it's indiscernible to decipher where I stop and Henry starts. "Maybe nothing would make me happier than watching you succeed."

I raise my chin, refusing to falter at his proximity or the way I can count the trail of light freckles dancing across the bridge of his perfectly aligned nose. How this near to him, I can see the laugh lines outlining his mouth, years of happiness etched on his face.

Henry pauses his verbal onslaught, eyes taking a moment to traverse over the expanse of my face like he's studying a roadmap or difficult math problem.

He's never looked at me like this before.

It's intimate. Questioning. Alarming.

And... heart-stopping. My pulse quickens the longer his attention stays on me.

"You don't mean that," I whisper. I can smell him, traces of peppermint and pine, with a faint hint of spice clinging to his body. It's a lethal combination that mystifies the hell out of me. I shouldn't be inhaling deeper, the scent whirling through me, eager for *more, more, more.* Yet here I am, leaning a fraction of an inch closer to his sturdy stature, wondering if he would catch me if I fall.

These musings are new and unfounded. His charm *never* works on me, but for some unexplainable reason, it's as if I'm under a spell, brought on by Henry's hands.

"Maybe I do," he continues. "Or maybe I'm going to relish in competing against you, head-to-head. It's always been my favorite game."

"I will go to war for this. I'm not going to yield. I'm not afraid."

He grins, wide and bright, and I feel it deep within my soul.

For the first time, I realize we could kiss if we wanted to. He'd have to shuffle forward one step. I'd have to stand on my tiptoes. And then it could happen, our lips fusing together like our previous battles, a fight of wit and skill.

A feather-light puff of air caresses my cheek and I rear back, startled, plummeting to reality. I put my hand on his chest and *push*, trying to get away.

Henry, to his credit, doesn't crack a joke. Doesn't smirk. Doesn't laugh. His gleefulness disappears as he stares at me, eyebrows pinching together.

A coldness washes over me. The contact between us snaps in half, leaving me rattled and displaced.

And empty.

As if a part of me is missing, and I'm no longer whole.

"I know you'll put up a valiant fight, Emma. You always do."

Before I can retaliate or process if what he said was sarcastic or sincere, Henry disappears, leaving me alone outside my office, watching him walk away for longer than I care to admit.

"Okay, what the hell is going on? You're drinking a martini with a stupid ass grin on your face. You never agree to dinner reservations before 7 because work always comes first. Did you get laid?" My best friend, Nicole, asks later that evening. She's sitting across from me, anxiously awaiting my news.

We've known each other for decades, growing up next to each other, and our friendship continued into adulthood. She's always the first to know anything that happens in my life, so when I cryptically texted her earlier in the day after the meeting in Wallace's office and asked if she was free for to meet up, I had to ignore seven missed calls and a barrage of messages demanding I tell her what was going on.

I laugh, shaking my head. "I freaking wish. No. This is more important. Wallace pulled me into his office today and told me I'm being considered for partner," I squeal.

"What? Holy shit, Emma! That's amazing! Congratulations," she exclaims, reaching across the table to squeeze my hand.

"Thank you! There's a caveat, though."

"Please don't tell me that dickbag asked you to sleep with him."

"Ew, stop it, no! That is not a picture I need in my head. Henry is the other person being considered."

Nicole flops back in the booth, frowning. "Of course he is. Instead of giving the position to the overqualified, lone woman in the office, he has to make you compete against another douchebag who doesn't deserve the spot."

"I know. It's frustrating as hell, but this is the opportunity of a lifetime and not a competition."

"With you and Henry, it's always a competition."

"That's not true!"

"Emma, you wrote angsty LiveJournal entries about him. Don't try to deny the poem titled 'Broken Dreams by Your Hands' isn't referencing Henry Dawson. I remember you lamenting about him winning valedictorian after you got the only A- of your academic career. He snatched the accolade out from under your nose. This is another notch on your battle belt. Who will get hurt this time?"

"Okay, no one is going to die. I'm sure Henry will stoop to his usual immature antics: taking the paper I like from the printer, making sure the file folders are out of my reach on the top shelf, and covering my door with Post-It notes. Once Wallace realizes how unprofessional he's acting, the position will be mine."

I never retaliate to his pranks which drives him up a wall. It's as if he wants me to engage with him, seeking out ways to get my attention. I'm not naive enough to think he's attracted to me. He's simply not used to someone rejecting him and is persistent as hell. I, meanwhile, get immense joy out of befuddling him. Someone needed to put him in his place, and I'm glad it can be me.

"You're good," she says slyly. "You're going to let him self-implode."

"He may charm some people, but that shit doesn't work on me. It hasn't for years. Two months of his stupidity will be worth it if it means becoming partner."

"You're so deserving of this, Emma!"

I blush bashfully. "Thanks, Nic. I've worked really hard. It's important for girls and women to know we can do anything we set our minds to, and we're equally qualified to do any job a man is. If not more so."

She raises her drink in my direction. "To all the badass women out there. Anything men can do, we can do better!"

"Here, here," I agree, clinking my glass against hers.

THREE

HENRY

"WILL someone please tell me what the hell is going on?" My best friend, Neil, asks, taking a swig of his beer. "Rebecca and I had a fight this morning and I've already apologized a million times. The sex is going to be incredible when I get home."

My group of friends and I are squished together in a booth at our favorite local restaurant, which is an arduous task given all but one of us over six feet tall.

After the news from Wallace today, I frantically messaged the gang asking if we could meet up tonight instead of our usual Friday night plans. The speculation started flooding in, and I'm on the edge of my seat, waiting to share the news.

Patrick, the second member of our group, rolls his eyes. "For once, I'd like to get through a night without hearing about your sex life. You talk about it so frequently, it's like we're there with you. And trust me, that's not something any of us want."

"At least you haven't walked in on them doing it," Jack, another buddy, grumbles. "I'm scarred for life."

Neil snorts. "My ass is divine, Lancaster. Besides, it's not my fault someone has the hots for their best friend and refuses to do anything about it. Being bitter isn't a cute look, Walker."

Patrick throws up both of his middle fingers. "Contrary to

popular belief and your small-ass brain, men and women can have a platonic relationship and not sleep with each other. Lola and I have never done anything physical, and I'm not arguing about this with you again."

"Doesn't mean you don't think about it."

"We aren't here to talk about me." Patrick's life-long friendship with Lola is always a frequent topic of debate amongst our group, and I know he hates when she gets brought up. "This is Henry's 911 Bro Call."

Our 911 Bro Calls, while carrying a pathetic name, are sacred. When enacted, the five of us do our best to drop everything and meet up immediately, knowing an important decision or announcement is about to take place. Patrick, Jack, Noah, and Neil have all initiated one in the last three years. This is my first time, and I'm sweating bullets.

"Sorry I'm late," Noah says, sliding into the empty chair at the head of the table, the last to arrive. "What did I miss?"

"I have an announcement to make," I start, taking a deep breath.

"You're pregnant."

"You're dying."

"You got someone pregnant."

"You killed someone," Jack says flatly.

"Wait. Shit. What do lawyers do when *they* need a lawyer?"

"I think they'd get their own lawyer. Right?" Patrick doesn't sound too convinced.

"Are you all finished?" I huff, anxious to share. They all nod in unison, and I break out into a grin. "I'm being considered for partner at my firm."

The guys are silent for two seconds before they erupt in boisterous cheers, loud enough for the surrounding patrons to crane their necks, trying to find the source of the outburst.

"Holy shit!"

"Congratulations, H!"

"That's well deserved, man!"

"So proud of you!"

It's five minutes of their hands clasping my shoulder, ruffling my hair, and hooting excitedly. When they finally settle down, I begin speaking again.

"Wallace told us today and the decision is going to come in the next couple of months. I'm already stressed out. I bet we both are. There's going to be interviews, an outside board, reviews. It's a lot to process."

I rub my temples, the intensity of what lies ahead hitting me. I've gone through a whirlwind of emotions today, ranging from elated and honored to horrified and nauseous. I like to think I'm good at what I do—my success rate and client feedback justifies that assumption—but self-doubt frequently lurks around, paralyzing me with fear.

I hate that slithery awareness of insufficiency. Of thinking I might not be good enough. Of competing against an equally qualified individual. Of all the negative thoughts that have trumped any positivity I've experienced the last six hours.

"Hang on. You said we. And us. Clarification, please?" Jack asks.

"I'm, uh, up for the position, but so is another person. It's Emma. Emma Burns."

"Em? No shit," Noah laughs. "That's kind of cute. It's like the universe is begging you two to get together."

"Whoa. What the hell are you talking about?"

"I'm a big believer in everything happening for a reason, Hen. Call it fate. Call it luck. But you two going after the same job? Sounds like a good story to me."

"Are you implying I have—Jesus Christ, I can't believe I'm saying this out loud—feelings toward Emma?"

Noah shrugs, unbothered by the raised pitch of my voice. "I'm not implying anything. Just an interesting observation."

"Well you can shut up, because it's unequivocally not true. I don't feel anything toward her physically, and I would appreciate it if you would stop insinuating as much. We're colleagues. Nothing more. That's it."

The exception to that statement is our moment in the hallway today after the meeting with Wallace. Me, pinned against the door. Emma, inches away, blinking up at me through long eyelashes. Something was *different*. There was a shift. A murmur traveled through the hallway, static energy cackling between us. I had the urge to pull her into my arms, bury my face in her golden hair, and hug her tight.

She was so close, I could smell her shampoo and soap. It was a delicious mixture of apples and sweet vanilla, the sweet scents tickling my nose and causing me to hastily flee in a panic, seeking refuge in my office the rest of the afternoon, afraid to get close to her again.

"Earth to Dawson."

A napkin gets thrown at my face and I blink, the recollection of our encounter fading away into a hazy memory.

"Sorry. I'll go grab us a fresh round. Be back soon." Sliding out of the booth, I walk to the bar, waiting my turn behind a woman who's leaning over the counter. I can only see the back half of her, but *damn* it's a nice half.

Her jeans hug her hips and ass in all the right spots as she stands on her tiptoes, bare shoulders displaying freckles up and down her arms. I glance at her left hand, grinning when I see it empty of a ring. A familiar tug draws me in, like I've experienced this woman before in some capacity. Instinctively, I step forward, approaching her, a moth to a flame.

"Hey, gorgeous," I say near her ear, resting my elbow on the counter.

My greeting initiates a frenzy of spinning and drink spilling. Half the contents of her cup end up on my jeans as her hip rubs against my upper thigh.

"Can I help you with so—Henry?"

It's not just any woman standing here.

It's Emma.

Gaping at me while looking like a fucking angel made out of sunshine.

An angel with an ass that's perfect and round.

An angel that looks like she might murder me.

What the hell?

"Sorry about that. I thought you were someone else." I toss her what I hope is a believable lie, wincing at how stupid it sounds.

"Someone else? Do you frequently accost women waiting for drinks who want nothing to do with you?" she snaps. The beverages in her hands slosh over the side and into the crevice between her thumb and pointer finger. It's the same finger she jabbed into my chest earlier, the press of her fingertip still embedded in my muscles.

"I can assure you I didn't know who you were. If I had, I would have gone down to the hot bartender and not wasted another second on an inevitable rejection. You're far from my type."

An emotion akin to disappointment and hurt flashes through her blue eyes. It's so subtle, so covert, I can't legitimize it actually happening. Then, she blinks, and the fire returns, blazing hotter than before.

"What are you even doing here? Don't you have a woman to be with?"

"Jealous?" I ask. "I'm with my buddies tonight. We're celebrating. Kind of a big day and all. What are you doing here?"

"I'm with my friend. Also celebrating," she fires back.

That bite in her tone is something else. I've always fucking loved and appreciated how feisty she gets. Emma is never meek or submissive, and I enjoy her tenacity, even when it's directed at me.

"Look at us both celebrating. Sounds like the start of a great movie." I grin. "Maybe we'll fall in love and live happily ever after. How many kids should we have? Three? Four? You want a house with a white picket fence?"

I'm pushing her buttons, teetering way too close to a dangerous ledge without a safety restraint, unable to stop.

Why the fuck am I asking her these questions?

Does she really want a white picket fence?

Would she prefer an apartment or condo?

How about a yard?

And why the fuck do I care?

The confusion swirls with the unresolved conundrum from earlier when I accidentally admitted I'd be happy to watch her succeed in the role.

It was the truth, not some bullshit said in jest to rile her up. She'd never believe me, though, so I didn't bother arguing when she insisted as much.

"Just… leave me alone, Henry," She huffs out, pushing past me. Her elbow digs into my side. "You can dream about a house all you want. The last thing I would ever do is fall in love with *you.*"

"Famous last words," I bark out without any bite, turning back to the bar so I don't have to watch her walk away. Nodding my thanks for the prepared drinks, I grab the tray and shuffle back over to the guys, plopping the fresh round on the table and trying to ignore how the knowledge of Emma being somewhere nearby rattles my thoughts, disrupting my focus.

"Took you long enough," Neil says, taking his beverage.

"I need some advice," I admit, rubbing my jaw. "I'm aware I've acted childish in the office and I want to spend the next two months being better."

"I know firsthand how it might be enjoyable and fun to annoy certain people in the workplace. Hell, I taunted Jo daily after she closed the elevator doors in my face," Jack says, smiling secretly into his glass. He's so infatuated with his girlfriend, it's not even worth making jokes about them anymore. "And, sure, it was my pathetic attempt at flirting and getting her attention, but it didn't have a purpose. It didn't benefit anyone. If you want to be taken seriously, maybe lay off the pranks and jokes."

I nod in agreement. "I see exactly what you mean. Any other suggestions?"

"It might be beneficial to watch what you say around other people," Noah suggests. "Commenting on a woman's looks unprovoked is teetering toward antagonizing and sexist."

My mouth falls open. "You think I'm sexist?"

"No, I don't think you're sexist. Remarks about, say, a woman's glasses is a good example. Calling an article of clothing *hot* or *not hot* is fairly derogatory. Words matter, H. Keep that shit out of your professional life. And your personal life, too."

Repulsion and shame inch down my spine as my neck heats. I take a sip of my drink to stop the mortification. "Fuck. I didn't think of it like that. I always thought it was in good fun, you know? Something to laugh about. But... Jesus, I don't want to bully anyone. That's gotta change immediately."

"Acknowledging and being willing to try something different is a step in the right direction," Patrick says kindly. "None of us think you're an asshole, and if you said something in our talks that was inappropriate, we would call it out. But stopping off-handed comments like Noah mentioned is a good idea."

"I never recognized how those words might make someone feel." I hang my head, pinching the bridge of my nose. "It would probably be smart to put some distance between me and Emma."

"I didn't think you two were... What's the romance trope the girls like?"

"Enemies-to-lovers," Neil supplies, and Jack nods.

"Right. That. Don't you two get along fairly well?"

I shrug. "Yeah, I guess. It's hard to describe the dynamics of our office life. We don't interact a whole lot. When we do, it's strictly professional. There's no sexual chemistry. There's barely any friend chemistry. Is she a good-looking woman? Yeah, she is. But I don't want to bang her over my desk or anything."

"All the desk banging spaces have been taken by Jack and Jo," Patrick says smugly, lightening the mood. Jack chokes on his drink.

"You fucker," he mumbles. "I told you that in confidence. Joke all you want, but it's hot as hell. Even better with windows."

"Windows?" I repeat, grinning. "Lancaster has moves. That is hot."

"Jo dubbed me as a stern brunch daddy once, whatever the fuck that is. She spends so much time on Instagram looking up book accounts, I'm terrified to learn what the nickname means."

"She calls you daddy?!"

"Once. She whispered in my ear, 'I want you to make me come, daddy,' then burst out laughing. Like, full-on tears and wouldn't stop giggling. I've learned that when the woman of your dreams wants to try something new in bed, whether that be positions, places, or names, you fucking listen. And then you laugh with her and vow to never do it again."

"Wow," I say, impressed. "Should I be taking notes? Is Jack really the best one out of all of us? When did I lose my groove?"

"Didn't you hook up with someone last night?" Patrick asks and I smile fondly at the memory from twenty-four hours ago.

Yeah, I did hook up with someone last night. Brianna. I was so worked up from the conversation with my mom and Noah's suggestion about hiring someone to take to the party, I needed to work out my frustrations. Lucky for me, the brunette was more than willing to help.

It definitely put me in a better mood. Her sucking my dick and smiling up at me with a mouthful of my cum helped me forget the stress from earlier in the day. It's amazing what an orgasm or two can do. I was so blissed out when I woke up this morning—alone of course—like I had returned from a lengthy yoga retreat, good as new.

"Uh oh," Jack says. "He's got that look."

"Just daydreaming about blindfolds. Anyway, these suggestions have been helpful. I'm really fucking excited for this opportunity, and I don't want to mess anything up."

"Hooking up with your coworker would definitely mess it up," Neil warns me. "So don't get any ideas."

I roll my eyes. "I do know how to keep my dick in my pants, believe it or not. No one is hooking up with anybody. Why is it so hard to think I don't possess any sort of feelings for Emma?"

"Because we know you. And you like everyone."

"Yeah, well, I don't like her," I say quickly, sipping my drink.

Something rumbles in my chest at the statement, like a beast clawing to get free. My hand becomes sweaty, nearly losing its grip on my glass. The sensation is almost debilitating, its motive for arrival untraceable.

I don't *like her*, I repeat to myself, hoping it sounds more emphatic this time around.

Out of the corner of my eye, I see Jack watching me, his lips pursing together like he's seconds away from calling me out. Dipping my chin, I shake my head. It would do me good to focus on this potential promotion and not *Emma*.

For some reason, I can't get her out of my fucking mind.

And I don't hate it as much as I should.

FOUR

EMMA

IT'S Friday and I'm in *love*.

This week has utterly drained me. My mental battery is depleted and in desperate need of a recharge. My body aches, muscles I didn't even know existed throb painfully, screaming at me to go to the gym and use them so they aren't overexerted and underworked. My eyes hurt from staring at computer screens, straining and squinting to dampen the blue light shining in my face for hours on end. Reading glasses do nothing to help, either.

In the eight days since Wallace shared the partner news, I've let work consume my life more than it already does. I'm knocking out my to-do list more swiftly and effectively than ever before. I kind of feel like Wonder Woman. Badass. Heroic. Ready to exhaustedly take on the world.

The backlog of cases and files I need to get through is rapidly dwindling, and, at this rate, I won't know what to do with my twelve-hour shifts soon. I might have a second to actually breathe.

The gargantuan workload is only half the battle I'm fighting.

The other half?

Henry.

Quizzical, confusing, way-too-freaking-good-looking Henry Dawson.

He's been suspiciously quiet this week. The interaction we share has shrunk to insubstantial and nonexistent. I even went out of my way yesterday, meandering over to his side of the building to check and make sure he's still alive because all signs point toward him disappearing into thin air. Correspondence that he might have personally delivered to me, using the chance to goad me into hearing a joke or being subjected to his pointless, never-ending stories I've learned to tune out, has gone through Lisa, who's equally perplexed.

If it weren't for the light on in his office when I get to work and still glowing into the late-hours of the evening when I slog home, I'd assume he had fallen off the face of the earth.

I keep checking over my shoulder, literally, waiting for the other shoe to drop and for him to give up this reformed act. To stop whatever game he's planning and crack, the usual goofiness prevalent again.

Strangely enough, nothing comes.

I didn't even see him leaving for lunch with Noah on Wednesday, and I know that's a long-standing tradition, one they haven't missed in years.

A rational individual would deduce Henry is finally evolving. Maturing and starting to act professional and dignified, the rowdy behavior a thing of the past.

I'm not entirely convinced.

I think he has ulterior motives, trying to appear like the perfect paradigm of what a partner of a prestigious law firm *should* be while simultaneously plotting a hostile takeover of the position, ready to swoop in and steal it out from under my nose with a nonchalant shrug of his shoulders. It's in my nature to consider all sides of a problem, and Henry Dawson is, without a doubt, a big freaking problem.

Walking into my house after another strenuous week, I sigh in relief as the door shuts firmly behind me. I kick off my shoes in the small foyer before heading to the kitchen. Pulling out leftovers from the night before, I pop the plate into the microwave, set the timer, and grab my personal laptop.

Scanning my email, my eyes catch on an unread message waiting for me. I double click it open.

To: RBCompanions
From: JD7683
Subject: New Inquiry
Date: September 1

Hi, there.

I hope this isn't weird, but a friend of mine gave me your information, and I have a few questions.

I have a family gathering in six weeks I need to attend. The itinerary spans from Wednesday to Sunday. Do you do multi-day events? If it's not part of your typical package, I'd be happy to pay extra for it. Just name the price.

I'm nervous to send you this message. Maybe you're not real, and my friend is messing with me. He'd get a kick out of that.

I debated hitting send for thirty minutes. A glass of whiskey later, here we are. Close to pleading for help. I'm sure I sound like a lunatic, and for that, I apologize. I'm not always like this, I promise.

Thanks,

JD

The email is referencing my super private, super secret company, RB's Companions, founded thanks to the American education system being wildly expensive and borderline unaffordable. The debt I, like many students, amassed over the course of my undergraduate education and law school tenure was demoralizing. I almost fainted when I saw the amount of my loans; the number had far too many zeros while my bank account had far too few.

How the hell do people outright pay a number that high without any assistance?

Between what I owed for seven years of school, living expenses, and a meager starting salary, I discovered I needed to figure out a plan to help with my finances and start searching for a supplemental income so I could afford to eat dinner.

I found a part-time job on the weekends out of law school, quickly learning it hardly earned me enough money to cover the gas it took to drive to and from the clothing store.

Joining an MLM pyramid scheme and selling products to people I haven't talked to since high school was out, and I didn't want to sell an organ.

Running out of ideas and close to panicking, a friend from law school invited me to attend a banquet with him to cheer me up. Little did I know dinner in a crowded conference room would be what changed my life.

"You're an awesome date," Matthew exclaimed over champagne. It wasn't flirtatious—he was gay—and while we didn't share a romantic attraction, we enjoyed each other immensely.

"Is it because I know how to sit quietly on your arm and smile real pretty?"

"Stop!" he laughed, bumping my shoulder. "I'm serious! You're great at holding conversations, and, no matter who you talk to, you're genuinely interested in learning about them. I don't know how you fake it so well. If I have to hear one more story about that woman in the hat's taxidermy collection, I might saw my ears off a la Vincent van Gogh."

"Wow. That's extremely aggressive," I joked with a chuckle. "I don't know; I've always enjoyed talking to other people. Learning their stories and history. It comes naturally, I guess."

"Have you ever considered doing something like this on the side? In addition to the soul-sucking path of corporate America?"

"What do you mean? I love my job."

"Trust me, Em, I know you do. I'm talking about people hiring you to accompany them to events. Weddings, galas, banquets… All of it."

"That sounds like a logistical nightmare. How in the world would I pull it off? How would they know who I am? And I would charge them? For what?"

"There's this thing called the internet. Maybe you're familiar with it? People always need a date to things. Set up a website and see what happens. I bet you could pay your debt off in a few years just by escorting people places. I, on the other hand, will be dealing with autopay withdrawals until I'm 97."

I pondered his proposal, the mountain of money I owed swimming in my vision. A few years of debt sounded a helluva lot more enticing and appealing than decades and decades of growing interest rates and monthly payments that drained my bank account.

"Do you really think it's feasible?"

"Definitely. You're the total package, Em. Think about it."

Matthew gave me a lot to consider that evening. I ran the numbers and created spreadsheets, factoring in every expense I could think of—items like a website, dress rentals, a background check person, a private investigator, as well as a plethora of other miscellaneous costs. Slowly, I started to see the profit margin form. After a deep-dive down an internet rabbit hole, I found some forums and message boards from people who did similar things. I was cautiously optimistic in attempting to see if this plan could work.

RB's Companions was born.

My first event was with an up-and-coming football player I knew casually through mutual acquaintances. He agreed to be my test subject, inviting me to a low-stress team dinner. Once the nerves wore off, I realized I had *fun*, enjoying my life outside the rigidity of legal jargon and court cases I was accustomed to. I'm an introvert through and through, and stepping outside my comfort zone was exhilarating.

In the six years since, I've attended weddings, office parties, birthdays, graduations, and every other type of event imaginable.

It felt slimy taking people's money in the beginning months, guilt hanging in the air as I lied about my association with clients. Brutal honesty is one of my character traits, and it made me uneasy to be part of a plan that involved fibbing and inaccuracies.

Over time, I've settled into the role, understanding that this extracurricular job helps men who don't want to be hounded all night about why they're single. I felt less like a fake and more like a friend who genuinely wanted the best for them.

More often than not, the men I interact with have an obscene amount of money, hiring me because they don't have time for relationships, too focused on work and their businesses to care about finding a forever sweetheart. Knowing there was no pressure to give anyone a happily ever after took most of the stress off my shoulders.

I've worked hundreds of outings, but I've never done an overnight trip. I'm not opposed to the idea; I've just never broached the possibility of giving up so much of my precious free time to devote my attention elsewhere.

Four days is a long time. An extended assignment calls for a thorough background check, lots of patience, and a ton of prep. It's easy to fake a partnership for a couple of hours in a ballroom while eating a meal. Multiple days, however, means being on for a prolonged period of time, no escape in sight.

I'm going to have to really get to know this guy.

The foundation of my business is anonymity. I never expect clients to share their real names or photos of themselves off the bat. A handful of the men are high-profile individuals, hesitant to reveal who they are until the last possible minute.

I get it. I don't want my services to seem like a traditional dating app. As long as background checks come back clean, and I don't get any uncomfortable vibes from the man on the other side of the computer and phone, I couldn't care less about what they might look like. I'm not doing this to date the hottest man in the city; limiting myself to events with only the most subjectively handsome men hinders how much money I can make.

And I really want to make money. I'm tired of living paycheck to paycheck, and ready for financial freedom once and for all.

All the inquiries I receive, including JD's, follow a strict procedure: We start by sharing basic information and submitting a background check. After the data comes back clean, we begin the process of getting to know each other, diving deeper into why they want to hire me.

Communication with a client starts strictly via email. It's more open-ended and formal, giving the man time to back out without divulging too much information if they don't feel like continuing the arrangement.

After a week of computer interactions, we transition to texting, done through a third-party app. Safety is paramount to me; I don't need random people knowing my phone number in the off-chance things go south and take a steep nosedive toward freaking weird.

There's nothing monumentally profound discussed in the text messages, but it's significantly less rigid, more friendly, and super laid-back.

The last and final step is meeting in person for an hour. This happens a couple of weeks before the event and is always in a neutral location picked by me. Awkward at first, it's a crucial milestone on the journey with the client, making sure everyone's still onboard with the plan.

Nicole always asks how I'm able to not become romantically involved with the men I talk to. I've found it's easy to disassociate emotionally from them; they aren't interested in love. I'm not interested in convincing them to find love.

It's a win-win for everyone.

For six years, my business model has been fool-proof.

For six years, nothing has gone wrong.

I intend to keep it that way, even if I might agree to a multi-day event.

I read JD's email again.

It's funny. Kind of awkward, but also endearing. It's clear he doesn't ask random people for help often, and it's... cute. In a weird I-have-no-idea-who-you-are-but-you-made-me-laugh way.

My eyes pinpoint the sentence that made my heart speed up when I read it originally.

Just name the price.

I tap my finger on my chin, pulling up the spreadsheet that outlines my debt history. I've always wanted to be a lawyer, and it became my sole focus when I turned ten years old, determined to do anything to achieve the dream.

Yeah, the debt was worth it because I adore my job, but I had over $100,000 in student loans when I graduated from my final year of law school, a staggering number that still overwhelms me anytime I think about it for too long. Looking at my data, I find that I only owe $3,800 on my loans.

$3,800, and I'll be financially free.

I take a deep breath, knowing the man on the other side of the screen will never agree to a price that high.

Am I unethical for trying? Probably.

But it's worth a shot.

Clicking reply, I type out a response, fingers trembling with every press of the keyboard. I didn't detect any bad vibes from JD's first message, so I'm going to go with my gut.

I can trust him.

To: JD7683
From: RBCompanions
Subject: Re: New Inquiry
Date: September 1

Hi, JD!

Thank you so much for your message.

I do multi-day events and the cost would be $3,800. In addition to the background check you need to submit, I would also like my private investigator to look into where we'll be staying, who else will be there, etc. You might not be comfortable sharing this information with me directly, but I hope you understand the need to broach this situation cautiously. As a woman, I'm aware of the many risks involved with my services, especially at a private location.

Payment won't be needed until the background check comes through. Once it does, I'd be happy to continue this conversation further. Until then, I've attached a sheet with the information you'll need to provide. Don't worry, I won't see any of it! I'm also attaching my contract outlining the premise of our tentative arrangement.

Please note that explicit sexual activities of any nature are forbidden.

Let me know if you have any questions!

Thanks,
RB

I never use my real name, operating under an alias until I meet the man in real life. My initials are vague enough where in the off-chance someone I know contacts me, I won't be discoverable. That hasn't happened yet, and I intend to keep it that way.

I hit send, watching the message disappear. At this point, it's probably inconsequential. No one is going to agree to such a lucrative price.

Too late now.

Nothing I can do besides wait for the rejection.

Shoveling the now cold food in my mouth, I close my laptop and grab a wine glass. After spending 60 hours at the office this week, I'm mentally tapped out. Nothing sounds more relaxing than a bath while I watch Netflix and drink wine. Pouring a glass of red, I head into the bathroom, starting the faucet on my claw-foot tub.

The bath fills with water, steam rising above the porcelain as I discard my clothes. As I lower myself into the basin, heat and warmth encompass my aching muscles. Between work and a late-night event earlier this week that stretched past midnight and messed up my sleep schedule, my body is a mess.

I take a sip of my drink and swirl the beverage around, letting out a sigh. Each day down is another day closer to my goal. My dream. And what a feeling of relief that is.

My phone buzzes next to me, distracting my restful thoughts. Carefully reaching for the device so I don't drop it straight into the water, I open my inbox again.

To: RBCompanions
From: JD7683
Subject: Re: New Inquiry
Date: September 1

RB,

Hey, thanks for the swift reply. I hate when people take forever to answer emails. $3,800 is reasonable and fair. $42 an hour? Perfectly fine.

I'm also good with the background check and P.I. stuff, so I'll get those documents filled out ASAP.

If you need a deposit to secure my spot for the dates, let me know. I'm sure it's a competitive market, and I'm not above strong holding my way into your calendar. It's October 17-21.

I know I'm reaching out well in advance, but I want to make sure I get all of this figured out with plenty of time to spare.

JD

·   ·   ·

That was not the response I was anticipating. I was expecting an expletive-laced reply, berating me and telling me where I could shove my out-of-control price tag. It's obvious this is an extremely important event to JD, and it sounds significantly deeper than a simple dinner party, holding substantial weight and purpose.

Guilt makes its way up my throat as I reread his speedy agreement. He didn't bother to ask any additional questions or challenge the total. Booking me for a single night out only runs my clients between $300 and $500. I'm seriously price gouging this dude.

Shit. I feel bad.

I *never* feel bad.

Why is this one different?

Shaking off the remorse, I read the email again, then a third time, picking the loose skin around my pointer finger as I digest his approval. Finally satisfied with my decision, I type out words my brain has yet to process.

To: JD7683
From: RBCompanions
Subject: Re: New Inquiry
Date: September 1

JD,

I'm on my phone a lot for work, so I'll always answer quickly. That's a pet peeve of mine, too. The P.I. is going to reach out to you to conduct a background check, so keep an eye on your (fake, I'm guessing, but still super original) email account so you can get that completed.

Looking forward to talking to you more soon!

Thanks,

RB

• • •

I click my phone off for good, hiding it under the towel on the edge of the tub. After that October weekend, I'll *finally* be debt free—something I never thought would happen. I could jump for joy right now, and I let out an excited, high-pitched squeal.

I found my one good thing of the day.

JD.

And not because he's paying off the last remaining bit of my debt. A handful of messages back and forth, and I'm already intrigued by this mystery man, eager to learn more.

FIVE

EMMA

EXHAUSTION.

Population: Me.

It's becoming a trend at this point. I'm a permanent resident.

Every inch of my body groans and protests as I rub my eyes, staring blearily at my computer screen. The first round of interviews for the partner position are happening soon, and to say I'm anxious would be the understatement of the century.

All of my work is triple-checked, ensuring its accuracy. I arrive at the office early, and I stay late. I'm taking on additional cases and reviewing interview techniques online, practicing the STAR method while jotting down questions to ask my interviewers.

I'm doing nineteen different things at once and attempting to juggle a work/life/social event balance. It's becoming more and more difficult. I'm ready for this madness to be over already.

An alarm pings on my phone, reminding me I need to leave for the event I'm scheduled to attend in twenty minutes if I want to make it on time. I *need* to make it on time; the man I'm accompanying is giving a welcome speech at a gala along with a nice donation to charity.

Grabbing the long garment bag hanging on the back of my door, I head into the bathroom and lock the door behind me. I peel off my business attire and unhook my bra, letting it fall to floor. Shimmying the emerald green dress I'm wearing down my body, I attempt to zip it up. It stops halfway, snagging on an unidentifiable roadblock. I bend and twist my arms and shoulders awkwardly, attempting to become a contortionist and fix the problem I've caused. I'm not coordinated enough to be successful, but I don't have time to fix it.

My phone buzzes on the counter and I pick it up, seeing my P.I. has texted me.

Shelia: Wanted to follow up about the potential inquiry you sent my way.
Shelia: I read all the info he provided, and everything checked out.
Shelia: I'm not going to lie, he sounds like a real catch!
Shelia: Nothing to worry about with this one!

I grin, excited to hear the positive news about JD. Next up will be sending him an official email tomorrow with the good news. Taking one last look at myself in the mirror, I grab my things off the counter and hurry back toward my office. Distracted while looking at my phone, my path gets halted by running headfirst into a firm barrier in the middle of the hallway. I bounce back, almost stumbling to the floor.

A large hand reaches out, catching me under my upper arm and preventing an inevitable face-plant into the carpet. A jolt of electricity whooshes up my spine with the touch, and I let out a gasp of surprise. It starts in my lower back, creeping up stealthily until it reaches my neck, causing me to *burn*, a heat encompassing every inch of my skin.

Steadying myself, I pull away, breaking the physical contact and the overwhelming pleasantness washing over me.

"Emma? What are you still doing here?"

I blink, looking up to find Henry staring at me, a perplexed expression on his face. His eyebrows furrow and the corner of his mouth turns down, something akin to a frown taking over the spot of his usual grin.

I open and close my mouth, mimicking a blubbering fish, unable to vocalize a coherent string of words while my heart rate speeds up, spiking as I glance at his hand hovering in the air, the apparent hero saving me from tripping over the hem of my dress.

Henry… *touched* me.

And it felt… *incredible.*

Swallowing thickly, I realize I haven't answered him yet. "I'm, uh, leaving. Right now. Yes. Leaving."

"In that?" he asks incredulously, emphasizing the last syllable. His dark eyes sweep over my outfit slowly, unhurriedly, careful to not miss an inch.

The meticulous assessment warms me further, following the previous path of electricity and knocking every nerve along the way. When I think he's finished, ready to step away, his gaze dips to my hips for a fraction of a second. His mouth parts, and he inhales sharply, muttering a string of words that sounds suspiciously like *fucking hell* before snapping his attention back to my face like he's done something very, very wrong.

"Yeah." I clear my throat and roll my shoulders back, hoping to show I'm undeterred by this increasingly intimate encounter when, in actuality, I'm close to combusting.

"You must have somewhere really important to be. You definitely weren't wearing this ensemble earlier."

"You saw me this morning?"

"Er. In passing." The tips of his ears turn pink, and his hands disappearing into his pockets.

"Oh. I'm just going to a thing."

"A thing," Henry repeats. "Like a regatta gala?"

I sputter, surprised by his joke. "Regatta galas happen during the daytime, allegedly."

The right side of his mouth turns up at my retort, a small smile present. A wretched half-dimple appears with the raise, partially revealing itself and blatantly showing off.

God.

Life would be so much easier if I hated this man.

Henry is a dangerous specimen. His personality is captivating and enchanting; every single time he speaks, he puts you under a spell. His voice is warm and rich as it seeps into your veins, taking on the role of an IV providing life. A bright aura surrounds him, others gravitating toward him like a magnet. He's popular with everyone in the office, exceedingly kind and funny while also being wicked intelligent and having a thirst for knowledge.

His looks? Downright devastating. Panty-dropping. Giggle-inducing and blush-creating. He's frighteningly tall, well over six feet. His body is long and lithe, veins running up his arms and muscles filling out his shirts. Moving away from his stature, the rest of him is equally imposing and daunting.

He's handsome.

Hot.

Suave and charming.

Absurdly so.

His dark, inky onyx hair is always perfectly kept, floppy up top and cut close to his ears on the sides. Now and then a piece will fall out of place and mask his warm, chocolate brown eyes. Eyes that frequently dance with mischief, mayhem, and excitement. Eyes I've had memorized for well over a decade, the first time I encountered them head-on permanently ingrained in my memory, refusing to be forgotten.

It was the first day of high school and I was walking down the hall, an awkward freshman rocking a puka shell necklace, Rainbow flip-flops, and wearing two layered collared shirts from American Eagle. I passed Henry's locker where he was surrounded by a large group of friends, even though we had only been in the building for an hour.

He doesn't remember our encounter, of course. Why would he? I was another nondescript body in a throng of many excited people. My chest was as flat as a board, my hair was frizzy, and I was pasty pale, a stark contrast to the girls that flanked his sides, fully developed and already beautiful. I was hardly a distraction then.

Or now.

His head turned at the exact moment I shimmied by his group, gleeful eyes meeting mine. The playfulness behind the cool facade he wore faltered temporarily. Our gazes remained interlocked for three long seconds while his lips pursed like he was trying to solve a difficult math problem. I audibly gasped, never having seen someone so blatantly good-looking in real life. Up to that point, I relied on *Cosmogirl!* and *Seventeen* for pictures of hot guys.

But there he was. A beautiful boy. Staring at *me.*

He looked away first, abruptly severing our contact as his attention slid from my face and refocused on his group. A friend clasped him on his shoulder and Henry shook his head, grin falling back into place, clearly unaffected by the insignificant moment we shared.

I happily faded away into the background for the rest of our high school years while Henry thrived. He was always the star, front and center. He played basketball and baseball, was student government president and homecoming king. He talked to a slew of classmates between lessons and exchanged high fives by his locker.

The only person he didn't talk to?

Me.

We never interacted again after that first day, narrowly missing each other over the course of four years. No shared classes. No nearby lockers. Different lunch periods. Zero casual comments tossed my way while leaving the library.

It was radio silent. A careful reflection on our time together leads me to believe he purposely avoided me, going out of his way to prevent any crisscrossing of paths. Our school wasn't *that* small, and I saw plenty of the rest of his gang.

Never him.

I blink and the Henry of the present returns, the young boy of the past shifting into a man. He shrugs, the shoulders of his immaculately tailored suit jacket tensing then relaxing, hugging his limbs in a salacious way.

"Only the fake ones do, I hear," he says. "Fascinating. I, too, have a thing tonight."

"Cool. I'm running extremely late, so if you'll excuse me, I'll be on my way."

I sidestep around him, my shoulder brushing his arm as I pass. Shuffling to my office, I know his eyes are still on me, watching my retreat. The continued attention makes it hard to breathe, my inhales becoming more ragged.

"Your zipper isn't all the way up." Henry's voice carries down the desolate hall, a velvety softness behind the observation.

I freeze, shoulders tensing. "It's stuck."

"Would you like my help?"

"No. I can handle it." I wince at the unintended sharpness.

"I didn't mean to imply you can't. Trust me," he says mildly, a low chuckle occupying the gap between us. "I thought I'd offer since I'm here and readily available. It's up to you."

Making a split second decision, I nod twice, conveying my acceptance of his offer. "Okay. Yes. I'd like your help. Please."

His approaching footsteps are heavy, magnified by the quiet stretch of space. I keep my back to him, focusing intently on the peeling paint on the wall. As he gets closer, I try my best to not dwell on the way his scent wraps around me like a vine clinging to a tree.

The aroma is comforting. Grounding. Familiar.

"I'm going to touch you now, okay?" An octave lower than before, his voice is gruff and full of steel while he patiently waits for my approval or refusal.

I nod feebly, enraptured by Henry's desire for my consent before proceeding. His hands—the same ones that caught me moments ago—lightly graze my lower back over the fabric, tackling the snag I've created. There's a slight tremor to his touch as he works skillfully, solving the problem in a few short seconds that stretch on for eternity, each one longer than the last, but somehow not long enough.

The gentle contact doesn't linger anywhere excessively. Doesn't explore or roam outside the strict boundary he established. Besides the slightest brush of his thumb against the base of my neck as he finishes zipping me up, you never would have known we had this moment.

The care hurts my heart, muscles constricting and coiling with a tidal wave of gratitude, awe and appreciation.

"There you go. Perfect." His hands fall from my bare skin, taking the heat with them.

"Thank you," I whisper, body shaking from standing still.

"My pleasure," he rasps. The tone lacks his normal confidence, trading in swagger for unsureness. "I hope you have fun tonight."

"You too, Henry."

Being late to the event is no longer at the forefront of my mind; getting away from him is my only goal, afraid of what might happen if I stay.

And how much I think I'd like it.

"Hey, Emma?"

I stop near my office door, daring a glance over my shoulder. Henry hasn't moved, still rooted in place as his polished dress shoe rubs the carpet. My name is shaky, like he's bewildered he even has the luxury of speaking to me and never wants to say anything else for the rest of his life.

"Yes?" I answer, coxing him, *encouraging him*, wondering what he's going to say next and ready to hang on to every word.

"You look positively stunning."

The compliment is so soft, so heartfelt, I'm uncertain he said it aloud. He raises his chin to stare at me, and the white-hot heat behind his chestnut eyes is scorching. Blazing. A dangerous inferno.

I'm burning from the inside out, yearning for more of his fire.

For more of... *him.*

I hold back a gasp, afraid to believe he meant those four

precious words. If he did, it would forever alter the dynamics of us, our charted trajectory of neutrality disrupted and interrupted.

"Thank you."

Throwing myself into my office, I close the door firmly shut, pressing my back against the wood.

I've never been so disjointed after an interaction with him before. The memory of his skin on mine is an image I wish I could have seen, desire rising from my toes and settling between my thighs.

I have to escape this building, afraid of how Henry will change my opinion of him if I don't. Or, even worse, what I might do knowing we could exist as something other than coworkers. As I grab my purse, I can't help but wonder something, a niggle of imagination I'm embarrassed to even entertain.

If this is how I reacted from a single touch of his, what would happen if he gave me everything he had?

For the first time in all the years I've known him, I'm achingly desperate to find the answer to that question.

SIX

To: JD7683
From: RBCompanions
Subject: Hooray!
Date: September 3

JD,

Hey! I thought I'd send you an email with the exciting news. Everything from your background check and the P.I. came back great. We're clear to go ahead with planning!

Can you give me the specifics of the event? If you have an itinerary, that would be even better. What sort of role do you need me to play? Friend? Girlfriend? Business partner?

Let me know!

Looking forward to hearing from you,

RB

To: RBCompanions
From: JD7683
Subject: Re: Hooray!

Date: September 3

My savior, RB,

That's great to hear. I'm excited to get the ball rolling. If you have follow-up questions that will ease your mind, ask away. I'm an open book.

The event is my parents' 40th wedding anniversary. They're doing an extended weekend celebration. Here's the tentative plan so far:

Wednesday: arrive at the house/dinner with my parents
Thursday: close family gathering (there are rumors of a game night—I hope you like charades?)
Friday: large event (dinner, dancing, etc)
Saturday: send-off event (dinner and fireworks)
Sunday: head home

It's a lot, I know. During the day, we'll be on our own or hanging out with my immediate family. Low-key stuff, nothing overwhelming.

Who am I kidding? This whole thing is going to be over-whelming, especially because I'm hiring you.

Sorry. I don't mean it as a dig. Simply lamenting about my own idiocy. As far as your role… Girlfriend would be best. I'll explain why at a later date, but posing as my other half would be ideal.

I'm rambling now. How often are we going to communicate? Are there rules? How's your day going so far?

Ecstatically,
    JD

To: JD7683
From: RBCompanions
Subject: Re:re: Hooray!
Date: September 4

JD,

Sounds like we're going to have a loaded few days, but at least it gives us plenty of chances to sell our 'relationship' to your parents.

We can communicate as much or as little as you'd like. Within reason, of course. I have a full-time job that occupies most of my time.

My day is going pretty well, thanks for asking! It's almost the weekend. Work has been okay. I'm going to an event with fireworks—that's a first. Overall, there isn't much room to complain. How about you? How's your day?

Conspiratorially,
   RB

To: RBCompanions
From: JD7683
Subject: Apologies
Date: September 6

RB,

Hey, happy Friday. Sorry it took me so long to get back to you. Work got chaotic, and when that happens, it consumes me. Suffice to say, I'm stoked it's the weekend. Do you have any fun plans?

The fireworks are going to be over the top. You don't have to pretend it doesn't sound pretentious, because it absolutely is.

Selling this very fake relationship to my parents, my mother in particular, is the *only* goal of our time together. Whatever I have to do for it to be believable, I'm all in. One could say that I made a very regrettable error, and now I'm suffering from the consequences.

If I have to hold your hand nonstop for four nights, I'm in. I'll superglue our palms together. I can also whisper sweet nothings in your ear if it's going to put a realistic smile on your face.

If that's allowed, of course. Please don't let me cross a line.

Searching for Elmers,

JD

To: JD7683
From: RBCompanions
Subject: Re: Apologies
Date: September 7

JD,

No apologies needed about work. I totally get it, and I've been in the same boat as of late. If it makes you feel better, I read this email yesterday and forgot to respond. Now it's my turn to apologize! I hope you have some time to decompress this weekend. All I'm planning on doing is baking cupcakes.

Don't worry, I've been doing this long enough that the smiles become realistic. You don't have to whisper too many sweet nothings. I'll accept a joke or two, though.

I'm excited about meeting your family! And some good food. And you too, I guess.

In Baked Goods We Trust,

RB

To: RBCompanions
From: JD7683
Subject: It's been one week since you messaged me...
Date: September 10

RB,

Can you believe we've been talking for over a week? This is already my most successful relationship.

Yikes. I probably shouldn't say that like it's something to celebrate.

My weekend was good. I spent some time working, and got sucked into an Apple TV show, so any productivity went out the window shortly thereafter. Pretty sure I binged 8 episodes on Sunday. Does that count as decompressing? I did remember to shower, so the weekend wasn't a total wash (get it?). I'm about to head out with some buddies of mine now.

How did your cupcakes turn out? I'm really jealous. What's your favorite flavor? Maybe one day you could bake me some. Or we could bake some together. Is that moving too fast? I promise I'm not proposing marriage. I just want cupcakes.

I should probably go eat dinner.

Starvingly,
   JD

To: JD7683
From: RBCompanions
Subject: Re: It's been one week since you messaged at me...
Date: September 12

JD,

You can't mention a bingeable show without telling me what it is! Spill!

What does it say about me if carrot cake cupcakes are my favorite? I know, I know. Not a traditional flavor, but it's so good. Buttercream frosting? Check. Feeling like you're healthy because the dessert has carrots? Check. Eliminating raisins because I hate them? Also check.

I'm not very talented, but baking calms me down. What's your ideal cupcake flavor? Favorite dessert?

You strike me as a chocolate and chocolate kind of guy. I'm probably reading you all wrong. It's only been a few days.

As far as baking together... I'm always looking for a sous-chef. I'll let you know when applications open. Hope you had fun with your friends!

Now I'm craving carrots.

Eh, what's up Doc?
RB

To: RBCompanions
From: JD7683
Subject: Rain, rain, go away...
Date: September 13

RB,

I'm assuming you live in the Northeast, too? If so, this weather fits my mood today. I'm rarely gloomy, yet today I woke up feeling kind of... down? It's hard to explain. I'm irritable. Annoyed. Tired.

I would've been perfectly content staying hidden under my comforter.

Perhaps it's the torrential downpour occurring outside my window, rain droplets slowly sliding down the glass and falling into puddles stories below. Maybe it's because I tossed and turned all night, anxiety dancing around in my head for no reason whatsoever. Whatever the cause, I don't like it, and I very much wish it would go away.

I think seasonal depression is kicking in, and I'm not looking forward to the sun setting at 4 p.m. soon.

Another week down. Time flies when you're having fun. Or, more appropriately, time flies when you're up to your neck at work and really need coffee and a nap.

Oh. The show was *Ted Lasso*. Have you seen it?

Yours in a severely decaffeinated state,
    JD

To: JD7683
From: RBCompanions
Subject: Come again some other day…
Date: September 13, 2022

JD,

Those feelings are valid, you know, and shouldn't be repressed all the time. I understand the desire of not wanting them to dominate your life, but sometimes I think feeling—pardon my French—shitty in the way you described reminds me I'm alive.

One thing I try to do every day is find something *good*. It could be a delicious meal. A warm sweater. A cold beverage. Anything that lifts your spirits.

No matter how dark and stormy the day might be, the clouds will eventually break. The sun will rise again tomorrow. And that's weirdly beautiful, I think.

Even if the bad days make little sense right now, they make the happy days appear so much brighter and better when we get to them.

We can share an umbrella. There's plenty of space.

Also, I love *Ted Lasso*.

To rainbows ahead,
RB

To: RBCompanions
From: JD7683
Subject: Thank U, Next
Date: September 14

RB,

Thank you.

I wish I could verbalize how much what you said meant to me, especially coming from a stranger.

Well, not a stranger.

You know what I mean.

What I shared yesterday is an extremely rare occurrence. Feelings in general are typically an off-limits discussion for me. I know; typical man. Hold the eye roll you're probably doing.

They've always been shoved aside, hoping to be forgotten as they fade away and the happiness returns. I appreciate you suggesting I should welcome the emotions and to find the good in every day. An insightful and optimistic way to look at things. Perhaps I'll give it a try.

How is it already the weekend? We must be highly successful individuals if the bulk of our conversations take place at the end of the week.

Or...

Wait.

You're a superhero who's out fighting crime.

I knew it. You're Spider-Man, aren't you?

Tucking away my umbrella-ella-ella-a-a for the time being,

JD

P.S. If you aren't Spider-Man, who's your favorite?

P.P.S. My good thing of the day was a slice of pizza. Greasy. Cheesy. Delicious. What was yours?

To: JD7683
From: RBCompanions
Subject: Talent show entry?
Date: September 15

JD,

Do you have any secret hidden talents a girlfriend would know about? I wish I could sing like Rihanna, but alas, I cannot.

I'm surprised my shower walls haven't cracked from the shrill flatness of my voice. I'm trying to think if there's anything cool in my repertoire.

Oh! I can lick my elbow!

No one has ever asked me to demonstrate said gift, so maybe I should think of something else.

I guess I could also just say I'm the real Peter Parker. Web-slinging would be an awesome party trick.

Fighting crime one street at a time,

RB

P.S. It's impossible to rank my fellow friendly neighborhood

Spidey, but if you're forcing me to answer, it would be Miles Morales. Wait. Tom. Shoot. Tobey. Andrew? Ughhhh.

P.P.S. Today my good thing was sleeping all the way until my alarm went off and getting to snooze for ten extra minutes.

To: RBCompanions
From: JD7683
Subject: Re: Talent show entry?
Date: September 16

RB,

It's now mandatory I hear you sing one of these days. Maybe when we're baking cupcakes and you're bossing me around. If you tell my mother you got me to cook, she'll think I'm locked down for life.

Please don't call me an idiot sandwich.

I'd buckle under pressure.

Okay. Secret talents. I can bowl. I played other sports growing up and was a college athlete, but bowling is probably my favorite hobby. I once rolled a 293—the closest I've come to a perfect game. With my lack of free time these days, I'd definitely need the gutters up.

Sparingly & strikingly,

JD

P.S. What if you're throwing me off your trail and you're actually Batman? Can I ride in the Batmobile? Pretty please?

P.P.S. A solo run without music, nothing but trees and sidewalk with me. My good thing.

To: JD7683
From: RBCompanions
Subject: Happy anniversary!
Date: September 18

JD,

Happy two-week anniversary!

I didn't get you a present.

Don't hate me.

Speaking of anniversaries, we only have a month until the event. We can shift this to text messaging if you want. Totally okay if not, just thought I'd offer since we exchange quite a few emails. If you feel so inclined, here's my number.

834-247-2400

Don't worry, it's a third-party app thing. You won't find me on Google with that!

Empty-handedly,

RB

P.S. Plot twist: I'm Superman.

P.P.S. Puppy kisses. A very, very good thing.

SEVEN

HENRY

RB'S EMAIL left the ball in my court about switching our conversation to texting. I mulled over the decision for three days, weighing the pros and cons before finally relenting to the idea. She wasn't aggressive in her suggestion. In fact, I haven't heard a peep from her since, which I find slightly worrisome.

RB, whoever she is, is the only answer to my predicament right now. I need her. Badly. Up to this point, she's come off as laid back. Cool. Nothing about her dialogue has caused me to panic. I'm starting to hesitantly believe this farce might work.

I don't sit around all day, constantly refreshing my inbox, hoping one from her arrives and ignoring my responsibilities. That would be absurd. I do enjoy hearing from her, though.

And, sure, I get excited when I see her name pop up.

Happy, too.

It's not a big deal.

I've never been one to put in such effort to casually converse with a woman. Normally it's all done in person, indulging in time-killing bullshit until it's been long enough where we can climb into a cab and go back to my apartment without feeling like total strangers while we fuck into the late hours of the night.

Now look at me. I just spent 30 minutes scrolling through

Google, searching for the best opening lines to use in a text message for the first time. That's literally what I typed into the search bar, not wanting to ooze total desperation when I speak to her next, no matter how dire my situation is becoming. Mild, panicked hysteria will suffice.

My mother called me yesterday, inquiring again about my date's name for place cards.

Goddamn place cards.

I've been itching to ask my friends for their advice on how to handle this whole fiasco, but that would lead to questions.

Questions I don't have the answer to.

Questions I'm not sure I want to know the answer to.

We'll tackle that shit at a later date.

I'm out here all alone, up a creek without a paddle.

Well, might as well dive in.

My fingers type out the opener I've constructed and deleted no short of 15 times. I've argued in courtrooms and helped design some of the most lucrative contracts in baseball history, but a *text message* to a *woman* is going to be my demise.

The boys are going to have a fucking field day with me when they find out.

After six laps pacing around my kitchen island, I finally grow a pair and hit send before I can think twice and chuck the device into the garbage disposal.

> **JD:** We're going on a road trip.
> **JD:** What two snacks are you bringing?

There we go. That's not so bad, is it?

Except…

Shit.

I double texted her. I'm still a novice when it comes to electronic etiquette, but I'm pretty sure there are strict rules about bombarding someone off the bat.

Cool. Five seconds in and I've already messed up. That's probably a world record.

I click my phone closed and turn the screen over. Out of sight, out of mind. Whenever RB decides to answer, I don't want to be overzealous to respond. Before I can walk out of the kitchen and put on my running clothes to distract myself, the phone dings. I stare at the blasted thing for eight seconds before snatching it up and reading the response waiting for me.

Not overzealous, my ass.

RB: Hi. That might be the most interesting first message I've ever received.
RB: I'm going to go out on a limb and guess this is JD?
RB: And if it's not... This is awkward.

I exhale, rolling my shoulders back and shaking out my limbs.

JD: Guilty! I'm not ashamed to admit I used Google to find a unique line.
JD: I can't take all the credit for that gem. It comes at the hands of some reddit user named w0m@nwhisp3r3r69.
JD: In hindsight, he probably wasn't the best person to take advice from with that as a username.

RB: Honestly, it worked pretty well.
RB: Are we each bringing two? I get two and you get two? Or is it two total?
RB: That will dictate my answer.

JD: You're a smart one.

RB: Consider me investigative.
RB: I like to have all the facts before I proceed.

JD: We each get two. Ladies first.

RB: This might be the most difficult part of my day, and that's saying something.

RB: Give me a minute. I want to do this correctly.

JD: Please. Take all the time you need.

RB: I'm going to pick Flamin' Hot Cheetos. So worth the heartburn after.

RB: Then I'll have to go with Zebra Cakes. Takes me back to my childhood.

RB: My mom used to put one in my lunchbox every day. A Zebra Cake and a pizza Lunchable? Those were the good ole days.

JD: Hang on.

JD: For clarification purposes, did you grow up in a Little Debbie factory?

RB: Ah, the rival actually. Hostess.

RB: What about you?

I grin at her answer.

Sarcastic.

Funny.

Quick to retaliate with a joke of her own.

I like it.

I like it a lot.

One of my favorite traits in a woman is humor. Right off the bat, I'm sucked in.

JD: Great choices.

JD: I would pick Combos. And peanut M&Ms.

RB: I'm intrigued by this picnic we've planned. What kind of music are we going to listen to?

JD: A mix of early 2000s and classic rock. Thoughts?

RB: Sounds like the only music I can stand. So far, so good.
RB: I'll make sure to wear a choker and bring an inflatable plastic chair.

JD: I'll spike my hair.
JD: How's your Wednesday night going?

RB: It's only Wednesday? This week is dragging, but today has been pretty good. I can't complain.

JD: Glad to hear it.
JD: Do you have any ground rules for texting? It feels more personal than emails, so wanted to do a quick vibe check.
JD: Are road trip snack discussions allowed?

RB: Snack discussions are always permitted.
RB: As for rules… No pictures of our faces until we meet in person. Photos of food and screenshots are totally fine. Send me all the memes you can find.

JD: So you don't want to know how handsome I am yet.
JD: Got it.

RB: Cocky, I see.
RB: No sharing specifics about work or names of friends.
RB: If things go south and we void our agreement, we don't know who was on the other side.

JD: Total anonymity.
JD: That makes it easier to walk away.
JD: I'm not saying I want to walk away or anything, by the way.

RB: I understand what you mean.

RB: It should go without saying, but no sexually explicit photos or conversations either.

JD: Don't worry.
JD: It never even crossed my mind.

RB: Ouch.

JD: Not what I meant. I'm looking forward to getting to know you. And what you like.
JD: Fuck. Not in a sexual way. I'm not going to send you a dick pic. That's so tacky. I didn't mean to imply I wouldn't want to send one to you. I'm sure you're an attractive woman.
JD: Oh my God, I will never speak again.

RB: Wow.
RB: I was just messing with you, but that was kind of funny.

JD: I'm almost having a meltdown, RB.
JD: My face has never been this red.

RB: Thanks for the comedic relief.
RB: I've had to cancel a few contracts because the man thought I was an actual… you know.
RB: Let me be clear, I have zero qualms about men and women who do that as a profession.
RB: It's just not what I'm promoting, and I don't want anyone to get the wrong idea or have false expectations.

JD: When you put it that way, I can understand.
JD: I'm sure that required some uncomfortable conversations and end up in some unsolicited images.

RB: Should you feel inclined to send me an unprompted dick pic, it will be shown to my friends and thoroughly analyzed.

RB: And then promptly made fun of.

JD: Hold off on the dick pics. I can do that.

RB: I don't get creeper vibes from you.
RB: You're doing great so far!

JD: I never thought I would be happy to hear that from a stranger on the internet.

RB: Stranger? I thought I was your girlfriend. Are we going to have our first fight already?

JD: I just laughed out loud. You're right.
JD: From henceforth, I shall call you my Very Real Girlfriend.
JD: VRG. How does that sound?

RB: Incredibly romantic. You certainly know how to woo a woman.
RB: When we meet, don't even bother to call me by my real name.

JD: Speaking of real names, I assume we aren't going to share ours until we meet in person?

RB: It's what works best.

JD: Got it.
JD: How often are we allowed to communicate?
JD: Times when texting is off limits? I'm sure you have a life outside of this and your career.

RB: I work pretty heavy hours during the week, so my responses will be less frequent.
RB: Nights are my rare free time, so I'm available to talk.

RB: Be warned, however, I won't drop everything I'm doing to answer you.

JD: God, I'd never ask you to.

RB: Phew. Glad that goes over well with you.
RB: We can put our first fight to rest for another day.

JD: Anything for you, VRG.

Never in my wildest dreams did I think talking like this would be *fun*. I blink, and midnight is rapidly approaching. I haven't showered. My cheeks hurt from smiling. My run didn't happen, and all I ate for dinner was a peanut butter and jelly sandwich that didn't have proportionate condiments because I was too busy reading RB's messages to pay attention to the amount of peanut butter on the knife. The evening has slipped away from me, and my usual routine has been infiltrated and interrupted by this woman.

Weirdly enough, I don't hate it.

We've been talking on and off for the better part of five hours, the conversation ebbing and flowing, teetering more toward flowing in the last 45 minutes. I had to plug my phone in earlier; the battery keeps draining rapidly at the consistency and frequency of the messages we've exchanged.

We've escalated from basic pleasantries to slowly asking more personal questions. What we wanted to be when we grew up. Favorite ice cream flavors. Which restaurant has the best crushed ice. Disappointment is not the sensation I expect to be conquered by when the ping of a new message comes through.

RB: I should probably get ready for bed.
RB: I didn't realize it was so late.

JD: Sorry about that.

JD: I hope I didn't break too many rules on my first day.

RB: Trust me, I'll tell you if something is wrong.
RB: I'm just exhausted.

JD: Thank goodness. Made it past stage one!
JD: I hope you get some good sleep.

RB: Now all that's left is learning small details about each other that a couple would know and knocking out a family event.

JD: I think I just had a heart attack.
JD: When I pass, tell my parents I love them, and I'm sorry I disappointed them. Scatter the crumbs of your Zebra Cakes over the plot of dirt in my memory.

RB: Baby steps. We'll get there together.
RB: I'm here to help.

JD: Good night, RB. Thanks for chatting with me.

RB: Good night, JD.
RB: Talk to you soon.

When I click my phone off, I'm off-center. Discombobulated. I've ignored work emails and the never-ending group messages from my friends, our chat blowing up with discussions I don't care about. I even deleted an invitation to meet up at a bar for drinks with an old fling, rejecting the sex that would have inevitably occurred, because I was too focused on discussing which villain from *Stranger Things* is the most powerful with this mysterious woman.

Maybe I should take a step back. Let her initiate contact the next few days. It was nice to talk to her, but I don't want to come across as too much like a... like a committed boyfriend who's going to answer every message right away.

That's not me.

That'll never be me.

That's not what this arrangement is.

It's fake. Not real. It has an end date. Nothing is going to change that, no matter how much she's fascinated me.

EIGHT

September 21st

                RB: Why do you need a date for this party?
      RB: I had three glasses of wine with dinner and I'm feeling bold.
RB: Is there an ex-girlfriend who will be there? Shoot. Sorry. Or an
ex-boyfriend. I shouldn't assume. Are you the overlooked middle
child, trying to win their attention?
RB: Whatever the reason, I'm here to support you and won't think
any less of you.

JD: Wow. I put my phone down for five minutes and come back to
an avalanche of text messages.

                                   RB: Sorry.

JD: No need to apologize. This sounds more fun than listening to
my friends talk about state-mandated testing.

                      RB: That's incredibly random.

JD: My buddy is a principal.

RB: Ah. Makes sense!

JD: Let's take this from the top. Three glasses of wine? You didn't drive, did you?

RB: Nope. Rideshare.

JD: Okay, good. Your guesses aren't bad. The real answer is stupid.

RB: Tell me!

JD: Fine, but no making fun of me, okay?

RB: I promise!

JD: I'm in my 30s (the young end, by the way) and I've never had a serious relationship. Or any relationship.

RB: Never? Not even a high school sweetheart? A college fling?

JD: Nope. Never. I lied to my mom and told her I had a date when I didn't, mainly because she's been insistent on setting me up with the daughter of a family friend.
JD: I don't speak poorly about women, but this girl is truly diabolical.
JD: My brother and sister have spouses, so that only adds to the glaringly obvious notion I am the only one without another half.
JD: My mom was so happy when I said I was bringing someone—I knew I couldn't reveal the truth to her once I started fibbing. That's where you come in.
JD: I know it's horrible.

RB: Tsk, tsk, JD. It's not cool you lied to your mom, but I can understand why you did.

RB: You were pressured and thought of an immediate solution. Deceiving people can be tough. It's one thing to say you have a significant other. Bringing someone to an event is a serious commitment to the lie. I want to make sure you understand that.

JD: Shit. I never thought of it like that. I'm an asshole for roping you into the lie.
JD: I know it's your job, but is it ever icky to you?

RB: Occasionally. It's a tough line to toe.
RB: On one hand, I'm helping someone out who appreciates me being there. On the other hand, I'm encouraging dishonest behavior. I go back and forth.
RB: Regardless, I'm here to help you. And I'll do that however I can.

JD: That's great to hear. Hopefully you don't think I'm an asshole right off the bat.
JD: I've felt sick over it ever since. I debated not even reaching out to you.

RB: You seem sincerely upset. You don't strike me as a bad person, and I'm sticking with my gut instinct.

JD: I'm glad I have your stamp of approval.
JD: What are you up to?

RB: I'll tell you, only if you don't judge me.

JD: I think it's pretty obvious I'm not in any position to judge anyone.

RB: Fair. I'm sitting on my couch.

JD: That's hardly lame.

RB: In my sweatpants.

JD: Also not lame. Sweatpants are my jam.
JD: Honestly, RB. You're kind of letting me down here.

RB: Watching *The Great British Bake Off*!

JD: What in the world is that?

RB: You've never heard of GBBO?!

JD: I can't say that I have and now I feel like I'm missing out. Tell me more.

RB: Oh it's incredible! A British baking show where they eat biscuits, drink tea, and bake cakes.

JD: Biscuits are my favorite breakfast food. Top them with some gravy? Divine.

RB: I regret to inform you that biscuits over there are called cookies over here.

JD: Even better. Cookies are my demise. You know that meme with the clown holding the balloon and beckoning you into the gutter?
JD: If he said, "I have cookies," I'd be halfway into the sewer before he finished his sentence.

RB: I love cookies too!

JD: There's a television series dedicated to people making cookies?
JD: I could get behind this.

RB: Not only cookies. Pies, too. When things get really wild, they make macaroons.

JD: Shit, macaroons?! Party animals. Is it on Netflix?

RB: Mhm! I apologize in advance for all the time you're going to waste watching it. It's my comfort show!

JD: Uh oh. Rough day?

RB: Not really. More like a confusing day? It's work stuff. Which is off-limits for our discussion.
RB: Short version: A coworker and I don't see eye to eye on things, and it takes a toll on me sometimes.
RB: But lately, it feels like we've reached a turning point of neutrality. A fork stuck in the road.

JD: Okay, Green Day.
JD: Want me to go Liam Neeson on your coworker's ass? Because I will.
JD: No questions asked.

RB: I just laughed out loud in my empty house.
RB: I appreciate the offer, but that's okay. I think our future will only improve from here.

JD: Does that make you happy?

RB: Yeah. I think it does.
RB: I'll keep you on speed dial, though, just in case I need some backup.

JD: While I have no clue where you work or how I'd help, the offer still stands.

RB: You must get along with all your colleagues, huh?

JD: For the most part. There's one person I have a history with, but it's no big deal.

RB: Sounds like there's a good story there.

JD: We've known each other for years.
JD: To be fair, I'm probably a dick frequently. And I instigate a lot of hostility between us.
JD: Hm. Hostility isn't the right word. Tension, perhaps? Weirdness? Orbiting just outside the zone of friendship?
JD: I think deep down I want them to pay attention to me. I'm trying to be cognizant of my behavior.

RB: That makes you a big person if you're willing to admit you've maybe not been the best.

JD: Enough with my melodramatics.
JD: You said you like to make cupcakes, Bugs Bunny. What else do you bake?

RB: You remember that?

JD: Of course.

RB: Baking is my favorite thing to do. It's a great stress reliever.

JD: I've never baked anything in my life.

RB: What?! How is that possible?
RB: What kind of childhood did you have? Or adulthood?
RB: How do you survive?

JD: On takeout and delivery meal services with already prepared dishes. Someone always cooked for me growing up.

RB: Wow.
RB: Did you type that with your pinky up, oh privileged one?

JD: Upon reflection, I'm aware of how pretentious it sounds.
JD: Also, to answer your earlier email question, my preferred flavor is chocolate with vanilla frosting.

RB: With or without the expensive gold shavings on top, Your Highness?

JD: Now I'm laughing. Damn you, RB. You're good.

NINE

September 22nd

JD: Tell me something good.
JD: I'm having a miserable day.

> **RB:** Hello to you too, Mr. Sunshine!
> **RB:** Why the bad day?

JD: Work is running me into the ground. I'm up for a promotion, and I'm doing my best to showcase my talents without coming across as arrogant.
JD: It's hard to stay focused. The other person who's going for the position is equally deserving.
JD: No. They're more deserving. 100%.
JD: I have an interview this week with a couple of people, and I'm second-guessing everything about myself. My work ethic. My career path in general. It's draining.

> **RB:** Congratulations on the promotion! That's awesome.
> **RB:** It sounds like a tough position to be in. I'm sorry you're going through all those emotions (which are all valid, by the way).

RB: You should try to devote your attention to smaller tasks, instead of the big, scary end task.

RB: Break up your week, interviews, and workload into tiny chunks. Cross one off when you complete it, that way you can see how much you're accomplishing and all the good you've done.

JD: Whoa.

JD: I really like that idea.

JD: One of my buddies suggested something similar. Maybe I'll make that a priority this week.

JD: Anyway. Enough talking about me. You're up. Something good. Go.

RB: My birthday is on Saturday!

JD: You're just now telling me this?! Don't you think I should know when your birthday is, VRG?

RB: Good point. Well, surprise! It's Saturday!

JD: Happy early birthday! Do you have any fun plans?

RB: My best friend and I are getting dinner, and then…

JD: I'm waiting on the edge of my seat with those dot dot dots.

RB: You mean the ellipsis?

JD: Okay, smarty-pants.

RB: We're going bowling!

JD: I knew you were a resident of the senior citizens' home, scooting around in a wheelchair, snacking on Zebra Cakes, and bowling on the weekend.

JD: My dream girl.

RB: Do you have a thing for older women? And by older, I mean four decades older?

JD: Guilty.

RB: You don't think I'm lame and boring? I know you said you enjoy bowling, but I feel like it's different when it's the subject of my 32nd birthday and not a drunken expedition.

JD: Lame? I'm incredibly jealous.

RB: I'm pretty abysmal, so it's going to be hilarious. How old are you? When's your birthday?

JD: I'm 31. My birthday is in the summer. July 17th.

RB: I'm older than you by a couple of months!
RB: Do you have a favorite birthday memory?

JD: Probably when I did a laser tag party for my 16th. I finally felt like I was cool since my parents didn't have to be there for supervision.
JD: What about you?

RB: We didn't have a lot of money when I was a kid, so frivolous spending was minimal.
RB: But for my 8th birthday, my mom took me to Toys 'R Us and let me pick out any three toys I wanted.
RB: To a lot of people, three toys sounds like nothing. To me, it was the best day of my life.

JD: What a great memory. What three did you pick? Do you remember?

RB: I do! A new Barbie (they used to be my favorite toys). A tamagotchi (which died after three days). And a Sky Dancer doll (which almost took my eye out).
RB: They're still in a box somewhere. I can't bear to part with them.

JD: I would hope not. They're special to you.
JD: That's so cool.

RB: Sorry. This got real deep real fast.

JD: Don't apologize.
JD: I like learning things about you.

September 23rd

JD: Hey, RB. How's your day?

RB: Not bad! I'm running late, so it could be better!

JD: Anything exciting happening tonight? Another event?

RB: Actually, this one isn't business.
RB: I have a date.

JD: Way better than business stuff. Fun!

RB: My friend set me up with him.
RB: He sounds nice!
RB: Wait. Is it weird I'm sharing this with you?

JD: Not at all. We're friends, right? Online friends count for something, I hope.

JD: Oh my God. Do you remember SmarterChild on AOL instant message?

RB: Yes! The original Siri!

RB: I tried to get him? Her? Them? It? To say so many inappropriate things. It never worked.

JD: RB. You scandalous woman. Trying to seduce a computer.

RB: Stop!!

JD: Just messing with you!

JD: For the record, I tried to do that, too. You aren't alone.

RB: I knew I wasn't the only weirdo!

JD: Where are you all going?

RB: Some restaurant in the city. Mexican, I think.

RB: Tacos are my favorite!

JD: The most important question is: hard or soft tacos?

RB: Hard. 100%.

JD: You're speaking my language.

RB: Can I ask you a favor? It's kind of awkward.

JD: I live for awkward. What's up?

RB: This is going to sound so strange. Can I send you a photo (not of my face, of course) and, as a guy, you can be honest about my outfit?

RB: My friend says it looks great. She's my forever hype-women, though, and required to compliment me.

RB: I want to make sure I look okay.

JD: Yeah, of course. As long as you're comfortable with that.

RB: I am. Hang on, give me a second.

RB: *Attachment: 1 Image*

RB: Thoughts?

JD: I love the color. The green looks great.

RB: Are you sure? You don't have to lie to me! I won't be upset!

JD: At the risk of sounding like a creep, you look fucking gorgeous, and I can't even see your face.

RB: Thank you so much. I'm nervous.

RB: I haven't been on a date in years, so I'm hoping it goes well. Ugh.

JD: I think you're a brilliant conversationalist.

JD: I look forward to hearing from you.

RB: Therein lies the problem.

RB: Sometimes it's as if I'm two different people with two different personas being yanked back and forth like a game of tug-of-war.

RB: There's the virtual side of me, which you've seen, that can come up with witty answers and make people laugh.

RB: In real life, I'm fairly quiet, which is often construed as weakness.

RB: Trust me, if we met before we started messaging, you wouldn't bat an eye at me.
RB: In fact, there's no way you would willingly come up to me in a bar even if I was standing right next to you.

JD: Hey, don't say that. You're making an assumption.
JD: So what if you're quiet? I can be loud enough for the two of us.

RB: Thank you. That means a lot.

JD: I hope you have a good time tonight.
JD: If something goes wrong, text me and I'll give you an escape plan.

RB: I appreciate it :)

JD: Possible escape scenarios: My goldfish died. My house plants need watering. I got food poisoning from eating too many Zebra Cakes.

RB: Hey! Don't hate on my Zebra Cakes! Also, I could talk about house plants for hours, so I need to shut this conversation down so I can walk out the door.
RB: Talk to you later!

JD: See ya later, VRG! Good luck!

TEN

HENRY

"WHY ARE YOU SCOWLING?"

I nearly jump out of my skin, looking up from my phone to find Neil staring at me.

Shit.

I haven't listened to him in minutes, too busy studying the photo RB sent to remember what he last said. The outfit she asked my opinion on is undeniably sexy, a dark green velvet top and a pair of jeans that sit low on her hips. There's a small sliver of skin showing between the hems of the clothing, and I'm... distracted.

My eyebrows pinch together as I zoom in on the picture. The image seems almost familiar in a way, like I've seen this person somewhere before. I know the sentiment is impossible, because I would *definitely* remember this outfit. It's my favorite color. It's hard to put my finger on it, but a sense of attachment pricks my memory the longer I stare.

It's the first time I'm seeing any indication from RB that she's a real human, and I allow myself precisely one minute to wonder what the rest of her might look like. Her face. Her hair. Her smile. Her laugh.

Do her eyes crinkle in the corners when she gets excited about something?

Does she have a dimple when she smiles? Two? None at all?

How tall is she?

Blinking, I break the reverie and return to earth.

"It's nothing." Placing my phone face down on the table, I give him a shrug.

Neil raises his eyebrows. "Nothing? You've checked your phone six times in four minutes. Are you meeting someone after this?"

"No, I'm not meeting someone after this," I snap, irritated by the assumption. "I'm just…"

Just *what*?

Just talking to a random person non-stop, several hours of the day dedicated to carrying on a conversation I look forward to having?

Just continuously checking my phone even though I'm aware nothing is waiting for me because I made sure there wasn't a new notification six seconds ago?

Just dealing with some unpleasant cackling sensation in my chest at the thought of RB spending time with someone else?

This is the opening I've been waiting for to tell Neil about hiring a companion for my parents' party. He wouldn't care. Sure, I'd probably get ribbed for a few minutes, but he'd understand the severity of my situation and realize it was one of my only options.

What I don't want to share is how I can't stop thinking about RB. Even though I've never met the woman, heard her voice, or seen her face, her digital presence is profound, lodged between the other important parts of my life—work, family, and the guys —a constant reminder she's working her way into becoming a regular fixture.

A fixture I want to be there, sturdy and solid and *real*.

"It's nothing important. I'm expecting communication from someone."

"You look like you're about to pull your hair out."

"I'm fine. Anyway, let's hear it. What gives? Why did you drag me out this late?"

Neil grins. "I'm going to ask Rebecca to marry me."

"No shit!" I exclaim, reaching over to pat his shoulder. "That's awesome, man! Congratulations!"

"All I have to do is buy the diamond and hope she says yes. Have you heard of Pinterest? That place is a goldmine."

"She's going to say yes," I laugh, motioning for the approaching waitress. "Can we get two shots of vodka, please? My boy here is getting married."

"How fun! I'll bring them over in a second. On the house, since it doesn't look like *you're* getting married." She winks at me, eyes darting to my ring finger.

"Thanks, Hen," Neil says when we're alone again. "I'm freaking the hell out. Me, a married man. Did you ever think you'd see the day?"

I didn't. Neil's a great guy; arrogant at times and occasionally crass, sure. Being with Rebecca has mellowed him out, though. Gone are the late nights, closing down the bar with giggling girls draped on our arms. Now he picks couples game nights over getting hammered and throws around words like *babies* and *registries* as frequently as his own name.

"Here we go," the waitress says, reappearing with two glasses. She slides them on the table, leaving a folded piece of paper under the one she scoots my way.

"To love!" Neil announces, raising the clear liquid in the air. I mimic him, knocking the drink against his and throwing back the liquid.

"The guys will be bummed they're missing out on the news."

"There's no news. I haven't done it yet. I was in the kitchen, cleaning the dishes, and it hit me. I want to spend the rest of my life with her. I called you before I could start freaking out. We'll have a full meeting with everyone to sort through ring options."

"Lovely," I groan. "I can't wait."

"Hold back the enthusiasm, please," he draws out. "Are you going to do anything with that piece of paper?"

I unfold the note, seeing the waitress' name scrawled on the torn paper. *Lexi.* With a little heart above the i.

"I don't know. Yes? No? Maybe?"

"You're turning down a woman. Are you ill?"

"I've turned down plenty of women. Last night. Saturday night. Do you want me to keep going?"

"Whoa. Are you sure you're okay?"

"I'm fine," I assure him, lying through my teeth.

I don't have time to add anything else, to share the truth about what's been plaguing me, because now my phone is lighting up and I snatch it off the table greedily, pulling up my messages.

> **RB:** What are you up to tonight?

I bite back the grin brought on by seeing her name.

JD: Hey. I'm out with a buddy right now. He just told me he's going to propose to his girlfriend.

> **RB:** That's exciting! Congratulations to him!

JD: Want me to pass along the message?

> **RB:** Eek! No! Don't do that!
> **RB:** Unless he already knows about me…?

JD: No, he doesn't. I'm not ready to share you with my friends yet.
JD: Wow. Pretend that didn't sound incredibly possessive. You know what I mean.

> **RB:** Why not?
> **RB:** Sorry, that was accusatory. I'm just curious.

JD: I'm not sure. They've all done questionable shit in their lives, so there's no room for judgment.

JD: They're going to tease me mercilessly. I'm enjoying keeping this easy right now.

RB: That makes sense.
RB: I think it's perfectly valid to be hesitant.

JD: Thank you. I'm sure you're used to this. I'm not. This is all new to me. Talking to women, I mean.

JD: Not that I don't talk to women. Trust me, I do. I mean in a non-sexual way or a "you're my fake girlfriend" way. I'm still learning the ropes.

RB: I'm happy to be your guide :)

JD: My hero! *insert Olive gif here*

RB: Haha, okay, Popeye! I'll let you go. I don't want your friend to think I'm taking up too much of your time.

JD: Probably for the best. He's very demanding of my attention.
JD: I'll text you later?
JD: How was your date?

RB: I'm turning in early, so I'll talk to you sometime soon.
RB: The date wasn't great. Not a good match.
RB: Have a good night!

Why am I relieved to hear her date didn't go well? Why is there a burst of satisfaction knowing she's already home, not still out with someone? Why am I a jerk who is about to jump for joy knowing she had a terrible time?

Maybe banging a hot woman would help take my mind off this confusion swirling around my brain. Maybe it would point me in the right direction and nudge me down the path I should take. Maybe it'll provide the clarity I'm seeking, so fucking over this uncertainty.

When our waitress returns with our check, I sit up straighter in the booth. "Are you doing anything tonight, Lexi?"

She grins, leaning her forearms on the table just enough to where her cleavage is threatening to tumble out of her shirt.

"Nope. You're my last table."

"What a coincidence. Want a ride home?"

"I'd love that," she purrs, taking my card to ring us out. "I'll be back in a few."

"I'm so glad I got to witness that little sex fest," he observes, pretending to gag.

"Shut up. You're just jealous."

"Jealous? Of what? Hooking up with a random woman one time and forgetting her name in the morning? No way. I think deep down, you're the jealous one, wishing you had something like what Rebecca and I have. Something like what Jack and Jo have. You're 31, man. Do you really still enjoy this casual hookup shit?"

"Maybe I am jealous," I admit.

A committed relationship like what my friends have has never, ever been a desire of mine. I don't want to wait up for a girlfriend to come home from work and make dinner with them. I don't want to cuddle in the morning and drink coffee together in bed, our matching pajamas discarded on the floor while our naked limbs tangle together.

At least... I don't *think* I do?

These days it seems I don't know left from right, too distracted by other things.

Things being...

Her.

"Whoa. Back up. Are you serious?"

"I don't know, Neil. I don't know what I want. Has the idea of one woman filtered through my mind lately? Yeah, it has, and it doesn't sound like the worst thing in the world. Look at you! You're happy. You don't hate your life. Maybe I can be happy, too."

"Cut the bullshit, Dawson. I know that wasn't a client texting you."

"I'm not ready to talk about it."

"But you're ready to go home with someone else? How does that make any sense?"

"It doesn't," I grumble, knowing he has a point.

I'm conflicted. The Henry of the past would have already tumbled out of my seat, pulling Lexi into a dark alcove and dropping to my knees.

But now, even the suggestion of hooking up with someone makes me feel like I'm doing something wrong.

Like I'm betraying RB.

Being unfaithful to a woman who's not even mine.

A woman who has me in a goddamn chokehold because the guilt pumping through my blood is unceasing.

It won't stop screaming at me to *go the fuck home*. To walk away. To climb into bed, eagerly waiting for morning so I can text her again.

Leveling me with a stern look, Neil slides out of the booth. "It's your life, Hen, and you can do what you want. But actions have consequences. Don't forget that." He pats my shoulder and walks away, leaving me all alone.

I used to think learning someone's favorite color and food was bullshit. I didn't care. I didn't see the point. I asked the polite, rudimentary questions required of me so I didn't come off like a total sleazeball. All I wanted was to have a woman on her back, my head between her knees while I ate her out then fucked her til dawn, delighted moans music to my ears. There were no promises to call or meet up again, repeating the cycle again and again until my dick was sore and I couldn't remember anyone's name.

These days, I'm constantly thinking about all the questions I want to ask RB while hopelessly wishing there were more hours in the day to hear her answers.

I can't get enough.

Every minute I wait for a response is another minute wasted. A minute that's escaped us, never to return, a grain of sand in an hourglass ticking away toward a conclusion.

A dreaded ending.

There's so much I've already learned, but I know there's still mountains left to discover. For the first time in my life, I find myself wanting to lace up my hiking boots, grab a backpack and traverse all the trails and hills and expansive terrain of *her*.

I want to know every diminutive detail and prod her for stories and tales and experiences until she's sick of me. I want to hear about all of her favorite things in life in excruciating, elaborate ways. Things like holidays and movies. Seasons and songs.

I'm certain I could listen to her talk for hours. I want to learn what makes her smile. What makes her laugh. What she hates and an exhaustive list of her pet peeves.

She's gotten under my skin. An itch I can't scratch. A delightful anomaly and blip in my life I'm in no rush to get rid of.

My phone buzzes again.

RB: I know I said I was going to bed, but I lied.
RB: This BuzzFeed ranking of road trip foods seemed like a time-sensitive article to share.
RB: One of us has good taste (and it isn't you).
RB: *Attachment: 1 Image*

Something hits me square in the chest, almost knocking me to the ground. It's powerful and painful and extremely difficult to ignore. I grin victoriously, like I won a race in the last few meters, sprinting toward the finish line.

She's thinking about me.

I'm thinking about you too, RB.

"Ready to get out of here?"

I look up to find Lexi standing above me, batting her eyes and popping her hip.

"Shit," I mumble, tucking my phone away. "Hey, sorry, Lexi, but I'm going to head home. Alone."

"Oh." Her face falls. "You have a girlfriend, don't you?"

"No. Not a girlfriend. Just a maybe. A somebody. Nothing will probably ever happen from it, but I—"

"You don't want to mess anything up with a quick blow job."

"Yeah." My hand runs through my hair. "I'm sorry. I didn't mean to lead you on."

"Can I give you a piece of advice?"

"Is it about how much of an asshole I am? Because I agree wholeheartedly."

"No way," she laughs. "It's a little cheesy, but life's too short to let things build inside you. It doesn't do anyone any good to not share them. They need to be out in the world, delivered to people's ears. If you like someone, you should tell them."

I nod, digesting her words. "Thanks for the tips. I know I offered to give you a ride home. Do you still need one? Platonically, of course."

"That's okay! My friend can take me. Good luck with everything." With a wave, she turns and heads back to the kitchen.

"Hey, Lexi?" I call out, needing to know the answer to the question that's been incessantly present for days. "Why is it so terrifying? Why has it never felt like this before? Why is this... this *maybe* sending me into a tailspin, wanting to do everything right?"

She smiles over her shoulder, and it seems like it's full of hope. "I think you'll find out soon enough."

The parting words scare me fucking shitless.

ELEVEN

JD: Happy birthday! I hope you have the best day full of sweet treats!

    RB: Thank you! I woke up this morning and my back cracked so loudly, I'm sure my next door neighbors could hear it.
    RB: Starting the year off right, I guess. Why does everything hurt?!

JD: How is 32 so far?

    RB: Not bad! I got a delicious coffee from my favorite local store, full of sugar, whipped cream, and caffeine. Extra large, too!

JD: Wow. That sounds... elaborate? But also weirdly good?

    RB: The more elaborate, the better!

JD: Hey, speaking of elaborate…
JD: We're three weeks away from the event. I wanted to make

sure everything is still going according to plan. No hesitation or anything?

RB: Nope. Not on my end.
RB: This is the part where we start talking about meeting up in person.

JD: Is it embarrassing to say I'm completely petrified?
JD: Not because I think you've been fooling me or anything like that. Just because it makes everything REAL.
JD: And I really don't want to fuck this up.

RB: Not to inflate your ego or anything, but this is the most nervous I've been to see a commitment through.

JD: *Activate inflated ego mode*

RB: Are you Inspector Gadget now?

JD: You kind of make me laugh.

RB: Yeah, well, you really make me laugh. So I guess I need to step my game up.
RB: I know we both work a lot during the week, so I'd prefer to rule out a weeknight.

JD: How about next Sunday?
JD: What's the name of the coffee shop where you got your drink this morning?
JD: If it's a place where you're comfortable, why don't we pick there?

RB: It's called Beans and Brews. Have you heard of it?

JD: Yeah, it's near my office in the city.

RB: Oh, cool. Mine too.
Is 8 a.m. too early?

JD: I'm an early riser, so 8 is perfect.

RB: Wow. Okay. We're really doing this.
RB: I'm worried you're going to be disappointed when you see me.

JD: Disappointed? Elaborate, please.

RB: It's easy to be someone over text messaging. I hope you enjoy the real me, too.

JD: VRG, unless you turn out to be a 55-year-old man, there's no way I'm going to be disappointed.
JD: I've genuinely enjoyed getting to know you. Meeting in person won't change that.

RB: You only get a few more days to call me VRG. Then you're going to have to use my actual name.

JD: Nope. I intend to introduce you as such:
JD: "Mom. Meet VRG! My spectacular and wonderful girlfriend. She's very real, and not at all fake. Here, let me show you the contract she sent me to seal the deal."

RB: I'm giggling.

JD: I can't wait to hear what that sounds like in real life.
JD: Shit. Sorry. That was weird.

RB: It wasn't weird at all.

JD: Phew. Okay. Sunday at 8 a.m. it is.

RB: I'm looking forward to it :)

JD: Have a wonderful birthday, VRG! Don't bowl too many gutter balls. I hope you get a Zebra Cakes cake! See ya in eight days.
JD: Go go Gadget Birthday Mode!

September 26th

JD: How was your night? I hope you didn't stay out too late.
JD: I know the old folks home has a curfew.

RB: It was great, thank you! Bowling was so much fun, and dinner was delicious!
RB: How was your evening?

JD: Good! I hung out with my friends.
JD: My buddy had a full PowerPoint slideshow of engagement ring options. We had to sit through the entire presentation and give feedback about which one we liked best and why. There was a numeric ranking system, too.

RB: That sounds incredibly sweet.

JD: If by sweet, you mean cumbersome and exhausting, then yes, it was very sweet.
JD: I had no idea so many different rings existed. What the hell?

RB: I take it you don't believe in marriage?
RB: Ack. Sorry. That was incredibly forward of me.
RB: I'm going off our previous dialogue.

JD: To be honest, I haven't entertained the thought deeply enough to lean strongly to one side.

JD: No woman has been present in my life for more than a few nights, so thinking about marriage, a life-long commitment, is hard to envision.

JD: I do think if I ever found someone who makes me laugh, loves me for my stubbornness, and makes me grin when she walks into a room, I wouldn't be opposed to the idea.

JD: I truly don't believe that'll happen. It all seems kind of fake, to be honest. How is that kind of person possible?

JD: I'll believe it when I see it.

JD: What about you?

RB: I think I could be married, sure. With a family and the whole shebang. No one has caught my eye, though. And I'm not in a rush. I'm doing a lot with my career right now, and it might make me sound selfish, but I'd rather dedicate my time to *that* instead of picking out china patterns and centerpieces, you know?

JD: You're preaching to the choir, RB.

RB: It's a waiting game.

JD: What's your favorite flower?

RB: What a random question.

JD: C'mon, ZC. Is this your first day here? You know I live for the random questions.

RB: Sunflowers.

JD: Ah.

RB: That's a vague response.

RB: Is my flower choice not good enough for you?

JD: On the contrary.
JD: Sunflowers are so vibrant and bright. Beautiful. They stand tall, even when they aren't getting the light they require to survive, persevering, stretching, seeking warmth even under a cloudy sky. You strike me as being cut from the same cloth.

RB: JD...

JD: I think I'm going to call you Sunflower from now on.
JD: Sunflower Zebra Cakes.

RB: I don't hate that.
RB: I kind of love it.

JD: Good.

September 27th

JD: Are you ready for the world's strangest question?

RB: Good morning to you, too.
RB: I guess I am. Should I be worried? Are we playing a game?
RB: I had leftover birthday cake before coming into work and now my stomach is revolting against me.

JD: I'm jealous and living vicariously through you, Sunflower, since all I had for breakfast this morning was a meh bowl of cereal.

RB: What kind of cereal?

JD: Cheerios. Trying to make my heart healthy and they seemed like the better choice over Lucky Charms. That little sticker on the box really sold me.

RB: But Lucky Charms are magically delicious!

JD: You're telling me. I've been bitter since I woke up.

RB: Which is your favorite marshmallow shape? I'm partial to the rainbows.

JD: Red balloons. They are superior in taste.

RB: You're so weird. They all taste the same.

JD: Oh, Zebra Cakes. How wrong you are.

RB: Ask your strange question. I'm excited!

JD: Let's say you live in the prehistoric times.

RB: Like Jurassic Park? Or the 1800s without cell phones and technology?

JD: Jurassic Park. The actual time period and not the theme park where everyone got eaten.

RB: Okay, sure. I'm picturing it. Seems a bit quiet and dull. How would I pass the time?

JD: If you had to pick one dinosaur to have as a sidekick, which one would you pick?

RB: Wow.
RB: Give me a minute.

JD: I know. It's a tough question.

RB: Tough? It's an easy question. I'm processing the fact that you actually asked me and you're serious.

JD: Of course I'm serious! It's a valid thing to want to know! What if we're at the party and someone asks me your favorite dinosaur? How the hell am I going to respond?

RB: Okay. Here we go.
RB: A raptor or T-Rex might be the obvious choice. You think they could protect you because they're tough and feared. Revered beasts of the old world. In reality, I think those two would make you a target.
RB: You don't think the Iguanodons would gang up on the big, bad guys? They totally would.
RB: With that being said, I think the Brontosaurus would be the way to go. One of those guys (or gals) would be friends with all the dinosaurs, thus eliminating any potential enemies.
RB: No enemies = greatest chance of survival.
RB: But if I needed to pick one for a fight, I'd take the Stegosaurus.

JD: Holy fuck.

RB: ???

JD: Holy fucking shit.

RB: Why all the goddamn expletives?

JD: I'm speechless. Never in my wildest dreams did I suspect I would get such a thorough and extravagant answer to that asinine question.

RB: Someone's showing off their SAT vocabulary.

RB: Did you think I wouldn't play along?

RB: I can't tell you how long I've waited for someone to ask me what dinosaurs I want as a friend.

JD: You're mocking me.

RB: I'm not! I swear!

RB: Tell me your answer.

JD: I'm embarrassed to share after your stellar picks.

RB: Come on!

RB: Pleaseeeeeee?

JD: I'd pick the Triceratops. They were always my favorite in *The Land Before Time*.

RB: I loved that movie! I haven't seen it in forever!

JD: Maybe after we meet we could have a movie night.

JD: Construct a fort. There's gotta be a tent too, obviously. We'll make popcorn. Eat junk food until the wee hours of the morning.

JD: Break out our Tamagotchis and relive the 90s while watching one of the greatest cinematic achievements of our time.

JD: ...Man, I'm good with crossing lines, aren't I?

RB: To be honest...

JD: I think we need to establish a rule. From now on, we'll promise to be honest, open, and share whatever the hell we're thinking, no matter the consequences or repercussions.

JD: We don't have anything to lose, so why not?

JD: Ready when you are, Sunflower.

RB: You're right.

RB: It sounds like a great plan. Perfect, really. I'd love to have a fort movie night with you. But only if we get the movie theater butter popcorn.

JD: Is there an option besides movie theater butter? We're on the same wavelength with that one.

RB: I should probably get back to work. I've been staring at my phone for 30 minutes.

JD: Sorry. I know you're busy.

JD: I didn't mean to interfere with your day.

RB: You can interfere with my day whenever you'd like.

RB: Especially when it involves dinosaurs. See you in six days!

September 28th

RB: What was your favorite subject in school?

JD: Math. My brain has always enjoyed numbers.

RB: Does your job involve numbers?

JD: Trying to break the rules, Zebra Cakes?

JD: In a way, yes. But not in a purely mathematical sense. What about you?

RB: What a cryptic response.

RB: History. There's something romantic about different time periods in history. Regency England. Paris during Impressionism. It makes our world today seem almost dull.

JD: If you could live at any point in history, what would it be?

RB: I think when art was in it's heyday. Monet. Van Gogh. Ugh, he's my favorite artist and has such a tragic past.
RB: I'd like to exist when he did, just so I could tell him how beautiful his work is.

JD: You strike me as the kind of person who likes to let others know they're loved.

RB: Hitting the nail on the head, JD.
RB: It's one of my biggest flaws. I put others first at an alarming rate. Sometimes I forget about myself.

JD: Can I ask you a personal question?

RB: Sure.

JD: Past relationships. I'm assuming you've had a couple?
JD: I think I'm the only thirty-something who is woefully abysmal in the dating category.

RB: Yes, I have.

JD: What happened? When were they?
JD: I don't mean to pry, but everything I've learned about you has been, well, pretty incredible. You seem like such a wonderful woman.
JD: I guess I'm confused why you have to do this instead of having an actual relationship.

RB: It's only fair I share some of my past with you.
RB: For starters, I don't do this for the social aspect. It's a nice perk, but not the driving force.
RB: As for my personal life, I have some tendencies others have

found difficult in the past. I obsess about things. Sometimes I have depressive thoughts.

RB: It's easy for you to see this fun, friendly side of me on your screen. There's also a portion that's not pretty. It's ugly. It's flawed. It's dark. And a lot of people fear the darkness. They're afraid of what might be lurking beyond the shadow of light.

RB: My dad left when I was younger. For a while growing up, I blamed myself. Maybe I was a taxing child, or a burden and cried too much. I think that lingering hesitancy has haunted me in relationships.

RB: I never want to appear like I'm too much. Or, on the flip side, not enough. Finding someone who accepts me, exactly as I am, is a scary dream.

RB: And a dream I'm not sure will ever happen.

RB: One of my ex-boyfriends cheated on me. The most recent one didn't see a future with me. He said I was too difficult to handle.

RB: So, after all of that, I'll sum it up: You aren't missing much by not having relationships. For as much joy as they can bring, they can also bring immense pain and self-loathing.

JD: I wish I knew your real name. And that I was with you right now.

RB: What? Why?

JD: So I could hug you tight and let you know you're enough. MORE than enough.

JD: You're not too much or too difficult. You're perfect exactly as you are, "flaws" and all.

JD: Though, to me, those aren't flaws at all. They make you, you.

JD: And I'm not going to lie, RB. I cannot wait to meet you so I can experience all of these parts of you myself.

JD: I have a flashlight. We can navigate the darkness together.

RB: That's the nicest thing anyone has ever said to me.

JD: My opinion of you won't change when we meet in real life. I don't want you to act differently around me.
JD: I'm doing this with *you*, and that includes all of you.
JD: Don't hold back. I want every piece of you.
JD: Got it?

> **RB:** You're an extraordinary man, JD.
> **RB:** I can't wait to meet you either.

JD: Five days.

> **RB:** But who's counting?

September 29th

JD: Favorite fight scene from a movie?

> **RB:** Hello.

JD: Oh, yeah, hey.
JD: I'm watching *Creed.* I know, wild Wednesday night over here.
JD: The movie has me all amped up and wanting to take up boxing. So, I'm curious what the best fight scene of all time is.

> **RB:** Honestly, JD. You need to make your questions more difficult.
> **RB:** The answer is the ending to *Thor: Ragnarok.* With Zeppelin playing and everyone kicking ass? Iconic.

JD: Wow. You're totally right.

> **RB:** What song would YOU want to play in the background as you throttle your enemies?

JD: I appreciate you thinking I would throttle my enemies and not crumble like a piece of paper.

JD: That's tough. Do I go the obvious route and pick something punk rock? Or do I go totally into left field and say "Girls Just Wanna Have Fun"?

JD: Screw it. I'm taking Cyndi Lauper. Final answer.

RB: I'm giggling. You're so weird.

JD: I made you laugh, didn't I?

RB: Fair point. You did.

JD: Time for you to answer your own question.

RB: Dang it! Okay. Let's see.

JD: I paused my movie and I'm sitting on the edge of my seat, waiting for your answer.

RB: Hey! I'm not worthy of stopping a movie!

JD: Trust me. You are.

RB: Okay. "Tubthumping" by Chumbawamba.
RB: Or "It's Raining Men" by The Weather Girls.

JD: I'm cracking up. RB!!!!! You have some jokes, woman!

RB: Oh! Or "Why Can't We Be Friends?"

JD: You might be my favorite person who has ever existed.
JD: Four days, Sunflower. Four days.

TWELVE

EMMA

JD: What do you like to do in your spare time? What's your ideal night look like? Spill.

RB: Staying in. A night on the couch reading is my idea of heaven. A blanket. A cup of tea. My warm socks.

JD: That sounds nice. A lot of my time is spent going out.
JD: Sure, some of it is for work, networking and all that.
JD: The older I get, the more your kind of night sounds ideal. Even if it means I'll have to move into a senior citizens home.

RB: There's plenty of room! We eat dinner at 4 p.m. and we're asleep by 8. Do you like shuffleboard?

JD: I'm laughing out loud right now.
JD: You know how people say 'lol' when they have a blank expression on their face?
JD: Laughter is audibly coming out of my mouth. I'm getting the weirdest look from my friend. He's asking if I'm drunk.

RB: Is getting drunk at 1 p.m. something you do often?

RB: Because now I have a lot of questions.

JD: Nah. Sometimes my job makes me want to drink excessively, but I reserve it for after hours.

RB: Yeah? I'm intrigued. Tell me more. What else do you like to do after hours, JD?

THE MESSAGE CHANGES from **delivered** to **read** instantly, like he's *waiting* for me to ask a question along these rapidly blurring lines.

"Shoot," I hiss, throwing the cursed phone across my office. It hits the floor and skids away, sliding under my bookshelf.

The messages JD and I have exchanged so far have been strictly platonic. Funny, interesting, and peppered with hints of deep discussions and thoughtful conversation. What we *haven't* talked about is nighttime activities, what he sleeps in or his favorite sex position. I might as well have just invited him to bang on my desk.

I sneak a glance at the wood, my stomach twisting at the thought, a deep, dark feeling of pleasure greeting me. Would JD be strong enough to balance me on the edge, back flush against the surface while my legs wrapped around his waist? Or would he crawl on top of me, knees bracketing my hips as he caressed my face and whispered those sweet nothings he suggested early on in my ear while I trembled beneath him?

A couple of weeks ago I would have shut this arrangement down the minute any visualization of sexual activity crossed my mind or weaseled its way into our talks. Now I'm itching to know what response waits for me. Will he back down? Use this as an opportunity to meet me, toe to toe?

And which road do I want him to take?

Jumping up from my chair, I scurry to the corner where my phone has made its home. I crouch down, scooping it up.

No answer.

Read.

No answer.

Not even three dots appear to let me know he's actively typing out a response.

I can't text him again. That would be way too aggressive. Maybe I can just burn the device and never talk to him ag—

"Drop something?"

Henry's voice startles me, and I hit my head on the corner bookshelf.

"Ow." I wince, rubbing my forehead, a small bump already forming near my hairline.

"Shit, are you okay?" he asks, crouching next to me and holding my bicep to keep me from toppling over. His eyes rake over my face, checking for any signs of damage. "Emma. Are you okay?" Henry repeats, sharper this time. I blink at his concern and the pressure of his warm, large palm wrapped protectively around my skin. Again.

I think I've missed it.

"I'm fine." After a beat, I scoot out of his hold. "What are you doing here?"

"I knocked. It appears you're having too much of an existential crisis to have heard me. Anything I can help with? Do you need some ice?"

"Nope. Not unless you know how to hack into an iPhone and delete an unintended text message that's already been delivered."

"I'm going to need more details. What kind of message? Is this like a dick pic scenario? A cute photo of a puppy dog? Quoting an entire song from *Hamilton*? Telling someone off for not knowing the difference between your and you're?" He sounds amused as he stands, towering over me.

Damn him. He gets me to crack a small smile even in my panicky despair.

"Why would I want to unsend a song from *Hamilton*?" I ask, peeling myself off the carpet.

"Maybe the person doesn't like musicals."

"True. What's up?"

"I'm dropping off a file for you. An actual file. Since we're friends now."

"Are we friends?" It's a valid question I ponder as I walk back to my desk, plopping in my chair. Every time we interact now, it's less awkward, becoming more natural and… compatible.

"What about amiable associates? Casual colleagues? Blasé business buddies? Dutiful desk mates? Tubular teammates?"

Now I can't resist the smile sneaking all the way through. "Wow. Better. Thanks. An army of alliteration is always appreciated." I take the folder from his outstretched hand.

"How's your day going?"

"Not too bad."

"Until you freaked out over a text you sent and tried to break your phone and your head in the aftermath?"

"Yup. Up until that point, it's been great."

"Next time, if you put your phone on airplane mode while the message is being sent, it won't deliver the text."

"Really? How the heck do you know that?"

"I've been a member of the drunk texting community before, and it's good to know a way to stop your alcohol-infused thoughts from being shared with the rest of the sober world. Trust me, they don't need to hear the eight-paragraph diatribe about why Taco Bell's Crunch Wrap Supremes are the superior menu item. One of my more elegant tirades."

The small giggle escapes accidentally, thunderously loud in the quiet room. When it reaches his ears, Henry perks, up, beaming at me in response. I'm inundated with a fresh wave of heat warming my body all thanks to a perfectly placed dimple.

A perfectly placed dimple I've never had an issue with before.

Now it might be my downfall.

"Thanks for the advice. Are you a verbose drunk or are the Taco Bell poems an anomaly?"

"I'm way too talkative for my own good. Talking means spilling secrets. And secrets have no place out in the open."

"I wasn't aware the outgoing, vocal Henry Dawson has things he doesn't want the world to know."

We don't tease. We don't joke. Yet here I am, lobbing a sarcastic remark his way like we're playing a leisurely game of friendship tennis.

Game.

Set.

Match.

Instead of taking the bait like I thought he would, Henry runs his hand through his hair and I detect an oddly placed smidge of anxious energy. "Not the world. Only certain people. Anyway, Noah says hello."

"It's Wednesday already? Good grief. Tell him I say hi back."

"I love being a messenger between folks who know each other and can interact on their own accord but use me instead, so I'll be sure to pass it along. Have you eaten lunch yet?" His eyes scan my desk and the trash can sitting against the wall for any lingering remnants of food. Finding none, his smile disintegrates into a frown and his shoulders tense.

"I haven't. My best friend is meeting me for a late lunch."

"When is she getting here?"

He asks as if I'm lying to him and trying to evade a meal all together. I hold up my phone, letting him see the message from Nicole announcing her arrival and ignoring the hurricane of unease churning inside me from the lack of messages from *other* parties, hoping JD doesn't pick this moment to answer my question.

"Right now."

Mollified, he nods. "Good. I'll leave you to it. Have a good day, Emma."

"Thanks, Henry. You, too."

He turns and leaves my office, strutting down the hall. The

room doesn't stay empty for long, Nicole taking the chair across from my desk seconds later.

"I know you aren't his biggest fan, but you cannot deny that Henry Dawson is a hot man," she says, greeting me. "Holy hell. He's got to be a ten in the bedroom. Do you think he has a sex swing?"

"Wow, Nic, say it a little louder next time so he hears you."

"And would that be the worst thing in the world?"

"For Henry to know I find him attractive? Yes. Yes, it would. I'm not sure his ego can sustain much more inflation. Poor thing stands to burst any day now."

"I knew it!" Nicole says, hitting my desk. "I knew I could get you to admit he's hot. It might have taken years, but it's finally happened. Hallelujah!"

"Who cares? He knows he's hot. Everyone else in the world knows he's hot. It doesn't matter if I agree with them. My opinion doesn't sway the vote."

"Mhm. Whatever you have to tell yourself," she laughs, pulling out our food from the bag she brought. "Salad and a slice of pizza for you."

"Thank you!" I take the wrapped package and set it on my desk. As soon as I open the plastic covering, my phone buzzes. I grab it, disregarding the steaming slice of cheese waiting for me. JD's name appears.

JD: That depends, Zebra Cakes. What kind of answer do you want to hear?
JD: The nice guy version? Or the not-so-nice guy?

He's letting me dictate how this conversation proceeds. I have a choice, and I weigh the options. Deciding what I want, I type out my response.

RB: It's open for interpretation. However, I distinctly remember us agreeing to be open and honest with each other.

RB: I'm also partial to the not-so-nice guy.
RB: So, take that however you'd like.

JD: Let's see… I go out with friends.
JD: Lately, though, a lot of my nights have been spent at home.
JD: Thinking about you.
JD: For some reason, I can't get you out of my goddamn head.
JD: I've tried. Really fucking hard, Sunflower. But nothing works.

RB: What about me?

"You're smiling and, oh my God, are you blushing?"

"No!" I say, momentarily forgetting I'm in a very public place embarking on what might turn into a very private conversation. It thrills me to know he's going along with this. And, *holy hell*, every time he calls me Sunflower I almost crumble.

"Yes, you are! You never smile at your phone! Your cheeks are so pink."

"That's not true! I smile at my phone plenty!"

"You're avoiding the question. Who is he?" Nicole demands. Dammit. There's no fooling her.

"No one," I sigh, shaking my head.

It's not allowed to be anyone. I'm in unchartered territory, dropped in the ocean without a lifeboat, deadly waves crashing around me.

A visceral connection has been forged with this anonymous human and I'm beginning to worry. The rational, sensible part of my brain is screaming at me to get out of this assignment before it's too late; I'm going to mess up what I've been hired to do and someone is going to get hurt in the process. The money should be my one and only focus, not falling for the guy I'm supposed to be helping.

The other part of my brain—the part infrequently used and often associated with *attraction* and *infatuation*—is hellbent to learn who is on the other side. I'm not sure I can carry on through life without discovering who I've been talking to late into the nights, the glow of my screen blinding in the dark bedroom, minutes slowly ticking by as the time of my set alarm comes closer and closer and I don't want to fall asleep, afraid to miss any sort of communication from *him*.

"It sure looks like someone."

I groan, dropping my head into my hands. "Swear you won't make fun of me?"

"Em, the only time I made fun of you was when you gave yourself bangs. You're beautiful, but they looked atrocious."

She isn't lying. I cried for three days, begging my mom to buy me a wig to hide the disaster on my forehead.

"I think I have a crush on a client," I admit.

"I'm going to need some more details."

Nicole knows the strict no-involvement and no-intimacy clauses both parties sign prior to meeting. There's also the unwritten, moral obligation I follow to keep my private life separate from the business aspect of the job. Over the last few weeks, I've failed miserably, the two mixing and bleeding into each other.

"He understands me, like I've known him for years, if that makes any sense. He's thoughtful and kind, asking how my day is and apologizing for sporadic texts because of work. He makes me laugh. I always look forward to what he has to say. We stay up late talking and learning the most random things about each other. Things I never thought someone would be interested in, like which side of a sandwich the peanut butter goes on, and knowing he despises olives with a passion. When morning comes, we pick right back up, like we were beside each other through the night. I'm distracted at work. I can't focus. All I want to do is talk to him. If this connection had formed from a dating app, we'd be approaching double digit hangouts at this point. It makes sense I'm enjoying him."

"This sounds like more than a crush."

"Fine. Maybe it's a very big crush."

"When's your first meeting?" she asks, tapping her red nails against her cheek.

"Sunday."

"Would you let yourself consider something more serious and personal with this guy outside your agreement?"

"Absolutely not. It's not how this works."

"Hang on. This is your last assignment, right?"

"Right," I agree slowly.

"If there won't be any more clients, maybe it's not the worst thing to open up and consider pursuing something deeper with this one."

"We'll see how the party goes. Four days with a person is a big deal. There might not be any chemistry in person. Good conversation over text messages doesn't translate to sparks when we see each other."

"You look so happy, Em. Joyful. Lighter. I haven't seen you act like this in years. Whatever he's doing, I hope he keeps it up. Stop damning a future before it happens. Go in with an open mind, no expectations, and let it be. Where are you meeting?"

"Beans and Brews."

"You're nervous," she observes.

"I'm petrified."

"I can't wait to find out who it is!"

"That makes two of us. After Sunday, everything will change. And I kind of can't wait to see where it goes."

Buried under the terrified jitters, I'm really, really excited, too.

Bidding Nicole goodbye with a hug, I close the door to my office. My phone buzzed five additional times while we were eating, and it took all of my self-control to not pick it up and read what was waiting for me.

JD: I'm going to give you both versions since you deserve to hear the truth. The nice guy thinks about your personality. I know you're kind, and I can't wait to see exactly how nice and wonderful you are. I can't wait to learn about your job and hear you laugh. I can't wait to see you smile in real life. I'm sure it lights up a room.

JD: Now for what might get me in trouble. But I don't care.

JD: I wonder if your hair is long or short. How much can I fist in my hand and yank so I can stare into your eyes? Can I lift you up and back us into a wall? Or do you prefer traditional spots, like a bed? What do your lips look like? And how do you taste? Sweet? Savory? A delicious combination of both? Are you a good girl who knows how to listen, or do you prefer to be in charge? And, most importantly, I wonder what you sound like when you come. Is it beautiful and quiet? Or is it rough, loud, and unrestrained? God. I need to know, Sunflower.

JD: I won't get those things. Can't have those things. Maybe that's why I want them so fucking bad.

My muscles start to quake, his words seeping into my bloodstream. I'm hot. Turned on. So fucking aroused I'm panting merely from written *words*.

Bad. This is bad. He's in just as deep as I am.

Would JD be sweet and considerate, letting me finish first while he stares into my eyes and tells me I'm beautiful? Or is he fierce and powerful, exerting dominance over me in a way I've craved yet never vocalized? Constructing my reply, my heart overpowers my logical brain, giving in to what Nicole said. What I know I want to do, consequences be damned.

Open up.

Screw it.

RB: I think... I think I want them, too.

RB: So maybe after some time, you can have them.

JD: Yeah?

RB: Yeah.

JD: Sunday needs to hurry up.

RB: Four days.

JD: I'm counting down the minutes.

THIRTEEN

HENRY

I'M ZONING OUT, twirling a pencil absentmindedly between my fingers and not paying attention to the men chattering around me in the conference room as we wait for the meeting Wallace called to start. He mass-emailed everyone yesterday afternoon, letting us know about an important announcement taking place, and attendance was mandatory.

I'm fairly certain he's going to tell everyone about Richards' departure, which also means he's going to be sharing the news that Emma and I are both up for partner.

Dread notches its way down my spine. I'm not quite ready for the rest of the firm to know we're going against each other. We've pleasantly coexisted as of late, and I'm enjoying this new dynamic between us. We're not full-fledged friends yet, but I think we could get there with time.

Hopefully.

She even awarded me a polite nod in the hallway the other day when I walked to lunch, a minuscule gesture that made my heart skip a literal beat. That's never happened before, and I rubbed my chest the rest of the afternoon, trying to find the source of the unrhythmic shift.

Emma and I are taking small baby steps in the right direction, but after the announcement, the jokes will roll in. Mumbled comments mentioning our inexperience will follow, and I don't want her to get caught in the crossfire.

I have the urge to send RB a message and ask for advice. Talking about work and our occupations is off-limits, I know, but I could use some motivation or encouragement leading into this inevitable shitstorm. That woman always says the right things, making me feel better when I'm down.

As if on cue, my phone buzzes in my pocket. I know it's her. It's weird, but I can tell when she's the one to message me. We don't have a strict communication schedule, but I light up when my phone vibrates at specific times during the day, knowing RB's sneaking in a message to me during her free moments at work.

I smile, leaving the device hidden away. I don't need any taunting or teasing from the surrounding assholes who think they're better than everyone else just because they went to Harvard fucking Law.

Big deal.

These people aren't my friends. I dislike a lot of them, hating the frat boy atmosphere that always develops when we're altogether. They're smart, though, dropping the stupid shit before Wallace or one of the other partners sees.

The men sniff out any signs of weakness, rejoicing when they find a way to catapult themselves to the top of the employee list, not caring who they damage in the process.

There won't be any congratulations tossed my way when the announcement is made. No one will wish me luck. They'll all be plotting ways to expose some dark secret of mine, wanting the position for themselves.

Selfish bastards.

My phone buzzes again, and my smile grows. I smile a lot more often these days, and I know RB is the source of this newfound excitement. We haven't spoken since yesterday's confessional, and I feel guilty.

I didn't intend to push as far as I did, sharing the thoughts that have formed in the dark corner of my mind. They're out there now, and I can't take them back.

I don't think I would if I could.

There are only hours until we meet. Friday and Saturday are going to crawl by, cruelly mocking me as I wait patiently to meet the woman who's rocked my world.

God, I can't wait to answer her in a few minutes.

A jarring laugh from the man to my right causes me to blink, focus returning to the scattered papers taking over my spot at the table and away from the hole burning in my pocket.

"Take Emma for example. She spends more time here than anyone else. There's no way she's getting laid." Brad, one of my unfortunate colleagues, smirks.

A smatter of dull laugher accompanies the comment, the rambunctious amusement from seconds ago quieting. Only a festering pool of ugly testosterone occupies the room. While we have a few other female employees at the firm, Emma is the lone woman attorney. Our lack of diversity has always pissed me off. The majority of the employees are straight, white men who are so out of touch with reality and today's world it hurts. If I get the partner spot, adding someone other than a person who looks like me is the top priority.

Fucking bullshit.

"Dude, come on. She'll be here in a minute."

"So? You can't tell me she doesn't know what she's doing when she wears those skirts. Her ass is so round. I want to bend her over this table and let all of you watch. God, she'd probably be a dream, spread out for us. A fucking buffet, and the perfect little slut. It's always the quiet ones. I bet she likes to take it like a whore. A little birdie told me she's up for partner. There's no way that'll happen. Unless she fucks Wallace first. Maybe she already has."

A cord inside me snaps. I'm blind with anger. Brimming with rage. Before I can think twice, my palm is slamming against the table and I'm on my feet. We passed my breaking point eight sentences ago. Those comments crossed a line and I'm awake now, revving for a fight. Eager to hurt. Ready to inflict unfixable pain.

"You need to shut up," I snarl, glaring at the perpetrator.

"What was that?" Brad asks. He's grinning, eyes full of mirth, no trace of remorse to be found. He doesn't care what he said to his fellow colleagues in a public domain, the brazenness and crassness loud enough for anyone in the building to hear. He's flaunting it and shoving it down our throats.

I'm two seconds away from lunging at this piece of trash and letting my fists run wild, giving him a piece of my mind and showing everyone exactly what I think about his remarks.

Fucking bastard.

"I said, you need to shut the fuck up," I repeat, louder this time. I'm done being soft-spoken, no longer the nice guy. I'm a wolf now, snarling in the face of a man I want to destroy for tearing *her* down. "How dare you sit there and talk about a colleague that way? Would you speak about one of us like that? Is it because she's a woman? Emma has been here for years—eons longer than you—and does an exceptional job. She's changed the community, and helps people day in and day out, which is more than I can say for you." Every pair of eyes is on me, and I power on, unfazed by the attention. "If I ever hear you disrespecting her or any other woman like that again, I'll make sure they revoke your bar license and you'll never practice again. Mark my fucking words."

"Are you going to call in a favor to daddy?" Brad jokes, knowingly hitting a nerve.

I hate when people imply I've earned my success because of my father. I love the man to pieces, but all of my accomplishments in life have been on my own, not from his hand.

I've never been a violent man. I'm a lover, not a fighter. The temptation to pulverize this asshole to a pathetic pile of mush is strong, though. Fury rips through me, a wildfire spreading in a drought-dry field. A lightning strike on a dead tree in a summer storm. Flames envelope my vision, and I see every shade of red imaginable. I have an urge to *protect*.

Defend.

Keep *safe* and *free* from harm.

"We don't pull that kind of shit here." My voice has settled to an eerie calm. "Emma is an outstanding attorney. She posted one of the highest bar scores in the last 50 years and is a better human being than your sorry ass will ever be. One more word out of your mouth about her, and I will not be responsible for my actions. Your face will be covered in blood when I'm done with you. I will rip you to pieces. I will destroy your entire life. Want to know the best part? I don't give a fuck about the consequences. Losing my job would be worth it to permanently shut you the fuck up."

I storm through the door, leaving the conference room behind. I need to get out of here before I act on my words and do something drastic. Every threat was real, and I'd yell it through a megaphone if I could. Fuck what HR has to say.

I forgo the elevator and take the stairs down, all ten flights of them, legs and muscles screaming in protest as I descend the concrete again and again, pounding away from the war zone I almost created. When I reach the bottom floor, I shove the door to the outside world open so forcefully, a woman passing on the sidewalk shrieks at the noise.

"Sorry," I apologize, not intending to take my wrath out on anyone else. My head lifts toward the sun and I close my eyes, letting the warmth wash over my body.

"Henry?"

My eyes fly open to find Emma biting her lip, a cautious distance of space between us.

"Hey." I rub the back of my neck, attempting to steady my breathing. "What's up?"

Hopefully my voice comes out neutral and not dripping with malice and contempt. I'm not mad at *her*. Far from it. I want to reach out and hug her, shielding her from the shitheads sitting ten stories up.

"Are you okay? You stormed out of the building pretty quickly."

"I'm fine. I needed a minute."

The rage might be deteriorating, but pure adrenaline is still very much prevalent. I could run lap after lap with how amped up I am.

"Sorry. I don't mean to interrupt. I can leave you alone."

"No. You can stay. Please stay."

She nods, turning her attention away from me. We stand in companionable silence for a handful of minutes, our gazes both transfixed on the traffic clogging the street. A soothing breeze flutters through the air, cooling my skin, and I sigh in relief.

Emma has a calming presence, and it's obvious she's letting me have a moment to relax, for which I'm grateful. She clears her throat, giving me ample warning she's going to speak and to leave if I want.

I don't. I want to hear what she has to say.

"Are we going to stand in the middle of the sidewalk until it's time to go home?" she asks, wearing a small smile.

The slight tip of her lips could power an entire city.

"I needed to get out of the building before I killed someone. And I mean that literally."

"Your day seems a lot worse than mine. Anything I can help with?"

"Not unless you know how to deal with sexist pricks."

"I've kind of been doing that my entire life. You have to brush it off. I learned long ago that HR can't really do anything regarding a complaint unless there's evidence to back it up. Unfortunately, people are more apt to keep their heads down and mouths closed when they witness that kind of behavior. You think the guys in the office want to challenge Brad? No way. They're fearful of him. Or they agree with what he says."

Of course Emma knows how to tackle sexist pricks. I'm sure she's heard some of the comments from our coworkers. It doesn't deter her, though, and she barely acknowledges their existence, not letting the rude remarks rile her up. The audacity of Brad to speak about Emma like that. To speak about *any* woman in that way.

Does RB deal with this kind of behavior? Is she harassed too? The anger from before starts to regrow, a fresh coat of red painting my blood.

I sigh defeatedly, so fucking frustrated that situations like this occur daily and no one steps in to do anything.

"I'm sorry," I whisper, knowing it holds little weight in the grand scheme of what women—what Emma and RB—face every day.

"Why are you apologizing?"

"I know I've said it before, but it needs to be said again. I'm so sorry, Emma, for every stupid, pathetic attempt at humor that's come at your expense. I also want to apologize for all the horribly offensive things a man has ever said to you. You deserve to hear it, even if it doesn't heal old wounds."

She's quiet for a moment, and I think I've overstepped a boundary or made this about me somehow, deflecting away from the problems at hand. She stares at me with such a piercing look. Her blue eyes give nothing away, not a hint of what she might be thinking. When she finally speaks, her words are quiet. Fractured. Hesitant. Cautiously trusting.

"I heard what you said; how you stood up for me. For all women, really. Thank you, Henry. It's rare for a man to call out inappropriate behavior in the workplace. I've never heard someone do it before."

What the fuck have the men in her life been doing to keep her safe? And how the hell is she so calm right now?

How can I help, Emma?

Let me help you carry this burden.

"What that scumbag said about you crossed a line. Multiple lines. I know you can fight your own battles. Fuck, you're the best attorney in the building. I don't think you need me to swoop in and help you in a situation like that, exerting some masculine power and considering you a damsel in distress. I just couldn't sit there silently and laugh. I'd do the same if someone talked about my mother that way. Or my sister. I protect people I care about, Emma, and that includes you. It always includes you."

Her hand touches my arm, soft fingers pressing into the exposed skin under my rolled-up sleeves. The contact has an immediate effect; my lungs deflate, greedily inhaling air. My shoulders sag. The world appears a little brighter and less bleak.

The gesture awakens me, climbing out of the cave of slumber I've been in.

She inhales sharply, head tilting down to study where we're joined, observing the skin-on-skin contact. I see the moment pass through her mind where she knows she should let go; she should release me from her hold. It's been too long now, well past a friendly, reassuring moment. Instead, her thumb rubs down my forearm to my wrist and back up toward my elbow, a comforting motion that has me shifting on my feet, heat following her trail.

I think I'd be okay with her touching me forever, never letting go.

"I can fight my own battles," she starts, severing our contact. I'm cold without her. Lost, too. "But it's nice to have someone on my side. Sometimes I need backup. We all do."

"Consider it done. Going forward, no more jokes. Only fighting words."

"Don't say that. You wouldn't be Henry without the jokes!"

"I'll have to come up with some new material when you get the partner position."

"Do you really think I'll get it?"

I smile proudly. "Yeah, I do. How could you not? You're overqualified. Everyone enjoys working with you. You're wicked smart. Wallace would be a fool to pick me. I meant what I said in the hallway, Emma. I *want* you to you to be the one who gets it."

The smile she gives me is sad. Her eyes are dim. Muted. Tired. So exhausted from putting up with the same shit again and again.

"As nice as it is to hear the flattery, it doesn't change what

Brad said. There's truth in his words. As long as men like him exist and continue to think archaically, being a partner will never be enough. Nothing will ever be good enough. It won't stop the inappropriate jokes. It won't stop people from wondering if I got the job because I slept with someone."

"I hate that you're subjected to such crap," I grumble, shoving my hands in my pockets to prevent myself from doing something stupid, like reaching out and giving her a hug or pressing a comforting kiss to her forehead—things I've never wanted to do before. "Maybe one day there will be a firm full of progressive, diverse lawyers who will change the world, like you're doing here. Everyone else can fuck right off."

Emma laughs, and it's the most beautiful, heart-warming sound I've ever heard. Her giggles are cute, but they don't hold a candle to hearing the sound of her pure, unfiltered happiness. Out here, in the open, the noise is so freeing. We're two ordinary people enjoying a conversation, the ties that have tethered us together for so long have snapped, allowing us to start anew. There's no history. No past. No future. Just… us.

"We should make that elegant saying into a t-shirt. Come on. We have a meeting to get to."

"Do we have to?" I groan.

"We do. We'll suffer through it and be fine."

"Together," I add. "We're in this together. Your fight is my fight. And even though they'll crown one of us a winner in a few short weeks, we face *this* challenge together. Deal?"

Emma contemplates the offering, searching my face.

I let her.

I let her see my honesty, meaning every syllable.

I let her see that I'll punch a guy in the face for being disrespectful toward her.

I let her see how angry I am, determined to help find a solution to all these goddamn problems.

Satisfied with what she finds, she nods, looking away. I swear her eyes glisten with tears.

"Together," she agrees firmly, marching back into the building, head held high.

A goddamn superhero. That's what Emma is. That's what all women are. I'll kill anyone who says otherwise. Especially to someone like Emma or RB, two of the most dynamic women in my life.

I haven't even met the latter yet, but I already know she's done something so profound to me.

FOURTEEN

HENRY

JD: This might sound creepy.

RB: Have you murdered someone? Are you stalking me? Wait, are you one of those guys who buys people's underwear off the internet?

JD: A. That's disgusting.
JD: B. I'm offended.

RB: Glad we got those off the table. Let's hear it.

JD: I'm excited to put a face to these messages. How dorky does that sound?

RB: What if I'm some ugly troll?

JD: Even if you were, which I doubt is true, I wouldn't care. I've really enjoyed getting to know you, and I just…
JD: I have this image of you built up in my head and I'm excited to see if I'm right.
JD: And even if I'm NOT right, I think you're still going to be

incredible.

RB: Try guessing. If you get something correct, I'll let you know.

JD: I imagine you liking oversized sweatshirts and mismatched socks, but you don't care, because they're cozy and warm and make you happy even if the colors contradict each other.
JD: You'd be content sitting on the couch, reading a book, with a candle burning on the end table. You strike me as very low maintenance, so you probably pull your hair back.
JD: Maybe a messy bun or whatever it's called?

RB: Are you in my house with me? This is all weirdly accurate.

JD: I knew it!

RB: What color do you think my hair is?

JD: I want to say brunette, but I'm leaning toward blonde.

RB: Now I'm freaked out.

JD: You're probably a fan of bubble baths and spending time with a small group of friends. You'd prefer going to the library or museum over a club or trendy restaurant. Low key, but still social.

RB: All correct. The history museum is one of my favorite places in the world. When I was younger, I wanted to spend the night there. I tried to make it happen once. I hid in the bathroom, hoping no one would notice I was missing.
RB: My mom found me ten minutes later.

JD: So shutting the history museum down for you would earn me a lot of points?

RB: I can neither confirm nor deny that completely accurate question.

JD: Got it. I'll tuck that tidbit of information away for a later date.

RB: And do what with it?!

JD: Have it on the back burner in case I need to woo you or make up for stealing all your Zebra Cakes or something.
JD: I gotta have plans, Sunflower.

RB: Now I'm wondering what kind of person you are to have the power to shut down a museum...
RB: Unless you work at the museum. In which case, I have so many questions about all the dinosaur bones.

JD: I don't work at the museum.
JD: Back to you. I like talking about you. I think you're short.
JD: Like I could pick you up and you'd wrap your legs around me and it wouldn't feel like I was holding you at all.

RB: That depends on how tall YOU are.

JD: How tall do you think I am?

RB: A giant, easily towering over me and the rest of the world, probably.
RB: I bet you're able to get people to do what you want because you're so imposing.
RB: You boss people around and they listen to you, because otherwise you'll squish them with your long legs and authoritative voice.

JD: How do you feel about authoritative voices?

RB: I... like them.

JD: Noted. And I am tall. 6'4. An honest 6'4. Not 5'10 rounded up to 6'4.

RB: Why do men feel the need to lie about their height?

JD: It's definitely a confidence thing. They don't think women are going to go around carrying yardsticks.
JD: We're also dumb. That's the easiest answer.
JD: Besides my staggering height, tell me what else you envision about me.
JD: Yeah, I'm selfish for asking.

RB: I think you're kind. Not in the sense you hold the door open for everyone walking in.

JD: Wow! I love holding the door open for people. I also always return my shopping cart.

RB: What I mean is you're probably loyal to your friends and stick up for them. You also probably help the occasional elderly woman cross the street and flirt with her afterwards.
RB: This next part might be a little bold...
RB: I think you're going to be handsome AND hot. A combination of the two, which, yes, is a thing. People probably gawk at you when they pass.
RB: I already know you're way out of my league.

JD: Doubtful. I think it's the other way around.

RB: We'll see soon, won't we? 36ish hours.

JD: Time isn't moving fast enough.
JD: What are you up to tonight?

> **RB:** Speaking of bubble baths…
> **RB:** *Attachment: 1 Image*

MY JAW DROPS and I bite my knuckles to suppress the groan that wants to escape from my mouth.

"What the hell is wrong with you?" Neil asks, staring at me like I'm insane.

It's Friday night, and the guys and I are together for our weekend-kickoff drinks and food.

"Nothing," I say quickly, clicking away from the photo before anyone can spot the source of my excitement.

RB sent me a picture of her in the bath.

Okay, sure, there are bubbles everywhere and only her ankles and painted toes are barely visible through the suds. The rest of her body is *heavily* obscured and the lighting is dim.

Still.

It's a photo.

And she's naked in it.

She's talking to me naked.

She's never sent me a picture so personal before, and thank fuck she hasn't, because now I'm useless. My brain cells are melting and disintegrating one at a time.

Holy fuck.

I've received private photos from women in the past. Images with seductive lighting and perfectly curated posed positions have filtered across my screen. This one from RB is different. It's private. Intimate. Not staged. The angle is wonky and it's a little dark.

But it's designed for only *me* because she's thinking about *me*, right now, and not using a photo from a batch that might get sent to another guy down the road.

"He's talking to his girlfriend," Noah supplies and I slap his arm.

"Girlfriend?!" Patrick asks. "Excuse me?"

"I don't have a girlfriend!"

"I know you talk to her at work. And when we're at lunch," Noah says casually. He's an instigator and knows exactly what he's doing.

"Can someone please explain what the hell is going on?" Neil asks. "You two have a secret the rest of us don't know and it blows."

A part of me was secretly hoping I could keep this whole situation under wraps, not disclosing any information to the guys until after the party when I could brush it off and laugh over a few beers.

It's no longer going to be that easy, given we're meeting soon and she's currently sending me bathtub photos that are causing me to melt into a puddle on this damn bench.

My friends deserve to know what's going on, especially because I'm going to need some serious advice on how to proceed from here. It's time to come clean.

Heaving a sigh, I get ready to begin the tale.

God, they're going to laugh their asses off.

"Noah already knows. He got me into this predicament."

"I did no such thing. I pushed you in the right direction. You're the one who decided to jump."

"What the hell are you jumping into? Spill," Patrick demands.

I launch into the full story, telling them about Noah passing along RB's contact information, and the messages that have transpired. I share about our frequent communication, and that she's going to be attending the anniversary party with me. When I let them know I'm going to be meeting her in a few days, in person, for the very first time, Patrick audibly *gasps* and Jack drops his fork onto the table.

When I finish talking ten minutes later, no one says a word.

"Will someone please speak? You're freaking me out," I mumble.

"Let's run this back so I can make sure I'm understanding this correctly," Neil says. "Henry Dawson, notoriously anti-relationships and dating, hired someone to be his girlfriend."

"Yeah."

"You're paying them a fuck ton of money."

"It's not that much."

"You have no clue who they might be or what they look like. They don't know who you are."

"Correct." I fidget, fingers tapping on my thigh.

"You don't know their name or anything about them at all."

"Mhm."

"And, despite all of the aforementioned illogical facts, you're still planning on meeting up with this definitely-not-real person and going through with this plan?"

"Yup, you got everything right, except for the part about not knowing anything about her. I know plenty about her."

"This is a terrible idea!" Neil exclaims.

"I can't think of anyone I can stand long enough to be around for multiple days," I challenge, crossing my arms over my chest defiantly. "The only girl I've hooked up with more than once, Shelby, drives me up a wall when I spend too much time with her, so she's out. I also don't want to be attached to a woman after my money, which is exactly who my mom was unknowingly trying to set me up with. Whoever is on the other end of the phone makes me laugh, has a good head on their shoulders, and likes talking to me. What else can I ask for?"

"Or they're a dude in their mom's basement fucking with you?" Patrick supplies.

"I can vouch for him. It's legit. My buddy used the services and said she's great," Noah chimes in.

Neil pinches the bridge of his nose. "It sounds so wild. It's literally like one of those books Rebecca reads."

"Jo reads those books too," Jack adds. "It makes it more believable, I think. Why go to these great lengths just to mess with you?"

"It's great the two of you are in happy and loving relationships," I say, gesturing to Neil and Jack. "Not all of us are with someone who can easily accompany us to events where we're going to be badgered with endless questions about the future. It's embarrassing and humiliating enough having to pay someone to pretend they like me.

"My mom was thrilled when I told her. It's only going to be a few days. We aren't getting married. We aren't falling in love. It's a business transaction. I'm paying her for her goods and services."

At the end of the day, RB is going to collect her paycheck, we're going to part ways, and I'll never hear from her again. It pains me to vocalize the truth; to bulldoze the strong foundation we've built and reduce it to a pile of rubble, no trace of emotional connections surviving. That's the reality of our situation, even if we talk about movie nights and hanging out normally. We're doing a good job at playing pretend for a future outside the four days I've hired her for.

I fucking *hate* pretend.

"What was the photo?" Patrick asks.

"Pardon?"

"The photo that made you moan when you saw it?"

"I wasn't moaning!"

"Yeah, sure, whatever you have to tell yourself."

"It was a generic, nondescript photo."

"She sent you a nude?!"

"No!" I practically holler, blushing deeply at the implication.

I'm not sure I *want* to receive a nude photo from her. Sure, objectively, I wouldn't be disappointed. I'm already convinced she's a stunning woman.

Have I considered lifting her up, pinning her against a wall, and ravishing her? Yeah. Repeatedly.

I've also dreamed about pulling her hair and driving her wild, learning all the things that make her want to lose control. I told her as much the other day.

Fuck, I want to taste her. *All* of her. So fucking bad. Her mouth. Her skin. What I would give to eat her out for hours, devouring her wicked flavor again and again until she was a spineless, withering mess, the aftermath of her orgasms dribbling down my chin as I beamed with pride and awe.

I wouldn't bother cleaning up.

Those are all far-off ideas, though; fleeting desires and passing musings. If I ever was fortunate enough to be with her intimately, I would want to discover her body for myself.

I'd want to study every curve of her muscles, and the way they move and ripple when my fingers trace over them, learning the sculpted, defined lines of her body. I'd like to memorize the number of freckles she might have, counting them one by one like constellations and creating an art project out of their locations. Perhaps there's one on her inner thigh I could kiss, up near her hip bone. Or behind her ear, near the column of her neck. I'd take my time, going slowly, steadily, appreciating her skin under mine as my palm runs across the expanse of her beautiful shape.

One stupid nude wouldn't be sufficient.

It would be like trying to capture the wonder of the star-covered sky with your phone. The photo never does it justice; the lighting isn't perfect. It's grainy. A little dark and a little hazy. The final product doesn't encompass the sheer splendor of nature's beauty, failing to highlight the best parts you're unable to put into words.

The same could be said about a picture from RB.

I can't deny the bath photo ignites me, however. I want to be in there *with* her, pulling her onto my lap to see how well we fit together. Her damp hair clinging to my skin like a persistent weed, strands of blonde latching on and never letting go.

What is this woman going to do to me when I actually see her? Kill me with a single piercing look? Have me dropping to my knees, ready to beg and bend to her every ask and demand?

"It's her in a bubble bath and all I can see are her feet."

"That made you excited?" Neil scoffs.

"For fuck's sake, not all of us have a fiancé at home who can give us a blow job whenever we ask," I snap. "It's been a while since I've had sex. I'm a little wound up."

"I'll say," Jack mutters. "I like Getting Laid Every Night Henry better."

"How long is a while?"

"Three weeks. Almost four."

Since RB's first email.

Since I felt a strong, noticeable presence lodge in my chest and refuse to leave, taking up a permeant residence after the very first question I asked.

Since a swarm of butterflies fluttered in my stomach, an excitement going through me with every flash of her name across my phone.

An amount of time that's seemed infinite but has also passed in the blink of an eye.

When I talk to her, I don't measure it in seconds and minutes and hours and days like I would with anyone else. I measure it in smiles. Laughs. Late nights. Early mornings. Dreams. Hopes. Fears. Sunflowers. Zebra Cakes. My lips tug upward at the mere thought of her.

When I talk to her, problems and irritations and all the other negative things in the world cease to exist.

When I talk to her, nothing else matters.

When I talk to her, I'm... home.

"Holy shit. You didn't hook up with that waitress?" Neil asks.

"Nope."

"No one from a bar?"

"No."

"You're never like this," Jack observes. "She must be special."

I don't think special is even close to what she is.

"You keep glaring at your phone, hoping it lights up," Patrick adds.

"He also smiles, too," Noah sings, pinching my cheek. "Our little Henry, all grown up and in love."

"Have we all gotten our jokes out? Good. In all seriousness, Hen, are you going to go through with this?" Patrick asks, and all eyes are on me.

"Yeah. I am."

"Is your mom excited?"

"She's ecstatic, but I'm terrified she's going to see right through this charade and call us out."

"I so wish I could be there to see her reaction," Noah groans. "Damn work trip."

"Are you two going to kiss? When Jo and I pretended to fake date, I made it very clear kissing was off the table," Jack says. "I knew if and when I finally got to touch her, it was game over."

"Was it difficult not to?"

"I've never jerked off so many times in my life," he mumbles and we all chuckle. "In the end, it was worth it."

"Kissing wasn't something I planned to do," I admit.

There's a heaviness in my statement, because despite the accuracy of it, it doesn't eliminate the temptation. The longing, pulsing need to have her mouth on mine. To feel her shiver beneath me as I claimed her again and again and again, not bothering to come up for air. I have the strangest suspicion I'll only need her to survive.

The no physical contact is one of her steadfast rules; the same ones I agreed to with a signature I sent to a goddamn private investigator. The same ones she reiterated when we started talking. The same ones that are becoming more blurred by the second, every seemingly polite message laced with a deep-rooted lust and push for *more*.

If—and when—any physical contact beyond the pretend boundary of fake partners happens, she's going to have to be the one to initiate it. If she wants me to touch her, she's going to have to say it. If she wants me to touch her, she's going to have to touch me first.

And *fuck*, I hope she does.

"How are you going to convince your family you're dating someone if you don't even kiss them?" Neil interjects.

"We can do things other than kissing. Hand holding. Stop laughing, you assholes!"

"You're going to spend four days with the woman you're calling your girlfriend, not kiss her, and expect your family to go along with it? They're going to see straight through your bullshit."

"Enough," I say firmly, my voice signifying the finality of the incessant teasing and jokes. My friends blink at me in surprise, caught off-guard by the sharp tone. It's out of character for me, but I'm done with the sarcasm. "I've weighed all the pros and cons. Numerous times. For the first time in my life, I'm excited to get to know a woman, and not just because I want to sleep with her. No matter how fake this might be, it's a big step for me."

"You're right, H. This is important, and we're not discrediting that at all. We want to make sure you've thought about all the potential outcomes here. And that you don't get hurt," Jack says kindly, lacking any judgment.

"This is what I'm doing."

"You really don't know anything about her? No physical features? What she does for work?" Patrick asks.

"I'm going into this blind and it's really scary. There's a connection here, at least on my end, and I'm excited to see if it's reciprocated."

"Has she given you any signs that it isn't?"

"Nah. I don't want to get my hopes up, you know? I'm literally counting down the hours. The minutes. The seconds. I pick up my phone, stare at the clock, and do the mental math until Sunday. And I hate these fucking feelings. She's all I can think about. I don't care what she looks like or what her voice sounds like. She can be short or tall, skinny or curvy, and I won't care. The only thing I do care about is finally seeing her, and hoping that when I do, everything makes sense."

"What kind of feelings?" Patrick asks.

"I'm discombobulated. My brain isn't processing anything but her, and I don't know what the fuck it all means."

"What else?" Jack encourages me, goading me to keep talking.

"My chest aches when I go all day without hearing from her,

anxiously wondering if I did or said something wrong. And when my goddamn screen lights up and I see her name there? Everything is right in the world. I'm calm. Peaceful. Steady. I fall asleep thinking about her and I wake up excited to hear from her again— a vicious, wonderful cycle that can't be broken. I'd build a rocket ship, fly to outer space, and find a way to give her a corner of the fucking sun if she asked for it, not batting an eye at the burns I'd earn. I'm the biggest idiot because this shit isn't me. This isn't what I do. I fuck then I leave. Yet for some unexplained, stupid reason, it's what I want to do with *her*, and it's driving me insane."

"Henry," Jack starts. "You are not an idiot. Get that shit out of your head. You're looking at four men who have all been tortured and broken by a woman at some point in our lives. I was stupid every time I talked to Jo. I felt like a loser for even daring to think about her in something other than a coworker capacity. I thought I was a fraud for imagining she would want anything to do with fucked up, asshole me. The bright, shining princess settling down with the messed up guy who carried all sorts of baggage? No way in hell. Every day was fucking agony."

"You want to talk about tortured? Do you know how much it hurts to look at someone and know you can never have them? To recognize you'll spend the rest of your life pretending to be excited for them, all while your soul fractures as you watch them find happiness with someone else?" Patrick asks, voice cracking and barely above a whisper. "Walking away hurts too damn much, so I put up with the pain. I'm too much of a coward to voice how I feel. I can't, because if I do, I'll lose her forever. And I cannot lose her. She means too much to me."

"I let the one woman who loved me for me, and not my finances or fame, get away," Noah adds, hanging his head. "All because I wouldn't move to be with her. Now she's happily married, and I'm constantly wondering *what if*? What if I had chased after her? What if we made it work?"

"I wake up every day fearful Rebecca is going to realize she can do so much better than me," Neil sighs. "I'm selfish and arrogant. She sees the good in me and doesn't leave. But that could change any minute."

"You see?" Jack asks, his hand grasping my shoulder. "You're not in this alone. You're not an idiot. Far from it. You're a man who cares about someone, which is *allowed*. It's scary because it's new and different from what you know. Trust me, I get it. We all get it. No matter what does or doesn't happen on Sunday, your feelings are valid, and we love you a whole fucking lot. Worry about the complications later. You gotta do what makes you happy, Hen. And if this girl brings you even an ounce of joy, you gotta fucking go for it, man. You'll hate yourself if you don't."

"Fuck," I curse, dipping my head and wiping my eyes. They're damp with tears and I brush the moisture away, grateful for the solidarity from the men surrounding me. The raw honesty shared by them—my brothers—to help make me feel better pierces my heart like a sharp dagger. Deep.

I'm not alone.

"Thank you," I get out, raising my chin to look at each of them individually. "All of you. I love you guys."

"We love you too," Patrick says, voice quivering. "But now that the moment is over, I think we need some alcohol and fries because that was deep as hell. We're never talking about it again."

I huff out a laugh. "Alcohol. Carbs. And trying not to have a panic attack thinking about the next 36 hours. Bring it on."

FIFTEEN

JD: I need to tell you something, and I need to say it before we meet tomorrow.
JD: I don't want you to get mad at me.

RB: Why would I get mad at you?

JD: It goes against your rules.

RB: Let's hear it.
RB: Full disclosure, I'm probably going to share it with my best friend.
RB: She'll help me dissect every word. Proceed with caution.

JD: Okay. Here goes nothing.
JD: Over the last few weeks, I've slowly had this vision coming together in my mind. Of you. Of us. Being together for real. As partners. Equals. Companions and counterparts.
JD: I know that violates everything you've spoken about up to this point.
JD: I know I signed an agreement stating to not engage in anything physical with you, but I wanted to be honest.

JD: I would NEVER act on these feelings, or coerce you into anything. I can keep my hands to myself. I know no means no. And I respect that thoroughly.

JD: I thought you should know all of this before tomorrow because I'm terrible at hiding stuff, Sunflower, and I don't want to keep anything from you.

JD: I know this connection has been formed on not whole truths. But YOU deserve the truth. I know we could meet and have NO sparks or chemistry, and if that's the case, it's totally fine.

JD: Now that I'm reading this back, you have every right to not show up in the morning. I crossed a line here. Shit, I'm sorry, RB.

RB: In the spirit of transparency...

RB: I've been thinking about that a lot, too.

JD: Really?

RB: Yeah. I think after we finish the weekend, I'd be open to exploring something more real with you, JD. I can't say what that looks like exactly, but I know I've enjoyed the last month immensely, and I don't want to walk away from whatever this might be after only a few days together.

JD: I'm grinning like an idiot. I'm watching football with my friends and missed the game-winning touchdown because I can't stop smiling.

JD: Totally worth it. We'll get through the weekend, then we can see what happens. Deal?

RB: Deal.

JD: And Zebra Cakes?

RB: Yeah?

JD: I can't wait to see you tomorrow morning and finally learn your name.

JD: I'm going to hug the shit out of you.

SIXTEEN

EMMA

NERVES.

So many freaking nerves.

My heart is beating erratically in my chest, the *thump, thump, thumps* nearly loud enough for the other patrons of Beans and Brews to hear, ricocheting off my lungs like pinballs. I've never been this stressed out about a meetup before. Trepidation and excitement rattle my bones, shake my insides and drown me with a maelstrom of thoughts and *what ifs*?

JD and I have quickly migrated from casual to the dangerous precipice of something more serious. Permanent. Lasting.

Forever, almost.

The possibility excites me, swirling in my belly with an exhilarating energy that doesn't want to go away. Not when I can't stop thinking about *him* and what a future might look like together.

I barely slept last night, spending the early hours of the morning tossing and turning, sheets tangled around my legs while my emotions flip-flopped from anxious to positively giddy. Thousands of scenarios have run through my head; who am I talking to? What does he look like? Will he actually show up or ghost me, never to be heard from again as he fades away and I'm left picking up the cracked remnants of a man who finally captivated me?

I've been stewing since sunrise, and my inability to calm down enough to relax for longer than three seconds is why I'm sitting in Beans and Brews twenty minutes early. I snagged a table in the corner, far away from the entrance, so I can observe everyone who comes inside.

My clammy hands want to grab a coffee to give the jittery appendages something to do while I wait instead of running up and down the length of my denim-clad thighs again and again, palms growing damper by the minute.

I don't want to be rude and order without JD. Will we sit for a while, laughing over steaming mugs of caffeine and swapping stories? Will he offer to split a pastry, letting me have the last bite?

My foot taps on the floor, going against the beat of the jazz music crooning softly over the speakers, and I pull out my phone, glancing at the messages we shared before sunrise. He was awake earlier than I was, and it thrills me to know he's waiting for this moment, too, counting down the painstakingly slow seconds.

JD: Good morning. I'm nervous to meet you. But so fucking excited.
JD: I'll be there at 8 sharp, wearing a purple baseball hat.
JD: Please don't run when you see me. Let's give this a chance.

RB: I'm freaking petrified.
RB: I'll be the one in long overalls and a pink, long-sleeve shirt. Blonde hair.
RB: I'm not running anywhere. I promise.

Every flash of purple and streak of violet has my head spinning and neck craning, wondering if I've spotted my mystery man. Grinning stupidly at the smiley face he sent, I'm about to text him again to let him know I'm already inside when a shadow covers my phone.

"Emma?"

I look up at the familiar voice, finding Henry Dawson standing above me wearing… a purple baseball hat on his head?

It's obstructing the hair I'm so accustomed to seeing him run his hands through, but it is unmistakably a purple ball cap.

The next moments occur in slow motion. Henry's eyes rake over my outfit, widening slightly as he takes in my overalls and shirt. He takes a step away from the table. Away from *me*. My mouth parts in understanding, realization hitting me like a bundle of dynamite, exploding as I begin to process what I'm seeing.

"You," I finally say. My voice is shaky, and I can hear the uncertainty behind the single syllable.

Henry is JD?

Henry is who I've spent hours and hours talking to, giggling at his words and blushing at his compliments at 3 a.m. when he probably had a naked woman next to him?

Henry wants to fist my hair and wrap my legs around his waist while he kisses my mouth, finding out how I taste?

Henry wants to learn about my past, talk about a future and offer to… to bring a flashlight to navigate the dark moments of my life together?

This can't be happening.

"What are you doing here?" I bravely ask, hoping for some purely coincidental twist of fate that has led him to the same coffee shop, wearing the same outfit JD said he'd have on, arriving at the exact time JD told me he'd be here.

"I… I'm JD." His voice is barely above a whisper, almost indiscernible over the noises around us, the world continuing to spin on its axis without knowing the severity of what's occurring feet away. The magnitude of the brewing catastrophe, two lives becoming interwoven even more so than they previously were.

Perhaps they've been destined to intersect this closely all along.

I have two options. Two choices glaring at me, forcing me to decide and pick which road I want to travel down. Which hand of cards I want to show. Do I want to up the ante and shove my chips to the center, bellowing out an enthusiastic "all in"? Would I rather fold, admit defeat and quietly exit the premises, never looking back?

"And I'm RB."

The truth weasels its way into the universe before I can clamp down on the admission and reel it back in. It's all I can say, the previous weeks of a budding relationship and emotional connection coming to a screeching halt as I feel my heart almost break in two at the understanding of there never, ever being an *us*. Not anymore.

A thousand thoughts fire through my brain, synapses working on overdrive as the questions begin to plague me.

Did he set me up? Is this all a game? Has Henry known who I was the whole time, laughing on the other side of the phone while I revealed more and more of myself to him? My stomach clenches at the negativity and I grind my teeth together, willing myself to stay strong and to get to the bottom of this.

When I dare to raise my chin and look at him, I expect to find him smirking, gleeful of his triumphant conquest. Instead, he's wearing a heavy frown, the corners of his lips tugging down, down, down. His brow is furrowed and pinched. His eyes look mystified and quizzical, unasked questions hiding behind those dark doors of devastation.

"May I sit?" Henry asks, cautiously approaching the chair. I nod once, jerking my head and averting my gaze, studying the rings on the weathered table that were left behind by old beverages. He slides into the seat across from me, his knees knocking against mine. I don't bother pulling away. He clears his throat once. Twice. Three times.

"This is unexpected."

"Are you joking? You must have planned this."

"Planned this?" Henry lobs back, having the gall to sound aghast. "I didn't plan anything, Emma. I'm as surprised as you are, if my sweaty palms are any indication of how freaking mind blown I currently am." He rubs his hands on his distressed, worn jeans—which look unfairly good on him—and offers me a feeble chuckle.

He's so… timorous. Bashful and lacking his typical confidence. He argues in courtrooms and represents some of the most powerful multi-million-dollar athletes, but I catch him fidgeting. Adjusting the bill of his hat. Scrubbing his hand over his cheeks, grazing the faint stubble lining his face. Shifting in his chair, his foot kicking mine.

"You're lying," I deadpan, half-heartedly tossing the accusation his way. It doesn't hold a lot of weight. If it did, I would have left long ago.

Somehow, I'm motionless.

Somehow, I'm not walking away.

Somehow, I'm staying.

It's baffling to consider the man before me is the same one who made me laugh until my sides hurt and comforted me on the bad days, offering words of encouragement. It's almost implausible I fell asleep talking to Henry and dreamed about what his mouth would feel like against mine, tongue running over the crease of my lips as he coaxed another round of pleasure out of me, telling me to *let go* and he's *got me* and *again* and *again* and *again.*

"I'm not lying, I swear," he says firmly. The conviction and despair behind his declaration makes me pause. Consider. Reassess and reevaluate. This is a surprise to him, too. "I was out to lunch with Noah last month and told him I lied to my mom about having a date. He has a friend, Jamal, who used RB's—your services. I had no clue you were on the other end of the phone. Noah didn't either, obviously, unless he thought this would be a hilarious joke, which I'm not finding funny."

I digest his story, fact-checking every line, every exhale, looking for a hole or flaw. It adds up. It all adds up.

Suddenly, a memory comes flying back to me and I sit up straighter.

"I remember that day. I was worried about you. You were particularly grouchy and I wanted to check on you. That's why I came to your office. You said you did something stupid."

"You were worried about me?"

I blush, picking at the loose skin on my pointer finger. "Yeah. It was so out of the ordinary for you. Of course I was concerned."

His mouth twitches a minuscule amount before settling back into a thin line. "Noah gave me your contact info."

"You shared that you were up for a promotion and competing against someone. You were talking about me."

Was I truly oblivious, too absorbed and enamored in our conversations to miss a major part of Henry's identity being revealed? I'm mortified he's found out I do this for a living. Clearly he's a man who's never had to worry about money throughout his life if he's willing to pay such an exuberant amount for a freaking date to a wedding anniversary.

Is he going to tease me and throw more jokes my way? Will he use this as blackmail to get whatever he wants career-wise? My cheeks burn, not thinking for a second JD would do something so malicious. I don't think Henry would either, but everything is so topsy-turvy, I'm not sure what's going to happen now.

My eyes meet his. They're flooded with heat, no trace of amusement or humor dancing on his face. "Emma. I'm freaking the fuck out. If I had known it was you at any point, I would have shut this down. Immediately."

I try not to flinch at his dismissiveness. I remember the night we were in the same restaurant and he came up behind me, assuming I was someone else. When he realized his error, Henry was adamant he wouldn't have approached me if he had seen my face.

I wouldn't have wasted another second.

The exact words he tossed so casually and callously my way

are seared into my memory. They stung like little needles on my skin for hours after, a prickly reminder I'm not what he wants. The same thorny sensation stabs me again.

Everything we've built as JD and RB is tumbling down, a house made out of a deck of cards trying to withstand a hurricane.

I hate it.

"Shit, no. I mean I wouldn't have wanted you to think I was using you. I wasn't implying I would have rejected you. Fuck, I'm saying all the wrong things. Can we talk about this?" he asks, gesturing across the table.

"Fine," I relent. "We might as well get everything out in the open. We've come this far."

Henry sighs, shoulders sagging, cinder blocks weighing him down. "I knew I felt something familiar and natural when I talked to you. Toward the end, the same spark was present when I talked to you in person, too. Everything I said as JD was true. I've never been the guy to spend hours talking to a woman, especially if the possibility of sex is off the table. You were different. I craved checking my phone. I wondered what you were doing. I hoped you were having a good day. I'd find something silly to send you because I *missed* you, Emma. You're special. It was like I knew you, deep down."

"It was the same for me," I admit, ambivalent about sharing the truth with him. Ignoring the heaviness of severe consequences that could come from sharing what I'm about to say, there's an urge to speak candidly and let him know he's not alone. "I've never talked to a client this much. Seriously, it's normally only a couple messages once or twice a week. It was easy to converse with you, and I wanted to answer your questions and ask my own. I thought—think—you're extraordinary."

"That's good, right? If it's a mutual feeling, we can figure this out. It's salvageable. I meant every word I said to you in those messages. It doesn't change because it turned out to be you."

"I need to think about this," I murmur. It's a lot to process. Is it worth the risk of the unknown? How badly will we get hurt in the process?

"I understand. There's no rush. If you say no and change your mind, I respect your decision. I won't badmouth you. I won't share your identity, or mention this to anyone. Ever. Emma, I swear on my life. You have my word. I'll sign an affidavit if it will put your mind at ease. Forget about me. I want you to be okay with this, no matter which direction it goes."

He looks, for a lack of better words, pathetic. Achingly pathetic, the sliver of hope and possibility slipping out of his fingers.

I want to hug him. Bury my face in his shirt, lace my arms around his waist, and squeeze him tight, promising to find a solution.

Together.

"The last thing I want is for you to be uneasy around me or my family for an extended period of time," he continues. "I'm a big boy. I can handle rejection. The ball is in your court. Let me know what you decide."

Henry doesn't give me a chance to make a dramatic exit. After asking me not to run, he's the one abandoning me. He stands from the table and walks to the door, leaving me alone, heart hurting in my chest, unsure of what to do and terrified to find out what's next.

This changes *e v e r y t h i n g.*

Do the feelings I've developed for JD translate to feelings for Henry? Can I mix the two personalities together, welcoming them both? Henry's a good man. No matter the name, that *was* him I was talking to.

Taking a moment to quell the negativity, I rework the emotions I experienced in finding out JD's identity, sifting through the residual leftovers: fear, frustration, and sadness.

There's one other emotion hiding in the trenches, barely poking its face out, trying to remain unseen, out of sight, out of mind.

It's a teeny, tiny, microscopic thing. Nothing important, really, and undeserving of the recognition.

My brain fixates on it, pulling the curtain back for a big reveal. Thrilled.

I was totally fucking thrilled.

SEVENTEEN

HENRY

THE FOUR DAYS since I discovered RB and Emma are the same person have felt like a long lifetime, stretching for decades and centuries and millennia, time standing still, crawling along at a snail's pace.

I'm out of sorts. Exhausted. Confused and miserably wishing I could see her again while also dreading our next encounter.

There have been no text messages. No passings in the hallway. No check-ins or assurances she's okay.

It's been quiet. And I fucking *loathe* it.

Our conversations are on repeat in my head. Were there any clues hiding in plain sight pointing toward her? Where were the flashing neon lights belting her name and screeching, "*Henry. Are you stupid? It's so obvious.*" Did I simply not notice, too preoccupied and caught up in the moments of stolen benevolence and happiness to catch on?

Fucking hell.

Emma.

Sunflower.

Zebra Cakes.

Everything is a goddamn mess. Where the hell do we go from here?

When I saw her in the coffee shop last Sunday morning, the pink shirt and adorable overalls stuck out to me like the North Star, a bright light I couldn't look away from. I was drawn to her immediately, yanked forward against my will, belonging at her side. I was elated. Relieved. Confused. A tempest of emotions I'm still attempting to process and understand. There's one thing I know for certain.

I'm not disappointed. At all.

I'm delighted. Excited. So fucking… happy.

Holy shit.

Can I stand next to her at the copy machine while picturing her legs around my waist and her hair in my hands?

Can I sit across from her in a meeting, contemplating the ways I'd make her dinner, remembering she likes her steak cooked medium well and hates Brussels sprouts?

Can we ride the elevator together while I hold back everything I want to whisper in her ear?

I don't like RB any less now that I know it's Emma. The feelings might be pulsing stronger than ever, piece by piece falling into place, a neat arrangement finally making sense.

My ego won't be the only thing bruised and battered when, naturally, she trudges away from our agreement. I won't blame her, either, and I'll have to pick up the pieces of a crushed relationship left behind.

Relationship, I scoff to myself.

There's a word I never thought would be in my vocabulary. Fuck buddies? Sure, I've had plenty. One-night stands? Absolutely. I love 'em. Spring fling? Summer fling? Been there, done that. A plethora of times. Quick bang sessions only lasting an hour in the back of my truck, in the bathroom at a bar, and in my office during an extended lunch break? Check, check, and check.

But *relationship*?

The entire decade of my twenties was dedicated to moving up the ranks at my job and then enjoying life, which meant enjoying women. Lots of women. However I wanted them. Respectfully, consensually, and safely, of course.

Settling down with one person isn't what I'm afraid of. I would never want to share a woman who's *mine* while I'm *hers,* unless it was a fantasy she wanted to act out.

Truth be told, I'm terrified of failing. It's one of my biggest fears in life, and the driving force behind me staying far, far, away from any woman who wants me to settle down. I don't know how to be a good partner.

Scratch that.

I don't know how to be a partner at all. I'm designed to give a woman a few mind-blowing orgasms, help her forget about the problems in her life for the night, and then go on my merry way. That shit is easy. I do it well. I'm fucking *fantastic* at it. Anything deeper than acting on physical attraction is daunting. Intimidating. It requires remembering birthdays and anniversaries. Planning date nights and agreeing to be a plus one to a wedding eighteen months away, a permanence to the obligation as the RSVP gets dropped in the mail. Scary shit. Shit I've never in my wildest dreams considered doing.

And RB... Emma... She deserves more than a romp in the sheets or a couple of rounds. She deserves the world. A kingdom to rule and a knight in shining armor who would slay a dragon and swim across a moat to protect her from life's evilest villains.

There's no way in hell she'll allow an asshole like me to be the one to reign by her side.

My phone buzzes and I snatch it off the desk.

RB: Can you meet?

Seeing her name, even as RB, makes my heart ache. God, I've missed her.

This is it. The end of RB and JD. Doomed before we even began. We never got a chance.

I think we could have worked, Sunflower.

I sigh, fingers moving across the keyboard in a death march, four letters cementing my funeral, concluded with a period to show I haven't been obsessively waiting to hear from her.

Me: Sure.

I turn my phone over, vowing to not touch it, no matter how badly I want to know what she's going to say. I need to focus on work and not the unfamiliar pain radiating across my pectoral muscles and lodging its way on the left side of my chest. The pestering presence is noticeable, and I fucking hate it.

"Henry?"

Without an invitation, Emma's walking into my office and shutting the door behind her.

That was quick.

Swallowing the batch of nerves nearly suffocating me, I do my best to appear composed. "Hey," I croak out, bringing my eyes to meet hers.

Her hair is down today, blonde waves spilling over the top of her shoulders. On her body is a forest green dress, showcasing bare arms that are doted with freckles. I inhale sharply at the color of the material—it's my favorite, and the sight of her in it rattles me.

It's the exact shade she wore the night I helped zip her up in the hallway. In the weeks that have passed, I can't get the image of her out of my mind. The vision of her warm skin under my palm is seared in my memory.

She's so fucking pretty.

"Is now a good time?" she asks.

I gesture to the two leather chairs opposite me. Emma lowers herself into the one on the right, crossing her feet at the ankles. Judging by her stance, she's here to discuss business.

"What can I do for you, Emma?"

I'm going to keep this interaction professional as I erase any lingering remnants of *what could have been* from my memory.

"I wanted to talk to you about your parents' party."

"What about it?"

"I'll do it."

"Look, I understand wh—Wait, what?" I stare, not sure I heard her correctly.

"I said I'll do it."

"Why?"

"We had an agreement, and I always honor my agreements. There's a caveat, however. I don't want your money."

"Why wouldn't you take the money?"

"I don't need your pity payment." She juts her lip out and I run my fingers through my hair.

Yup.

Definitely want to sink my teeth into that plump bottom lip of hers and revel in the sounds she'd make.

"Pity? I'm not paying you because I pity you, Emma. You would have taken the money if it wasn't me, right?"

"Right."

"So why can't you take what I owe you?"

"I don't want you to pay for my…" She stops herself from going any further, looking away. If I didn't know any better, I'd say she's ashamed.

"Your what?"

"It's none of your business," she replies with a razor-sharp intensity, and what do you know? I've hit a nerve.

"Clearly it's a big deal if you go around doing *this*."

Dammit.

That was the wrong thing to say. I hate the implication behind the demeaning statement, frantically wishing I could grab the words and bring them back, erasing the previous twenty seconds and starting anew.

She's out of the chair in a blink of the eye, palms splayed out on my desk, face near mine. I don't bother retreating, wanting to absorb all of her wrath.

Give it to me, Sunflower.

"This? What do you mean by *this*, Henry? Some of us have to work hard to make a living and don't have an inheritance to blow through whenever we want. Some of us have to hustle and pick up side jobs wherever we can to afford basic necessities like rent and shit. So forgive me if I resort to doing things like *this*, something that's so obviously beneath you and your tax bracket. You didn't seem to have an issue with it when it was beneficial to you."

It's the most passionate and animated I've ever seen her. She's lighting up like a Christmas tree in December. I won't lie. The fervent tirade and fiery persona are hot as hell, a side I'm so unused to seeing from her. Her eyes are full of steel and practically feral, focused on the subject of her lashing.

Me.

No objections here. She can keep her attention here as long as she'd like.

Beautiful, determined woman.

My curiosity is piqued about why she needs the money. I imagine we make roughly the same salary, and it's more than generous. Even with factoring in cost of living in a major city, there's still plenty of income left over to survive comfortably. Emma doesn't strike me as the kind of woman who needs an overflowing bank account or spends her wealth on mindless items. Does she have a child? Is it for medical bills? How much money does she donate to charity?

I won't push her to tell me now, yet there's still a persistent urge flowing through me, wanting to make sure she's okay. Making sure she has enough. Making sure she's not struggling to get by.

I stand up and she retreats half a foot, the back of her thighs hitting the edge of the chair. She lets out an *oof* at the contact, and heat flares through me with the sound. I want to reach out and steady her on her feet. Drag her onto my lap while I comfort her and learn what the fuck she needs help paying for.

So many things I want, I want, *I want*.

"I'm sorry, Emma," I apologize sincerely. Hanging my head, I sigh. "I didn't mean it offensively. I want you to have the money because it's important to you. I'm not telling you what to do, and I'm not demanding you listen to me. I'm doing a shitty job of communicating how much I want to help."

"We can discuss it at a later time," she answers, jaw relaxing a fraction of a degree. I concede her vigorous brush-off as a temporary victory. "Moving on. Let's talk about logistics. While I'm not 100% comfortable around you as Henry yet, I do trust you. We're off to a good start."

"You trust me?"

"Yeah. I know you aren't going to lure me into the woods and cut me into tiny pieces."

"Is the standard for men being just above serial killer level? How badly have we fucked up over the years for not murdering someone to be the bare minimum of chivalry?"

Her lips twitch in amusement. "It's obvious we don't have a sexual connection in person, so we don't need to worry about that becoming an issue."

"Ah. I suppose that's good."

"It is, otherwise I wouldn't agree to continue this. I plan to follow my strict rules. You aren't the exception. "

"I see. It's reassuring to know you find me hideous and annoying. Definitely not the hot, handsome man you assumed me to be, right? The not-so-nice guy who could pin you to the wall with only one of my arms is totally unappealing. I get it. Tell me, Emma, exactly how repulsive do you find me?"

The air between us is charged and electric, ions of lust bouncing back and forth and rapidly filling the room, raising the temperature to an insufferable degree. We're seconds away from either launching into a yelling match or clawing at the other's clothes, dresses and shirts flying out of the way. I want her so fucking bad, and I think I might die without her.

It's a travesty she doesn't feel the same. Not anymore.

She blushes, a faint shade of pink creeping up her chest to her neck, millimeter by millimeter. The color spreads to her sharp cheekbones, splotching them with a rosy hue. She swallows, and I track the movement down her throat.

I perk up at the shift in her demeanor. Maybe it's not a lost cause after all. Emma is many wonderful things, but a good liar is *not* included on the long list.

A for effort though, Sunflower.

"We aren't here to talk about how attractive I may find you. Which I don't."

"Of course. My apologies. Maybe we can discuss this later, not in my office? Are you free tonight? Or this weekend?"

She smooths out her dress, picking a piece of invisible lint off the material and flicking it away. Wow. She's really trying to avoid looking at me.

It's cute.

"I'm unavailable tonight."

"Do you have an event? With another guy?"

"I didn't stop working when I agreed to accompany you, and I don't intend to do so now. You're not my sole priority."

My fists clench involuntarily at the thought of someone else spending intimate time with her. Someone else learning her secrets and ambitions, goals and dreams. Someone else turning her on, goosebumps erupting on her skin as they whisper bullshit lovey dovey words in her ear, her proud, stoic facade changing to a giggly pile of goop.

She's not yours, Dawson. Reel it the fuck back.

"What about this weekend?" I begin to tap my thigh. Emma watches my fingers drum on my slacks and her face softens.

"Why don't we meet for coffee Sunday morning? This time we'll actually get drinks, instead of one of us storming out. That's only a few days away."

"I can do Sunday."

"Good. 8 a.m. at Beans and Brews again. Until then, have a good rest of your week, Henry." She gives me a parting half-smile before dipping out of my office, leaving me alone.

I groan, collapsing back into my chair. Fumbling with my phone, I pull up my group chat with the guys.

HD: I need to talk to someone.
HD: Please tell me you all are free later.

JL: I am. Jo's out with her best friend tonight and told me I better not sit at home alone.
NR: Sorry, I have a thing. Everything okay? Is this a 911?
PW: Talent show night at school, so I'm busy until late. Are you okay?
NL: I have to go look at wedding venues tonight, but I can meet after.
JL: H, come over. I have beer and I can make some burgers.

HD: Thanks, J. I'll be there around 7.

EIGHTEEN

HENRY

"I KNOW you didn't come over here to eat my food. You better start spilling what's going on," Jack says later that evening, handing me a heaping pile of homemade food.

"Where the hell do I start?" I groan. "Remember how I told you guys about the anniversary party my parents are having? And how I hired someone to be my girlfriend?"

"Yeah. You met up with her, right? You've barely talked in the group chat, so I assumed you two hit it off and were spending time together because it went well."

"There's been a snag in the plan."

"Define snag. Everything okay?"

"Uh, yes. And also no. A mix of both. The woman is Emma."

Jack's hand freezes, the burger he's about to inhale stopping short of his mouth. His eyebrows raise. "Wait. Like, Emma Emma?"

"Yup."

"Emma, who you work with?"

"Mhm. That's her."

"Emma, who you most certainly do not have a crush on but you sure like to talk about a lot? That Emma?"

"Hey!" I exclaim, licking a drop of mustard off my thumb. "There is no crush."

"It's funny you think I don't know when you're lying, Dawson. When you hired her, are you sure you didn't know it was her?"

"No! When I walked into the coffee shop and saw it was her who was wearing the overalls and pink shirt…" I trail off, trying to string together my words in a coherent way without sounding like a total sap. "My heart fucking fluttered, man."

"Fluttered, huh? Are you still going to try to lie out of your ass about no crush?"

"Shut up."

"Okay, what's the problem? It's good you were happy, right?"

"I guess so. She agreed to stick to our plan but refused to take my money."

"Whoa, hold up. I thought you were joking about monetary compensation."

"Nope. We decided on a price weeks ago. I want to honor it, but she's insistent."

"I'm sure there's a whole bunch of legal shit that might encompass this which I'm clueless about. You aren't paying her for sex, are you? Just want to make sure we're on the same page."

I snort. "Believe me, there's no sex. She's made it abundantly clear it's off the table. Even if we talked about… things… in our messages, it's not going to happen."

"What kind of things?"

"When we were still communicating under our aliases, I told her I wanted to hear what she sounded like when she came."

Jack drops his burger onto his plate, ketchup landing on his shirt. "I beg your pardon?"

"Yeah."

He whistles. "What did she say?"

"That she wants those things, too."

"So intimacy was off the table, but you talked about it, so it was potentially back on the table, but now it's probably off again because it's you and her. Am I understanding this correctly?"

"Nailed it."

"Are you attracted to Emma?"

"Yeah, I am. I've always been weirdly drawn to her, and knowing she's both Emma *and* RB only heightens the attraction. It's strange. Emma would always take up my attention in person; I'd go out of my way to get her to notice me or acknowledge my presence. RB takes up my attention on my phone. Now the two are converging and I'm so confused."

"And you still want to..."

"Jack, I've never wanted something so bad in my life and I'm going fucking insane."

He whistles again. "Okay. Let's brainstorm this."

Before we can formulate a plan, the front door to his house opens and slams shut.

"Jack?" Jo, his girlfriend, calls his name down the hall.

Not only did I win the friend lottery with my guys, but their other halves are equally amazing, too. Jo's no different, and I owe her everything in the world for saving Jack after his last relationship and bringing him back to the light. She's incredible.

"Sorry," he apologizes, standing from the table.

"No worries."

"There you are. Oh, hey, Henry!" Jo says, greeting me with a smile.

"Hey, Jo. What's up?"

"Everything okay with Abby?" Jack asks, frowning.

"The babysitter was queasy and Raul is still working so Abby rushed home in a panic. I'm going to hide so you two can talk about whatever dudes talk about. Please don't break out any rulers."

"Actually, let me get your opinion on something," I interject. "A hypothetical, totally not true situation at all."

"Okay..." she says slowly, climbing into Jack's lap as he sits back in the chair. He wraps his arms around her and rests his chin on her shoulder, gazing at her adoringly like she hung the fucking moon.

I feel… lonely looking at them. Jealous. Isolated and introspective. Not because it's Jo on his lap, but because he has *someone* to be affectionate with. The awareness spears me, roaring in my head and building to an almost deafening crescendo, wishing I had what they have. Wishing there was someone on my lap, folding into me, hugging me tight.

"Let's pretend you need a date for an important function. You told someone you're bringing a significant other, which is a lie, because you're single as hell. Would you consider it weird to hire a person to be your date and pay them for their time?"

Jo laughs. "Of course not. You aren't going to marry the person. It's a favor. They're helping you out. It's not shady or illegal. Heck, it could even be fun."

"What if it's someone you have a long history with, you're both competing to be partner at the same law firm, you may or may not be attracted to each other, and you talk about wanting to be physical with each other?"

She steals a fry off Jack's plate, contemplating my question. "Long history?"

"We went to high school together. We weren't friends. Only recently have we become amicable."

"I don't understand what the problem is. She's agreeing to help you."

"We talked for a month without knowing who was on the other side. I started to re—"

"You didn't know it was her?!" Jo squeals excitedly, almost tumbling off Jack's lap. He squeezes her hip to keep her in place, fingers dipping under her shirt.

"Nope. We used an app that didn't show our real names or numbers."

"Stop it! You're making me want to write a book. Let me guess. You've really liked talking to her. You were surprised when you finally met in person, shocked and confused by the sight of *her,* and now you don't know how to proceed or what to do yet you still want to see her again."

I gape at her. "How did you... What the hell?!"

"She reads a lot of romance novels," Jack offers, unfazed by her ability to figure all of this out so quickly.

"Okay, yes, to all of the above. What the fuck should I do?"

"You go to the party with her. You have a good time, then see what happens. If she's still willing to go after finding out it was you, I'd say it's a good sign."

"What do you mean?"

"You mentioned knowing each other for a while. She clearly doesn't dislike you. Maybe she feels similarly and hasn't voiced it yet. Maybe she's also excited to find out it was you."

"Huh. I never considered a world where she, as Emma, could like me, as Henry. What should I do going forward?"

"Act like you would normally act."

"He normally wouldn't talk to a woman after a night with her," Jack offers.

"Stop berating him." Jo nudges his shoulder before returning her attention back to me. "Henry, enjoy her company, and don't put too much pressure on yourself."

"Women," I mutter, shaking my head. "How do they do it?"

"You've got me," Jack responds, moving the hair away from Jo's shoulder and kissing the top of her arm. "She's right, though. Things can't get any worse. Might as well have a good time."

"Is it normal for my heart to beat so fast when I talk to her? Or check my phone constantly to see if she's responded to my messages? I mean, I look forward to hearing from you guys, so it can't be that different, right? We didn't talk for a few days after we met up, and I almost lost my mind wanting to know how she was doing."

The couple exchanges a look, and Jo tosses me an encouraging smile. "It's perfectly normal. Stop overthinking! Send her a text, say hello, and relax. You're going to be fine. You're a great guy."

"Can you send a message on my behalf and talk me up? I don't know what to say."

"You can tell her you want to hear what she sounds like when she comes, but saying hello is the problem?" Jack asks sarcastically and I toss a napkin at him.

"Whoa, what?" Jo asks. "You were sexting?!"

"Don't listen to your stupid boyfriend," I grumble.

"That's hot." Jo grins. "Anyway, you can figure out how to interact with a woman without trying to bang her. Pick up your phone. It's not that difficult."

"There needs to be a class on this shit. Texting 101. How to Woo a Woman in Ten Days. Best Desk Banging Positions." I throw in the jab as retaliation for Jack's joke.

"Lancaster here could teach a seminar on the latter topic," Jo says brightly. "Speaking of, I'm going to take a bath." She leans into Jack, whispering in his ear, and I don't miss the shade of crimson he turns or how his eyes dart to me.

"Oh, please don't stop on my account," I tease, leaning back in my chair. "I'm enjoying the show."

"What, you want to watch?" Jo grins at me.

"Don't tempt me with a good time. Two hot people getting it on? Sign me up. I've heard about some of his techniques. Maybe I need a clinic."

"Jesus, this is why you two can't be alone together," Jack mumbles. "Too many ideas. Leave, sweetheart. Please. You're provoking him, and I know what you're thinking. It has to be a *stranger*, not one of my friends."

"But it's so fun," she whines, climbing off his lap. "You deserve to be happy, Henry. Go in with an open mind and see what happens. I'm rooting for you." With a wave, she leaves and Jack exhales.

"I swear that woman is going to kill me; at least I'd die happy."

"A stranger, huh? Thinking of adding a third?" I ask.

"Adding? No. Watching? Yes. And if you try to say some shit about what she likes, I'll punch you."

"Are you kidding me? That's sexy as hell. Does it bother you when I joke with her?"

"No. I'd tell you if it did. I like that you two are friends."

"Okay, good. I would never touch her. None of us would."

"Are you calling my girlfriend ugly, Dawson?"

"You know I think she's a beautiful woman. I meant regarding your past. That shit isn't going to happen again."

Jack's last relationship ended with his fiancée leaving him for his best friend right before their wedding. Needless to say, his faith in other people took a severe turn after the fiasco. Jo and I playfully push each other's buttons regularly, but I would never want to take things too far or give Jack the wrong idea about us. I value his friendship too damn much to overstep a line.

"I know. I trust you guys." His phone buzzes on the table. "I'm kicking you out. Right now. Or stay and get a show. I don't care at this point."

I laugh heartily, already feeling more at ease. "You win. Go bang your awesome girlfriend and I'll go home to my empty apartment and mull over my pathetic, dull life, not having any sex because I can't get the woman I think I want to be with but I'm not sure if she wants to be with me out of my damn head."

"Never say never. Maybe you'll be surprised."

"Thanks, man. This helped a lot. I'll let you know how things turn out. Wish me luck."

NINETEEN

HENRY

SLEEP WAS the last thing on my mind last night. I tried counting sheep. Listening to a meditation podcast. Attempting breathing techniques. Turning the air conditioning down in my apartment to cool off the energy causing me to stare at the ceiling, unable to find a comfortable position while my mind raced a million miles an hour.

I'm meeting with Emma this morning, and to say I'm freaking out is putting the panic mildly. I'm on the verge of a heart attack, torn on whether to be afraid she won't show up or optimistic she's willing to give this a shot.

Are we supposed to pick up our plan like we didn't have an earth-shattering discovery? Start fresh? Act like best friends? Act like colleagues? Act like... boyfriend and girlfriend? *Be* boyfriend and girlfriend?

The worst part about this process is the goddamn feelings I possess for her haven't changed.

Nope.

They're still right there, persistent and mulish with every blonde woman I pass on the street. Every chime of my phone. Every hour I check the clock, wondering if it's Sunday yet.

I pull open the door to Beans and Brews, the bells over the

door chiming obnoxiously and announcing my presence. Offering a polite nod to the two giggling baristas behind the counter, I slide into a small table off to the side and check my phone to see if she texted me. The entry bell chimes again, and I whip my head around to see Emma walking through the door, a halo of sunshine following behind her.

The world stops spinning. It's silent. Still. I'm not sure if I'm breathing. I can't hear anything. I can't see anything. I can't process anything.

Only her.

Every movement is smooth and purposeful. She glides across the floor with a ballerina-like grace. Her cheeks are rosy while the rest of her face is pale, the exhaustion and reluctance mirroring my own. Brilliant crystalline eyes that are usually challenging and alive are dim, a bright flame snuffed out. I want to howl at the moon for being a source of her discomfort.

Joining me at the table, she silently folds her legs under the wood as she sits, angling her body to the side so our knees don't collide.

She stays.

She doesn't flee.

I think she's giving me a chance.

My shoulders roll back, hopefulness warily making its way into the room.

"Hi," she says disconsolately, and I offer her a tentative smile.

"Hey. How are you?"

"Tired. I didn't sleep very well."

"Oh? Was there something terrifying waiting for you today?" I joke. Her lips quirk up on the right side—the side her slightly crooked smile tends to favor—and her body relaxes marginally at the humor.

"I'm going to be honest, Henry. Up until twenty minutes ago, I went back and forth about coming at all. Even after talking in your office, I wasn't sure about my decision."

I anticipated hearing the words. Knew they were coming. It doesn't alleviate the blow.

A goddamn sucker punch.

"Emma, listen to me. I didn't know it was you. What do I have to do to prove it to you? Say it—whatever it is—and I'll do it."

I'm not sure I'm above begging at this point, dangerously close to dropping to my knees and weeping repentantly at her feet, asking for forgiveness for uncommitted sins.

Her hand reaches out, fingers folding over my forearm, mirroring the way she's touched me before. Never anything provocative or flirtatious. It's a comforting gesture. Grounding. One intended to soothe. Dispel fear. Reaffirm hope.

I'm frozen, her touch making me an ice statue. The press of her fingertips has become a part of me, stitched to my person. Even through the barrier of my cashmere sweater, her warmth penetrates the fabric, radiating and traveling to every part of my body. She grips me lightly, the hair on my arm standing up, ready for battle, ready to fight, electricity zapping me like a live wire sparking in a puddle of gasoline.

I melt, pleading for more. It's an entirely different sensation from the sensual touches I'm accustomed to encountering. It's not frenzied or hurried, rushing down the length of my body to grope or tease or unbutton. She's selflessly making sure I'm okay.

She cares.

The realization of those two words barrels into me because *holy hell*, do I care about her, too.

"Hey. Take a deep breath. I'm going to honor my commitment, okay? Now, let's get to work." She breaks our contact, slicing it in two, and I miss her instantly.

"That's it? No fight? No arguing?"

She shrugs, a simple raise and lower of her shoulders. The neck of her sweater slips down, revealing milky white skin before she pushes it back up, unbothered by the distraction. "I'm sure we're going to fight at some point. I'm not going to kiss your ass right away like everyone else in the world. But there's no denying I enjoy... you."

I tilt my head and laugh, genuine happiness pouring out of me. This is the first ounce of relief I've felt in days.

There she is.

Hey, Sunflower. I missed you.

"I promise no ass kissing is involved. Okay. So. The party is my parents' wedding anniversary, like I've mentioned before. They said if they lasted 40 years, they'd have a big celebration."

"Did they argue a lot when you were younger or make you think they might have gotten a divorce?"

"On the contrary. They've always loved each other fiercely. There were no screaming matches or silent treatments. They've had to put in a lot of work and effort, between stressful careers and raising three kids. They're still as stupidly happy as the first day they met."

"That's so sweet. You mentioned part of it would be a bigger celebration with quite a few people, and part of it would be more immediate family. How many folks are you thinking it'll be total? Two dozen? Three dozen?"

"Oh, you naive thing," I chuckle. "There's going to be over 100 guests, easily. They're inviting folks I've never met, family members I didn't think were still alive, and fourth and fifth cousins."

"Holy shit," she curses, and the surprising vulgarity makes me smile. "We need some coffee before we start talking logistics. My caffeine supply is severely depleted."

I follow her to the register, hot on her heels like an obedient dog, ordering a regular coffee while she selects a concoction I've never heard of before. Her eyes grow wide at the sight of the whipped cream overflowing out of the top of her waiting cup. After we collect our beverages, I see her checking out the pastry display with a wistful glance, and I covertly add two chocolate chip muffins to our order, shaking my head as she tries to use her credit card to pay.

"Thank you for this," she says, unwrapping the treat, face alight with excitement and glee. The bleariness from earlier has worn off, making way for a cheerful woman that makes *me* happier just by being across from her.

"I know you like baking. What's your favorite thing to make?" I bite into the sweet pastry, almost moaning at the taste.

"Cookies. There's something comforting and nostalgic about a regular chocolate chip cookie."

"You could make something to bring to the party."

"The party that's going to be catered by professional chefs?" she asks inquisitively.

"Yeah, sorry, that was my pathetic, roundabout way of hoping you'll make me cookies."

"If you want cookies so bad, you can do it yourself!"

"What if I say please? Would that work?"

"You've heard of this little website called YouTube, right? They spell it out for you there," Emma jokes, taking a bite of the muffin. I try to avoid staring at her mouth as it closes around the chocolate treat. How her tongue wipes the crumbs clean off her small, pouty lips. How her eyes flutter closed, enjoying the decadence of the dessert. *Fuck*, I can't look away. "No more cookie talk! You're distracting me from the important topics! Will I have to know everyone's name?"

"God, no. I barely know everyone's name and I'm related to them. I doubt they expect my girlfriend of... How many months are we saying?"

One of the many, many questions we need to have a precise answer for to ensure this goes off without a hitch.

She taps her cheek, thinking hard. "Four months. That's a decent relationship length in today's world, and it's enough time for your mom to not be upset you haven't introduced us."

"Smart. I knew I hired you for a reason. I'll bring you up to speed on my immediate family and fill in the gaps with the others as we go. We'll be spending most of our time with them and I want you to feel comfortable with their names and anything else you think is prudent."

"Perfect."

"Also, before we go any further, I want to talk about your contract and PDA."

"What about it?" she asks curiously, taking another delectable bite. The way her mouth forms a perfect O around the chocolate is borderline obscene. What I would give to scatter crumbs over her body and lick them off.

"I want to make sure you're okay with *me* being the one who's touching you."

"Oh. I didn't think about it that way."

"I'm not going to make out with you in front of my parents. Are you fine with holding my hand? Please be honest; you aren't going to hurt my feelings."

"Yes, I am."

"Arms over your shoulder? Around your waist?"

"Yes, that's fine," she answers. Her voice sounds strained.

"Kissing your cheek?"

"Yes, but that's the only kissing allowed."

"Got it. Sorry. I hope I wasn't implying anything with that question."

"You weren't. I want to cover all our bases so we don't find ourselves in an awkward position. No matter what we might have discussed previously about things we want, we need to keep the line of no intimate contact well established. This is business. Nothing else."

"Right. Business," I echo. The agreement punctures me.

"Good. Now that we're covered that, I'd like to hear more about your family, if you're comfortable sharing about them."

I tell her about my parents and their life together. I show her pictures of Elizabeth and Drew, my sister and brother, as well as their families. She laughs at the photos of my nails painted bright purple, courtesy of my four-year-old niece, Rosie. I share about my childhood and the bits and pieces hardly anyone knows; how some days were better than others but a lot of times I felt alone, painfully high standards demanded of me, no room for negotiations. I talk about the grueling experience of balancing school, extracurricular activities, a social life, and my mental health. The words flow from me effortlessly like I'm catching up with an old friend, and when my stomach rumbles, I notice it's already lunchtime, the morning lost between us in enlightening and enthusiastic conversation.

"Wow, I spoke about myself for 99% of our time together and didn't let you share anything," I say sheepishly, rubbing the back of my neck.

"That's okay. We can meet up this week and I can give you some of my history. It's nothing special, so don't get too excited."

"I get to see you again?"

"Of course you do. This isn't going to be easy to sell if you don't know my middle name."

I hum, nodding in agreement. "When do you want to hang out again?"

"How about Friday?"

"That could work. What did you have in mind?"

"How about an escape room and baking cookies?"

"That sounds—"

"Incredibly stupid, sorry. I thought it would be a good trust-building thing. And fun." Emma's talking quickly, like she wishes she never suggested the idea.

"I was going to say awesome. I'm totally down."

"Really?" Her face splits into a wide grin, stretching across her face, illuminated and elated. It's now, right here in the middle of a crowded coffee shop on a Sunday afternoon, patrons bustling around us and machines whirling in the background, where I realize for the first time that I will do anything and everything in my power to make sure Emma smiles like this every single day. And that I get to witness it. Never have I seen a more beautiful sight. It's mesmerizing and soul-crushing in the best way.

Is this what my buddies see when they look at their partners?

Is this reaction why they bend over backwards to make their significant other happy, ready and willing to travel to the ends of the globe to give them whatever their heart desires?

That's exactly what's running through my mind. What mountains would I move or rivers would I cross to find the things that make Emma light up like a beautiful sunrise?

Deep down, I think I know the answer.

Deep down, I think I've known the answer for a while. Ever since RB—Emma—blazed into my life and changed me for the better.

All of them. There's not a body of water too deep or peak too tall.

I pinch the inside of my wrist to derail the sickeningly romantic thoughts, doing my best to damper the nausea I'm beginning to experience.

And I still haven't answered her. I need to speak. To say *something* coherent and rational, not letting her see what the hell is happening inside my head.

"Really. I can book it and send you the info."

Nice, Dawson. Neutral and chill. Exactly what we're going for.

"Perfect! I have a busy week coming up, so this will be a good stress reliever before we head to the party."

"Lots going on at work?"

"I have my first interview with Wallace and the review board on Wednesday," she admits, picking at the skin on her pointer finger before cursing under her breath and quickly wrapping a used, stained napkin around the spot sprouting droplets of blood.

The picking is a habit I've learned she does when she's stressed or uncomfortable. It's always a subtle action when she thinks no one is watching, usually during meetings or when she's working hard, peeling away the loose skin inadvertently. It's something I noticed years ago, but I wouldn't dare share that information with her. The last thing I want is to make her think she's on display, every move scrutinized.

"That's awesome! You'll have to tell me how it goes."

Emma frowns, shifting in her seat. "You want to know?"

"Why wouldn't I? I'm cheering for you and I support you. I already told you I think you deserve the spot more than I do. Of course I want to hear about the interview."

She blushes again, and as much as I like seeing a smile on her face, watching her skin flush with color might be my favorite sight.

How red can she get?

What kind of filthy words can I whisper in her ear to get her to change colors?

The things I want to say...

The things I want to do...

Are you a good girl who knows how to listen, Emma?

"Thank you."

I run my hand through my hair, edgy to ask the next question. "Would it, ah, be okay if we texted this week? I look forward to hearing from you. It's kind of become the thing that gets me through the day. I would never want you to feel obligated to communicate with me bu—"

"Henry," she interrupts, voice gentle like a calm, serene ocean. "You can text me. I'd like that. Do you have my real number?"

I exhale in relief, shoulders drooping with her agreement. "No, I don't. Here, add it to my phone." I extract the device from my pocket and watch her type away on the keyboard before handing it back to me.

Glancing at the contact she created, I snort. "Bold of you to put yourself in my phone as VRG. How would I explain that to anyone that asks, besides the obvious fake girlfriend answer?"

"You're a smart man. I'm sure you can think of something." She gathers her cup and plate, a small smile ghosting over her lips as she stands from the table. "It was good to see you."

"You, too. I hope the interview goes well."

"Thanks." She gives my shoulder a gentle squeeze before walking away.

"Hey, Emma," I call after her. She turns her head, eyes meeting mine. The blue almost sparkles, and I break out into a grin. "What does RB stand for?"

"What do you think it stands for?"

"Hm. Refreshingly beautiful? Radiantly beaming? Really bored?"

She giggles, shaking her head. "It's my middle name. Emma Reagan Burns. It's not very creative, I know."

"At least you didn't stick to your lawyer letters like some other dummy I know."

"God, how did I not pick up on that?! It's so obvious!"

"I'm glad you didn't. It gave me an opportunity to finally outsmart you for once."

"Don't get used to it, Henry Dawson. See you later."

With a wave, she departs, disappearing through the door. I reach over and let my hand rest where hers laid, trying to ignore the butterflies fluttering in my stomach and the way I miss her already.

TWENTY

HD: Test, test.

HD: Is this thing on?

HD: We're going on a road trip. What two snacks are you bringing?

VRG: This sounds strangely familiar.

VRG: I hate to burst your bubble, but I've heard that one before. Totally unoriginal.

HD: Do I get an A for effort?

VRG: Too generous. B-minus is more realistic.

HD: You wound me, Zebra Cakes.

VRG: What does it say about me as a person that through all the conversations we've had, you calling me Zebra Cakes are Sunflower are some of my favorite things?

HD: I'm glad it makes you smile.

HD: Kind of weird we're like, 20 feet away from each other, isn't it? I miss seeing JD and RB on my screen.

HD: But I like knowing it's you.

VRG: Remember the day you came into my office and I hit my head on the bookshelf?

VRG: I was freaking out that I asked you what you liked to do in your free time.

VRG: It's kind of funny to think you were giving me advice about a message delivered to you.

HD: For the record, I'm glad you asked for advice about how to stop a message from being delivered AFTER you sent that one to me.

HD: How's your day going?

VRG: Not too bad!

VRG: I'm starving. I haven't had a chance to eat lunch yet. It's next on the agenda.

HD: …it's 2 o'clock.

VRG: I've been busy!

HD: Want me to bring you something?

VRG: That's okay, I'm walking to the kitchen as we speak.

HD: *Attachment: 1 Image*

HD: Made reservations for the escape room at 7 on Friday night. That cool?

VRG: That's perfect!

VRG: Is it okay if I meet you there?

HD: Of course.

HD: I'll also grab some cookie supplies, too, should the mood strike.

                                               VRG: I'm excited.

HD: Me, too.

HD: Good luck on your interview tomorrow! You're going to nail it.

                              VRG: Thanks, Henry. Talk to you later!

October 11th

                                    VRG: I'm craving Cheetos.

     VRG: Except I'm about to go into my interview and can't walk around with orange dust on my fingers.

HD: No? I think it would make a great first impression.

HD: Professional. Dignified. We need to drop the stigma surrounding clean hands.

                               VRG: You're so weird.

HD: I bet you laughed.

                               VRG: Maybe. Off I go!

HD: Go kill it, Emma!

October 12th

VRG: Do you have anything to do with the bag of Cheetos sitting on my desk?

HD: Hm? Me?
HD: I have no clue what you're talking about.

VRG: Henry.

HD: Emma.
HD: Fine. Yes. I might have stumbled into the vending machine earlier. A bag of Cheetos might have popped out. And I might have put them on your desk when you were away.

VRG: Thank you so much! These made my day!

HD: Always happy to help, Sunflower.
HD: Quick vibe check—still good for tomorrow?

VRG: Yup. I'll meet you out front at 7.

HD: Cool. See you then!

TWENTY-ONE

EMMA

"I CAN'T BELIEVE you've been talking to *Henry*!" Nicole gushes through the phone while I pull on my jeans, almost toppling over as my foot gets caught in the bottom part of the denim.

"It was a surprise for sure. It's also kind of cool; there's so much more to him than meets the eye. I almost feel bad for all the things I used to assume about him."

"Oh, so he's more than a guy who sticks up for women at work? A guy who loves his family enough to lie to them to make his mom happy? A man who has a solid friend group, a successful job, and is financially stable? Not to mention is hot as hell? What did I miss?"

I laugh at her thorough list, grabbing my sweater off the back of a chair. "Okay, yes, when you say all of those things, he kind of sounds like the perfect guy. I'm sure he has flaws, though. Probably spends hours getting ready in the morning. I bet he only sleeps with a top sheet and no blankets or comforters."

"Wow. Is that our standard now? Men who have duvets on their bed are instantly more attractive than men who don't and should be bumped up to marriage material?"

"Remember that guy you dated who didn't even have a mattress? He slept with a pile of sheets on the floor."

"We're not talking about my mistakes here. You're deflecting!"

"Do you want to accompany Henry instead? I'm sure he'd be more than willing to let you be by his side next weekend."

"You know he's not my type. Besides, it would be pointless. He's clearly taken an interest in you."

"He's not my type either!" I exclaim.

"He could be your type."

"What does that mean?"

"It's obvious you're attracted to him. For one freaking second, will you allow yourself the opportunity to enjoy spending time with another human being? A *male* human being? Even if that human being is your former-academic-rival-current-coworker, Henry? You've got a good job, Em. You're up for a big promotion. While I'd certainly never advocate for finding a guy to make you happy, why not explore the idea of having a man by your side, too? Even if it's a causal, get-to-know-you thing? You owe it to yourself."

I pause, considering her words.

Nicole's right.

The entire stint of my twenties was spent becoming successful in my field. It didn't happen overnight; I gave up dinners with friends to spend hours studying legal statutes and documents. Trips home were reduced to two visits a year, plane tickets unaffordable while working my way up the corporate ladder. Exhaustion became my personality while romance took a backseat. Since my last breakup, where he told me I spent "too much time helping others" and not enough time "helping him," dating hasn't interested me. I've guarded my heart fiercely.

Up to this point, my life hasn't felt like it was missing anything monumental or substantial. There's no void I needed filled. I'm content being alone. My house isn't empty without a testosterone power present. It's been a *soon* but *not now* aspiration, personal fulfillment taking priority over anyone else.

In the last month, however, the satisfaction and contentment that have become familiar have shifted to curiosity, mingling with sadness and loneliness. The longer I'm alone, the less whole I'm becoming. The more I talked to JD—Henry—the more I understood how nice it was to have a person to share the small moments of the day with.

Someone to send a picture of my pretzel to, asking if it resembled a goldfish.

Someone to laugh about the Weekend Update skit on SNL with, exchanging YouTube videos of our favorite cold openings.

Someone to share my hopes and dreams, fears and hesitations with, and listening to theirs in return. Learning that Henry's afraid of not meeting expectations from several different sources, and deep down he wants to be *happy*, in every sense of the word.

It was nice to be heard. Acknowledged and recognized. It made my heart soar, an optimistic beat lulling me to sleep with every text message we exchanged in the late-night hours as I curled up in my sheets, dreaming about what it would be like with him next to me, warm body pressing against mine.

If I had known it was Henry on the other side of the phone outright, I would have frantically shot down the idea of pursuing anything with him. Other than our job, we have nothing in common; he's outgoing and loud while I'm more quiet and reserved. He prefers spending time out while I enjoy staying in. He's the leading man, the center of attention, the life of every party, and I'm the extra in the background, overlooked and unseen.

Despite these stark differences, we drifted toward each other. No longer was indifference the sole emotion I harbored toward his presence. It morphed to passion. Excitement. Joy.

I was honest with JD when I said I would be interested in exploring a more meaningful arrangement with him. Has that changed now that I know it's Henry?

I'm confused. Getting whiplash from the back and forth between keeping up with the two different identities, ultimately whittling down to one single person I can't stop thinking about, no matter how hard I try.

Him.

Maybe tonight will help me sort through the bewilderment. Maybe the universe will give me a clear sign. A beacon. An omen that says: *Yes, Emma, he's safe. You can trust him.* Or, more aptly: *That's attraction you're feeling. Accept it. Welcome it.*

"You might have a point," I acquiesce, slipping the leather strap of my satchel over my tense shoulder. I need to relax. My body is as stiff as drying cement, unsure of what comes next. Do we pick up where we left off? Start over? Erase everything I've learned about Henry up to this point? My face falls into a frown at the thought of forgetting what I've discovered about him. I hate the idea. "But this is only a fun get together. He's not attracted to me like that."

Except for when he said he wondered if I'd be able to wrap my legs around his waist and wanted to know what I tasted like. I also didn't miss the way his eyes watched me devour the muffin at the coffee shop the other morning, gaze lingering on my mouth, molten lava staring back at me. An unsolicited shudder courses through my body and I swallow, the sweater around my body becoming constricting.

"Whatever you need to tell yourself. What are you two doing tonight?"

"An escape room and baking cookies at his apartment."

"Sounds awfully like a date."

"It's not a date," I groan. "It's an opportunity for us to figure out how the hell we're going to navigate this."

"Mhm. I see. So you're doing a pre-date with a client before the main event. Is that part of your package?"

She knows the answer, and somehow voicing no, Henry is the first, and I'm doing this because I want to, makes everything more... real.

"I should get going. We're meeting up soon."

"Can you at least promise me you'll try to have fun? Forget it's Henry. Forget you're two people competing against each other for one job. Let yourself have an enjoyable night out, okay?"

I sigh. "Fine. I promise."

"Good. Send me your location so if I don't hear from you by the end of the night, I know where to send the cops!"

The escape room is the most fun I've had in months. Henry and I are partnered up with another young couple. At first, it was tricky working with people we didn't know. Once we found the first clue, letters written on the wall in invisible ink, the awkwardness dissolved and we ended up having a great time.

"It was so great to meet you," Annabelle, part of the pair we worked with, says as we stand on the sidewalk outside, celebrating our success. "We moved to the city a few months ago for Derek's job, and it's been a struggle to meet new people and find friends our age. We were reluctant to come out tonight, but I'm so glad we did!"

"I haven't laughed that hard in a long time," I say, smiling as I recall Henry sticking his whole arm in a toilet to retrieve a hidden key. The look of disgust on his face was priceless and worth every penny. "I know how hard it can be to put yourself out there. You and Derek are awesome."

"How long have you and Henry been dating? Probably a couple years, I'm guessing?" Annabelle asks.

There wasn't a lot of time for small talk during our quest for freedom, and certainly not enough to exchange pleasantries like dating history or meet-cute stories.

"We're not a couple," I say, tucking a piece of hair behind my ear.

"Oh. Friends with benefits?"

I snort, shaking my head. "Nope."

"I like you too much for you to be having an affair with a married man. Please don't tell me that's the case."

I laugh. "No! No one is cheating! We work together and I'm kind of helping him with a project. I'm going to be his fake girlfriend next weekend at a family event. Tonight was a trial run to see how well we mesh outside the office."

"You could've fooled me! I don't think you have anything to worry about. I thought you were together this whole time. It's totally believable. The sweet glances he kept tossing your way? Ugh, it melted my heart!"

"What are you talking about?" I didn't notice anything out of the ordinary from Henry.

"When you figured out a clue, his eyes got all bright and he positively beamed," she gushes. "He was so proud. But also not surprised? Like, he knew you would be the one to figure it out and still wanted to celebrate you."

"Oh," is all I can whisper, skin too tight on my body. It prickles with awareness at Annabelle's observation. Was he really that blatant in his nonverbal affection? I wish I could have seen it for myself so I could categorize every grin, every visible groove of the dip of his dimple, every alleged awed expression. "Henry's a charismatic person. I'm sure it doesn't mean anything."

She gives me a look, sensing my deflection. "You're probably right. You know him better than I do! Anyway, it was so great to meet you, Emma. Good luck next weekend!"

Henry and Derek stroll up to us from where they were chatting off to the side, shaking hands.

"Ready, Zebra Cakes?" Henry asks, smiling down at me.

I become weak in the knees with the quirk of his lips.

How have I survived so long, immune to his charm, when it's staring me straight in the face, practically mocking me and reducing me to a puddle on the pavement?

"Yeah," I answer, returning his smile enthusiastically. "I am."

Henry and I start down the sidewalk alone, no buffer of other people or solving riddles between us, heading in the direction of what I imagine is his apartment. We take a few steps before he disappears temporarily. Reappearing, he shifts from my right side to the left, falling back in place and walking on the outer edge of the sidewalk, closest to the street, thus nudging me away from the passing cars and bicyclists and toward the safety of the row of brownstones we pass.

You can trust him.

You're safe.

"Did you have fun?" he asks. The air is crisper now that the sun has set, and I shiver under my sweater, cursing myself for not bringing my larger jacket.

"That was so much fun. I've never done an escape room before, but I'm definitely going back!"

"Are you still up for making cookies? Or was that a polite excuse to step away so you could reject my proposal of sweet treats in private?"

The teasing tone causes me to giggle. I glance up at him, a gleam in my eye. "The only reason I suggested this idea was for the cookies. Don't think you're special or anything."

"Oh, so you didn't want to be stuck in a room with me for an hour?" Henry places his hand over his heart, sounding outraged. His face betrays him, another full grin splitting across his mouth. "I knew you were ruthless. I'm seriously concerned about your sugar intake. Might I propose a vegetable board instead? I could set out carrots and cele—" His elation falters as he watches me shiver again, an action I try to disguise with a maneuver around a spilled ice cream cone. "Shit, Emma. You're freezing." He stops in the middle of the sidewalk and pulls off his peacoat, placing it around my shoulders and hugging it snug to my body. "Better?"

I nod aggressively, cocooning myself in the warmth, the telltale scent of *Henry* filling my nostrils, causing me to emit an unintentional sigh. "Much. Thank you." I smile to reassure him, and he nods, placated with my heat level before we resume walking.

"I'm on the next block. Not too much further."

We cross an intersection and approach a large brick building. Henry waves to the security guard planted out front.

"Evening, Charlie!" he calls out as he opens the door, holding it for me and touching the small of my back to guide me inside. Charlie waves in return and I follow Henry into the small elevator and watch as he pushes the button for the twelfth floor, his hand no longer on me. It's colder without his touch.

"What kind of cookies are we making?"

"Chocolate chip. Does that pass the Emma Burns Sweets Lover test?"

"My favorite!"

"How are you feeling about next week? I think tonight went well."

The vestibule dings as we ride up each floor. "I think it did, too. Annabelle thought we were actually a couple." I don't know why the admission causes me to blush, but it does, my cheeks turning pink.

"Fooling strangers is a good start."

"I've been studying the list you sent me."

Earlier this week, Henry forwarded over a document with information about his parents, siblings, and other close relatives. I'm blown away by his successful family. His father served on the Massachusetts Supreme Court for twelve years. His mother was a state representative for 20 years and helped pass a bill requiring all feminine hygiene products to be tax-free. Henry's sister, Elizabeth, is the Dean of Admissions at a private high school, while his brother, Andrew—Drew, for short—is the CEO of a leading engineering firm.

Intimidated is an understatement. I'm freaking out. It doesn't matter that I've been around high-profile folks, executives, sports stars, and millionaires; the Dawson's are a daunting bunch. I expected to find articles addressing how terrible they are—conniving, greedy, and dangerous, rich assholes. Instead, I found they weren't terrible at all.

They're philanthropic, generous, and exceedingly kind. I watched the cutest interview where Henry's mother sat down with a young Girl Scout, answering all her questions in a gracious way, speaking as if she was the most important person in the world. It was admirable.

"You're thinking hard over there," Henry interjects. "Tell me what's going through your brain. How can I help?"

"Sorry. Your family is just…" I trail off, not knowing the politically correct way to voice my thoughts.

"A lot? Yeah, I know." Walking down the hall, we stop at #4. He unlocks the door with a key fob. "They're more down to earth than you think they might be."

"I'll be better by next weekend, I promise."

"I don't have any doubts, VRG."

When he pushes the door to his apartment ajar, my jaw drops open at the sight greeting me.

Massive. The place is huge and sprawling, bigger than my house by a landslide. Floor-to-ceiling windows show off the entire city below us, dazzling, twinkling lights blinking at me like fireflies in a field on a hot summer night.

"Holy shit," I curse, walking inside and straight for the glass. My nose presses against the cool material, scoping out as much of the view as I can.

"Do you want something to drink?"

"No, I'm fine. Thank you." I stare outside, mesmerized by how beautiful the world looks this high in the sky.

"It's even prettier at sunset," Henry says from my side. "It's rarely get to see it, though, with work and everything. When I do, I'm reminded how lucky I am to be alive." He pauses, considering the statement. "That's cliché, I know."

"Not at all," I say hurriedly, facing him. "It's a wonderful way to look at life."

"Well, someone very wise once told me the sun always rises again after a dark day. And when it does, it makes the happy days so much better. I started to see the proof of that firsthand."

"That person sounds like a genius," I whisper, attempting to diffuse the heaviness settling in the enclosed atmosphere. My heart twists at his easy memory of my words.

"Smartest person I know. Hey, how did your interview go? I

was going to ask earlier in the week, but I figured you were probably decompressing."

"Really well, I think. I answered all the questions they threw at me. I might have come across as a bit aggressive with my vision for the future of the firm, but I don't have any regrets."

There's almost an invisible nudge against my back when Henry smiles, trying to propel me closer to the man in front of me.

That's attraction you're feeling.

"I'm not surprised; I'm sure you knocked it out of the park. Those men deserve to be challenged. Things shouldn't always be comfortable and cushy in our job; you're the one who can make them look at things differently."

I fiddle with the ends of my hair, blushing at the direct compliment. "It's scary to put yourself out there. I say I don't care about the opinions of others, and I try not dwell on what small-minded people like Brad think. I can't help but wonder, though, how I'll be treated if I get the position, no matter how badly I want it." I cringe at the implication. "I'm sorry. I don't want this to be weird to talk about."

"Don't you dare apologize for manifesting a dream," Henry says fiercely, taking a step toward me. "Speak that shit into existence and don't hold back on my account. It's going to happen whether we address it or not. We might as well be open and talk about it. I'm cheering for you, Emma. I'm always cheering for you. That job is yours."

"I'm cheering for you, too, Henry."

Silence again. This high up, I can't hear any of the outside sounds of the world. It's just me and him, two confused souls staring at each other, wondering how to proceed from here.

He breaks first, clearing his throat and cocking his head to the side. "Ready to get busy in the kitchen?"

"That's awfully forward of you. I don't get a tour first?"

"Where are my manners? Of course you do. Come on."

Henry guides me through the space. A dining room sits off the kitchen and a hallway leads us to the master bedroom, passing a spare bedroom and guest bathroom.

I'm surprised to find it doesn't look like the bachelor pad I thought he'd reside in. There aren't women's bras scattered about or half-naked centerfolds taped to the wall. No boxers hang from a lamp and the bedside table is free from old pizza boxes and beer bottles.

It's freakishly clean.

A large bed sits on one side, and navy-blue curtains cover hidden windows. A dresser is against the opposite wall, a large television mounted over it. A thin bookshelf is smushed into the corner, overflowing with books. Pictures hang sporadically on the eggshell white walls, no design or pattern to them.

I run my finger over the glass protecting a particularly weathered photo and frown. Henry's in his graduation outfit, and it's like I'm transported back to the days when we were young teenagers, blissfully oblivious to the real world and the challenges that awaited us.

"Everything okay?"

"Yeah," I reply, studying the young Henry. He was scrawnier back then, with messier hair that nearly covered his eyes. Age has been kind to him. His body has filled out and his shoulders are more broad and toned. He grew taller. Wider. In the photo he's smiling, but I can tell it doesn't reach his eyes. It doesn't rival the one he tossed my way a few minutes ago. The brown orbs look sad and dull, a far-off glance hovering there, searching for someone or something right out of the frame, unseen to the viewer.

"Ah. Graduation day," he says, voice dipping near my ear.

"You don't look happy."

"I wasn't. In that particular moment, I was having a crisis."

I turn to stare at him. "Why?"

The day is a distant memory; I vaguely remember going through the required motions of the event. I wore the gown. I walked across the stage. I collected my diploma, shook hands with teachers, and walked off. I threw my hat in the air with the rest of my classmates.

"Do you know what happened the moment this photo was captured?"

"No." I gaze at the photo then back at him. My eyes are glued to his. Even now, they look more alive than in the snapshot, dancing with fulfillment. "Why would I? I'm not in it."

"You walked past me and didn't glance my way. Didn't stop to wish me a happy summer vacation or good luck with college. Some sick, twisted part of me was holding out hope you'd turn your head and nod, or at least give me some sort of sign letting me know it was okay. Okay that I took valedictorian away from you when everyone knew it was your dream and I just got lucky. Okay that we didn't speak for over 48 months. 48 months, Emma. What the fuck was I thinking? Okay that we were leaving a common ground and parting ways without getting to know each other, with no desire to try. When you didn't so much as blink... I realized that was it for us. The rest of my life would go on, without you there. I just... I held onto a thin, pathetic thread of hope that maybe someday we'd be able to put everything behind us. We'd run into each other at a reunion and laugh about everything, clearing the air and saying how stupid we were to not speak. Instead, 17 years later, here we are. Still intertwined. Still connected. Still in each other's lives for a reason I have yet to discover. I don't believe in fate or destiny or any of that other bullshit. But this can't be a coincidence, can it, Sunflower?"

"I-I had no idea you even knew I existed," I whisper. "You never... I never..."

Four years of walking the same halls, going to the same classes, and never once did we speak. Besides that first day, the split second of eye contact and visceral heat passing between us, he never looked in my direction again. I assumed he made it obvious what his intentions were, but now I'm second guessing everything I thought I knew.

No. It can't be a coincidence.

Henry rocks on his feet, breaking our staring contest, one I'm sad to win. "Now you do."

We fall into a quiet, ponderous moment. There's so much more I want to say and learn about this man, desperate to make up for years and years of unknowing.

The hush surrounding us isn't awkward or stilted. It's full of memories. Of regret. Of *what ifs* and *what could have beens.*

Could we have been friends back then? Possibly. Maybe. There's no way to tell for sure.

Are we both trying now? With every fiber of our being and with every tool in our arsenal.

Is this the sign I've been waiting for?

You're safe.

Deciding to switch topics before we start professing even more declarations we might regret, I gesture around the room. "Your place is nice. Now I know what color your sheets are in case I'm asked during an interrogation from your mother. Navy blue. Just like the curtains."

"Speaking of, I don't think we should live together yet. My mother might outright disown me if she learns I have a live-in partner and this is the first she's heard about it. Fake live-in partner. God, this is confusing."

"Who's saying I'd agree to move in with you after four months, anyway?" I challenge. Another foot. Another step. Another inch. I have to tilt my chin to look at him, and I'm met with another grin in return. "I'm very independent."

"Tell me something I don't know. I'm not going to introduce you to everyone as, 'My girlfriend, Emma.' Are you kidding? You'll always be Emma first. Whatever title you want to tack onto it after is up to you."

My pulse speeds up. "Really?"

"Really. You're your own person. Fake dating doesn't change that. Hell, even real dating shouldn't change that."

"I'm not sure anyone's ever treated me like that before. Like I exist as my own person outside a relationship with someone."

Henry's eyes darken. "Sounds like you haven't been with the right men, then."

We're standing too close. My chest is pushing into his stomach and my entire neck is bared to him. A not-so-gentle reminder how dominating his presence is and how it's still not enough.

"We should get to the cookies," I whisper.

It's the only rational thing I can say without confessing that no, I obviously haven't been with the right men, because standing inches away from him, looking into those destructive eyes, a half-dimple peering at me from his cheek, I feel more of a desire than I have with any of my long-term relationships in the past. I feel more at peace. I feel more cared for and seen. I feel more... at home.

A fleeting, unreadable look flashes across his face and he retreats backwards, away from me, the distance feeling like miles.

"Right. Cookies."

I may not be able to decipher what his face is conveying, but the disappointment in his tone is all I can hear, ringing in my ears as I follow him to the kitchen.

TWENTY-TWO

EMMA

HENRY IS AN ABYSMAL SOUS-CHEF.

It's so bad, it's comical.

I'm doing my best to not laugh at him, because he's working really hard, but I can't help it, tucking my chin into my shoulder to smother the fit of giggles racking through me.

His determination and perseverance, however, is astonishing. I thought he would have given up 20 minutes ago when raw egg ended up on his foot. He's persisted, sticking out the treacherous task, biting his lip in concentration as he finishes rolling the last ball of raw dough, refusing to be a quitter.

Sticky, gooey cookie dough covers the countertops and my fingers. There's a chocolate chip stuck to his cheek. Flour coats the floor, resembling freshly fallen snow against the sleek black tile.

"I never knew making cookies would be this difficult," he grunts, wiping his forehead and leaving a trail of sugar behind, the white substance sticking to his sweat-soaked brow. "There. That's the last of them. Please tell me we can bake these fuckers now."

I can't stifle the laugher that bursts out of me any longer. Taking the two full trays, I carefully place them in his oven. "After eleven to thirteen minutes, Henry, we can eat these fuckers, too."

"I've never been so hungry in my life," he whines, collapsing onto the barstool on the other side of the island, lips sticking out in a pout. "If I had known it was going to take us years to make 24 cookies, I would have eaten a bigger dinner. Properly hydrated. Paced out my food throughout the day. I'm not sure I can make it. Go on without me." He drops his head onto his arms, hiding his face.

"Remind me to never ask you to help me bake a cake. Or bread. You might lose all your sanity."

"Oh, forget it. I wouldn't stand a chance. I'll keep picking up baked goods from the grocery store and passing them off as my own."

I gasp. "I can never trust you now!"

"This is why I order all my food or purchase it pre-made. I don't want to have to work for my meals."

"Poor, poor, spoiled Henry," I joke, squealing as a handful of chocolate chips gets launched my way, joining the flour on the floor. A rogue rebel lands in my hair.

"What do I have to do to make you my professional cookie maker?"

"You can start by not throwing precious chocolate chips at my face! I could've eaten those! They're valuable!"

"Five second rule?" he offers, grinning boyishly at me. There's the dimple again. In all its sugar-coated glory.

"Doubtful. These floors probably haven't been cleaned in weeks."

"When did you start baking?" Henry asks. "You make it seem so natural."

"I think I made my first batch of cookies around the age of six. I was watching an episode of *Little Bear* while I mixed ingredients together. The aftermath looked mysteriously like this and the cookies were charred. Burnt to a crisp."

"Tell me more about your childhood. I like learning about you. There's this whole life of yours I never knew existed since we're not—"

"Friends?" I finish for him. Henry frowns.

"I hate how negative it sounds. Friendly is the more appropriate word, I think. I want to know everything, Emma Burns. Have you ever been to a concert or broken a bone? What's your favorite band? Favorite Nickelodeon cartoon? I swear if you say something dumb, like *CatDog*, we're going to have an issue."

"Wow! That's a little harsh. You're putting me on the spot! Why don't we play a game while we wait for the cookies to finish? I'll ask you a question, you answer. Then you ask me a question," I suggest, leaning my elbows on the corner of the island. It's the only surface in the kitchen that hasn't been turned into a hazard zone.

"I like this idea. You start. No thinking. Answer right away. First thing that comes to mind."

"How deep are we getting here? Is anything off limits?"

"Emma, I mentioned a cartoon from the 90s with a dog and cat sown together. I can assure you I won't be asking you your favorite philosopher, or how you'd establish world peace. Hit me with your best shot, ZC."

"Oh! Can I amend my fight scene song? I love that tune!"

"Fire away. I'll allow it."

"Good. Okay! Here we go. Favorite color?" I ask, lobbing him an easy one to start. Henry hesitates, obviously weighing his answer. His nose scrunches up and his mouth turns down in the corner, ever so slightly.

"Red. Favorite food?"

"Tacos. Favorite season?"

"Fall. Love the sound of crunching leaves. What do you sleep in?"

Oh. Okay. This took a quick turn. I blush. "A big t-shirt. What do you sleep in?"

"Boxers. Long pants when it's cold. Dresses or skirts?"

"Dresses. Shorts or pants?"

"Shorts. Day or night?"

"Night. Wine or beer?"

"Beer. Romance books or thrillers?" he asks.

"Romance. Bowling or baseball?"

"Baseball, but I hate that you're making me pick. Cruel woman. Chocolate or vanilla?"

"Chocolate. Or swirl! Beach or mountains?"

"Mountains. Car or plane?"

"Car. Radio or playlist?" I ask.

"Playlist. And I already have a great one for our road trip. Soup or salad?"

"Soup, always. Hotdog or hamburger?"

Henry scoffs. "Hamburger. French fries or tater tots?"

"French fries, but I wouldn't refuse either! Favorite city?"

"London. Sweet or sour?" he asks.

"Sweet. Dogs or cats?"

"Dogs. Favorite Nickelodeon cartoon?"

"*Rocket Power*. Duh. My first crush on a fictional character was Twister. Same question."

"*Rocket Power*. My first crush on a fictional character was Reggie Rocket. I've always liked spunky women. First concert?"

"Simple Plan. Have you ever broken a bone?"

"My ankle, when I was twelve, while attempting to skateboard in my Etnies. I was a total poser. You?"

"Never. I did staple my finger with a staple gun once. Fav—"

"Whoa. Wait a minute," Henry interrupts. "You can't give me this tidbit of knowledge and bypass a story I need to know. How does an accident like that even happen?"

"I don't want to tell you because your opinion of me will change! I like you thinking I'm smart!"

"Emma Burns, I swear to God, if you don't tell me the story, I'm withholding any and all cookies of tonight and the future from you. Don't think I won't hold them above your head and use our height difference to my advantage."

"Fine! Only in the name of sweets. I was twelve at the time of the incident," I begin, speaking as if I'm being questioned for murder. "I guess the last hoorah before our teenage years was rough for both of us. I went into my mom's bedroom to look for my summer homework. I picked up the staple gun, not knowing what it was, then pressed *down* on said staple gun, thus lodging a nice piece of steel wire into my finger. I went to my grandmother who was babysitting me and showed her my pinky. She almost fainted. There was no pain, only disappointment. I was supposed to see the new *Hey Arnold!* movie in theaters that afternoon. We spent five hours in the emergency room. Four days later, I ended up back in the same ER after cutting my foot open on the 4th of July at Nicole's house. I needed eight stitches."

Henry tips his head back, low, rumbly laughter filling the kitchen. "You're really freaking incredible. That might be the best story I've ever heard."

I busy myself with a patch of crumbs on the counter, wiping them into the sink. His praise notches its way into my bones while a rush of satisfaction zooms up my spine. "Incredible? Hardly."

"Unfortunately for you, it's not up for debate. Did you eventually get to see the movie?"

"I did! Three times."

"Good. If you hadn't, I would download an illegal version from somewhere off the dark web so we could watch it right now."

"You'd do that for me?"

He shrugs casually, like the words have no significance, hold zero weight, and it's *no big deal* to hunt down an animated movie from 2002, added to the grocery list below tomatoes and above butter.

"Of course I would. Do you have a scar on your pinky? Any memorabilia left behind from the incident?"

I hold up the previously injured finger. "No. It's kind of bent. Still functions fine."

"Please tell me you haven't picked up a staple gun again?"

"God, no. Now if I don't know what an item is, I observe from a distance like an intelligent adult. My adolescent brain didn't comprehend the idea of pain like I would today. I'd like to avoid any and all hospital visits. Not my cup of tea."

"So you're saying I should nix the tool belt I was going to get you for our fake first anniversary?" Henry asks, and I chuckle.

"I consider myself self-sufficient, but please keep all hammers and other household items that might cause bodily injury out of my reach. A thoughtful gift, though."

"I'll settle for a small, handheld stapler instead."

"Gee, now you're really going above and beyond."

"Back to the game, my friend. Our cookie countdown is almost over. Up or down?"

"Down. Top or bottom?" The question slips out before I can think twice. Henry breaks into a wicked grin, dropping his chin into the palm of his hand and staring at me intently, hot flames nearly cackling from his body. "I didn't… That's not…" I fumble, eyes widening, words ceasing, utterly mortified by my mistake while simultaneously drawing nearer to him, waiting with bated breath to hear the answer.

"Mmm. Top. I've always liked to be in control, and it gives such marvelous views. Now tell me, Emma, top or bottom?" His voice is husky. Deep. Powerful. The tone causes me to shudder, my nipples pebbling under my shirt. It echoes through my body from the top of my head to my stomach, sliding lower and lower, enveloping me in long-awaited aching, yearning *want.*

I know I don't have to answer. I could dismiss the game and walk away. I could throw something at his face and snap at him for being derogatory. I could roll my eyes and laugh it off, ignoring the concealed interest in answering openly, anguished to know just how far this might go.

Eyes trained on him, I speak with as much gusto and confidence as I can. "Bottom," I rasp, refusing to look away.

"Good," he croons.

I almost burst into flames. I'm on fire; his scorching gaze is burning me alive. It's too hot in here. We're close. We're not close enough. I want to take back what I said. I want to say more. I'm suppressed by *Henry* all around me as my imagination runs wild, picturing all the depraved, delicious ways he could electrify my empty world.

And how I would let him.

Never have I had such a physical reaction to someone without so much as a touch or caress. My underwear is growing wetter by the second as fantasy after fantasy dances through my head. My breathing is becoming erratic. I'm about to throw myself at him, casting my morals to the side and asking him to show me how to live dangerously and recklessly.

That's attraction you're feeling.

The oven timer beeps loudly, puncturing the unfinished discussion, air rapidly deflating from the room as I crash back to reality. I jump up, diving for the cookies, grateful for something— anything—to do.

"Where are your oven mitts?"

"I'll get them," Henry says, unfettered by the turn our conversation took. He opens a drawer and nudges next to me, my shoulder coming up to the middle of his chest. He sticks his mittened hands in the oven, withdrawing both trays with ease and setting them on the counter. "These look perfect."

I peer around his torso, admiring our work. "We have to let them cool."

"You're not serious."

"Two minutes! 120 seconds!"

"You're torturing me. Do you know how hard it is to have something right in front of you and not be able to touch it?" His eyes slide from the cookies to my face.

Considering the question, I'm aware we're no longer talking about bakery items. We've transitioned to something far deeper and more important.

Yeah, Henry, I think I do.

"We can eat them now," I whisper. He snatches one of the cookies and holds it out to me, challenging me. Daring me. I take the bait, an obvious glutton for punishment.

"Open up, Emma," he orders, the same husky voice embracing me. It's authoritative, guiding me to comply. And comply I gladly do. "You listen well, don't you?"

My thighs clench together as I stand on the tips of my toes and part my lips, closing around the treat. I'm greeted with the taste of chocolate and sugar, narrowly avoiding biting the pad of his thumb.

Good. So good. I hold back a moan at the taste. At the sensation of his warmth mingling with mine. At the charged energy circling us, smothering us in tension and chemistry. My hands want to reach out and fist his shirt, pull him to me and cover his lips with my own, letting him savor what we created together.

And me.

I want him to wreck my world.

"Delicious," I say hoarsely. Henry's thumb wipes a rogue crumb away from my mouth, lingering on the center of my lips before retreating away.

"My turn."

Realizing what he's asking me to do, I jump at the opportunity. Taking a cookie in my hand, I reach for his mouth. His lips open and he puts the whole damn thing in his mouth with a single swoop, tongue swiping over my finger, coating it in *him*. I gasp at the contact. I lurch forward. My heart stops. I'm on a roller coaster hurtling down a hill. I want to succumb to his every demand.

"I should stop," Henry murmurs.

"What if I don't want you to stop?"

I don't mean to say the question out loud. I don't mean for him to hear my desperation. I also don't want to take it back.

"Careful, Emma. If you keep saying those kinds of things, I might start to think this is might be real."

"It's not. It's fake. So fake."

"Then why does it feel so fucking right?"

I'm in so much trouble. My carefully laid plans have been tossed out the window, discarded and unremembered, along with the rules I abide by. I don't want to leave and walk away... but I need to. I *have* to. Extracting myself from the situation in this kitchen, putting the blinders on, and recalling what my *job* is has to take priority over whatever lust I'm experiencing.

My job isn't to fall in love with Henry Dawson and his swoony soliloquies, devastating looks, and hysterical, witty conversation starters. It's to get through a weekend with him as a paid helper. A role. As much as I want to entertain the idea of *more*, it's overwhelming. Implausible. It hurts to say the next words, but I do. They're necessary. It's for the best.

"I should go."

Rejection overtakes him. His smile falls. His eyes dart away, attention focusing out the windows. He nods, running his hand through his hair as a muscle in his jaw ticks, holding back words he doesn't speak, no matter how badly I want to hear them.

"Right. Yeah. It's getting late. Let me get some cookies for you to take home."

Shuffling away, he pulls out a Ziploc bag, shoving almost half our hard work into the plastic and handing it to me.

"Thanks," I mumble.

"I'll pick you up at 1 p.m. on Wednesday. Does that work?"

"That's perfect. I'll send you my address."

"Cool."

"Good night, Henry. I had a great time." I reach out, bravely hugging his middle when I know I shouldn't, my cheek resting on his chest. His arms circle around my waist, one hand moving to my hair and stroking through the blonde locks twice. His heart is a metronome in my ears, racing as fast as mine.

"So did I," he says gruffly. He untangles us, pulling away and stepping back. "Will you let me know when you get home?"

"Yeah," I nod. "I will."

"Good night, Emma."

I force myself to leave, force myself to trudge through the door, force myself to let it slam close behind me, mirroring the shift in my mood, tumbling from the highest high to a lowly low. As I head for the elevator, my chest constricts like it's been the patient to a defibrillator, an electric charge from every inch Henry touched me running through my veins. My hair. My waist. My fingers. My mouth.

My heart.

While I ride the elevator down, I try to ignore the passion that resided behind his eyes. It was ferocious. Tender. Kind. Aroused. Confused. Knowing.

It was all for me.

I half wish he would have picked me up, laid me across the counter, and ravaged me to within an inch of my life, leaving warm chocolate kisses down my body as a reminder of *him*. Of what he could do and what he could give.

I sprint out the front door of his complex, the cool air of the outside world a bucket of ice water, dousing the gnawing need residing within me.

This isn't going to be an easy itch to scratch.

TWENTY-THREE

HENRY

THE DRIVE to Emma's house to pick her up is an out-of-body experience, rivaling a funeral procession or another major event that might alter the course of my life forever. My brain is hundreds of miles away as I stop at red lights, use my blinker to turn right then left, motion for someone to merge ahead of me before finally pulling into her driveway and parking my car.

I take a moment to bask in the silence, collecting myself and studying her home through the windshield. It's small and unassuming, with a brick facade. There are flowers blooming in two wooden beds under a large bay window and the blue mailbox out front looks welcoming and inviting, adding a pinch of color to the monotone exterior.

Turning off the ignition, I hop out of my truck and walk toward her front door. Before I can climb the three small steps and knock, it's opening, revealing Emma, her suitcase, a bouquet of flowers, and a bottle of wine.

"Hey!" I greet her brightly.

"Hi," she answers, shifting on her feet.

We exchanged a handful of messages in the aftermath of Cookiegate the other night. I've tried to ignore the lingering scent in my kitchen she left behind; apples and vanilla with a hint of chocolate. I've attempted to forget how she felt in my arms, warm and content, the perfect fit. Like my favorite things: a nice hot shower, a good meal, hugs from my friends.

And, most importantly, I've done my best to block out how I wish she had never left and the loneliness that's engulfed me in the time we've been apart. I wanted to hear her talk all night about anything, everything, and nothing at all, her voice a soothing melody as we drifted to sleep under blinking city lights and dreaming about hopeful tomorrows.

I've failed miserably at all of these things. Emma's been at the forefront of my mind for days on end, and our time spent getting to know each other is about to come to fruition in a few short hours. Soon, we'll walk through the doorway of my child-hood home and begin what brought us together in the first place.

A lie.

A job.

A paid favor she does for dozens of men, not just *me*.

It's becoming clear why I've successfully avoided this type of commitment to a single person for over three decades; not knowing what the other person is thinking… what the other person is feeling… what the other person wants or doesn't want is fucking irritating. What am I supposed to do? Give her a hug and ask if she's been daydreaming about the other night, too, visions of chocolate chips haunting my thoughts? Play it off like nothing happened, pat her back, and call her *buddy* or *pal*?

God, help me. I'm a fucking mess.

"Ready to get going?" I ask, grasping for a neutral topic. "My parents want to have dinner with us tonight, and, being the senior citizens they are, if we aren't through the restaurant door by 5 on the dot, they get dangerous. I want to protect you at all costs, Zebra Cakes."

The joke and nickname earn me a tip of her lips and a slight hint of a grin. I cheer inwardly.

"Yeah, I'm ready. Thanks again for driving." Emma turns and

shuts the door, locking it with her key. I hurry up the stairs to take her suitcase and a full smile crosses her face.

She's beautiful. It's such a natural beauty; no makeup, no hair products, no fancy outfits or adornments. She's showing me all of her exactly as she is. And it's fucking exquisite.

"It'd probably be difficult for you to get us there without a car. I didn't realize you don't drive." Lifting her bag down the concrete, I hoist it in the bed of my truck next to mine.

"I can walk to the train station and take it into the city. Beats having to sit in traffic, since not all of us live in the heart of downtown in a nice apartment with a parking garage like you," she teases, flipping her hair behind her shoulder.

My eyes zero in on her skin, right above the collar of her shirt, finding the hollow spot of her neck I wanted to kiss the other night when we were together. Nostrils flaring, I look away, opening the passenger side door for her to climb in.

"Want me to put the flowers in the back?"

"That would be great. I got them for your mom. And the bottle of wine that's probably going to taste like shit compared to what they'll have at the party."

"It's the thought that counts, and this is very kind." Taking the items from her, I set them in the backseat next to the bag of snacks I brought. I slide into the driver's seat and adjust the rear-view mirror. "All set?"

Emma nods, shifting her body to get comfortable for the drive. Her left elbow rests on the center console between us, a few inches away from me. I could lace her fingers with mine if I wanted to, and caress my thumb over each knuckle. Her petite hands are probably smooth and soft, delicate things I would treat with care and reverence.

Jesus Christ.

When did I start caring about *hands*?

"How far do your parents live?" she asks, buckling her seatbelt.

"About an hour north of the city, depending on traffic."

"You spent two hours a day getting to and from school?"

"Yeah. They wanted me to be successful, and I'm thankful for the education I received. It'd be naive of me to not acknowledge how their advocacy impacted my future."

My parents thought the high school in the city had a better reputation than even the private schools up the road from our house. They fought tooth and nail for me, and other students, to be allowed to attend the school despite living outside the boundary for admittance. I love my parents immensely, and watching them fight for equal education everywhere, no matter one's tax bracket or socioeconomic status, reaffirmed how much respect I have for them not only as guardians, but humans, too.

"Did your brother and sister go to BPHS? Elizabeth and Andrew, right? I don't remember ever bumping into them."

"Hey, nice job with their names. Drew did. Who's older?"

"Give me a minute." Emma bites her lip, deep in thought, pensive and studious. I adore the expression of hers, when she's thinking hard about something that's *just* out of reach but still in her well of knowledge. "Your sister is four years older than you, and she has two kids. Your brother is the youngest, and he got married a few months ago."

"You deserve a gold star. I'm impressed."

"I do my research."

"So, what's our backstory? How did we meet? We probably should have talked about this beforehand."

"We can say we met at work. It's the least complicated answer. Why add another lie?"

"True. How about we worked on a case together, got to know each other as friends, one thing led to another and… here we are. Introducing you to my family."

"Have you ever been friends with a woman?"

I snort, merging onto the highway. "Unless you count the girl-friends of my friends? No. I've never had a platonic relationship with a woman before."

"Do your parents know about your aversion to finding a partner?"

"My mother knows I've never dated anyone, so prepare to be pestered. I apologize in advance for whatever gets said or insinuated."

"Don't worry, I can handle it. I'll charm the pants off them so hard, they'll wonder why you didn't scoop me up sooner."

Why didn't *I scoop her up sooner?*

Good question, Dawson.

"Want to hear the playlist I put together for our journey? There's enough Blink-182, Simple Plan, The Ataris, and Third Eye Blind to satisfy your cravings."

A small giggle tumbles from her lips and the wave of pride I feel almost makes me explode. *I made her laugh.* Okay, sure, it was barely a puff of air, and she probably only did it because she needed to breathe, but it's better than nothing.

I'll take it.

Small victories.

Little wins.

Another mile closer to our destination, her by my side.

"Before you serenade me with some of the greatest hits from the early 2000s which made up the majority of *Now That's What I Call Music!* discographies from volume 1 to 10, there's something important I need to tell you."

Fear slithers down my back, replacing my fleeting euphoria with panic and foreboding.

"Okay..." I brace myself, preparing for the worst and dreading what she might share.

"I'm a terrible copilot. I can't stay awake in cars and constantly fall asleep. You're going to be on your own."

I exhale, relieved at the admission. "Thank God. You can't scare me like that!"

"You should have seen your face!"

"Because it was cruel! I thought you were about to open the

door and roll onto the highway, road rash be damned! I thought you were about to tell me you're secretly married."

Emma lets out a full belly laugh and, *holy hell,* I love that sound. I don't think I'd ever get sick of hearing her infectious happiness.

Cheerful, bright, and radiant, it fills up the enclosed space like a blanket on a chilly winter night, wrapping around me. Reassuring me. She's not physically touching me, but I feel the lightness from my head to my toes. I want to lean into it. Bottle it up. Keep it for-fucking-ever.

"Do you forgive me?" Emma asks. She's biting her lip, trying to stop a smile.

"Yeah," I say automatically. "I do. Prop your feet up, Zebra Cakes. Get comfortable. I'll let you know when we're close."

"Hey, Emma. We're almost there." I nudge her shoulder as her eyes blink open, a sleepy fog hanging over her. I turn down the music, *Jumper* playing through the car speakers.

"Already?" Her voice cracks and I hand her the bottle of water I grabbed from the back seat. She smiles at me gratefully, bright enough to light up a night sky.

"Yeah, we beat rush hour traffic."

She takes a sip of the7 drink and almost spits it out when she looks out the window. "Holy cow, these houses are beautiful."

Turning onto the brick driveway, the long expanse of red disappears in front of us, behind tall trees. I punch in the gate code and the squeaky metal creaks open. Sneaking a look over at Emma, I find her mouth agape, taking in the monstrosity of our home and land. From an outsider's perspective, it's definitely opulent and gaudy. Large columns flank a wrap-around porch, appearing more like a hotel complex than a single-family residence. Inside, though, hidden from passing cars, is a place full of memories. Of joyous moments, worn hardwood floors, years of laughter, and photos lining old walls.

"Wow. This is your house? It's incredible!"

"Born and raised," I answer, stopping at the top of the driveway and parking the car. "Before we go in, I want to tell you something."

"What's up?"

"I know this is going to be overwhelming. I'm not discrediting you, because I know you've done things like this before. You're a professional. This isn't new. What is new is us being here for multiple days without an escape. At the end of the night, you don't get to go home. You don't get to stop pretending. You don't get to drop the facade. You're stuck here, being on all the time. If you need a breather, a minute alone, or Christ, a nap and a snack, *please* tell me. I don't want you to feel obligated to do things. If you need anything at all, say the word and we'll temporarily remove ourselves from the situation. Got it?"

Her eyes search my face and I let her. I let her see I'm laying all my cards on the table. I let her see my nerves and anxiousness. I let her see the fear and worry I have that she's going to stretch herself thin. I let her see the way I want to pull her into my lap, hug her tight, and thank her for standing by my side.

"I got it," she agrees, giving my arm a squeeze. "Thank you for being so considerate."

"Don't thank me yet. The fun's only beginning, my friend." I cut the ignition and jump out of the car. After helping her to the ground, I hand her the bottle of wine and flowers before unloading our suitcases.

"Ready?"

"I'm ready." Emma laces her free hand through mine.

I anticipated it gesture the whole solitary drive, wondering if she would initiate any PDA, and I wasn't prepared for the outcome.

I suck in a breath at the contact of our palms pressed together.

Sparks of lust and fire are climbing up my arm, clawing at my skin, wanting to consume and possess not only me but also her. I've touched plenty of women, but it's never been like this.

There's never been a flaring desire. A visceral ache and psychical pain to touch more of her. To explore her. To drag her back into my truck and lock the doors if she'll let me, having my way with her again and again and again while I study every inch, every dip, every groove of her body.

Instead of acting on these animalistic instincts, I level my breathing and gently squeeze her hand.

"Henry," she whispers, and I pause, almost to the front door and the start of our charade.

"Yeah, Sunflower?"

I turn to face her, a hesitant gaze meeting my own, measuring the passing seconds in birds chirping. Leaves rustling. Her heart beating in time with my own.

One.

Two.

Three.

Four.

Five.

Six.

Seven.

The count is interrupted by her squeezing my hand in return, smile returning to place. Eyes brighten. Frown creases soften. Shoulders roll back.

"We're tackling this together, okay? Just like we've tackled it so far. Just like the day in the conference room. It's you and me. Both of us. I'm here with you. I'll be next to you the whole time."

The air leaves my lungs at my new favorite word, and I beam at her.

Together.

"Together," I repeat emphatically, knocking on the door.

TWENTY-FOUR

EMMA

TWO BEATS.

I allow myself precisely two beats of panic before I pirouette, my face taking on a natural smile at the snap of a finger. The door flies open and a stunning woman with long gray hair and a bright expression greets us with outstretched arms.

"Henry!" she exclaims, wrapping him in a tight embrace. I sidestep to my right, giving him a moment alone with his mother. "I've missed you so much. Having a good job in the city doesn't prevent you from coming to visit. We haven't seen you in almost a month."

Henry chuckles, hugging her back before wiggling himself free. "I know, Mom. I'm sorry. This is Emma, the reason I've been so distracted."

His arm drapes over my shoulder, pulling me into the crook of his body. I'm slingshotted back to the night in his kitchen when I hugged him and pressed myself against his chest. I didn't realize how much I missed the closeness until I was back in the safe confines of his hold.

"Emma! It's so lovely to meet you," she says, and I hold out my hand for her to shake. She bypasses the formality, giving me a quick hug as well.

"It's so great to meet you, too, Mrs. Dawson. I brought you some flowers and wine. Henry mentioned red was your favorite."

"Oh, you're such a sweetheart! Thank you so much. And please, call me Anne," she says, taking the gifts. "Gosh, you are beautiful! How was your drive? Did you hit any traffic? Come inside!"

"The drive was great. Quick. No traffic," Henry says as he walks into the foyer and I follow behind. "This one slept the whole time. Worst copilot ever!"

"Hey! It's not my fault you didn't offer any of the snacks you brought to keep me awake!" I throw back, elbowing his ribs. "You promised Zebra Cakes, and here I am, famished."

"I'll spend the rest of the weekend feeding you whatever your heart desires to compensate for my sins."

"Aren't you two cute," Anne swoons. "I figured you'd want to relax this afternoon before the chaos ensues. I should have said screw the party and taken your father on a trip. Event planning is not for the faint of heart. How about Mexican food for dinner? We figured we could go out tonight, since we'll have most of the meals catered the rest of the weekend."

"Sounds delicious," I say.

"Wonderful. Hen, your room is ready for you. Towels are in the bathroom and fresh sheets are on the bed. If you need any more, let me know, and I'll dig some out."

"Perfect. Where are we putting Emma?"

Anne frowns. "What do you mean?"

"Where is she going to sleep?" he clarifies.

"With you in your room, of course. Where else would she go?" She sounds confused as she looks between us like we each have two heads.

My stomach drops straight to my feet so fast, I swear I'm free-falling from a plane without a parachute. Henry's grip tenses around me. It's a small flex of his muscles, but I notice it immediately. The tips of his fingers tap on my shirt repeatedly. It's his nervous habit, I've noticed, one he subconsciously does when he's anxious or on edge. He's clutching me tighter, almost using me for protection.

If I had to wager a guess, I'd bet this is the first time he's hearing about this, too.

It turns out sleeping arrangements are the only thing we haven't discussed in our weeks of communication. I know Henry is allergic to kiwi and adamantly declares black ink as the superior color when signing legally binding documents, but where we'll be resting our heads never got brought up.

Maybe that's my fault for assuming we'd spend time in separate hotel rooms, not shacked up together under the same roof as his parents.

The temperature in the foyer is steadily rising, becoming much hotter at the thought of spending four nights curled up beside him, bodies less than a foot apart as we slumber peacefully.

Henry speaks first, breaking the icy silence. "I'll take the guest room," he offers.

"It's your home," I interject. "I can take the guest room."

"No, really, please, my room is much bigger and I want you to be comf—"

"Don't be silly," Anne laughs, interrupting our battle. She's oblivious to our panic. "Not sharing a room would be weird, wouldn't it? Besides, the guest rooms are going to be occupied this weekend."

I gulp down the last remaining oxygen I can find, peering up at Henry and deferring our plan of action to him.

His deep inhale brushes his arm against mine, and I lean further into his embrace, hoping he can convey a sense of calm and rationality I'm unable of possess right now, attempting to quell the salacious scenes running through my head.

Henry, in only a pair of boxers, stretched out lazily on a mattress.

Henry, a sheet pooled around his chiseled waist, grinning at me as the sun rises.

Henry, staring at me as I wake up, studying me intimately while I figure out my surroundings.

Us together on a rumpled comforter as he holds my hands above my head, sweat sliding down his chest as he growls at me to *"come, Sunflower."*

Our gazes collide, and he lifts an eyebrow. With a bob of my throat and dip of my chin, Henry nods, turning back to his mom wearing a megawatt smile, doing his best to look unbothered.

"Sharing my room it is."

I sense the waver in his voice despite his emphatic declaration. The way his tapping resumes. How he holds me closer, still, our bodies fusing together not close enough.

"Perfect!" Anne says, clapping her hands. "We'll meet down here in a bit to head out. I'll be in the kitchen with the party planner if you need me. I can't wait to learn more about you, Emma."

"Come on," Henry says, taking my hand and guiding us out of the entryway. "I'll show you where we're staying."

"Your house is gorgeous," I observe, noting the twenty-foot ceilings and crystal chandeliers greeting us along our journey.

"People always say that, but I just see the four walls where I grew up. Lots of memories here. Lots of happy days. Some sad ones, too. The corner where I tripped and hit my head on the hardwood floor. The stairs Lizzie, Drew, and I would run down on Christmas morning. The hallway I would sneak down when I got back a little too late past curfew. First impressions always imply this place of wealth and prestige. Which, yeah, it is. But to me, it's just home. No different from anyone else's."

I smile as we ascend a large staircase in the center of the home that leads to a long hallway. "Please tell me you slide down the banisters."

"Every morning," he chuckles.

"You have your own wing?" I ask as he opens one of the many closed doors.

Henry hums. "Wing is a bit pretentious, don't you think? This isn't the White House."

"It could certainly rival it. Looks like a wing to me."

"Maybe we can compromise and agree that it's a not-wing wing. A separate area, away from the rest of the house. Welcome to my childhood bedroom."

I look around the space we've entered. The room is large. A king bed with a deep mahogany headboard sits in the middle under a tall window covered in curtains. There's a desk in the corner with notebooks and papers scattered over it, as well as an old computer monitor collecting dust. Posters line the cream-colored walls, an array of art from pictures of Derek Jeter to a Blink-182 concert image.

"I'm a little disappointed. I was expecting a swimming pool in the middle of the room, or a jacuzzi. Oh, or peacocks! This isn't nearly as outlandish as what I was picturing."

"You're cute when you're a smart-ass," Henry says. "We keep the peacocks in the gardens, and the swimming pool is in my sister's section of the house."

"A travesty."

"Talk to me, Emma. How are you feeling so far?"

"Not bad," I answer honestly. "To be fair, one person is a lot easier to handle than a dozen people. Or two dozen people."

"Or a hundred."

"Right."

"Does Mexican sound okay for dinner? I called Mom yesterday and suggested it. I know you love tacos."

Words of affirmation and acts of service have always been my love languages, and my heart bursts at his recollection of my favorite food. It's a small, inconsequential fact we only discussed once or twice. Still, he *remembered*, and accommodated me and the things I like.

"It sounds perfect."

"Cool. Want to set your suitcase up over there?"

He gestures to the far side of the bed, where a long ottoman sits in front of a lounge chair. I carry my bag over and lift it onto the piece, hoping I don't get any scuff marks on the wrinkle-free upholstery.

My shoulders are stiff, grimacing at the sight of the worn material against such nice, decorative furniture. The dirty wheels are a stark contrast against the white fabric that's probably never used for comfort, used primarily to bring the room together in interior design harmony.

"Hey." Henry's voice is soothing as it drifts across the room, like a cool breeze on a warm summer day, offering a reprieve from unrelenting sun. "What's wrong? Are you all right?"

"I'm fine," I answer, fumbling with my suitcase zipper.

He ambles over, moving to stand next to me. I tilt my chin up, meeting his troubled stare. Worry is etched on his face, prevalent in the frown he's wearing and the creases in the corner of his eyes. He looks tired. Exhausted. Yet still so strikingly handsome.

"It's you and me in here, Sunflower. You don't have to lie or pretend, okay? Your shoulders are up around your ears. You're wringing your hands together. We can pretend we aren't familiar with each other as Emma and Henry all we want, but I have a pretty good read on you. And right now, you're not okay. You're stressed out," he murmurs.

"It's stupid and pointless. Totally not a big deal. I'm just over-analyzing. I do it frequently."

His hand reaches out, thumb swiping over my cheek. "For the next few days, we need to be brutally honest with each other, even if it means saying the tough shit we don't think the other wants to hear. I'm asking a lot from you by being here. Having my mom think I'm dating someone is important, sure, but your feelings and well-being are more important to me. The *most* important to me. Nothing you say is stupid. I won't laugh. I'm not going to make fun of you. I'm going to listen and we're going to figure out a solution together, okay?"

The sincerity behind the words causes me to exhale a heavy

breath, a weight leaving my shoulders. He's right; they're tense and I feel relief when I let them relax, shaking out my arms.

"You know I've done this before. A lot of times, actually. With lots of different people."

Something akin to… anger? Agitation? Dislike? crosses Henry's face, so fleeting and fast it's hard to tell it was ever even there. "I'm aware," he says.

"I've been a little anxious in the past when I'm with high-profile men. But this is… next level. I'm scared. Nervous. Really not wanting to mess anything up for you."

"Nervous and being scared are okay." His palm cups my cheek, and I turn my head a fraction of an inch to nestle into his soft touch. "What else is on your mind?"

"It's difficult for me to process all these conflicting reactions. We have a history, and very specific and regimented roles we play at the office. I'm trying to find a balance between the two parts, and it's really freaking hard. Then, I see my stupid suitcase on your nice furniture, and I think about how laughable this is. No one who truly knows me would ever believe this is real. Look at you. Look at me. My socks have a hole in them and the watch you're wearing probably costs as much as my mortgage payment. I really enjoyed talking to JD; I'm struggling to remember that he's also you, too, Henry. I'm sorry."

"I am looking at you," he says vehemently. "I don't give a fuck about what your suitcase looks like or if your socks have fifteen holes in them. You know why?"

"Why?"

"Because you liked talking to me for me, just how I liked talking to you for you. You didn't care about my name or my family's name. Whatever gossip you've heard about me in bed is the last thing on your mind. You're not conniving or spiteful. You're the most gracious, generous person I've ever met, and anyone who thinks I wouldn't want to be with someone like you or couldn't be with someone like you, is so wrong, it's laughable. Jesus, Emma, you could live in a box and I'd still think you were one of the most magnificent people in the world."

My lip trembles. It's so thoughtful. So unlike anything Henry has said to me before, yet so also *normal*, and I feel rocked to my core. Is he always like this, and I've just failed to notice? If he is, I hate that I've missed out on such a sensitive man, regretting every second I spent being indifferent toward him and brushing him off.

There are so many things I want to say back.

Too many words and conflicting emotions, torn between wanting to laugh his admission off and jump into his arms, seeing if he would catch me.

"I-I think you might be one of the most magnificent people in the world too, Henry."

He beams, a joy on par with the best things in my life and the good in every day. I wish I had a camera to capture the moment, forever cementing it under the Start of a New Era of Us.

"Do you know what I was thinking when I saw you sitting in the coffee shop, wearing the same outfit RB told me she'd have on?"

I shake my head. I've been too afraid to ask. Too afraid to hear the truth. Not brave enough to push for details. What happens after we cross this line of sharing emotions and feelings? We can never go back to being two coworkers who exist under the same office roof. We'll be Henry and Emma with promises and bonds and shared intimacy.

I wonder what you sound like when you come.

I shiver at the memory. How the nine words are permanently stitched into my brain, right up there with *you look positively stunning*.

I might need to start a dictionary of phrases said by Henry Dawson that make me crumble.

"Overjoyed, Emma. I'm *still* overjoyed, and not because you're helping me out. Yeah, it's a nice perk, but it was so freeing to be authentically me. And to be accepted. And to fucking *laugh* with a woman who wasn't trying to... to get me to pay all this attention to her. We have a complex, twisty history. We've existed in each other's world for almost two decades, yet we know next to nothing about each other. We're here now. Together. I'm not asking you to fall in love with me or guarantee a life beyond this weekend. I'm just excited to spend the next few days as *us*. And whatever happens, happens. I'm so glad it was you on the phone, Emma, and I wouldn't want it any other way."

Something deep in my chest cracks, a fissure beginning between my breasts that spiderwebs out of control. I'm fighting back tears, the swell of raw emotion almost knocking me unconscious. I've never heard a man speak so openly or be so vulnerable.

Every second I'm with Henry, all of my attempt at keeping this casual and professional are close to snapping in half, giving way to what I truly want.

More.

More with this man.

More words. More touches. More glances and smiles. More learning and more guidance. More whispered sweet nothings followed by more dirty talk. More taking and giving.

More Henry.

I switch our positions, putting my hand on his cheek, the pinprick of his stubble grazing my palm. He inhales sharply, staring at me, and I stare right back, unafraid. This is the moment where I decide I'm going to get what I want, and savor every second.

What I want is him. Wholly and completely. In any and every way.

"I'm so glad it was you on the phone too, Henry."

TWENTY-FIVE

EMMA

"SO," George, Henry's father, says as we settle into a booth at the Mexican restaurant later that evening. "Tell us the story about how you two kids met."

I'm sitting next to my doting fake boyfriend, who lets me slide across the wood first, scooting beside me and offering an encouraging smile. The bench we're occupying isn't very large, and, thanks to Henry's stature, it barely accommodates both our bodies. Our shoulders brush, a glide of fabric against fabric. I jolt at the contact, still not used to this shared proximity, and how nice it is, in no hurry to pull away.

"Believe it or not, we work together. This is the same Emma..." Clearing his throat, he pauses, tugging at the collar around his neck. "The same Emma I've mentioned before." He finishes the sentence in a rush, the words blended and garbled together. Even in the darkened room, I notice his cheeks changing from tan to light pink from embarrassment.

"I knew it!" Anne announces, elbowing George. "I told you!"

"You know nothing!" Henry retaliates, shifting on the bench. The movement brings him even nearer, the side of his muscular thigh pressing into mine.

"I'm so out of the loop here," I laugh nervously, unsure what he might have said about me.

"Oh, Emma darling, it's nothing bad," Anne says quickly, shooting Henry a stern look. "It's quite funny. He would woefully lament about this woman he worked with, trying to figure out why his charm didn't work on you. He made an entire list once, a few years back, documenting reasons he was inferior to you, and my favorite one was that he—"

"Mother," Henry hisses. "Don't you dare finish that fucking sentence."

"Language!" Anne says, reaching across the table to swat his arm. "You don't want your girlfriend to hear about the time you walked through the house drunkenly waxing poetry about her and the... what was the phrase? *Hair like sunshine*? You had a conversation with a wall."

Henry groans, dropping his head to his hands. "I'm emancipating myself from this family. None of these events ever happened. You're all a bunch of liars."

I reach over, prying his fingers away from his face. Slipping his hand into mine, I bring our joined palms to rest on my thigh, squeezing reassuringly and doing my best to abate some of his distress. With our grips hidden, I tap his skin eight times, hoping he understands what I'm spelling.

Together.

He taps back.

"You've been talking about me for a while, huh?" I ask, keeping my voice low so only Henry can hear me.

He squeezes my hand tighter, thumb running along my pointer finger. "Can't help it, Sunflower. You've irked me in the best way for years."

There goes my heart again, stumbling, sputtering, and spiraling out of control as he speaks to me—just me—like I'm the only person in the world.

"Maybe one day you'll let me hear some of that drunken poetry," I say bravely, and the ghost of his lips dance across the top of my head.

"Maybe if you behave yourself this weekend, I'll recite poetry to you all night long," he whispers over the shell of my ear, breath hot on my skin.

I gape at him, blinking a dozen times. I can't find anything to say. I can't find anything to do. I'm frozen, staring at him as he smirks, the left side of his mouth tilting up in a taunting, promising way.

"So, Mom, what flavor is the cake Saturday night?"

The conversation continues around me, but I feel like I'm out of my body, nodding along without actually processing the discussions, finding it difficult to focus on anything. I've never, ever felt like this with a man at an event. Alive. Distracted. Concentrated. A battle of will and what the hell is going to happen next.

The only thing that pulls me out of the dark thoughts of desire is Anne and George sharing stories of a young Henry, and I can't stop my hysterical laughter when they recall how upset he was when, at six years old, he didn't get to go to the sleepover Elizabeth's friend was having.

"He wanted to have his nails painted and hair done. When I told him he wasn't allowed to go, he packed up a knapsack and walked down the road for ten minutes, claiming he was running away. All because he didn't get to play dress up."

———

After dinner, when we arrive back at the house, we wave good night to his parents. The climb up to his room is silent and Henry lets me use the bathroom first, washing my face, brushing my teeth, and changing into my pajamas.

Stepping back into the room, I watch him pull some pillows off the bed, setting them up on the carpeted floor. He unzips a large sleeping bag, laying it out flat.

"What are you doing?" I ask as I climb onto the mattress and pull the comforter up to my chin.

"I'm going to sleep down here."

"Why?"

Henry peers up at me, confused. "So we don't sleep together?"

"Is there a reason you aren't going to sleep in the actual bed?"

"Well, sharing isn't an option. It's okay, the floor is shockingly soft. That's what you get when your mother splurges on the high-end carpet."

"I don't care if we share the bed, Henry," I blurt out.

"You don't?" His head tilts to the side, crossing his arms over his chest. He's so much larger than me, taking up so much space. If he joined me up here, there wouldn't be any substantial distance between us. I try to keep my attention trained on his face and not on the pajama bottoms hanging dangerously low on his hips or the worn shirt that's almost see-through.

"Of course not. This is your home. I should be on the floor. I'm smaller anyway. Here, let's switch." I peel back the covers, swinging my legs to the side.

"Emma, I swear to God if you even think about getting out of that bed on my behalf." He crosses the floor, barely taking three steps before he's beside me, my wrist in his hand. I inhale sharply, seared by the contact. Realizing he's touching me, holding me, inches away from pressing my body against his, he stops, dropping my arm and retreating backwards. "Shit. I'm sorry. I would never ask you to sleep on the floor."

"If I'm not sleeping on the floor, and I'm not letting you sleep on the floor, the other option is sharing. Which I'm completely fine with."

Henry searches my face for any doubt or hesitation. I'm certain if I gave him even the smallest inkling of uncomfortableness, he'd adamantly refuse my proposal. And for some odd reason, the notion makes me tingly all over.

"Are you sure?"

"Positive. Now, let's be adults about this. Get in." I pat the space and Henry complies, slipping under the sheets.

"You win this round, Burns. If you change your mind at any point, even in the middle of the night, you better wake me up or shove me to the floor."

"I will, I promise. Besides, it's freezing down there. I can't have you shivering to death while I bask under all these covers. Seriously, how many layers are on this bed?"

"Ah, not having a 'let them eat cake' moment, are you? I knew you cared about me," he muses. "And I thought you wouldn't shed a tear if I disappeared off the face of the earth."

"Hm. Maybe one. A lone drop. Suffice to say, we've made progress over the last few weeks."

"We definitely have. Until we find out who they're selecting for the partner position soon."

I turn on my side, resting my head on my elbow so we're facing each other. "You should get it. You work so hard. You're intelligent. Your clients adore you. You have a great success rate, and you're a good guy."

"I only work with contracts. You're literally changing the world."

"That's not true."

"Are you kidding me? Emma." His hand reaches out again, stroking along the length of my elbow where my cheek is resting. "You're out there fighting for people others don't listen to. You tackle pressing issues. You save lives and keep families together. You work on changing the antiquated laws in this country, and you accept any client, no matter their socioeconomic status. You're not a paycheck pusher like half the asshats in our industry. You genuinely care, and that makes you special. And judging by the way your eyes are about to pop out of your head, you clearly don't hear it enough."

"That's incredibly kind of you to say," I whisper. "I know I alone cannot fix the world's problems, but every time I can help just *one* person, it reminds me I've done something good. Something worthwhile."

"*You're* good, Emma. So good. You're like... like a ray of sunshine on a cloudy, stormy day, peeking through the darkness and evil, shoving aside the sense of gloom for a hint of brightness and warmth. Which is mind-blowing, because if I encountered what you do on a day-to-day basis, I'd be sad as hell. You smile through it all, getting up the next morning, on a quest to kick more ass."

"I am a certified ass kicker," I agree, rolling onto my back and yawning.

"Glad I'm not the only one who's beat. Tomorrow is going to be more stressful."

"More family members, right?"

"Too many family members." The lamp clicks off, silence and darkness surrounding us. "I'm glad you're here, Emma."

"Me, too. Good night, Henry."

"Night, Sunflower."

TWENTY-SIX

EMMA

A BIRD CHIRPS outside the window, greeting the day and rousing me from my peaceful slumber. I stretch my arms above my head and adjust my position on the mattress. It's blissfully quiet in the room, and I savor the stillness. There are no car horns. No trash trucks. No lawn mowers or trains rumbling in the distance.

On instinct, my hands find their way to the mass next to me, burrowing myself further under the covers, not ready to get up just yet. Something hard presses against my stomach as I shift onto my side, leg perched on an elevated surface. Letting out a happy sigh, I reluctantly open my eyes.

The room comes into focus. The curtains are vaguely familiar from yesterday. A heater hums nearby, churning to life. As I turn my head to the side, gaze dropping, I see Henry staring at me, mouth agape and eyes widening.

It's the moment I realize I'm wrapped around him like a koala, my hair covering his neck and arms, pads of my fingers holding onto his middle in a clenching grip.

"Um. H-hi," I stammer out, voice thick with sleep. Carefully, I swing my leg off his hip.

"Er." Henry coughs twice, and when he moves, his dick—his *hard dick*—presses further into my belly, and I gasp.

"I... uh." Wiggling free, I try to break our contact completely before understanding his arms are around my thighs and ass, keeping me firmly in place and pinned provocatively against him.

"Hello." He extracts his limbs away from mine, careful to not touch me further.

"Well. This is fun, huh?" I blurt out.

Henry chuckles lazily, and it's the kind of laugh you can probably only hear before he climbs out of bed and starts his day. Running a hand through his sleep-mussed hair, he gives me a sheepish smile. "Sorry for accosting you."

"It definitely was my fault. I usually spoon a spare pillow at home and must have gotten confused."

"Are you comparing me to something fluffy, Burnsie?"

A giggle escapes me, the weirdness of waking up *literally* on top of him fading away with the morning chill. "Innocent until proven guilty, Your Honor. I think we both know you're far from fluffy."

My eyes flick to his covered body, the outline of defined abdominal muscles barely visible under the hem of his white tee. Henry is all sharp and firm lines. Hard work and dedication in all his projects: fitness, his career, his friendships. The only parts of him that *are* soft are his kind heart, sweet demeanor, passion for helping others, and the love and adoration for those closest to him.

He sits up, tossing me an apprehensive look. "Are you ready for today? Most of the gang will be here for brunch."

"I'm so excited to meet Drew and Elizabeth! Do you mind if I shower? What kind of outfit should I wear?"

"You can use my bathroom. Towels and stuff are all set up. I'm going to do a quick run to shake out some of these nerves, so take your time." He climbs out of bed, cracking his back. "As for clothes, wear whatever you want. Jeans. A sweater." Pausing, he taps his cheek, deep in thought. "A pillowcase. You look great in anything."

"Thanks." I take the compliment and tuck it close to my heart, keeping it safe in a special box.

I head into the bathroom and close the door. There's a Jacuzzi tub and a stand-alone shower that takes up the entire length of one wall. The white marble floors are warm under my feet.

Floor heaters.

Discarding my sleep clothes, I turn on the shower, water from four different heads filling the room with steam and heat. I step inside, grabbing the fresh bar of soap and cautious to not get my hair wet. I lather myself up, suds forming on my body as I relax under the hot water, tension from the last 24 hours sliding down the drain.

My mind wanders back to Henry's powerful arms, biceps flexing as he held me in his possession. The feel of him pushing against my body, long length making me ache for more. The absurdity of how good the press of his fingers on the swell of my ass felt, punishing and pleasurable.

My hand slides down my neck, water cascading over my shoulders. I bite my lip. I shouldn't be thinking about him while I'm in here. I shouldn't let my hand slip between my parted thighs and daydream about what it would be like to have him there, easing the worry from my bones and whispering encouragement in my ear as he brings me down from a high I so desperately want to climb.

The craving of wanting him hasn't faded away with the dawn of a new day. It's still there, in the forefront of my mind, the promises and desires he's insinuated being brought to fruition.

Do I wish he was here, a wicked gleam in his eye as his hand slides up my legs, higher and higher?

Do I want him on his knees before me, wet hair tickling my inner thigh?

Am I picturing him pushing me against the tiled wall, hiking my foot onto his hip while he goes to town, pounding into me until I can't take anymore?

Are you a good girl who knows how to listen?

Pressing my back against the smooth surface behind me, I give in, just for a second. A quick moment of weakness. I pinch my nipples, hands moving from my chest down to my stomach, thumb grazing against my clit. I reposition myself so the stream of water hits me in the perfect spot, replacing the need for my thumb.

Sliding a finger inside myself, my eyes snap closed, reveling in the sensation. The stretch. The fullness that encompasses me. I take a deep breath, about to add a second digit, when I hear the bedroom door slam closed.

"Emma? Are you still in there?"

Fuck.

Steadying my breathing, I resist the urge to bang my head against the sliding glass door.

"Yeah," I call back.

"Everything okay?"

"Yes! I just… it took me a minute to figure out how to turn the shower on." I wince at the horrible line, washing the rest of the soap off and ignoring the throbbing between my legs.

"Cool. I'm going to shower in my parents' room. I'll be back soon."

The door slams and I curse, turning off the water and snatching a towel off the rack.

I rummage through my suitcase, putting on a sweater, jeans, and a pair of boots. I style my hair in a quick French braid, tying a hair tie around the end when I hear a knock.

"Come in!"

Henry reenters the room, eyes downcast, and head bowed. "Are you decent?"

"Yeah. All clear."

"Running usually helps calm me down. Not the case today, it seems. I didn't get hit by a car, either. A shame."

"Was that your intention?" I laugh, checking my reflection in the mirror. He's also dressed casually, wearing jeans and a long-sleeved henley shirt with Converse on his feet. I've only seen him out of business attire twice this decade: the night we did the escape room and the night at the bar. This morning, he looks really freaking good, one of those men who can wear everything and wear it *well*. With the laid-back outfit and scuffed up sneakers, perhaps we aren't as different as I assumed we were.

Letting out a sigh, he pinches the bridge of his nose. "Sorry. I'm really stressing out and this isn't something I experience frequently."

"Hey. I got you." My hand rests on his shoulder. "It's okay to be freaked out. I'm here with you, remember?"

Giving my hand a pat, large palm covering mine, he tilts his head toward the door. "I want to show you something before we're ambushed. It's a surprise."

"Is it a kitchen full of Zebra Cakes? Or an all-you-can-eat cookie buffet?"

"Maybe I shouldn't show you. If those are your expectations, I think you're going to be sorely disappointed. Whoa, wait a second. Your face is flushed. Are you feeling okay?"

"What? Oh. Spent too much time in the shower, I guess."

Lacing our hands together, he tugs me to the hall. "Come on. I think you're going to like this."

As he leads me from his room, I don't miss the fact that he's still holding my hand. Despite not having an audience, despite being all alone, our fingers intertwine, wrapped around each other for survival.

I never want to let go.

TWENTY-SEVEN

HENRY

SCONCES LINE THE WALL, illuminating our journey through the quiet house. Much of my time as a kid was spent running these halls and I could walk them blindfolded and backwards, knowing exactly where to go. Exactly how many paces until I needed to turn right, and which floorboards along the way squeaked the loudest.

Reaching our destination, I stop in front of the entrance to the library, giving Emma a chance to take in the exterior of the hidden room. I haven't told her what lies beyond the door yet, and I'm bouncing with excitement to show off the other side.

"Wow. This looks like some shit out of a castle," she observes, her hand dropping from mine to reach out and trace the details along the eight-foot-high wooden frame.

"Just wait." I push open the decrepit door and she gasps at the sight.

"Henry," she whispers, walking to the center of the space. The library is circular, with floor-to-ceiling shelves and rolling ladders. Every inch is covered in literature or comfortable furniture. Her head tilts up, observing the rows and rows of books residing under a skylight, natural sunshine brightening the cozy, quiet haven. "I-I'm speechless."

"Pretty incredible, huh? It's my favorite room in the house. When I was younger, I'd spend my afternoons here, reading the classics and hiding away. It's where I discovered fictional worlds where there is no evil, only good. It's where I decided I wanted to be a lawyer. It's where I fell in love with words. A lot of people don't know this, but books make me happy, and I figured you could relate."

"I truly don't know what to say. It's amazing." Her eyes bounce back and forth, sweeping over every part of the shelves, trying to find where to land first.

"Take a look around. See what you can find. We've got some time before we need to be downstairs, and we can always come back up afterward, too."

"I'm afraid I'll mess something up! Some of these books have probably been here for a century!"

"You won't, trust me. My grubby fingers have already touched everything in sight."

Emma nods, walking over to one of the shelving units, fingers running down the spines, studying the names. Using her distractedness to my advantage, I, in turn, study her.

She's like a 1,000-piece puzzle: extremely complex to decipher in the beginning. You wonder how in the world you're going to figure her out. As the pieces start to come together, corner by corner, middle piece by middle piece, she becomes easier to understand. Easier to read, until it's as if you've known her your whole life.

When Emma likes something, she positively lights up. Her eyes widen in awe, the blue sparkling like firecrackers. Her smile stretches wide, covering her full, plump lips and turning up in the corners. Right now is no exception. She appears joyful. Excited. Elated. About to give herself whiplash as her neck turns right then left, scanning as many books as she can find. Her shoulders alternate between hunching then elongating to try and reach a book above her head. When pieces of her braid fall in her face, she tucks them away behind her ear, wanting an unobstructed view of what's in front of her, and continues her search. Every book she encounters is a rare prize. A jewel. A once-in-a-lifetime find. Despite the thousands of antique pages and historic titles surrounding me, I only see *her*. Her beauty. Her wonder. Her happiness, the exuberant excitement making me smile.

I know she likes to read. The bookshelf in her office is full of books, and I saw the way her eyes sparkled when she noticed the shelf in my apartment, too. I also noticed the three books tucked in her suitcase when she was unpacking yesterday. I'm curious how she reads, what she likes to read, and if she prefers physical books or an e-reader. Who's her favorite author? What's a quote from a book she's annotated and highlighted, going back to the comfort of familiarity in times of sorrow and despair? What's her favorite love story?

More questions I'm desperate to know the answer to.

The list is never-ending with her.

"I could spend all day here," she announces. "Seriously, how did you get anything done growing up? I would've flunked out if I had all these books waiting for me."

"It loses some of its grandeur when you're around it so much. Sometimes you have to take a step back to really appreciate its true beauty." My eyes stay locked on hers as I say the words, and I'm absolutely not talking about the library anymore. I think she knows it, too, because she swallows, taking a small step closer to me. "If you find a book that piques your interest, feel free to take it."

Take my heart while you're at it, Emma.

"Do you mean it?"

I don't think I've ever been more sure of something in my life.

"Of course. As many as you'd like."

"No one from the Dawson clan is going to hunt me down?"

"My parents won't care."

"Thank you," she says giddily. "I think I'll wait until we have more time. I don't want to make a rash decision."

Do you remember the first day we saw each other? I wish we had more time.

"They say absence makes the heart grow fonder." I offer her my hand again. "Ready to tackle this shindig?"

Her fingers slide into mine, a key in a lock. "Yeah. I am."

I nod, leading her from the library and down the winding stairs, halting at the glass door to the backyard. It's already chaos outside; children are running through the grass and servers carry full trays of mimosas and orange juice. The smell of prepared food wafts through the air, and brunch will be served shortly.

"Do you want to have a secret phrase in case we need to tap out for a minute?" I ask, not sure what protocol might be.

"I've always wanted to be a spy. How about 'can I get you another plate?' What do you think? Not too obvious?"

"It's perfect. You're going to be fresh meat to these people. Sure you don't want to back out?"

"I'm ready, Henry." She pats my forearm, reassuring me. "This isn't my first rodeo."

Her words are acid on my skin. How could I forget? She's helped numerous men in situations like this. Does she hold their hand, too? Wrap her arms around their bodies? Does she blush when they look at her like I do—like she's the only woman in the world?

I plaster on a smile. "Right. You're a professional." Turning the knob on the door, I gently nudge her over the threshold of safety and into the throes of hell.

In almost perfect unison, all eyes snap up to us the moment we walk outside. I keep the smile on as we approach the mass of people, and Emma does the same, her demeanor relaxed and effortless, like we're strolling through the park on a lazy Sunday afternoon and not walking straight into a lion's den. There are hushed whispers, murmurs of shock and surprise, and shaking heads.

Why the fuck do these people care so much about my personal

life? I don't know half of them, and here they are, judging me and making assumptions without bothering to speak to either of us. The last fucking thing I'm doing is grabbing a microphone and announcing our arrival to these nosy assholes when I really want to flip them all off.

Out of the corner of my eye I see Betsy, the girl my mother wanted to set me up with, whispering into another woman's ear. They both sneer at us, directing most of their disdain toward Emma. I gulp, drawing her in closer to me. I'm not going to be able to protect her forever, so a temporary shield will have to do.

I grab two flutes of mimosas off the first tray I find, handing one to her and ignoring the receiving line beckoning us for introductions. "Drink?" I ask.

"God, yes," she replies, sipping it greedily. Half the contents disappear in a single gulp.

Okay. Maybe she's not as immune to nerves as she thinks she is.

"Small sips, princess. Can't have you getting sick."

She nods, bringing the glass away from her mouth and licking her bottom lip. *Fuck,* I want to help her clean up the mess.

"Henry? Is this the girlfriend I've heard rumblings about?" Grandma Jean, my mother's mother, calls from across the field, the first to strike. I flinch, wondering how the hell an 89-year-old woman's voice is able to carry so far.

I can't *ignore* her. That would be cruel.

"Hi, GJ, yeah, this is her," I call back, keeping my voice neutral. "So much for trying to lay low," I hiss to Emma.

"You said it yourself: You with a woman is a sight to behold. I'll go introduce myself. You mingle with your family and I'll come find you in a bit."

"Are you sure?" I ask, afraid to release her into the wild alone.

"I'm positive. Grandmas are my jam. I'll see you in a few."

She stands on her tiptoes, pressing her lips to my cheek in a fleeting, chaste kiss. Emma moves away so fast, I'm not sure it even happened, and I'm left staring after her, resisting the urge to touch where her mouth met my skin. That would be a dead fucking giveaway.

Pull it together, Dawson. You can do this.

I can see why people shell out money for Emma's services. She's believable and really sells this shit, spending the last thirty minutes sitting with GJ, a genuine smile on her face the entire time, even though I *know* my grandmother is incessantly chattering away, leaving her no room to escape.

The late-autumn breeze keeps pushing her hair into her face and she bats it away without pausing the conversation. I've kept one eye on her, making sure no one harasses her too forcibly and she doesn't drink too much without any nourishment to back it up. She might do this frequently, but my family will push and prod for any information they can scour. I should go and save her, but my cousin Michael is currently giving me an earful about a topic I'm no longer paying attention to. I hear the words, but I'm not processing the content behind them, too focused on *her*.

"Dude, are you even listening to me?" He snaps his fingers in my face, close to flicking my nose.

"No, I'm not," I answer, eyes sliding away from Emma and back to him.

"I've never seen you so distracted," Michael says, following my gaze.

"Nothing has ever kept my attention before."

"She's hot, dude. I'd fuck her."

I growl in warning, not appreciating the way he's sizing her up from across the field like some conquest or game he might win. My jaw flexes at his lecherous eyes and the knowing smirk he's wearing. "Shut up," I seethe.

"How long have you two been dating?" Michael asks. "Is it

serious? Or can I snatch her away from you when you inevitably get bored? I'll give it another week. Tops."

My fingers tighten around the champagne flute, the glass close to cracking. He's always been a flirt like me, and when we were younger we would help talk each other up until we both left for the night with someone by our side. His value of morals is a lot lower than mine, though; the more unattainable the woman, the more he wants her, not caring if she is married or taken.

Or mine.

"Four months. Yes, it's serious, and if you *think* about touching her, I will pummel you into the ground. She's mine. Back the fuck up, asshole."

"Four months and this is somehow the first time anyone in our family is hearing about her?" Lizzie asks, inserting herself into our conversation. "Were you hiding her away in your penthouse apartment tied to your bed frame? Or did you pluck her off the streets last night before you got here?"

"I didn't want to put it in the family newsletter and overshadow Drew and Luke's wedding. You saw the way the sharks reacted when we walked outside. It's insane."

"Exactly, and right when you know Mom and Dad are going to pester you and set you up with someone, you suddenly have a woman on your arm? I'm calling bullshit."

Lizzie doesn't mean it maliciously; she's a traditional woman, following my mother's way of thinking. Why *wouldn't* I settle down right after college with the first girl to catch my eye? That's how her and her husband Shawn met years ago, and she thinks everyone else should follow suit. She doesn't understand friends with benefits, one-night stands, or the desire to hook up with someone in my office during my lunch break.

And, yeah, it's probably my own fault for living my life in such a gregarious way that the notion of having a woman accompany me to a family event is a bigger fucking deal than the four decades my parents have been together, but it's too late to back down from this scheme now. It's also too early in the weekend for anyone to catch onto us.

"I think you two are friends, and she's helping you out as a favor," Lizzie continues. "If you ruin this weekend for Mom and Dad with some little game of yours, I'm going to be pissed."

Sweat forms near my hairline. My throat is parched. I yank my sleeves farther up my arms, trying to cool off, and my fingers begin to tap my thigh.

"Hey, sweetie," a comforting voice says from behind me. I look down to find Emma sliding next to me. "Are you all having a good time over here?"

I could cry with joy knowing she's here now, rescuing me, and I try not to hug her too tightly as I put my arm around her. I want to wrap her into my embrace and keep her here for a very, very long time.

"There you are. Lizzie was joking with me about how she doesn't think we're actually dating."

Emma laughs lightly, a calming noise that doesn't sound irritated or annoyed. "I know, right? Trust me, I get how it looks. The truth is, he's really freaking persistent and wouldn't stop blowing up my email. One message on the computer turned into a text message. A text message turned into a phone call which turned into dinner. Four months later, here we are. I gave in, just to put him out of his misery. Jury's still out on whether I like him or not."

"Wow. I was thinking things were going well. I didn't realize you pitied me."

"Don't flatter yourself," she jokes, turning her attention back to my cousin and sister. "I know it's hard to believe and seems like convenient timing. For what it's worth, I think we're really happy. I enjoy spending time with him."

"She helped me learn to bake cookies."

"Yeah, except more ended up on your hands and face than in the oven!"

"It's not my fault the dough was delicious." My hand drops to between her shoulder blades, rubbing her back in small circles.

"Wow, okay, get a room, you two," Michael laughs.

"We have one, thanks," I throw back, resisting the urge to flip him off.

"Okay. Stop. I've seen enough cute bullshit to know this isn't some elaborate scheme you two concocted. Emma, I can't believe you're the one who got him to settle down, but good job. He better treat you right."

Emma looks up at me and grins. Her eyes sparkle like diamonds. Her cheeks are flushed. Her entire face is lit up. I have the crippling urge to kiss her. To have her lips on mine. One time and I'd probably be fucking addicted, needing her like plants need sunshine.

I'm so far gone for this woman.

"Mom and Dad should be doing the toast soon. You guys want to head to the table?"

"We'll meet you over there." I nod, turning to Emma as they walk away, leaving us alone. "Hey. How're you doing? Sorry I didn't save you from GJ."

"It's okay. She kept telling me all these stories about how sweet you used to be. What happened?"

I playfully pinch her side, delighting in the yelp she emits. "I'm still plenty sweet, thank you very much."

"Your mom invited me to get my nails done with her and your sister this afternoon."

"Whoa, moving up the ranks, Burns. Are you cool with that kind of alone time?"

"Yeah. I think it'll be fun! What color should I get?" She wiggles her fingers in my face and I take her hand back in mine.

"Hmm. I'm thinking red," I say softly, kissing the back of her palm without thinking. Her lips part and her breathing changes, a slight hitch that would go unnoticed if you weren't listening intently. "Red is sexy."

"Red it is," she whispers. "It'll go well with the black dress I'm wearing tomorrow night."

I raise my eyebrows, already picturing the devilish getup. "Black dress, huh? Are you trying to kill me?"

"I know red is your favorite color. Totally not impactful on my decision."

"I lied. The real answer is green."

"Green? What's the story behind that pick?"

I freeze, the blurry past coming into focus. I can't venture down the rocky road. Not right now. Not here. Not surrounded by anyone who could hear me admit the truth I've held close for years and years. Instead, I offer her a smile. "A story for a different day." A fork clinking against a glass breaks our private moment.

Saved by the toast.

Emma handles brunch effortlessly. She engages with all my family members, being gracious and polite. Everyone wants to talk to her, vying for her attention and the opportunity to pick her brain. She's asked about her career, family history, and hobbies. The shocked exclamations about her presence don't rattle or faze her at all, and she juggles multiple conversations while devouring an entire plate of food seamlessly.

I'm in awe.

She's a strong warrior, returning from battle without a single scrape or bruise, and looks gorgeous as hell while she slaughters the naysayers.

At the end of the meal, I bring her in for another hug, my arms snaking around her trim waist. I would keep her here forever, flush against me, if she asked me to. I'd never let her go.

"Hey, Sunflower."

"Hey," she smiles. "I need to find a nickname for you."

"Nah. I'm not special enough for a nickname."

"That's not true. You're plenty special. I'm thinking something along the lines of…"

I tuck her further into me. It's still not close enough.

"All good?" I ask

"I wish there was more bacon."

I chuckle lightly, dropping my chin to the top of her head. "Food goblin. Have fun this afternoon. Text me if you need me."

"I can't wait to hear all the stories about you."

"Believe none of them," I scoff, pressing a kiss to her forehead. My lips leave her skin before I have time to process how it feels to touch her so openly and freely.

"I'll miss you," she whispers. With no one around, it's not for show. It's for *me*. My ears only.

"I'll miss you, too," I answer honestly. She's not out of my grasp yet and I'm already lonelier, counting down the minutes until she returns.

With Emma gone, I spend the day with my brother, dad, and a handful of cousins and relatives. We play a game of pickup basketball on the paved court on the side of the house. A welcomed distraction, because with initiating full court press and diving for rebounds, it gives little room for my brain to wander. The longer I can keep my mind off the woman absent from my side, the better. I make sure to shove Michael extra hard on defense for his earlier comments, and "accidentally" kick his shin.

After a few hours of sweaty exertion, we switch our attention to drinking beers and sitting in chairs around a fire pit, the blaze keeping my chilled hands warm. It's cooler up here outside the city, and with the sun already setting, the temperature is dropping. At dinnertime, my dad lights the grill, getting ready for the burgers and hotdogs he's making. With a smaller group sticking around this evening, he took it upon himself to play chef.

I use the opportunity in the break of action to head upstairs and rinse off in the shower, changing out of my gym clothes and into jeans. When I come out of the bathroom, Emma is unloading a pile of bags onto the floor, nearly hidden behind paper and plastic.

"Hey! You're back!" I hurry over and take the heavy bags from her hands. "Holy cow, you bought lots of stuff! How was your day?"

"So much fun." She smiles, shrugging off her purse and tossing it into the chair. "Your mom and sister are incredible."

"That makes me so happy. Show me what you got!"

"You really care about the shirt I bought in four colors?"

"Of course I do! I wouldn't have asked otherwise."

She pulls out her purchases, laying them out on the bed. There are a couple pairs of jeans, two pairs of shoes, some headbands, and a variety of tops. My eyes snag on a green sweater.

"I like that one."

"That's my favorite! I wanted to wear it tonight, so give me a second to change, and then we can head back downstairs."

Every time I see her, I swear it's like the first time. When she emerges from the bathroom in the new outfit, I smile, and it's another sucker punch to my gut.

She looks beautiful.

"Wow," I say softly. "I really like this." My hand hovers inches off her body, and I hesitantly ask the next question. "May I?"

She nods, and my palm falls to the top of her arm, running over her bicep and down to her fingertips. My touch skirts back up over her shoulder and to the base of her neck, wishing I could dip under the barrier and feel her bare skin.

"That feels good," she whispers.

Good.

Good isn't good enough. I want to make her feel *great. Sky high.* Transcend out of this room and into the stars, on top of the world.

"I should stop touching you now."

"Why?"

"Because if I keep going, I'm not sure I'll be able to stop. I want more, and I can't have it."

I drop my hand and step away. I know what she said in my kitchen. I saw how she wasn't flailing away this morning when we woke up on top of each other. I notice her mouth parting and her eyes fluttering closed right now as her feet shuffle another step toward me. But I'm doing my damn best to respect the lines she's drawn, because at the end of the day I respect *her*, and this isn't about me selfishly trying to get off.

"Henry?"

"Yeah, honey?"

She fidgets, biting her lip, searching for courage. I lean forward, silently encouraging her, letting her know it's okay to be honest. It's okay to tell me. I see the second she gives up, not voicing what she's really thinking. "We should head back to everyone."

At the flip of a switch, I go from hopeful, optimism flooding my veins, to a popped balloon, deflating in an instant.

She's not ready.

She might not ever be ready, these two identities unrelenting in confusing her. Pulling and tugging, no regard for what her heart might want.

I'll give her time. I wasn't lying when I told the guys I'd give her anything she wants. I'm not going anywhere, and she's worth the wait.

"You're right. Come on. Let's get some food."

We spend the rest of the night laughing with my family, playing games, and enjoying ourselves. It's easy and fun; Emma is the perfect addition to our little cluster of people. More than a few times my gaze drifts over to her across the fire, observing her laugher, merriment on her face. When I reluctantly cut my eyes away, I catch my mother staring at me, wearing a knowing smile.

Even with the friendly and welcoming atmosphere, there's a lingering, nagging voice whispering in my ear, barely loud enough to be heard over the crackle of embers and flowing conversations and wine. It's determined to not let up, a headache blooming at the base of my neck and radiating up to my temples. As much as I try to refuse to acknowledge it, the whisper persists, building into a mocking, cruel, smirking apex that sounds like a dull roar.

Don't get too attached, Henry, it laughs savagely.
This has an end date. One she's going to adhere to.
You don't stand a chance.

TWENTY-EIGHT

EMMA

WHEN I WAKE up the morning after the dinner of burgers and hotdogs, I'm relieved to find I stayed on my side of the bed, not migrating over to harass my co-inhabitant. There's a wide berth of space between us this time, the rumpled sheets forming a firm barrier. His hand rests in the middle of the bed, crossing the threshold we wordlessly established last night when we returned to his room after a fun time of backyard games and stories around the fire. His palm is face up, splayed open, as if he was just holding someone's hand in his own or gripping an object tightly, fearful to let go.

I turn on my side, seizing the opportunity of his continued sleep to study the man next to me. Henry and I have existed in each other's lives long enough where I have his physical features memorized. I know his hair and eye color and a lot of his mannerisms. He always has a pen stuck in his pocket. Wears a tie with or without a blazer on. Has at least ten pairs of fun socks he rotates through. His eyes are the same brown of the chocolate chips he threw at me.

Watching him while he sleeps peacefully is different. Awake, he's never quiet and contemplative. Under the light of a new day, he appears pensive and deep in thought, pondering the secrets of the universe through his dreams. His lips are slightly parted, soft, deep breaths puffing from his mouth. I wonder what he's thinking about. It almost looks like he's smiling serenely, keeping a secret only he's privy to. There's a slight curl to his hair. I noticed yesterday he didn't bother styling it, the strands falling to whatever natural position they wanted, winding up in disarray by the end of the evening. I like it better this way; relaxed. Unhinged. A part of him not everyone gets to see. It's not put together or trying too hard. It's simply *Henry*, no glitz or glamor required.

His jaw is chiseled and sharp, with flawless and unblemished skin. All the features of his face are proportionate, and there's something inherently *hot* and *sexy* about him. Maybe it's his eyes, or maybe it's the vulnerability he's given me glimpses of. Whatever it is, I can't bring myself to look away.

My assessment gets cut short as he stirs, shifting on the mattress. He extends his arm and pulls me flush against him, tugging me into his body. He expels a content sigh and I bite my lip, not wanting to move away. Not wanting space. I want to stay right here, in his hold, forever.

I haven't allowed myself to think about what might happen after this weekend. Yes, I want him, but daydreaming about a future with Henry never seemed plausible. Lying here, our legs intertwined, his warm feet tucked under my socked ones, I let my walls down, imagining what *maybe* feels like.

I snuggle further into him, inhaling his scent. His shirt smells clean and I rest my cheek against the thin material, listening to the rhythmic beating of his heart. Yesterday, he admitted he needed to stop touching me because he wants more. I was on the verge of telling him I want more, too, but something prevented me. I couldn't get the sentence out, too scared to reveal everything.

Like how I want him to touch me. I want him to kiss me. I want him to wrap me tightly in his arms and keep me safe from the world, a private oasis that's only us. Him and I. The comprehension hits me like a wrecking ball. Instead of drowning or being pulled out to sea, I'm anchored. Grounded. There's such an air of familiarity being here next to him, like we should have been doing this all along.

"This feels nice," he says, eyes remaining closed.

"Are you awake?"

"I think so. If not, this is a really fucking amazing dream." His voice is thick with sleep, half rasp, half whisper. It's sexy as hell. "Good morning."

"Good morning," I whisper back, the endearment seeping into my bones. His eyes open slowly, squinting into the sunlight starting to filter through the curtains. A beat passes, his brain catching up with his body, causing him to wince as he takes in our close embrace.

"Shit, I'm sorry," he mumbles, hands moving to my shoulders to reposition me away from him. "Can't seem to keep my hands to myself."

"I came over here willingly. And I'd like to stay."

Henry stares at me. "You sure?"

I nod, my head returning to his chest, a smile forming on my lips. "Yeah. I'm sure."

"We have a few minutes before we need to get up."

I hum. "It's going to suck going back to work and not getting to sleep in. I'm normally two cups of coffee and four file folders deep by now."

Yeah. I could definitely get used to waking up in the arms of a strong man. I wiggle my hips forward, met with hardness pressing below my belly.

I let out a gasp the same moment Henry curses, both of us freezing, unable to move.

"I'm sorry. That's not intentional."

"Right. Yeah. Of course not."

"Shit. I don't mean you don't get me hard or anything. Because you do. Fuck. Let me start over. I can't control that first thing in the morning and my brain is really jumbled right now. I'm sorry."

"It's fine. Totally fine."

"How'd you sleep?"

"Wonderfully. What's on the agenda today?"

"The big dinner. Dancing. Drinks. Lots of food. My parents are giving a speech. It should be fun."

"I'm excited. I think everything's going well. Minus that slip up we almost had with your sister yesterday, we're doing a great job at pretending this is real."

Henry stiffens, muscles growing rigid and taut. His grip around me falters and he scoots away.

"Yeah," he says curtly. I've been doused with a bucket of water and I shiver in his notable absence. "I'm going to take a shower downstairs. You can get ready here."

The heat from his body leaves as he moves off the bed, fumbling with his suitcase and keeping his back turned toward me.

"Is everything okay?" I ask.

"It's peachy, Emma." The coldness in his voice is still prevalent as he opens the bedroom door and closes it loudly behind him. I'm left staring at the wood, wondering where I went wrong.

I watch Henry pick up his nephew by the arms, the early afternoon sun beaming down on them. He swings the young boy around, high-pitched squeals escaping the little one's mouth. Henry's grinning too, careful to avoid the area being set up for the party. He never lifts the boy too high, keeping a cautious eye on him as he raises him in the air.

"Do you want children?" Anne asks. I draw my eyes away from the scene. It's a deeply personal question, one I've become accustomed to answering. Women face more scrutiny than men when it comes to our future choices, and the older I get, the more interested outsiders are about my personal life. Am I married? Do I have children? Do I *want* children? Why? Why not?

I understand the curiosity behind her asking. She assumes I'm in an actual relationship with her son. A deeply committed relationship where we've probably started talking about a potential next steps. When you reach your 30s, you don't date someone for fun. There's no more fucking around for a few months and parting ways. You date them because you see yourself being with them forever, a long-term partnership filled with love and future plans that include swing sets and house buying.

"I do, I think. If not with a partner, I'd love to adopt. I have no problem being a single parent." I've always loved children, and I'm a firm believer in the idea of not needing a man to have one. "There are so many kids out there who need a loving home."

I've seen firsthand how many young people in our country suffer from a broken family and get tossed around, forgotten in a system designed to hurt them.

"That's a wonderful thing to hear. I get sad with the state of the world sometimes. Well, frankly, a lot of the time these days. It makes me hopeful to know I raised three children who go out and do good every day, and will pass that on to their children if they feel inclined to have them. I hope if they do, they'll continue to visit and see our home as a safe haven for them. And if children aren't in the cards for them, that's okay, too."

"That's a wonderful sentiment."

"I'm so glad you came, Emma. It's obvious you mean a lot to Henry. Enough for him to bring you home and risk us all interrogating you," she chuckles.

"I'm honored to be here. Thank you for having me. I haven't met anyone too nosy yet, but I'm sure it's bound to happen tonight."

"I always worried about him. Why was he still single? Was he afraid to tell us who he liked or didn't like? Relationships never seemed to be a priority to him. Work always came first, and as he settled into his new job a few years ago, he placed more emphasis on finally enjoying life. Now I see *why* he was waiting. I haven't seen him this relaxed in years."

The admission confuses me, and I turn to watch Henry again.

His shoulders are loose, arms dangling at his sides as he pretends to run away from his nephew, making sure to move slow enough to be caught. He's laughing loudly, the sound carrying over the yard. He doesn't look any different to me. His typical manner is always happy-go-lucky and insouciant. Maybe he's perfected how to wear a mask, covering up self-doubts.

"I've enjoyed the time we've spent together. He's really special."

It's been scary to slowly recognize this acceptance of him, and to see him accepting me in return. I've wondered what being in a full-blown, head-on relationship with him would be like. Would he have the same personality and communication style as before, texting me late into the night and first thing again in the morning? Is he a flowers kind of guy, or does he shy away from PDA and grand gestures, preferring to keep physical activities to the bedroom?

"Emma? Everything okay?" Anne asks. I smile, schooling my face back to neutrality.

"Sorry. I think I might head inside for a nap before tonight."

"That's probably smart. Make sure you wear your dancing shoes!"

I wave goodbye to her, stealing one last glance at Henry. He doesn't follow me, and I don't expect him to. We don't need to be attached at the hip all day, and he's enjoying his time with his family. I don't want to interrupt that time. Slipping up the stairs and back into his bedroom, I close the door and grab my book.

I'm still perplexed by his behavior earlier. What did I say that caused his attitude to shift so drastically and suddenly? We were having a good time. I mentioned wanting to stay in his arms, which he liked. I said we were doing a good job of pretending.

Oh.

There it is.

Henry's upset I keep bringing up that this is fake.

Because... he doesn't want it to be.

He wants it to be real. And the more attention I put on the untruthfulness of the situation, the more agitated he grows.

Bingo.

I guess that's the sign that one of us needs to make a move and we're both unsure how. I'd never coerce him into doing something, but I'm going to make damn sure I make it difficult for him to hold back tonight.

TWENTY-NINE

HENRY

"EMMA! FIVE MINUTE WARNING!" I call through the bathroom door, knocking on it twice to get her attention. She's been locked inside for almost forty-five minutes, and I'm worrying. I know she's not having second thoughts; she was bopping around the bedroom before she disappeared behind the barrier, wearing a smile I couldn't quite place. Since she closed the door, she's been suspiciously quiet.

What the hell is she up to?

"One more minute!" Her voice is muffled and I walk to the bed, putting on my suit jacket and straightening my tie. As I button my blazer, I stare at the bed, unable to stop the grin that forms when I think back to this morning.

Waking up next to Emma, I got a glimpse of what every day could look like. Her messy hair and skin pressed against mine. Her hands on my body, coaxing me awake. I've been recklessly indulgent so far, seeing exactly how close to the dangerous ledge I can teeter with her before we crash to the ground. This morning I slipped, hanging on to the precipice with a single hand, and it's about time I reel back. If not, I really won't be able to stop.

And then there are her words.

Pretending.

Not real.

How can I tell her I want to kiss her senseless? Can I tell her how good it would be if I wasn't pretending? How badly I want to press her against a wall and chant *not real, not real* into her ear, again and again, while my hand travels down the slope of her neck, dips into her dress, and pinches her nipples that lie beneath luxurious fabric, delighting when she begs for more and asks to make her mine?

I'm about to send a text to the guys, asking if I should just go for it already, when I hear a throat clear from behind me. I turn around, coming face to face with Emma who looks...

Un-fucking-believable.

Holy shit.

Her blonde hair is curled, falling below her shoulders in soft waves, pinned off to the side and away from her face. She's wearing a black cocktail dress cut low enough to display a tease of tasteful cleavage I've never seen from her before. The article of clothing hits above her knee, a small, tantalizing slit creeping up her thigh.

On her feet?

Blood-red stiletto heels that elongate her half-bared legs. She's sin incarnate, brought here to utterly wreck me. I welcome her with open arms, a willing servant at her mercy.

She's a sight for sore eyes.

A vision I want to tattoo on my eyelids so I'll never forget it.

No one else will ever look as beautiful as she does at this moment.

I remember my senior year of high school I was in the outfield during a baseball game. A teammate and I ran toward a pop fly at the same time from opposite directions, colliding into each other and landing on the ground. The wind got knocked out of me and I was unable to breathe, fearful I was going to die.

This...

This feels eerily reminiscent of that moment. I'm gasping for air. Suffocating. Drowning.

I don't stand a chance of survival with her around.

Holy fucking shit.

She's talking, but I can't hear her because I'm in a trance. Blinking twice, I level my gaze back to her face and away from the figure I didn't know she had. Soft curves. Inches of flawless skin. A glow radiating from her body.

Thank God she doesn't wear dresses like this at work; I'd never get anything done and I'd have to kill all the men who would leer at her like hungry dogs. I'd leave a trail of bloody tongues in my wake.

Mine.

"Well?" she asks softly.

She has a hint of makeup on. It's nothing dramatic or obvious, but enough to draw attention to her naturally striking features. Her lips have a touch of color—red, of course—and her cheeks look pinker. Fuller. The lining under her eyes makes the blue *pop*, practically twinkling, and I want to jump into the pools of azure beckoning me. Emma in day-to-day clothing is a sight to behold. Right now, she's a fucking goddess.

"What do you think?" she asks again, and I hear the nerves hedged in the question.

I suck in a breath, genuinely afraid to answer. My cock is already stirring, thanks in part to the way the material of her dress hugs her hips so perfectly. It's form-fitting, leaving little to the imagination. For half a second, I'm dreading the thought of anyone but *me* seeing her in it.

"Divine," I manage to get out. "Elegant. Hot. Seductive. Fuck, Emma, forgive me for the vulgarities, but you're fucking unbelievable."

"Are you reciting all the adjectives in your repertoire?" she jokes, tossing her hair behind her shoulder and giving me an excellent view of her neck and the column of her throat. Her neck I want to kiss and suck and lick, my teeth running down her skin, leaving red hickeys behind, claiming her as *mine* and *mine alone*.

And then I'd proudly show her off to the world.

I am so unbelievably fucked.

"I'm struggling to find words adequate enough to convey how wonderful you look. I knew you were stunning that night in the office, when I helped zip up your dress. Trust me, I've been thinking about it ever since. And I know you're stunning every day of the week, even with muffin crumbs on your face. Knowing you're here with me tonight, wearing this, and I can stare at you all evening by my side, makes you even sexier."

She beams and spins slowly, letting me see the whole ensemble. When my eyes land on her ass, I suppress the groan building in my throat. So round. I want to run my hands under the material and grasp her cheeks, my fingers digging into her skin while I fuck her from behind, watching her bounce on my dick.

"Thank you." At the completion of her turn, she walks toward me, hips swaying threateningly. She's an assassin coming for her prey. She could behead me for all I care, and I'd thank her for it. Anything for one more second to appreciate her beauty. "You look very handsome," she remarks, stopping in front of me and looking me up and down, repeating the assessment I gave her.

"Shucks. This old thing?"

Emma lets out a chuckle, her hand resting on my tie and threading it through her fingers. The red nails from yesterday stand out, crimson against the black. A gentle tug has me leaning forward, closer to her. "I see you in suits all the time, but this looks different."

I cup her cheek with my palm, noticing how close her lips are. It takes restraint to not pounce and fuse our mouths together, mine over hers, relishing in the first taste of sweetness. "Are you ready for our big test?"

"Yeah. I think I am."

When we arrive at the door to the backyard, Emma peers through the window. "Wow," she breathes out. "This looks spectacular."

I'm not admiring the circular tables covering the massive lawn or the lantern lights dangling around the perimeter of the grass, illuminating the inky night sky. I'm not paying attention to the stage with instruments and the long buffet tables with metal containers of catered Italian food.

No. I couldn't care less.

A knot in my chest forms as I steal a glance at Emma's side profile. The pressure near my heart tightens, becoming almost painful. A million sights in the world, and all I can look at is her.

I wish I could immortalize this moment forever. Her hand in mine. The smoothness of her palm. The soft music filtering through the walls. A star-filled sky. The tip of her lips in a small smile tugging across her beautiful face. A calm, content joy slowly filling the surrounding space, reaching every nook and crevice. Waves of serenity and *finally* lapping at my ankles, beckoning me to tread deeper into the waters of complete bliss. Perfect doesn't do it justice. Perfect doesn't come close.

"Yeah," I agree. "Spectacular. Let's go make some memories together, Sunflower."

This woman continues to blow me away. Emma is truly phenomenal, saying hello to second uncles and divorced cousins like she's been to dozens of Dawson family events in the past. My hand rests on her lower back for the majority of the night while her side presses firmly into mine like we're stitched together. Two peas in a pod.

Occasionally, she threads her fingers with mine, giving my hand eight squeezes. I picked up on the attempted Morse Code two days ago at dinner when I was embarrassed by my mom sharing deeply personal memories of the blonde woman beside me. Memories no one knows. Memories I might not ever share because I don't know how to describe them. Memories I've thought about for years, unsure of how to voice them.

Together.

Eight letters bringing me joy and peace.

"Doing okay, honey?" I whisper in her ear when we take our seats for dinner thirty minutes later. I'm about to press a kiss to her cheek when she lets out a soft hiss. Looking down, I see a drop of blood forming on her pointer finger, the red matching her nails.

"Shit," she whispers, looking around frantically.

"Hey. I got you," I say, reaching into my jacket pocket for a Band-Aid. I peel back the paper and unwrap the bandage.

"What are you doing?" she asks.

I hum, carefully holding out her palm and covering the small wound. "Stopping the bleeding. There. Good as new."

"You have Band-Aids in your pocket?"

"I do."

"W-why?" Her voice trembles with the question.

"Because I noticed what you do when you're nervous years ago and I always carry one in my pocket, just in case. I knew there wouldn't be any disposable napkins tonight, only expensive cloth ones, and I didn't want you to feel like you couldn't clean up a mess if it happened." She opens her mouth to speak, but I continue before she can interrupt. "No, it's not obvious to anyone else, sweetheart. It's not a big deal. I promise. You talk all the time about how I don't see you. That's so far from the truth. I can't fucking look away, Emma. I see you. All of you. And I'm not afraid. If you think a nervous habit is going to deter me, think again. If you think having depressive thoughts is going to make me want to pack my bags, you're wrong. If you think I expect you to be smiley all the time, nice try. You can try and push me away. Tell me how different we are. Say there's no chemistry or heat between us. We both know that's a lie, don't we? You felt it upstairs in the bedroom. I feel it right now, staring at you, marveling at how fucking wonderful you are. I want you, and I think you want me, too. I'm not going anywhere, Sunflower. I want all your dreams, and all your nightmares, as well. I'm here for the long haul, and that includes accepting every single part of you, no matter how small. I'm in no rush."

She blinks rapidly, and suddenly her eyes are wet with tears. *Shit.* That wasn't the intended reaction I hoped to get. "I-I don't know what to say."

"You don't have to say anything."

"How can I not? You thought about me in advance. You carry bandages around with you, on the off chance you're nearby when I go too far. Henry..." she trails off, resting her cheek on my shoulder. "Thank you. You... You're so wonderful."

"Anything for you, princess."

Giving her knee a gentle squeeze, I turn my attention back to my parents, knowing Emma most likely doesn't want to linger on what just occurred. I don't either. I hope I didn't go too far or say something that might push her away with that spontaneous admission. Once I started talking, I couldn't stop.

The chaotic conversation around us allows me to try and forget my stupidity. Laughter and chatter fill the yard as everyone shares their favorite memories of my parents. We hear about their young love. The time my father messed up and tried to win my mother back after standing her up on a date. The trip they took to Europe, backpacking through the mountains for their honeymoon. The food is delicious, the wine is crisp, and I feel so completely *happy* and enamored sitting around the people I care about. And that includes Emma.

After dinner, champagne gets passed around in anticipation of the toast my parents are going to give. They walk onto the stage as the band ceases playing. A hush goes over the crowd.

"We appreciate all of you being here with us tonight. It's been an incredible 40 years." My mother beams at my father as he speaks. "To my wife, Anne. Not a day goes by where I'm not thankful that I get to do life by your side. We've dealt with challenges and hardships like every other couple, and we've persisted. I cannot thank you enough for staying by my side all these years. Not only were you a wife, but also a mother, a representative, a revolutionary, and an all-around incredible woman. I am so lucky to be loved by you."

Emma sniffs, and I wrap my arm around her shoulder. Guess she's a declarations kind of gal.

Noted.

"George," my mother starts. "You make life fun. You also make it annoying as hell sometimes, but every night I go to sleep thankful to have you by my side. I loved you then, I love you now, I love you always." The crowd around us breaks into applause as my parents share a brief kiss. "Thank you for taking the time out of your busy schedules to be here and celebrate with us. We'd like to invite all the couples, no matter how long you've been dating or married, to seal your relationship with a kiss!"

My hand nearly drops the glass I'm holding.

"Henry? Lizzie? Drew? Can you all join us up here with your partners please?"

"I-I didn't know this was happening," I whisper. "I swear. We do not need to go up there."

"It's one kiss, Henry," Emma says, standing from her chair. I follow her lead, rising to my feet. "It'll be fine. I trust you," she adds, walking toward the stage.

I chug the rest of my drink, bubbles popping on my tongue. I need more than liquid luck right now to calm me the hell down.

Emma stops at the bottom of the stairs and I hurry around her, offering my hand. I know she's not used to being in the spotlight; she loathes it. And I'm thrusting her to center stage, all for my own personal gain and glory. I'm a horrible human.

"I'm sure everyone knows our three wonderful children," my mom says, followed by another round of applause. Emma and I stand off to the side and I'm fully prepared to make a quick escape and tug her with me if needed. "For the first time ever, they're all in a happy and healthy relationship. I've been envisioning this picture for months and think it would be perfect in the house. The photographer is going to count down from three and then snap the photo, so get ready to kiss your other half!"

A murmur goes through the crowd as people stand. "Are you sure you're okay with this?" I ask quietly and she nods, pulling her shawl tightly over her exposed shoulders. I take off my jacket and drape it around her. "Give me the honest answer, honey. Not the one you think I want to hear."

"Yes, Henry. I'm okay with this."

"Places, everyone! 3!" The photographer calls out.

I bend down, pulling her close, my hand splaying wide on her waist. I angle my head and she stands on her tiptoes, our lips inches apart and nearly meeting.

"2!"

"Last chance to bail, baby."

My other hand rests on the nape of her neck, moving the rogue hairs away as my thumb presses into her skin. A sound escapes her and she puts her palm on my chest, fisting the fabric tightly. Our eyes meet. Gone is the timid unsureness. Now there's heat. Fire. Ardor and a fervor *need*.

"Kiss me, Henry. Like you mean it. Fuck the rules."

"1!"

My mouth touches hers, barely a graze, before I dive deeper, ready to drown.

THIRTY

HENRY

THE SECOND OUR LIPS MEET, it's fireworks instantly. An explosion of bright colors. A vehemence of passion. An axe of desire. A lifetime of waiting.

She tastes sweet like champagne and dangerous like the best kind of trouble.

Emma's mouth parts, opening wider, inviting me in—begging me in—as her arms fall around my neck. Needing more, the distance too much, I bring her flush against my body with a single tug. My tongue runs across the crease of her lips, learning. Exploring every inch of her mouth. She lets out a small, breathy moan. It's a seductive noise, my ears ringing long after I swallow it down, the aftermath ricocheting down to my dick.

I want to discover what other sounds I can get her to make. How loud can she be? How much can she let go? What does it take to get her there? Does she like dirty talk and praise, or would my touch be enough to let her finish?

I've never had such an immediate reaction to kissing someone before. My hands itch to touch her everywhere, caravanning across the swell of her ass, perky and firm. The golden ringlets of hair, silky and smooth. Her waist, trim and small.

Every. Goddamn. Inch. Of. Her.

This feels... right.

This feels like destiny.

It feels like the stars are aligning.

The heavens are opening.

A choir is singing.

It's intense. Passionate. Sweet. Hesitant. Lazy. Every emotion I've had bottled up for weeks releases with every second that ticks by.

Right now, there's no one else around. There's no crowd. No stage. No audience. It's just the two of us, she and I, alone in an open meadow. She's all I can see. All I can hear. All I can process.

My Sunflower.

All of my attention is on her and the minor details I've never noticed before. How our height difference doesn't feel so substantial as I angle my neck to capture her mouth further. Deeper. The press of her chest into mine, nipples hard and pointed through the thin material of her dress. The way she's holding onto me for dear life, both frightened and invigorated, the nails of her fingers digging into my shoulders for support, afraid of what might happen if she lets go.

I won't let you fall, honey.

Hold on tight.

I always thought a moment like this was an unobtainable phenomenon. Kissing is the precursor to sex; a part of foreplay I indulge in but never get a lot of satisfaction from. It's always fine. Okay. Decent enough to pass the time until clothes are shed.

It's never been like this before; mind-altering and world-bending. A fuse short-circuiting and electrifying all my nerves. Heightening my senses. Making me content to just do *this* for the rest of my life.

When Jack told us he saw stars when he kissed Jo for the first time, I thought he was a liar. The clichés surrounding those beginning moments are laughable and superficial.

Turns out, the bastard is right.

This is an unearthly experience I never want to come down

from. This is what the movies and books talk about; a moment so powerful, so life changing, you're rendered speechless. Unable to compute anything except the 5'5", independent, determined, beautiful, ass-kicking, powerhouse blonde angel before you.

Far, far too soon, Emma pulls away, disentangling our limbs as her mouth withdraws away from mine and breaks our connection. My eyes flutter open, reluctant to return to reality. I study her face for regret or disappointment. My search reveals no sign of contrition, only the faint etchings of terror and surprise.

I'm scared shitless, too.

Fingers shaking, she touches her swollen lips, tracing the path my tongue traversed moments ago. Her skin flushes, color splotching her chest and neck. "Wow," she whispers. "Um." A shiver racks her body, and I step toward her, pulling my jacket tighter around her.

"Should we..." I trail off, clearing my throat. "Uh. Do you want some dessert?" I spit out the most neutral, placid topic to bring us down from the uncertainty of our kiss.

"Yeah. Okay."

Tentatively, I slide my hand against hers, helping her down the stairs off the stage. We step to the side, in a darkened corner out of the spotlight, and Emma lets go of my grasp.

"I'm sorry," I say. The apology hangs in the air, weighing heavily.

Her eyes dart to mine, surprise morphing to confusion. "For what?"

"I... I feel like I did something wrong. I don't want you to think I purposely manipulated you."

Looking away, she tucks a piece of hair behind her ear. "I'm not mad. You don't need to apologize. I'm just..." She sighs, and I can hear the battle happening in her head through the exhale. "It's stupid."

"I promise you it's not. Tell me what's on your mind, Emma. I don't know if I should laugh because that was the best kiss I've ever had, hate myself for upsetting you, or roar into the wind because I waited too damn long to do it in the first place."

"I want to do that again, Henry. Badly."

My name is pure magic coming from her mouth, the two syllables a symphonic melody I don't think I'll ever tire of hearing.

And she wants to kiss me again.

Making a hasty decision, I throw her a half smile. "Do you trust me?"

"Of course," she answers automatically, and my chest bubbles with pride.

"Come on. I want to show you something."

I lead her away from the party. The sound of music subsides as we walk down a small path and into a thicket of trees. The grass gives way to dirt and mulch. Emma struggles for a minute with her heels on the rockier terrain before I kneel, offering her a piggyback ride. She jumps on my back, calves looping around my stomach. I run my palm up her bare shin, thumb swiping over the top of her knee.

We walk in silence for a few minutes until we enter a clearing. The moon is bright tonight, light filtering through the branches enough for us to see our surroundings. A bench and old wooden swing sit up ahead and nostalgia hits me as I slow my pace. It's been years since I've spent much time out here, besides a quick walk through the grounds, but it looks exactly how I left it.

"What is this place?" she asks curiously. Sliding off my back, she takes a seat on the bench and peers up at me, waiting for me to share.

"It's my spot," I begin, leaning against a nearby tree. "It's a little dilapidated and has definitely seen better days. When I was younger, I would come out here all the time and do my homework. Sometimes I would sit and stare at the sky wistfully, daydreaming about what the future might hold. Other days I would toss my calculus homework on the ground because it didn't make any sense, and I knew you were probably understanding it better than me. This was the only place in the world besides the library that felt like it was mine. I came out here when I was tired. Sad. Stressed out and confused. It became the place I ventured to when I needed a moment to breathe. I thought you might need that, too, with everything that went down back there. I didn't bring you here with any ulterior motives in mind. A few minutes of quiet sounded nice, and I'm happy to step away if you want some solitude."

Emma smiles at me, moonbeams bathing her face in a bright, perfect splendor. "Thank you for showing me. It's so beautiful." Her head swivels, surveying the surrounding land. A cricket chips in the distance, and leaves rustle overhead. "I don't want you to leave. Please stay."

"Okay," I agree, knowing I'd do anything she asked. "I'll stay."

Forever, if you'll let me.

"Henry, can we talk about earlier?"

"What happened earlier?"

"When we were in bed this morning. About what I said and how you left."

My spine stiffens. I suspected this conversation was coming. "I'm dejected you keep reminding me this isn't real. I'm confused. Everything is blurring together. You say we're doing a great job of pretending and then... Then we kiss like *that* and I can't believe any of this is fake. Not anymore. Not on my end."

"Ah. I thought that might be the case." Patting the empty space of wood beside her, I sit on the bench and turn to face her. "This morning was so perfect. I've thought about it all day and I can't get you out of my head. This," she gestures between us, "means something to me, and I'm sorry if what I said comes across as otherwise. I-I thought not real was what you wanted."

"I thought it was, too. Guess not."

Her head drops to my shoulder, hair tickling my neck. "Guess not," she repeats.

"When I visited my parents' house a month ago, you and I were already talking. I had this vision of kissing the woman on the other side of the phone. I had this grand plan if I ever had the chance to bring you here. I pictured sneaking you away, using a terrible line that had you laughing hysterically, pitying me and my pathetic jokes, and kissing you because I *wanted* to, not because we were *forced* to. Even after I found out it was you, I still had that thought."

"Really?"

"Really, Emma."

She stares at me for a moment. Neither one of us blinks, holding steady, deliberate eye contact. There's a heat building. A current. My blood runs hot through my veins. The air around us thickens, tension and lust stifling us in their grips. Something sparks at the base of my spine, almost catching fire.

My mouth hovers a hair's breadth above hers. "Tell me you want it," I say lowly, voice taking on the authoritative tone I save for courtrooms and client meetings. It's not nice. It's not pleasant. It's demanding. Coaxing. "Tell me you've thought about it, Emma. What it would be like, the two of us. No audience. Nothing pretend or fake. You told me to fuck the rules. Did you mean it?"

She inhales, and it's sharp enough to cut glass. I also see the moment she gives in. "Y-yes. Yes, I meant fuck the rules. Yes, I've thought about it. Kiss me again, Henry. I need it. Please."

The *please* is my undoing, annihilating the last remaining shred of my self-control. I want to attack. I want to bombard her. I want her so fucking bad.

This time when I kiss her, it's not cute. It's not flirty. It's more intimate. Sensual. My tongue swipes across her lips and they part, granting me access to her mouth. Her hand falls to my thigh, palm running up and down my slacks. I shudder, muscles flexing at the touch and the proximity of her hand moving further and further up my leg.

I bite her bottom lip, reveling in the startled gasp I receive. Taking the sound as acceptance, I pull her into my lap. Her legs fall to either side of my hips, and I groan at the feel of her nearly seated on my cock.

My hand threads through her hair and I tug it back, exposing her neck. My teeth drag up the length of her windpipe, and I press a soft kiss right below her ear. "I'm not going to touch you. Not yet."

"Why not?" Emma whines. She shifts in my lap, and the change presses her against the head of my dick. Scraps of material separate us, and it would be so easy to pull her underwear to the side and bury myself inside her.

But not yet.

"The first time my fingers are inside you, I want to be sure you're thinking clearly. Because once I touch you, Emma, I'm not going to fucking stop."

"I'm thinking clearly," she pants, grinding against me. Her hips are rolling. Her head is tilted back, offering the sky a prayer. Her nipples are hard and peaked through the thin fabric riding up her body. The dress might be black, but I can practically see the rosy pink.

"You're a terrible liar," I murmur into her collarbone, kissing the top of her chest. "And you're making it very difficult to behave."

"You're scrambling my brain."

God, I want her. Really fucking bad. Right here, right now, under the stars. Fuck the consequences. But I'll be damned if the first time I taste her is on a wobbly bench that might collapse under our weight. I want to *enjoy* her, not worry about putting her in harm's way.

"Oh, Emma. I'm going to do much, much more than that."

"So do it."

I hear the desperation in her voice. She's close to begging; if she asked me to slip my finger inside her and make her come, I'd do it in a heartbeat.

It pains me to say the next words, but I get them out, knowing it's what I *have* to say, not what I *want* to say.

"I wish I could, but we should get back to the party."

It's obvious she wasn't expecting the dismissal, and I didn't intend for it to be so... direct. The high she's chasing crashes and burns as her attitude changes. She nods curtly while her mouth droops and her eyes dim. Frowning, she adjusts the straps of her dress that have slipped down her arms, dangerously close to falling off completely. My jacket is in a heap on the grass. "Okay. Yeah. We've been gone for a while."

Taking her chin in my hands, I bring her gaze to look at me. "Don't think for a damn second I'm rejecting you. I'm trying my best to not ruin anything. To not move too fast. To not tell you all the filthy things going through my mind right now. All the creative ways we could use this bench. If I do, we're never leaving. You'll have twigs in your hair and dirt on your knees when I'm finished with you. They'll have to send a search party after us, and even then I wouldn't give you up willingly."

"Maybe I want to hear those things," she challenges.

"Is that so?" Moving quickly, I spin her around so her back is flush against my chest. "I could share how I'd love to bend you over the arm of this bench and slide my fingers into your tight, sweet pussy. I'd go slow, baby, so you can savor every second." I lift her arm, bringing her hand to run over the wood, weathered from age, careful to avoid any spots that might give her a splinter. She begins to pant, squirming in my lap. "Stop moving," I warn her, and she complies, stilling. "Should I tell you how I'd love to kneel in the dirt before you, my fucking queen, and go down on you, tasting how delicious you are? Open your legs, Emma." Her thighs part automatically and I hum my approval. "That's my good girl. I could share about how I want to paint your pretty face with my come. Or do you want to hear how turned on I am, thinking about fucking you here? I would give a lot of things to have you spread open beneath me, naked and begging for more."

"Henry," she whimpers. Her legs are trembling, pressing into mine. "I-I—"

"You told me you wanted to know, so now you're going to

listen. I want to fill your mouth with my cock so you stop taunting me, thinking you're going to get what you want. Not yet. You need to be patient."

I kiss down her neck, letting my free hand skate up the inside of her thigh. My fingers brush along the seam of her underwear, right over her slit, and she moans. Dampness greets me, and I grin. "I'm a selfish man, Emma. Anyone could hear us out here. Anyone could see. The only person who gets to experience what you sound like when you come for the first time is *me*, which is why we're going to wait. This isn't about me not wanting you, sweetheart. You feel my cock, don't you? *You* did that. I want you so. Fucking. Bad."

I lift my hips as I punctate each word, and she lets out a cry.

"A-are you implying someone can listen the second time?"

My lips skate over her ear. "Would that interest you?"

"I-I think so."

"Mm. Noted. Let that imagination run wild. I'm going to learn every one of your fantasies. I'll finger you under the tablecloth surrounded by my entire family if it's what you want."

She gasps, legs snapping closed. She doesn't have to verbalize it, but I know I just hit one of her desires on the head. Regretfully, I lift her off my lap and set her back down on the ground. Gritting my teeth together and thinking of anything except touching Emma, I lead us back to the party.

No one noticed our suspicious absence, but there's no way we can sneak out early. We spend the next two hours conversing with my family members, sharing a couple of dances, and eating chocolate hazelnut cake. At the end of the night, after saying goodbye to my parents, we depart back to my side of the house, climbing the stairs silently.

"Hey," I say softly when we enter my bedroom. "Are you okay? I can sleep in another room tonight. You don't owe me anything just because we kissed two times."

"It's not that," Emma says, closing the door behind us. "I'm... This is embarrassing. I'm nervous, I guess."

"Nervous how?" I ask. My thumb strokes her cheek, ready to help find a solution to all her problems.

"This is a whole new territory for us."

"It is. We can stop whenever we want, you know. It's not a nonstop flight. We can get off the plane and enjoy a layover."

"That's the thing. I don't want to stop. I want to keep going. I want *you* to keep going."

"You sure?" I sweep my eyes over her face.

"Positive."

"In that case..." I pick her up, gathering her in my arms. Walking four steps, I push her against the wall without using too much force. Emma lets out a squeak, legs instinctively wrapping around my waist. I stare at her for three never-ending seconds, letting her decide if she wants to run and hide or stay and play. She stares back, unflinching, and when she tilts her head to the side, a tempting smirk sitting on her face, I kiss her.

Game fucking on.

This time, the kiss is hungrier. Greedier. Sloppy and messy. Now that I've gotten to enjoy the tiniest fraction of her, I'm a starved man wanting to have the whole damn meal, gluttonously needing to taste every square inch of her. A moan falls from her mouth and my hand threads into her hair, tilting her neck backwards.

Fuck. I love seeing the blonde strands wrapped between my fingers like fine silk. My teeth travel over her pale skin, and she moans, louder than before.

I'm just getting started, Emma.

Her heels press into the small of my back, egging me on, driving us closer together. My dick is achingly hard again and pressing into her stomach, close to where I want to take her once and for all.

God, the first time is going to feel too fucking good.

She withdraws from my attack, blinking at me with stars in her eyes. She looks a little dizzy. A little disheveled. Very turned on. "I never knew kissing someone could feel so damn good."

"Me neither. I guess we've been kissing the wrong people."

I nip at her neck and down to her shoulder, lightly biting her skin. It's not enough to leave a mark, but it's on the list. The male satisfaction I would feel seeing her with *my* hickeys on her neck in the office, no one knowing where they came from, is indisputable.

She trembles in my arms as her thighs quake and I grin victoriously, already learning what drives her crazy. "I like how responsive you are."

"Are we going to have sex?"

The blunt question surprises me, and I can't help but burst out laughing. She frowns, folding her arms across her chest, trying to find the humor.

"Is that funny to you?" she presses.

"If it's not obvious enough already, I would absolutely *love* to fuck you right now."

I roll my hips forward so she can feel exactly *how badly* I want to sink into her. *How funny* it is we only have a layer of clothes keeping me from sinking deep into her heat. *How good* it would be to have her clench around me as I pound into her, again and again, finding the perfect angle and tempo. Holding her up under her thighs, the tips of my fingers grip the swell of her ass. Hard.

"I've been imagining at least seven different spots just in this room."

"Seven?" she sputters, eyes bouncing from the bed to the floor.

"Mhm. Believe it or not, I want to take this slow. I don't want to rush anything. The physical part will be a great reward, yeah, and I'm looking forward to it. I also just like being with you. You... You make me happy, simply by existing."

I'd be out of my mind if I didn't want to study and learn her body lazily, leisurely, working at an unhurried pace until I have every part of her committed to memory. More importantly, I want to lie on the mattress with her, listening to her talk until the early hours of the morning. I want to count the freckles on her arms. To hear her steady breathing while she sleeps soundly, knowing I'm the one keeping her safe and protected through the night.

I want so much more than a few minutes inside her, no matter how spectacular they might be.

Her legs loosen, dropping from my body, and I set her down, tucking a lock of hair behind her ear. I can't go a second without touching her, it seems. She stares back at me with understanding eyes, nodding, the weight of my admission heavy in the small sliver of space between us.

"I like just being with you, too. They've been some of my favorite moments the last few weeks, and I want more of them. I can take things slow."

"Why don't we take separate showers, get out of these outfits and into something more comfortable, then meet back here in thirty minutes?"

"I agree. Only if you bring me a Zebra Cake," she teases, and I press a kiss to her cheek.

"Check the bedside table, Sunflower. There's already one waiting for you."

THIRTY-ONE

HENRY

I DID nothing profound in our time apart.

I didn't find the solution to eradicate world hunger, and I certainly didn't win a Nobel Peace Prize. I didn't write the next great American novel. Even remembering my name is a hazy, distant memory.

I spent the majority of the agonizingly long minutes under an ice-cold shower, freezing water dripping down my shoulders and stomach as I aggressively gripped the temperature knobs to keep from fisting my dick and going to town.

Images of Emma's legs around my waist danced in my vision, and the sound of her sweet, breathy moans echoed in my ears. I vigorously washed the arousal away with a restrained grunt, doing my best to not think about her.

It was an impossible task.

Slow, Dawson.

You goddamn moron, with your goddamn big mouth.

After thirty minutes away, I'm curious what I'm going to find when I return to my room. Dozens of scenarios play out in my brain. I consider Emma might have turned the light off, feigning sleep so we didn't continue the building momentum from a short while ago. She might be lounging on the comforter in a sexy pose, arms draped seductively above her head while wearing a sultry expression.

Opening the door, neither of the ideas turn out to be accurate.

She's on the bed, yeah, but she's holding a book in her right hand and a Zebra Cake in her left. Every few seconds, she pauses, taking a bite of the sweet treat before resuming her reading.

The scene is so flawlessly *her*.

My heart skips a beat at the intimate moment. Fucking like animals is one thing, but allowing another person to share a bed with you when you're the most vulnerable and raw, half-asleep in the early morning hours? It's a big fucking step. It's promising. Bordering on the edge of forever.

It's why I've never had a sleepover before. No woman has infiltrated my space long enough to get comfortable in my sheets, making herself at home while we slumber peacefully, limbs intertwined and breathing in unison.

Until her.

Emma's upended everything I thought I knew about relationships and being with someone. These past few mornings I've woken up peacefully and in no rush to roll out of bed and disappear. It's almost like there's an invisible string tethering us together, linking us, preventing me from wanting to shove her away. Every moment with her I reel it in, inch by inch, wondering how close I can get, and what will happen when I do.

Closing the bedroom door behind me, I prop my elbow on the dresser and look at her. Because I'm finally *allowed* to look at her.

God, she's so effortlessly gorgeous.

Don't get me wrong, she was radiant tonight—waltzing around in a fancy dress and a pretty updo, menacing heels on her feet and lipstick painted on her lips. Here, in the dim lighting of my childhood bedroom, wearing her massive sleep shirt and pajama shorts, a dollop of frosting sitting on the corner of her mouth and crumbs on her fingers, she's never looked more beautiful.

Exquisite.

Perfect.

Mine.

Her hair is in a messy bun, the curls from earlier breaking apart and framing the soft features of her face. She's leaning back against the pillows, posture relaxed, feet tucked under her, and a small throw blanket covering her calves.

"Are you planning on standing there all night? You could try taking a photo. It would last longer." Her voice pulls me out of my stupor of admiration and I shake my head, clearing my thoughts.

"I'm just enjoying the view," I reply, walking to the bed and sitting on the edge of the mattress. "What're you reading? Doesn't look like work stuff."

"Definitely not career-oriented. It's a fantasy story about fairies. I'll spare you the details, but imagine wars, crowns, cauldrons. The usual."

"Fairies? Like Tinker Bell?"

"Try men who are taller than you and can fly."

"Ouch. You're making me jealous, Burnsie."

Instead of answering, she smiles a soft, shy smile that makes my heart beat faster. We're left with an easy quiet and I appreciate the stillness. The heater clicks on, a quiet hum filling the room, and her eyes drag ploddingly to meet mine.

They're wide, full of an aching need. Beneath those desires, though, hidden beyond the wants of physical affection, there's a timid vulnerability. An edginess, as if she's afraid I'm going to walk out of the room at any second, leaving her behind.

I'm not going any-goddamn-where.

She's giving me air and life, and if I go… I think I might die.

"What are you thinking about?" I finally ask, breaking the silence.

"It's warm in here. You look absurdly attractive without a shirt on. I think I have frosting in my hair. I'm still nervous. So, so nervous."

Her honest admission makes me smile. One of my favorite

things about Emma is her ability to speak her mind freely and unabashedly. She's quiet, sure, but also never holds back. If you ask her opinion on something, she's always going to tell you the truth.

I adjust my position on the bed, wanting to give her ample space. "Permission to speak openly?"

She nods auspiciously, encouraging me along.

"Emma," I start. "When we first started talking, I wasn't interested in pointless conversation with someone I didn't know. I figured we'd hash out the details of the event, go along our merry way, and call it a day. My plan didn't work. I checked my phone constantly, becoming distracted at work. I hoped I would hear from you, smiling like a fucking tool bag every time you answered. Each morning I woke up excited to talk to you, and every night I was sad when we said goodbye, trying to find ways to prolong our conversation so I could squeeze out more time with you.

"Then I'd see you in person, unknowingly drawn to you as Emma, too. Every time I walk into work, a magnetic force draws me by your office. I never stop in, not wanting to interrupt you, but I always pass by, wondering what you're doing on the opposite side of the wall. I kind of like that we built the foundation of our arrangement on anonymity. We have this... this structure of trust, happiness, humor, and attraction. Little pieces have grown into something sturdy. Something strong. Something worth working on."

"So where do we go from here?" Emma asks.

That's the million-dollar question.

I don't have a fucking clue.

Does this mean we're officially dating? Embarking on a non-exclusive friends-with-benefits track with no strings attached?

My stomach churns in disgust and my blood curdles at the thought of her spending time with another man. Bile rises in my throat as I picture myself with another woman, ignoring Emma's texts while I get someone else off.

Nope.

Not interested in non-exclusive.

Leveling a breath and gathering whatever strands of courage I can find, I speak. "I like watching you eat an entire basket of chips and queso, then wash it down with six tacos and ask about dessert. I like making cookies with you and how you squeal when I throw chocolate chips at your face. I like falling asleep beside you, and I like it even more when I wake up with you nestled in my arms."

Emma listens with a razor-sharp attentiveness. She's a logical, pragmatic woman, and I know she's assessing me for any fallacies I might be trying to spew. I have her undivided attention, and knowing she's not laughing in my face spurs me on, eager to share more.

"I'm attracted to you, both physically and emotionally, which sounds fucking stupid when I say it out loud, but it's the truth. I'm not going to pretend to know how to be in a relationship, and I'm fairly certain I'm going to be terrible at it, but I want to try to learn along the way with you, honey, because I like you a whole fucking lot. More than I've ever liked anyone else. I have no clue what that means or how to define this. Being a boyfriend or a partner or a significant other is a concept I'm wildly unfamiliar with. All I know is I can't get you out of my fucking head, Emma. And I don't want to."

I run my hand through my hair, averting my eyes from her scrutinizing gaze. I feel her studying my face, considering every word. Every syllable. I'm not sure what she's looking for, but I hope she finds it.

The silence is back, an ominous shadow lurking in the night. Holding my breath, I wait, content to give her as long as she needs.

"I like you too, Henry," she says. My head jerks up at the statement, the words of affirmation firing straight through my skin, new fireworks erupting behind my ribs. Behind my lungs. Behind my goddamn heart. "Let's do it."

"You're going to have to be very specific about what 'it' is, Emma, because I have a million and one ideas in my head, baby girl, and I'm not sure which one you're referring to."

Baby girl.

The endearment slips out far too easily, taking up residence on my new vocabulary list of Sweet Names I Want to Call Her. It's wedged between *honey* and *sweetheart*, a sandwich of affection and fondness I've never expressed before. I like how it sounds rolling off my tongue and the blush it elicits from the beautiful blonde across the bed from me.

"I-I want to try with you, too. It's been a long time since I've been in a relationship, so I'm going to be rusty. But I want to do this with you. Together."

Her hand reaches out, shaking as she grasps my arm and runs her thumb up my skin. It's a direct path from my fingertips to my shoulder, close to my heart. I thread her hand in mine, cradling her palm against my bare chest. The Band-Aid from earlier is wrapped securely around her finger, and I make a promise to myself here on the duvet cover from 2006 that I'll carry one in my pocket until the day I die.

Touching her in the privacy of my room, alone, because we *want* to, not because it's for show, is an overwhelming recognition.

A lump forms in my throat, a steel block making it difficult to breathe, as flashbacks of my life pop up like Polaroids.

How many women have I kissed in the past? Several.

How many hands have I held as I pinned them above a woman's head, mindlessly fucking them into oblivion? Dozens.

How many orgasms have I given and received? Hundreds.

Why is this proclamation, this intent to commit and this nonsexual contact shrouding me in anxiety, wanting to do every. Little. Thing. Right?

Because it's *her*.

I take notice of the four freckles spread out on the backside of her hand, aligned in an almost perfect geometrical square. I turn her hand over, relishing in the smoothness of her callous-free

289

palm. My fingers trace each lifeline, measuring their length and width. Details so minuscule and insignificant, I've never been bothered to look before. I'm usually too busy ripping clothes off to appreciate the small things, ready to bury my dick inside a woman instead of counting the breaths they take or the artwork of their beauty marks.

Now… Now I have to grip the mattress to steady myself. My hand tightens around hers, confirming she's here, in the flesh, beside me. I'm almost shaking proleptically, desperate to extend every second we have.

Jesus fuck. Who knew one person could have such control over me?

Plenty of women have tried to tame me. Plenty of women have argued they could make me happy. A parade of females have come and gone, insisting they *"aren't like the other girls"* and can be the one *"to change"* me.

It's ironic the person who never tried is the only one capable of those superpowers.

"You've been really surprising," Emma says. The lilt of her voice sounds reassured. Optimistic. A renewed faith in the man grasping her arm close to his body. "You're kind of wonderful. And I kind of hate myself for never realizing it before."

I snort, kissing her palm. "Believe me, Sunflower, I am far from wonderful. I have many, many flaws."

"So do I. You're wonderful to me, and I think in the grand scheme of life, that's the only thing that matters, right?"

Have I finally done the right thing? Gotten over my disdain and fear of commitment and monogamy? If this is what a relationship is like, why the hell have I been so unenthusiastic about having one?

We're trying.

Together.

And boy, that makes me giddy as fuck.

"Right," I agree, the tightness in my chest that's been persistently nagging me all evening reappearing. "I'm sorry I interrupted your book. I'm going to catch up on some emails before bed. Is that okay?"

"Of course." Giving my hand a parting squeeze, she severs our contact, reopening her reading material and curling back up against the pillows. I move to my side of the bed and pull out my phone, eyes nearly bugging out of my head when I see I have 247 unread texts in the group chat. I don't bother scrolling to the top, typing out a quick message to the guys.

HD: What's up?

NR: Well, well, well. Look who woke up from the dead.
PW: H! It's about time we heard from you.
JL: I swear to God if you don't have something interesting to tell us, I'm chucking my phone out of the window.

HD: Sorry, been distracted. Family stuff. Invasive questions.
Kissing Emma.

NR: ??!?!??!?!?!
JL: You can't say that then stop talking, you bastard.
NL: We need details!
PW: Who the fuck do you think you are slipping that in all casually?!
NR: Why? How long? Tongue? No tongue?
JL: Was it good?

HD: Nope.

PW: Yikes.

HD: Better.

NR: My man!

HD: I'll share more soon, but we had a talk. And I'm going to give this relationship thing a try.

NR: Thank fuck. Only took you, what, 15 years?
PW: Try 17, Noah. It's about time.
JL: Anyone else want to cry? My eyes are watering.
PW: Look at our boy. All grown up.
NL: It's not bad, H. Assume she's always right and you'll be fine.

HD: Thanks for the advice. Gotta go. Text soon.

Five more messages roll in, but I ignore them, chuckling as I put my phone on Do Not Disturb and click it off. Out of the corner of my eye, I catch Emma fidgeting. Her legs shift under the covers, brushing against mine. She lets out a soft *"oh."* Intrigued, I turn on my side, watching her read.

Finding nothing amiss, I frown, until—there. Her grip on the spine of the book tightens fractionally. It's such an infinitesimal movement, if I had blinked, I would've missed it.

But I didn't. And now I'm curious.

"You're restless," I say, understanding her body language.

Emma doesn't acknowledge me, but the blush staining her cheeks validates my observation. I allow myself precisely one second to wonder if the rest of her body matches her neck—what would her ass look like when it turned the same shade, an outline of my palm stark against the cherry hue?

Biting the inside of my cheek hard enough to draw blood, I stomp down on the thought, shoving it aside and ignoring the twitch of my dick at the image of her on all fours, bared to me, cheeks in the air and a sob tearing through her throat.

"I'm fine," she answers. The pitch is higher than her usual tone.

Fine, my ass.

My height grants me the perfect vantage point of her book,

and I scoot closer, following along with her finger as she devours the page she's reading.

His fingers threaded through her silky hair, giving a sharp and forceful tug. A cry escaped from her hungry, ravished mouth. It wasn't enough. She was so desperate. So ready. So eager to submit to him. She wanted him in more ways than she ever thought imaginable. There's nothing he could ask her that she wouldn't do. His wings spread out beneath her, coaxing her on her way to the first of many org—

"Fuck," I whisper, mouth hovering above her ear. She jumps, turning to look up at me. "You're not restless at all, are you? Tell me, Emma, what's going through your mind."

"The book is turning me on."

I let out a breath.

Hot.

So hot.

So sinfully hot she's reading filthy things next to me. I reach out and cup her face, thumb rubbing over her high cheekbones as I caress her flawless skin. "Look at how you're reacting just from reading. What would you be like if I were the one whispering in your ear? The one showing you what I want to do with you?"

She slams the book closed, shoving it away. It topples off the bed, landing on the floor with a pronounced *thunk*.

"Show me."

I hum, dragging my thumb from her cheek to her lips, grazing over the mouth I want to kiss. The mouth I want to fuck. The mouth I want to cherish. My eyes roam freely down her face, landing on her chest. She might be wearing a shirt, but her nipples are hard and pointed, peaked and outlined through the thin cotton. Her breathing is turning more and more ragged, rapidly increasing as it becomes shallower with every inhale.

"Are you wet, Emma?"

It's a simple question, one I already know the answer to, but I want to hear it from her. She's going to be the one to dictate our next steps.

Does she want to tell me?

Will she tell me?

How far does she want this to go tonight?

I've never been so anxious to hear someone speak.

Shifting on the sheets, she opens her mouth, and with one word, she nearly explodes my brain. "Yes," she rasps. The covers slip from her waist, down her thighs, milky white skin displaying itself to me. "What are you going to do about it?"

Slowly, I grin.

It's not a friendly, fun grin. It's not lighthearted or nurturing.

No.

It's a grin that promises wreckage. A grin that promises to expound on her desires. A grin that promises to obliterate her prior beliefs and experiences, setting a new standard. One that will be hard to beat.

"Do you want me to do something about it?"

Another reckless nod from Emma pushes me closer and closer to trouble.

It'll be worth the consequences.

"Please," she whispers breathlessly.

There's that goddamn word again, unhinging me and roaring in my ears. The plea makes me want to learn every fucking thing she likes and give it back to her tenfold.

So. That's what I'm going to do.

I bring my lips down, millimeters away from hers, ready to engage in a full-on war.

"As much as I love to hear you beg, you're going to have to tell me exactly what you want. I'm not touching you until you explicitly say it's okay, because the second I rip off your shorts and finally taste your sweet, delicious pussy, I'm never coming up for air, Sunflower. Even if it kills me."

She moans, and triumph and pride beat in my chest, a possessive kick to my libido. It's enough conveyance for me, and I kiss her—hard—delighting in the way she pulls me in. The way her hands scramble around my neck. Her mouth gluing itself to mine, afraid of letting me move too far away.

Honey, I'm here for good.

The noises she's making could destroy nations. Start battles. Little breaths and pants sneak out, and I swallow each one down greedily, a lead bullet to my heart.

"Henry," she gasps.

"What do you want?" I ask, resting my forehead against hers while my fingers trace the hem of her shirt, skimming across her stomach.

"You. I-I need you… I need you to touch me."

You.

Need. Need. Need.

I need you.

Funny. I'm beginning to feel the same way about her.

With permission, I tear the shirt from her body, heroically not ripping it to pieces. She moves backwards on the bed and tilts her hips up. Far too late, I realize she's taking off her shorts, and I snap my wandering eyes away from the disappearing shield protecting me from seeing all her glory.

Safe. It's safe up here.

Up here, I can't lose control.

Up here, I can't mess up.

Up here, I can prevent myself from driving into her straight away, feeling her wet heat around my throbbing dick.

My heart is thumping way too erratically, nervous as fuck wanting to get this right.

I *need* to get this right.

Need. Need. Need.

"You're shaking."

"I'm sorry." She takes a deep, steadying breath, and I frown.

"Why in the world are you apologizing?" I ask, tucking a tendril of hair behind her ear.

"I don't know. I don't want to disappoint you or anything."

"Disappoint me? Nothing you could disappoint— Emma." Understanding dawns on me. "You've had sex, right?" I ask it carefully, not wanting to offend or assume.

The answer is going to significantly impact what happens next.

"Of course I have," she scoffs, eyes snapping to mine. "It's just been awhile."

"Define awhile." I drop my hand to her hip, fingers dancing over the bare skin. The silence and tension in the room has grown thick and palpable. I wait patiently, not hurrying her along.

"Six years," she admits, and my brain almost implodes. "You know how much I work. I… I haven't had time for anyone."

"Fuck," I groan, grabbing her neck and bringing her mouth to mine, lips crashing together in a frenzied affection.

She's gone six long years without being appreciated. No one has tasted her. Touched her. Brought her over the edge repeatedly, body withering as orgasm after orgasm consumed her.

Good.

Now she's mine to worship and adore. To torment and ravish. To kiss and cuddle. To give the whole fucking world.

Mine.

"I still know what I want. I want you, Henry. I want you to fuck me." She arches her back, chest pressing into mine. Her hard nipples are like glass against my muscles and I almost spasm at the contact. "I might be a little difficult to work with, and I'm sorry in advance. I'm sure most of the girls you've been with have more… experience."

I cup her chin, tilting it up, bringing it to meet my gaze. "Hey. We're not going to do that."

"Do what?"

"Any sort of comparisons. I'm here with you. I want to be here with *you*, Emma. Only you. And you're goddamn perfect. You aren't going to be difficult. You aren't going to be a chore or too much work. You do not need to apologize. We're doing this together. Okay?"

She looks at me, her eyes warming and sparkling. "Okay," she agrees.

"Good girl. Now lie back, so I can make you come like you deserve."

Those luminescent blue orbs widen at my brazenness. After only two seconds, she nods, easing back on the pillows. Her blonde hair fans out above her head, reminiscent of an angel's halo, bright as day against the navy fabric. Once she gets comfortable, she drops her chin toward her chest—an approval—and I start my journey down her body.

One quick look at the wondrous sight under me, and I'm a weakened, ruined, wounded man.

Her tits are the perfect size, sitting evenly on her chest. The dusty pink nipples are pointed, aching to be pinched between my fingers. Continuing down, I notice the slight protrusion of her ribs, and a flat stomach. Fair skin leads to deceivingly voluptuous hips, the swell of her thighs begging me to sink my fingers into them. When my eyes reach her parted legs, I suck in a strangled breath.

A second bullet to my heart. And my dick.

"Emma," I croak, voice catching as I relax back onto my heels.

Her pussy is bare, not a strand of hair to be found. Moisture is staining her open thighs, glistening in the lamp-lit room. God fucking Almighty, she's practically leaking and I've barely touched her yet.

Whatever doubts I have sail out the window. She *wants* this, and she wants *me* to be the one to give it to her. I drop my head and close my eyes, praying to whatever deity is watching from above to please let me survive tonight.

I'm not sure I will.

"I need a minute."

"Did I do something wrong?" She sounds worried, fear and rejection evident in her timid tone.

Rage boils within me, a volcano on the verge of erupting. Did someone in her past accuse her of not being good enough? Make fun of her and say she was doing something incorrectly? Demand that she needs to be better?

Fuck every single asshole who's gotten to be with her before me. I hate them all.

"No, Emma, you didn't. I need a minute because you're going to annihilate me. I'm already destroyed, and I haven't even touched you yet. Haven't tasted you yet. You've gone years without being appreciated, honey, and we're going to remedy that immediately. And repeatedly. Until you're fucking sick of me."

"I don't think I could ever be sick of you."

The statement shouldn't make my chest tighten painfully again, but it does, a knife twisting into my skin. "I'm going to be the one to take care of you. Whatever you want, just ask, and I'll gladly give it to you."

"Whatever I want? I want you naked." Her face has changed from hesitant to hungry, and she licks her lips as her eyes wander down my bare chest. "This isn't fair."

"You're right," I agree, grabbing the waistband of my pajama bottoms and shucking them off. They get tossed into the abyss of the room, the fucks I give about anything except *her* flying away with the plaid cotton. "How's that?"

THIRTY-TWO

EMMA

THE SIGHT OF HENRY DAWSON—A man attractive enough to rival a Greek god—naked in front of me is really absurd.

Once he ditches the one article of clothing covering his body, I'm greeted with strong, defined muscles. His chest. His biceps. Sharp lines contouring the fine edges of his body, leaving no room for imagination. Abs traverse across his tan stomach into a perfectly chiseled V, a carving done out of marble by a Renaissance sculptor, mimicking an unworldly being. A small dusting of dark hair leads down the rest of his toned shape, an arrow to a cock that's incredibly hard, jutting to attention.

"Oh, good God," I mutter, burying my face in my hands like a blushing idiot.

"Something wrong?" The question is humorous, prodding me to share. The asshole knows he's a knockout and is trying to get me to admit it.

Fine. I will.

"No." Feeling brave enough to show my blazing cheeks again, I find Henry, assumed sex-god extraordinaire, grinning back at me. His sinfully dark eyes brim with lust and longing, a far cry from the family-friendly gaze he wore all night. "I've always begrudgingly thought you were hot."

"Don't make me twist your arm to admit it," he remarks, and I reach out to swat him. He catches my wrist, emitting a sultry laugh as he leans forward.

The laughter extinguishes when he catches my mouth in a kiss I return emphatically, pouring every ounce of my being into the display of affection. My arms climb up his stomach, over the firmness of his muscles, draping around his neck to pull him closer. Even flush against me he's too far away. His teeth sink into my bottom lip, hard enough for me to barely distinguish between pleasure and pain. It's a thin line I'm gleefully toeing, eager for more.

"Lie back," he instructs, running his hands up and down my arms. The large, warm palms cover the goosebumps he created with the instructions.

I nod, wiggling away and resuming my position against the mountain of pillows. I prop my head up so I can watch him, not wanting to miss a second of what might be waiting for me.

He doesn't move or attack. He… sits back and stares at me.

"What are you doing?" I ask as he takes his dick in his hands, giving himself a single stroke.

"Going slow," he responds roughly, and I shiver at the new timbre of his voice. He crawls up my body on all fours, thighs bracketing my hips. Thick, male hardness presses against the inside of my thigh and I whimper, hating the word *slow* and how often it's been repeated in the last few hours.

I don't want slow. I want *now*, instant gratification and immediate reward.

I never thought I could hate a man for being too nice or establishing boundaries. Enter Henry fucking Dawson, wanting to do things right.

Damn him.

His thoughtfulness and subdued reaction to the length of my unintended celibacy is appreciated. There was no laughter. No smirking. No questions about why I've shied away from intimacy with others. No quips said in jest.

He took it in stride, unflinching at the extensive time span, a possessive glint twinkling in his eye.

Never in a million years did I expect *him* to be the one to break my dry spell, yet here I am, knees parting automatically to give him more space, accommodating his tall frame.

"Okay," I agree. "Slow."

His palm traces down my neck in a straight line, running along my windpipe. He applies the slightest bit of pressure to my throat, eyebrow raising when I don't protest or ask him to ease up. Before I can open my mouth and ask for *more,* he pinches my nipple between the thumb and pointer finger of his other hand, turning them half a degree. My eyes roll to the back of my head at the exquisite pain.

He dips his head, kissing the sensitive skin around the elevated peak. I whimper at his path, a woefully pathetic noise discharging from my throat. I'm incapable of anything else. "You have come in the last six years, right, Emma?" he asks into my neck, inching to my other nipple and pinching it harder than the last. I groan, the start of a tsunami forming. His attack ceases when I don't answer, and *God,* I shouldn't like that as much as I do. "I asked you a question."

"Y-yes, I've come," I sputter, body prickling with an unidentifiable heat starting at the small of my back.

"How? Fingers? Toys?"

"B-both. It hasn't been very frequent."

I don't tell him it's been half-assed sessions in the bath after work when I'm almost too tired to function, giving up after ten minutes because all I want to do is crawl into bed. I keep my mouth shut about the nights when I have energy, hand under the waistband of my shorts, reading a book and picturing myself as the protagonist getting everything I want, even if it's something I haven't tried before. And I certainly don't share about the other day in his shower when he interrupted me.

Nothing has been noteworthy; it's barely enough to accomplish the job hurriedly then go on with my life.

Henry hums in response, offering me no insight to what he might be thinking. His thumb swipes at the juncture of my waist and thigh, dangerously close to where moisture is beginning to pool. I tip my hips up, trying to meet his hand before he withdraws his touch altogether.

"Don't move." His stern voice has an immediate effect on me.

I freeze, obeying his demand. I haven't shared with him what I dream about. There's no way he can know, even if the book excerpt he saw was a glaringly obvious clue.

He's an extremely smart man, and I wonder if he's picked up on my subtle hints. The way my body quivers in delight at his dominance. How I melt when he uses the two words that will be my ultimate ruin—*good girl*—the praise stealing my breath and singeing my skin.

"Tell me, Emma, if I slide my fingers inside your pussy, how wet am I going to find you?"

My abs clench from attempting to stay still and follow his directions, hands fisting the sheets like my life depends on them to keep me sane. To keep my head on straight and not beg and plead on my knees. The cool fabric anchors me, grounding me on Earth when all I want to do is fly.

A pinch to my thigh causes me to jerk. It's not hard, just enough to get my attention.

"That wasn't a rhetorical question."

Oh, God.

It's already too much stimulation. Too much desperation to find a release. A heady desire settles over me, engulfing me from the inside out. I'm an inferno, burning alive.

"Drenched," I whisper, admitting the truth. "For you, Henry."

"Show me."

"What?" My head snaps up to find him straddling my body, his hand gripping my inner thigh with nearly all his might.

It's still not hard enough.

"I said, show me. Show me how wet you are. Show me what you like. Show me how deep you can get your fingers. I want to see how wide you spread your legs open to me, so I can watch and learn everything you like."

He drops my thigh from his hold, reaching for his cock and jerking up and down over the pronounced length, eyes staying locked on mine.

I inhale, trying to calm my nerves. It's empowering to realize I have control over him. The man who seems invincible might fall at my hands. And now I really want to play.

"Sometimes I touch myself when I read my books," I start. My finger runs up my leg, exploring. Every inch higher is another drop of confidence I take with me, growing bolder and bolder.

"Like the one you were reading just now?" Henry's breath is near my ear, and his lips land on my neck. "I bet they give you a lot of ideas you want to try."

I nod, my shaky fingers close to my entrance. One more nudge forward and they'd be inside. "They do. Things I've never done but have always wanted to."

"You envision yourself being told what to do. Worshiped and possessed and praised." His mouth closes around my breast and I cry out. "Sweet girl," he murmurs, teeth lightly biting my nipple. "You must be so turned on right now."

I can't hold back any longer, finally giving in and letting my finger slide inside, gasping at the stretch. Arousal greets me immediately, and I position my thighs farther apart to get deeper.

I withdraw and plunge back in, a loud, guttural moan escaping my mouth. Anyone could hear me right now if they were listening hard enough, and the thought makes me even wetter.

"That's it, honey," Henry says. "Fuck what I said earlier. I think I want everyone still at the party to hear you. I want them to know who is going to make you finish all over these sheets."

"Henry," I beg, relaxing enough to get past my second knuckle.

His lips find their way back to mine, and it feels like a lifetime passed without them. We tango back and forth, falling into a rhythm only long-time lovers might know. I part my mouth, his tongue glides over my teeth, a savage assault on all my senses.

His scent—a mix of spices and the whiskey he was sipping on earlier.

His touch on my leg—alternating between soft and tentative to rough and unyielding.

His sounds—whispered encouragement and a gentle *"that's my girl"* ringing in my ear.

Him.

Everywhere.

I circle my clit with my thumb, running over the bundle of nerves and jolting at the connection. I'm seconds away from giving in. Seconds away from surrendering to ecstasy. Seconds away from soaring to the stratosphere, when I feel a tap on the inside of my wrist, halting my motions.

"Let me taste," Henry begs hoarsely, bringing my hand to his mouth. His tongue runs up the length of my finger, from the base of my palm to my fingertip, hooded eyes never leaving mine. "I need more, Emma." He kisses down my stomach, a devilish path with only one finish line. "It's not enough." Pushing my thighs apart with a quick flick of his wrist, he looks up from between my legs, waiting. "It'll never be enough."

My pulse flutters at his sensitivity and patience, even in the heat of the passionate moment. I nod once, conveying my acceptance of any destruction he might bring my way.

Seconds pass, and then his fingers trace over my slit, dipping just inside my pussy, but barely entering.

"Look how beautiful you are." He kisses near my bikini line, taunting me. Teasing me. "You're practically leaking, Emma. So perfect and ready. Just for me."

Without warning, his pointer finger pushes deep into me, replacing my own, and I almost combust.

My vision explodes, white spots forming.

My hands fly out to grab onto something stable—his sturdy

shoulders. His hair. His forearms. I'm ready to jump from the highest cliff and soar toward the sun.

"Just for you," I repeat, grinding unabashedly on his finger.

"Fuck, Emma. You're so tight. I wish you could see how you're pulling me in. You need this, don't you? Do you want to ride my finger and use me, or let me do the work?"

"You. Work."

He pulls his digit all the way out for the briefest of moments before spearing me again. My back rises off the mattress, hands digging into his hair, twisting the onyx locks and holding on.

Seconds. That's all it's going to take me to finish. I'm not ashamed. I'm not embarrassed. Not when Henry moves with such lethal precision and purpose, a determined man on his mission, greedily ready to be the one to bring me rapturous exaltation.

When an additional finger joins the first, I balk at the stretch. He stills, his unused hand rubbing my stomach in soothing circles.

"Too much?" he inquires, that same husky tone present. He remains unmoving, letting me acclimate to the new addition.

"Not even close."

"Thatta girl. You can take it," he says proudly, dropping a chaste kiss to my hip.

Never has someone's praise meant more and I light up, a bright star in a cloudless night sky.

He resumes moving, quickly finding the perfect sequence. When his thumb circles my clit while his middle and fourth finger dive inside me a final time, I'm on the cusp, an orgasm rapidly intensifying like a hurricane in the Atlantic.

Another circle and it's *right there*, closing in and just barely out of reach... And it vanishes into thin air.

"W-what?" My eyes fly open, disoriented and frustrated. "Henry!" I beg. I've said his name more times in the last five minutes than I have in 17 years.

I love how it sounds.

"Come on, honey. You're the most intelligent woman I know.

You really thought I'd let you finish on my fingers without tasting you properly?"

There's no time to process the oddly kind chastising before he hikes my feet up, placing them on his shoulders. His palms slide under my thighs as he yanks me toward him. I let out a yelp that transitions into a groan, the depraved sound bouncing around the room as his tongue *finally* mimics the torturous path his fingers previously created.

"I fucking knew it," Henry hisses, licking me brazenly as if I'm the last source of water on a desolate island at high noon. "I knew your pussy would taste like heaven. You're my new favorite meal, Emma. I want to devour you every hour of every goddamn day. I'll never get sick of how good you taste." Slick sounds—the effect he has on me—drown out my appreciation of his mastery. I can't bring myself to care, climbing back to the edge, so very, very close to euphoria. "I'm not one of those alpha assholes who's going to dictate when and where you come. But when you do, I'm going to drink up everything you give me. I want it all, honey. Every last fucking drop."

The filthy words I've waited so long to hear are my demise. The orgasm races through me, charging from the top of my head to the end of my toes. My whole body convulses and spirals, the most intense wave of satisfaction overtaking me. Henry never ceases his attack, guiding me through blinding bursts of pleasure. His tongue stays fully buried in me, fingers digging into my thighs to steady me.

After a length of time rivaling eternity, my limbs stop shaking. My exerted breathing subsides. My eyes flutter open, finding Henry lifting his head, lips and mouth damp and shimmering under the light. Carefully, he lowers my feet back to the mattress, kissing each ankle as my soles return from their suspension on his shoulders.

He moves up the bed, positioning himself behind me and gathering me in his arms. Spinning me so we're facing each other, his lips tackle mine and I'm able to taste myself—taste *us*—a fresh blossom of excitement stirring within me as I savor the residual aftermath.

I'm on top of the world.

He kisses me passionately. We're one person, fused together. My tongue darts out, cleaning up the mess I've created, running along the line of his lips, corner to corner.

"Do you see how delicious you are? Decadent. Sweet. One time and I'm fucking addicted, Emma."

This is a different man from whom I've encountered over the last 17 years. This is Henry unleashed and unrestrained. Not refined or polished. Not professional. He's raw and animalistic. Possessive and territorial. And, God, what a perfect version of him.

Is he like this with every woman, primal and in control? Has he whispered praises in *their* ears as they reached the peak of fulfillment by his hand?

This is my eternal downfall. Overthinking and worry begin to kick in, threatening to ruin a perfect moment. As if sensing my question, he kisses me gently, softly, more… *lovingly*, shoving the doubt far away and locking it in an unreachable compartment.

"You. Only *you* bring out this side of me, Sunflower. No one else."

I sniff, wiping my eyes, unintended tears escaping. I'm sated. My muscles are heavy. My body is pleased. I could either sleep for nine hours due to exhaustion or run eight miles due to adrenaline.

And that nickname.

Sunflower.

It pierces my heart more prominently than any other affectionate word he's used so far. It's personalized. Designed for *me* by *him*. A secret, private story behind the name that only we share and no one else will ever know.

"That was incredible."

"You're crying. Talk to me."

"I'm not crying. It's a side effect from your manhandling."

Henry kisses my hair, lips lingering in my defunct curls. "Manhandling, huh? So much for slow. I'm sorry."

"I'm fine, I promise. That was perfect."

"Should I grab you another Zebra Cake so you can regain some consciousness?"

I giggle, tears drying on my cheeks. "I think my appetite is all set for the time being. Well, the food part at least." My fingers brush over the tip of his cock. There's already pre-cum dripping from the slit, and I swipe my thumb over the moisture.

"You know exactly what you're doing, you sexy deviant," he says lowly. "It might have been a few years, but don't pretend like you're innocent. Tell me, Emma, do you want to suck my cock?"

Is blurting out *fuck yes* too aggressive?

Probably.

I settle on a simple, nonchalant shrug. "Yeah. I do."

Feeling bold, I escape his warm embrace and shift off the bed, not trusting myself to balance on the mattress with how weak my legs are feeling. Henry follows me, understanding the message, walking a few paces closer. He's such a daunting, powerful man.

"Then get on your knees, princess, and open up. It's yours."

My knees fall to the carpet, listening to his command. He's bigger than anyone I've ever been with before, both in size and girth. I run my tongue up the full length of him, getting accustomed to his size and taste, wetting the shaft. My hands rest on his thighs and a shudder rakes through his body.

"I want you to know something," Henry says. His hand cups my cheek, thumb running over my parted lips before tilting my chin to meet his gaze. "You might be on the floor for me, under me, below me, but you are not inferior to me in any way. I can't even begin to describe how sexy you look right now. You're fucking perfect, Emma. I respect you. I care about you. You've far exceeded any expectations I had about tonight, and you're going to be my undoing."

The admiration lights a fire inside me, a small match turning into an uncontrollable flame.

"Then give me what I want," I tease, finally taking the head of his cock in my mouth. My cheeks hollow out, and I unhurriedly suck him down, inch by inch. I blink up at him through my eyelashes, earning a moan of approval.

"You're going to take all of it, aren't you?" Henry strokes my hair, fingers lacing in the messy bun. "Because you're such a good fucking girl."

The praise relaxes me. My jaw loosens, enabling him to get deeper. He's near the back of my throat and I'm already finding it difficult to breathe. New tears spring to my eyes, formed not from pain or uncomfortableness but rather lust and determination.

Inhaling through my nose as steadily as I can, my mouth finally reaches his base. Henry groans loudly, hands grasping my hair tighter and tighter with every bob of my head.

It's clear he's restraining himself, trying to behave and be *good* and *courteous* without getting out of control.

What if I want him out of control?

What if I want him hanging on by a thread, pushing me to my limits and reacquainting me with old desires and new pleasures?

Releasing him with a pop, I look up and am met with a dangerous, dark gaze in return. My hand fists his slick cock and I stroke up and down, thumb running over the tip.

"Do you remember what you said to me in a text message once?"

"You're going to have to be more specific," he grunts.

"You asked if I wanted the nice guy or the not-so-nice guy. Don't be kind. Don't be sweet. Give me the one that's full of trouble, Henry."

My mouth covers him again, reaching the base easier this time, as a bead of drool slides down my chin. Another tremor passes over his body. His muscles are straining. Veins and tendons are flexing with attempted constraint, trying to rein in the monster he wants to unleash.

"Emma," he whispers reverently, like a prayer. His head drops back and his eyes shutter closed, the grip in my hair tightening.

I bring my free hand to cover his, jerking roughly, hoping he gets the idea.

His eyes fly open, and I see the moment he realizes what I'm asking.

"Use me," I say, repeating his own words back to him as my hand strokes in rapid succession, finding a good rhythm. The movement starts to become instinctive and familiar.

His resolve breaks, crumbling to the ground beside me. The next thing I know, my head is being yanked back with a rough tug. My throat strains at the angle.

"Is this what you want?" Henry demands, cock sliding back into my mouth, nearly choking me. I nod, unable to speak. "So rough you can barely breathe? Because I could watch you suck me down all fucking day, princess."

He thrusts past my lips without abandon, self-control disappearing with every shove of his hips. The aggressiveness and assertiveness reignite the heat in my belly, wetness inundating my thighs. I bring my touch back to my clit, moaning around his cock as I tease along my entrance.

"What are you doing?" Henry stills in my mouth and I freeze.

"N-nothing."

"Nothing? Is that why your hand is between your legs?"

"I-I needed to touch myself."

"Which part is turning you on the most, Emma? My hard cock in your mouth and knowing I can't wait to paint your throat with my cum? Me telling you what to do? When you trust me enough to surrender complete control to me, doing anything I ask?"

His words are musical, infiltrating my ears and causing me to squirm. I'm going to create a puddle on the floor. "All of it."

"And you really thought you could start touching yourself without me noticing? Stand up."

"What? But I want to—"

"I said, stand up," he repeats, firmer this time. Stealing a glance at him, I read the expression on his face. There's a softness to his features, and I know he's giving me a chance to refuse. There's an out, if I want it.

But I don't.

Shooting to my feet, my heart races, wondering where he's going with this.

Henry surprises me, positioning himself flat on his back on the floor and offering me his hand. "Come sit on my face."

My mouth drops open at the five words. "Pardon? I-I've never... I haven't..."

"Never?"

"Never."

"Even better. Let me eat you out, Emma. I told you one taste wasn't enough."

My face is heated, both from mortification and desire. I turn around, knees on either side of his hips. I've never been so close and intimate with someone before. He's going to have access to *everything*, and I won't be able to stop him. I shiver, a thrill running through me at the thought.

"Like this?"

"Yeah, honey. You know exactly what to do." His tongue licks over my still sensitive clit, lurching me forward, ass in the air. "Oh, fucking perfect. Just like that. This is a sight I'd like to see for the rest of my life. Grab my leg if you need me, okay? I'm right here."

I nod, refocusing on the mast in front of me. Using a combination of my mouth and hand, I work him back up, taking care to observe which moves he likes best. He particularly likes when I lightly graze my teeth behind the trail of my hand, running along the vein covering his entire length. It's almost impossible to stay upright, determined to take him deeper and deeper while my breathing becomes more shallow with every plunge of his finger.

"Henry," I whine. The name comes out garbled and disjointed, mirroring my diminishing cognitive activity. I'm seconds away from falling. He doesn't let up, tipping me over the ledge a second time, his hands sliding under my stomach to keep me from collapsing.

I moan around him through the aftershocks, my movements becoming sloppy and rushed, energy evaporating.

"Dammit," he curses. "I'm going to come, Emma. Pinch my thigh right this second if you want me to pull out. Otherwise, I want you to swallow every drop."

I ignore his warning, fingers forming a tight circle around the base of his cock and squeezing. Warm liquid coats my throat seconds later, and I swallow his release down happily. After two more bobs of my head, I free him from my mouth, cleaning up the mess as I go and making sure I don't leave anything behind.

He rubs a hand up my back and I climb off Henry's legs. He extends his hand to me, helping me off the ground. Pulling me close, he holds the base of my neck, looking at me like I'm the only girl in the world.

"Hey," he says softly, forehead resting against mine.

"Hi," I murmur.

"What are you thinking, pretty lady?"

"Did I... did I do okay?"

"You did more than okay," he says, moving my hair out of my eyes. "You're perfect."

"I want to kiss you."

He beams, granting my wish. When Henry kisses, it's a whole-body experience. It's enthusiastic. Toe-curling. Mind-blowing.

I could kiss him forever.

"Did you think I'd say no? You nearly wrecked me, Emma. I told you... Whatever you want, you get. No exceptions."

"Whatever I want, huh? Who knew the infamous Henry Dawson was so easy to destroy?"

"I'm not. You're my weakness, apparently. Thoughts on what happened down there? All good?"

I bury my face in his chest, firm muscles welcoming me. "I loved it. Sorry I'm inexperienced."

"Have you had to apologize a lot in your life?"

"Yeah. Kind of goes with the territory of being a woman, sadly."

"You don't ever need to apologize to me, okay? Do you know how hot it is, getting to be the one to do things with you others haven't? It doesn't get much better than being the first person whose face you rode. I might make a medal."

I gasp, pinching his side. "I did not ride your face, and you are not making a medal!"

He laughs, chin resting on top of my head. "Au contraire, my friend. You almost suffocated me with those luscious thighs of yours. Don't worry, I'm not complaining. Death at the hands of your pussy? There are far worse ways to go."

"I'm so glad you survived such an arduous adventure. Forgive me for the assassination attempt."

"It would've been worth it. Tomorrow is going to be another long day. We should get ready for bed, which means I'm going to pester you until sunrise, asking you questions I need to know the answer to."

"What kind of questions?"

"There's a long list, Sunflower." He pulls me toward the bed. "Why don't you get cleaned up and I'll get this catastrophe reorganized?"

I peck his cheek, gratefully disappearing to the bathroom for a few minutes alone to collect myself.

Physical intimacy has never been like this for me before. I haven't been with a a lot of men, but I always assumed it was okay for things in the bedroom to be… average. Good, but not great. Fine, but not unforgettable.

The last hour and a half with Henry has changed my belief.

That is what I've been missing out on. Holy hell, was it phenomenal. I can't wait for more.

I hurry through my nighttime routine, eager to return to his arms. When I reemerge in the bedroom, I find Henry propped up on the pillows, an arm behind his head. Throwing my shirt and shorts back on seems futile at this point, but I do it anyway, walking to my side of the mattress and crawling under the covers.

"Can I sleep near you?" I ask, not wanting to take over too much of his personal space. I know his usual M.O. after being with a woman is expeditiously escorting her away. I don't want to spook him or make him think I'm ready to swap house keys.

He smiles at me sleepily, eyes already closing. "Come here, honey. I missed you." He opens his arms in invitation and I scoot toward him, nestling in his embrace. My back presses against his chest, and I hear him sigh contently. The noise fills me up, warming my blood and reassuring my racing heart.

"It's kind of scary how natural this feels," I say, closing my eyes as Henry turns off the light, plunging the room into darkness.

"I know," he agrees, cheek resting in my hair and fingers intertwining with mine, seeking solace while sharing scary words. "You feel… right."

"You feel right, too." I yawn. "Save your questions for tomorrow. I'm too tired."

"Anything for you, Sunflower."

As my breathing evens out and I begin to step toward a dream, an echo of Henry's voice filters through the air. It's so soft, so sincere, so serene, I'm not sure it's real or part of my imagination.

"I think I'm falling for you, Emma."

THIRTY-THREE

HENRY

MY CHILDHOOD BEDROOM is warm when I wake up. I should have cracked open a window last night to let in the outside air.

I open my eyes and squint at the bright morning sun greeting me, blinking twice before darting my gaze to the sleeping form coiled tightly around me. I find the source of my rapidly approaching heat stroke and have zero complaints. The sweat prickling my forehead is worth it.

Emma.

My smile comes immediately. She's still sleeping soundly, off in a dream, and I stroke her cheek, reveling in the smooth skin under my palm. Her head is on my chest, hair tickling my nose with every inhale. Her hand rests on my stomach, rising and falling with my rhythmic breathing. Her legs are curled up against her chest, pressing into my hip.

"Good morning," I whisper, shifting forward to press a soft kiss to her forehead, not wanting to disturb her slumber.

I've decided waking up with Emma beside me is substantially better than waking up alone. There's no panic creeping up my throat. There's no urgency to throw the covers aside and escape as quickly as possible. I'm not annoyed by another human being. I'm not looking for an excuse about why I can't stick around.

My mind, which usually runs a million miles an hour categorizing all the things I need to accomplish, is calm. My muscles are relaxed, aches and pains wearing away. My lungs are full of fresh, clean air.

I turn on my side to study the blonde next to me. She's just as beautiful in the morning light as she is under the moonbeams of the star-streaked night.

My chest aches at the sight of her in my arms, fitting so nicely against me. Her chin has moved to the crook of my neck, body molding into mine.

I think I could get used to starting every day with her cheerful face smiling blearily as I hand her a cup of coffee or bring her a doughnut in bed.

She's perfection personified, and I'm beginning to think she was designed specifically for me.

There's so much left of her to explore. I want to learn all of her fantasies and what else gets her hot and bothered in bed, turning into a withering mess.

I also can't wait to discover more of her intellectual and emotional depth and beauty. I want to listen to her discuss current events. What cases she's been working on. Her highlighter preferences and what board game is better: Monopoly or Life.

I want to hear her biggest dreams and help protect her from her deepest nightmares.

From the moment I first kissed her, I knew this was going to be more than a one-night fling. That understanding is why I'm not crossing any boundary in the bedroom until we have an explicit conversation. I want to get every goddamn thing right. Last night I picked up on some of her preferences, taking mental notes and filing the observations away for further dissection.

Each gasp, each moan, each scrape of her fingernails over my skin is committed to memory.

Her hollowed-out cheeks, the dribble of drool on her chin, the bob of her throat as she swallowed down my cum in a single gulp, have all been seared in my mind.

The feel of her hand in mine, the soft laugh from her lips, and the twinkle in her eye have all been repeated in my brain a million times, a permanent reminder of exactly how fucking *perfect* she is.

Emma stirs, the sheet falling away from her shoulders and pooling at her waist. Her nipples poke through the fabric of her thin shirt, hard and pointed. I didn't get to enjoy them enough last night, too preoccupied with other parts of her.

Like her glistening pussy she presented to me willingly and eagerly, legs spread and bared to me.

How she sat on my face with no objections, trusting me to not lead her astray.

The lack of grimace or disgust on her face when she looked up at me with wide, proud eyes, mouth full with my cock.

I can't pick a favorite.

Again: Perfection personified.

Perfect for *me*.

"Morning," Emma says. Her voice is scratchy and I reach my arm out, grabbing the water bottle from my bedside table and handing it to her. She accepts the beverage, taking a small sip.

"Hey. How'd you sleep?"

"Really well. Again. How about you?"

"Same. I was just about to get up."

"That desperate to get away from me?" she asks, giving me a breathtaking smile.

It's brighter than the sun, lighting up the entire room. I want to keep it in my pocket for safekeeping for when the days get cold and bleak.

"Fuck, no. I just wanted to make sure you were doing okay this morning."

"Are you always this polite or am I just lucky? One minute you're pounding your dick into my mouth, nearly choking me, and the next you're asking me about my feelings."

"Well, for the record, I didn't hear any complaints from you last night about the alleged choking incident."

"And you certainly won't." Emma reaches her hand out,

tracing the outline of my abs. I suck in a breath at her examining touch. "I'm good. Are you good, Henry?"

I could listen to her say my name again and again for hours on end and never get bored with hearing it. It's melodic and sweet, a reminder of how wonderful she is.

"So good," I respond, shutting my eyes as her nails graze over my muscles.

Fuck.

"What are two people who are both good going to do now?"

Keep you in my bed from now until the end of time.

Give you anything you want and ask for nothing in return.

Kiss you until you want to get rid of me.

"As much as I'd like to have your mouth around me again, sweetheart, my parents are expecting us downstairs in fifteen minutes. And what I want to do with you will take much, much longer than that," I say, capturing her lips with mine.

Shifting onto my back, I pull Emma with me so she's straddling my lap. Her lips are swollen, the early morning affection and last night's rendezvous plumping them up. Her sleep shorts are bunched high on her legs near her hips, creamy white thighs exposed to me. I'm close to ripping them away and sinking her onto me once and for all.

Fuck slow.

I want her. Badly.

Fast.

Hard.

And every other kind of way.

My hand wanders down her body, running along the ridges of her shoulder blades to the valley of her back. I stop just above her ass. God, the things I want to do to her backside. I haven't even been inside her yet and my imagination is already spinning out of control.

I could live like this forever. I could throw my phone out the window and never speak to anyone again. Except her.

All at once, everything is clear and focused, an arrow heading directly for a bullseye.

My goddamn heart.

She shifts on my leg, and it's a dangerous game she's playing as she grinds against my dick. I can't stifle the groan sitting in my throat.

"Emma," I warn. There's no real threat behind her name. I wouldn't care if she rode me until dinnertime, tits bouncing and pussy clenching.

"I'm not doing anything bad."

I watch, transfixed as she brings herself up my length. Her lip catches between her teeth. She's determined. Concentrated. My hardworking girl.

"Of course you're not. You're so good." The pink flush tints her skin, and I *knew* she had a thing for praise. "You'd never do anything wrong, would you?" My thumb traces the hem of her shorts, dipping under the fabric and running across smooth skin.

"N-no. I just... I want you so bad. And it sounds so stupid, but after last night I—"

A spontaneous idea pops into my head. "Do you want to play a game?"

"A game? What kind of game?"

"We have four minutes until we need to get up. Which means you have four minutes to get off, Emma. If you don't, this stops, we go downstairs, and you don't get to come until tonight."

Orgasm denial isn't high on my list of preferred kinks; it's practically near the bottom. No shaming those who enjoy it, but *I* get off on my partner getting off. Something about this game, though, has me growing harder, curious to see if she'll accept the "rules" I've enacted.

"Will you help?"

"Like I'd ever say no to touching you. Three minutes and thirty seconds."

"I want to play," she says quickly. I start a timer on my phone, the countdown beginning.

"Tell me what you want. What you need. You're in charge here."

Her eyes dart to the ticking time. "Touch my chest," she says breathlessly, moving against my cock again. I'm going to be sporting the biggest fucking case of blue balls when we're finished.

It's going to be worth it.

Complying, my hands dip under her shirt and roam up her stomach to her chest. My fingers find her pebbled nipples and I pinch them in unison, eliciting another gasp from her mouth.

"What else?" I demand, hellbent on helping her finish. Knowing we have a time constraint, seconds speeding by, this is one of the hottest things I've ever experienced. A wet spot forms on my pants from Emma's out-of-control movements. I think I might wear them to breakfast and show off.

Perfection personified.

Made for me.

"Grab my ass," she pleads, hand disappearing into her shorts. I can see the circular motion her wrist is making and I add it to my mental list.

Clit play.

Ass attention.

Nipple squeezing.

Check, check, and fucking check.

"Henry," she whispers. I've only been rewarded with two orgasms from her so far, yet I can already read her body language so easily.

She's close.

Blonde hair cascades over her shoulders like liquid sunshine as her mouth opens and her lips separate. Her legs spread wider and wider, shorts no longer covering the pussy that's fucking *using me* in the most salacious way, frantically trying to reach a goal.

I lean forward, taking her nipple in my mouth through her shirt, dampening the material. The action rewards me with her loudest moan yet. It's feral and desperate. Rough and sloppy. Broken and stilted, but still absolutely beautiful.

As I kiss across her chest, ready for another taste, my alarm blares, jolting us both out of our stupor. I drop my hands from her body and Emma lets out a strangled sob.

"Time's up." Gently, I move her from my lap and back to the safety of the mattress.

"No," she says firmly. "I'm not finished. I was almost there. Dammit," she huffs through red cheeks.

The curse makes me chuckle, and she tosses a murderous look my way.

There she is.

She clambers off the bed, stomping to her suitcase as she mutters under her breath. I think I hear the words *bastard* and *asshat* slip through the mumbled words.

"We could have kept going. You know I wouldn't have actually told you no, right?" I grab a pair of boxers and my jeans, searching for a shirt.

"You gave me a task, and I lost." She yanks off her sleep attire, slipping on a light blue sweater that matches her eyes. I walk behind her, my front pressing against her back.

"I promise you'll come later," I say huskily in her ear. "However you like, with or without me. I'll pull you into the pantry and go down on you in there. Deal?"

Emma huffs again, extracting herself from my grasp. For a second, I'm worried I went too far. Pushed her past a limit too soon.

When she squeezes my hand reassuringly, murderous expression turning into only a highly agitated glare, the worry abates.

"It better be on your dick," she declares, walking to the bathroom and slamming the door shut.

I grin, staring at the barrier long after she's shut me out.

Perfection personified.

THIRTY-FOUR

EMMA

I'M GOING to catapult Henry Dawson across his parents' backyard.

He's been tormenting me all day with lingering touches, seductive winks, and deep chuckles that vibrate against my sizzling skin. I'm about to snap, tiptoeing toward the point where I lose all self-control and modesty. I'm close to pulling him into the kitchen pantry and begging him to go down on me right there under the cereal boxes and sugar containers like he suggested earlier.

He's a sorcerer, doing something inconceivable to my brain, yanking me under a dark oasis, offering me pleasure and satisfaction while being kind and attentive along the way. It's the perfect balance between the man I want in bed and the man I want beside me in real life. How does that make any sense?

I figured he'd be interested in vapid communication to fill the time and toss me half-assed remarks while he pushed for intimacy on his terms, dictating the way the weekend is going to play out. Turns out, it's the total opposite. It's patience. Care. *Are you okay*s and *You feel right*s. Check ins and warm embraces. Cuddling and hand holding. Smiling at me from across the lawn and lighting up when I grin back. Forehead kisses and gentle hugs. It's magical.

Astonishing. Any doubt I had about him and his lack of experience with relationships has vanished, and I'm left with a man willing to try and work and grow with me.

I could dwell on these musings, pondering them until the wee hours of the morning and cataloging each encounter, but it's our last night here and I want to be present. I want to enjoy the time we have left, soaking up the familial interactions and malice-free jokes at Henry's expense. Even if my underwear is soaked through.

We spent the afternoon mingling with guests and family, laughing at shared stories about Anne and George's early days of marriage and their children's memories of growing up with parents who were prominent in the world of politics and law.

As the sun sets, we dine on small plates while lounging in a less formal environment. Pulled pork sliders, fried macaroni and cheese bites, and flatbread pizzas are devoured over cocktail tables and lawn chairs. The last big event of the weekend is the fireworks show. I've been looking forward to this since Henry first told me about the party. It's funny to think about how far we've come since those first few messages.

"Are you warm enough?" Henry asks, sliding into the seat next to me. I'm wearing his suit jacket, passed over to me when I shivered once. He darted across the grass and deposited the garment around my shoulders without a second thought, like he was watching and waiting for me to get cold, ready to jump in.

"I'm great," I assure him, snuggling into his side. Out of the corner of my eye, I see someone glaring at us. It's the same woman who attempted to come up to me several times throughout the weekend, Henry diverting us away from her whenever he saw her approaching. "Hey. Who is that?" I subtly gesture to the scathing gaze being tossed our way.

"Ah. That gem of a human is Bailey. Shit. Betsy? Remember how I told you my mom was insistent on setting me up with a family friend?"

"Yeah. It was your reason for hiring me in the first place."

"That's her. She's bad news. She wants one thing and one thing only: money. I overheard her bragging to her friend a few years back about how easily she'd be able to get me to sleep with her and how much money she could get from me if she 'accidentally' wound up pregnant. Needless to say, I steer clear of her at all costs."

"How horrible." I frown in disgust. "I'm glad I'm here with you instead."

"You and me both," he agrees, pushing the hair away from the nape of my neck. He drops a kiss below my ear in the spot I'm learning is one of his favorites. The first launch of the fireworks display goes off, bursting rays of color against the dark night sky. "I don't want to spend our last few hours here talking about her."

"Me neither," I concur, nestling deeper into his chest. "I couldn't have asked for a better weekend."

"These have been some of the best days of my life, Emma, and that wouldn't have been the case if you weren't here. I know I've said this before, but thank you. Not only for joining me as my other half, fake or not, but for being so fucking wonderful. So caring and understanding. It makes me a terrible person to say this, but I'm so glad I lied to my mom. It gave me you. And I've never been happier."

My head drops to his shoulder and I wrap my arm around his bicep. "Before we got here, I had this idea of what you and your family were going to be like."

"What were you expecting?"

"More rigidity and uptightness. But there's no pretentious behavior. No showboating. Yeah, you all live comfortably, but everyone is also so down to earth and kind."

"My parents used to be different. More close-minded. I'm primarily talking about my dad. Mom has always been a strong advocate for women and women's issues. In the last decade, though, they've shifted their focus."

"What do you mean?" I ask, turning to face him so I can listen to his story properly.

Henry sighs, and I can hear the heaviness in the exhale.

"My dad made some comments in the past. They were never anything blatantly offensive, but more snide, you know? Off-handed. Said in jest. The older I got, though, the more I realized what he said wasn't okay."

"When we're younger, we don't understand the broad spectrum of words having weight yet," I say gently, curious to hear what else he might share. I hook my foot around his, pressing my ankle against his sock and hoping he can sense the comfort I'm sending his way.

"I know. But we all know being silent means you're being complicit. I wasn't a five-year-old. I was a teenager. I knew right from wrong. Something also happened at a basketball game in high school. We were on the road, playing an away game, and a fan called out some..." Henry trails off and his jaw flexes with anger. "Some racist things toward Noah. My dad heard was appalled. I got ejected for almost beating the fucker to a pulp. Noah just... shrugged. Why? Because he was so used to hearing that kind of shit tossed his way.

"It was kind of the straw that broke the camel's back. Dad realized after the game how much impact even a handful of words can have on a person, and he's been better since. A couple of weeks later, Drew came out to my parents. Lizzie and I knew, but it makes me sad to think Drew might have hid this really important part of himself all because of misguided beliefs.

"They've gotten more vocal and more involved in the local community. Mom and I attended the Women's March together a few years ago, and she and Drew marshaled the Boston Pride Parade last year. People can change. It takes time. Patience and learning. I've always been proud to be their son. And now I'm fucking honored to call them my parents."

"Henry," I whisper, enveloping his hand in mine and squeezing tight. "Thank you for sharing with me. It's incredible to hear about the growth they've gone through. You were a big part of that change."

"Sorry. I don't know what made me want to word vomit all of that to you. You're so easy to talk to, and you don't judge me. I want to share all this shit with you. The important stuff. The not important stuff."

"Don't apologize," I say fiercely. "I like that you can open up and tell me these things. You're such a good man. You spoke up when you saw something wrong happening, like you did for me at the office. You care about others, and it shows."

His eyes meet mine, the caring and sensual brown of earlier shifting to dangerous and dark. "There's a very short list of people I would burn the world down for, and you, Emma, are certainly one of them. I'd strike a match and welcome the flames."

My heart skips a beat. Then another. Then another. Powerful, destructive words. Enough to nearly make me fall out of my chair with the sincerity and promise behind each one. It's a far cry from an *I love you* and certainly not sweet and sugary. To me, it's the most romantic declaration anyone's ever said on my behalf.

"Please don't become an arsonist," I joke, feeling obligated to add a touch of humor to our conversation. I'm afraid to let him see how much the assertion is affecting me.

"I really brought the mood down, didn't I?"

"You didn't. Not once in the two months we've been talking have I ever wanted you to be quiet. Do you remember when you'd try to chat my ear off in the hallway, telling me a story I didn't care about? Did I ever tell you to shut up then?"

He hums. "No. I guess you didn't."

"I listened, even if you annoyed me. These are the kind of things I want to know more about. Things no one else knows. It makes me feel special."

His face softens and he kisses my cheek. "You are special, Emma."

It's like the universe pieced together my dream man and plopped him here in this backyard, sitting next to me on squeaky, folded chairs, pulling his suit jacket tighter around my frame and brushing rogue tendrils of wispy hair away from my face.

And he's been in front of me all along. How stupid have I been to miss him?

I'm curious to see what kind of relationship we could have. What kind of partner Henry would be. I can't wait to spend time with him as the two of us where we can learn even more.

"Do you want to head upstairs?" Henry asks at the end of the fireworks show.

"Yeah. I'd like that."

He stands, offering me his hand, and I take it. I'm ready for some peace and quiet. Tonight was a lot. Between the handshakes, laughter, stories, and jokes, I'm exhausted.

I rarely do back-to-back events, so all this interaction and communication with strangers is beginning to take a toll on me. My feet hurt. My cheeks ache. My head is pulsing from having to explain my job nine times, fielding questions about why I would ever want to work in such a sad branch of law. Socialization is part of the job, and I owe it to Henry to keep it together these last few minutes.

"I'm going to say good night to Drew and Lizzie. Meet you at the door in five minutes?"

"Perfect," I smile, kissing his cheek as we go separate ways.

"Emma, right?" Halfway across the grass, I look up at the source of my name, finding the woman Henry mentioned earlier blocking my way.

Lovely. This will be fun.

"Hi. I'm not sure we've met."

"Your boyfriend has made sure of that. I'm Betsy."

"Nice to meet you."

"Did you sabotage Henry? Is that why he's with you and not me?"

"Sabotage? We're colleagues and have known each other for years."

"It was supposed to be me. Our parents have been talking about setting us up for years, until you swooped in and snatched him up first."

I rub my temples. I'm not a catty girl, and the last thing I want to do is engage in some childish fight when I've had such a nice time this evening. And I absolutely don't want to make a scene and ruin the party.

"I'm sorry you feel that way. I'm sure it must be hard to see the guy you like with someone else, but he pursued me because he wanted to, not because he was forced to. We're happy, and I hope one day you find someone who makes you happy, too."

I sidestep away from her, approaching the backdoor and safe haven away from the woman whose face I want to throw a glass of red wine in.

"He'll get bored of you soon. He always does. I've heard the rumors about how fast he goes through women. A new one each night. Sometimes two or three at the same time. You're nothing special, so I wouldn't get too attached. Guys like him think they want something different when they find something shiny and new, but deep down they never change."

She slinks away and I deflate, hating how much her parting shot punches my gut.

They never change.

"Hey," Henry says, appearing at my side. His smile falls when he sees my face. "What's wrong?"

"Betsy cornered me. She's not a pleasant human."

"Dammit," he mumbles, pulling me into a hug. "What did she say?"

"It was supposed to be her and not me. Asked if I sabotaged you. Told me you'll get bored of me soon."

"That's bullshit. I could never get bored of you."

"Can we just forget it happened? Please?"

"I'm sorry I wasn't here when she came up. I should have diverted her away."

"It's okay. I'm fine."

"Come on, let's go upstairs. I can tell you're tapped out." Releasing me from the hug, he laces our hands together.

"Am I so easy to read?"

He shrugs, opening the door. We ascend the stairs to his room. "If you know what to look for you are. Here's what's going to happen. I'm going to get a bath going for you, then we'll reconvene after you've had some time to decompress, okay? That was a lot of talking, and your well is dry. Time to recharge."

My eyes fill with tears and I quickly wipe them away. "Thank you."

"Give me five minutes and the bathroom will be all yours."

He disappears, and I hear the faucet begin to run, rushing water filling the bathtub. I unclasp my necklace and pull off my heels, feet thankful at the chance to be free. Shaking my hair out, I throw it up in a ponytail and yawn, discarding his suit jacket on the dresser.

"Right this way, your majesty," Henry says, and I laugh when I find him bowing, gesturing to the awaiting tub.

"Thank you, kind sir." I walk into the steam-filled room, the floor heater in full effect.

"Need help with your dress? I seem to remember you being accident-prone when it comes to clothing and zippers."

"Yes, please. The last thing I need is to get stuck and drown in this massive jacuzzi."

His hand moves down my back, unzipping the garment. Upon completion, his lips press a kiss to my bare shoulder blades. "Please don't. I'd miss you a whole fucking lot. Take your time, okay? I'll be out here when you're finished."

Henry closes the door behind him, sealing me inside. Disrobing and kicking my dress and underwear to the side, I sink into the warm water and groan.

It's heavenly. My muscles relax and my head drops back. I had no idea I was so stressed out, but the longer I sit in the tub, the better I feel. My breathing evens out. My ears stop ringing. My vision becomes clearer. It's silent and quiet and so blissfully zen. This porcelain has healing powers, and, as much as I'd like to spend the remainder of my days in this sauna-like state, there's a great man beyond the door waiting for me.

Draining the bath after twenty minutes, I grab one of the fluffy towels and wrap it around my body, securing it under my arm. I crack the bathroom door open, spotting Henry. He's sitting on the bed, typing away on his phone. He doesn't hear me slip back inside and lean against the door, watching him. Taking him in. Marveling at his splendor.

His messy hair. The small grin on his lips. The wrinkles in his shirt and the way the tendons of his forearms flex with every keyboard stroke. The tap of his foot on the floor, a beat of four quick taps, a brief pause, followed by four more.

Have I missed all these parts of him when I passed him in the halls at work, content to roll my eyes in his direction instead of appreciating the small bits of him others might not know? Like how he struggles to tie his tie, biting his tongue in exasperation while he loops the fabric through the knot. The fact that he enjoys sleeping on the right side of the bed and keeps one leg outside the covers to regulate his body temperature, a phenomenon he tells me works. How he hugs me close during the night like I'm permanently his.

Forever.

"You're pretty when you smile," he says.

"You're hot when you wear a suit."

"I wear suits every day. Does that mean you think I'm always hot, Zebra Cakes?"

I shrug nonchalantly, biting back a grin at the nickname. "Maybe."

A drop of water slides down my arm and he watches it drip to the floor.

"How was your bath?" he asks, voice deep and husky.

"So refreshing. Thank you for thinking of me."

"Thank you for being so on this weekend. You were amazing." Henry stands, striding toward me.

"Were? Are you implying I'm not amazing every day, Dawson?" I tease and he chuckles.

"You are. All day every day."

"Good answer."

We stare at each other, eyes locked. Who will break first? Who will nudge us closer to what we both want but might be too afraid to ask for?

Without speaking, he begins to unknot his tie, fingers working quickly to rid the material from around his neck.

"What do you like, Emma?" He runs the accessory through his fingers. I swallow, acutely aware of how badly I wish that tie was around my wrists.

"Pardon?"

He's unbuttoning his shirt now, discarding it to the side, standing bare chested in front of me. "In bed. What do you like? I have an idea, but I need to hear it from you directly."

Oh. I guess we're jumping *all in*, then.

He's quiet, waiting for me to speak, not pressuring, only encouraging me to take my time.

"You saw an excerpt from my book," I start.

"I did. Sorry I can't do much about the lack of wings." He offers a boyish smile, and I relax with his lightheartedness.

"I think you make up for it in other areas."

"What else from your book do you like?"

Taking a deep breath, I gather my courage. "I want you to tell me what to do. I want to ache and be sore and be filled. Everywhere. I want you to take me. All of me. Any way you want and wherever you want."

He steps forward, rubbing the pulse point of my wrist. "What else? I know you're not finished."

"I spend so much of my life telling others what to do and helping everyone left and right. For once, I'd like to relinquish control and hand the responsibility over to someone else. To you. I want to enjoy without overthinking."

He nods in understanding. His face is schooled, incredibly neutral, and I wonder what he's thinking. "Let me get some clarification. Being told what to do... I doubt you want this to translate to your day-to-day life, correct? Can you be more specific? I want to get this right."

"The second we leave the bedroom, it stops. In here, I want you to tell me when and where to bend over. When to open my mouth. What to do next. That sort of thing. Last night was spot on."

Goosebumps sprout on my arms. I've revealed everything to him. Without answering, Henry unbuckles his belt, slides off his slacks, and kicks them away, leaving behind only black briefs.

"Is that what you really want, honey? Because I can be that guy for you."

"Yes, I want you to be that guy. I don't want you to be sweet. I want you to be rough. Powerful. Show me... Show me that..."

"Finish that sentence," he growls, closing the remaining distance between us. My shoulders hit the bathroom door and I hiss at the contact.

"Show me I'm yours," I blurt out. My heart races at the lofty implication, wondering how Henry will respond.

He licks his lips greedily and expectantly. "I don't own you, Emma. No one owns you, you amazingly independent woman. But I will make sure it's *my* name on your lips when you come, again and again. I'll make sure to remind you that only *I* can make you see the fucking stars. Because I'm yours, too."

His mouth lands on mine, finally devouring my lips, and I moan at his ferocity. His tenacity. His promise. Henry's a man of his word, and I already know he's going to be my demise. My downfall. Ruining me from the inside out before becoming my salvation, a vicious cycle I can't wait to stumble into.

"Yes," I repeat, groaning as my arms fall around his shoulders like we've been doing this for years, a practiced dance between two lovers and the closest of friends. My nails dig into his back, tracing down his spine as his muscles flex along my journey. I want to mark him so any other woman who might want to experience him after me knows I've been there first and staked my claim. The first one to ever keep him for more than 24 hours. "Please."

"I've been waiting for this moment since our first email," he whispers, lips dipping to kiss the crook of my neck. I arch off the door and further into his embrace. "I'm going to possess you like you've possessed my goddamn brain and every waking thought, week after agonizing week."

"Then take me, Henry."

THIRTY-FIVE

EMMA

HENRY AMBLES AWAY, creating unwanted distance. The moonlight trickling through the curtains bounces off his chiseled body with each step, making him look like a god-like hero sent to walk among mortals.

"I have one rule."

"What's that?"

"I don't come until you do."

I snort. "Oh yeah?"

He cocks his head to the side and crosses his arms. "Is that funny?"

"I think it's a really good line."

"Clearly I'm not doing a good enough job if you think I'm lying. I'm going to get you there slowly. Gradually. Haltingly. You know why?"

"Why?"

"Because I want to savor every moan, every sigh, every whimper that comes out of your beautiful mouth. For me. Because of me. Does *that* sound like a line?"

How did we get here? How did we gravitate away from Henry and Emma, amiable coworkers who don't socialize, to me nodding like a possessed fool at his promised torture, ready to do whatever he asks?

My tongue is heavy in my mouth, rivaling a piece of lead. I have to swallow a few times before I find my voice and can speak actual words. He's going to destroy me.

My demise. My downfall. My salvation.

"N-no it doesn't sound like a line."

"Good. I need a word from you."

"A word? For what?"

"In case it gets to be too much. I need to know you'll stop me so we don't go past your limits."

"A-are you going to hurt me?" Dread fills my stomach. Physical pain isn't close to what I'm insinuating.

Horror replaces the lust on Henry's face and he blanches. "I will never, ever hurt you. I promise. That's why I want you to pick a word, sweetheart. I know it's been a while for you. I'm not saying that to be a jerk. I want to keep you safe. Not overwhelmed or trapped."

"Do you think you're that good?"

The heat behind his gaze tells me all I need to know. "I know I'm that good."

"O-oh."

"A word, Emma."

"Cheesecake," I say quickly. His lips turn up and his eyes dance.

"Cheesecake," he repeats, kissing me softly. His hand rests on the terry cloth of my towel, fingers toying with the haphazard twist holding the covering in place.

"Do you remember the night you zipped me up in the office? When I was on my way to an event?"

"In great detail."

"When you touched me, it felt like electricity running through my veins. A spark, even then."

Henry cups my chin, a move I'm learning he enjoys, raising it to look me in the eyes. "That touch awakened my soul. You've utterly destroyed me for anyone else."

This kiss is so full of life. He guides us to the bed, undoing my towel along the way. When the backs of my legs hit the mattress, I tumble onto the sheets.

"Lay on the pillows, hold the headboard, and do not drop your hands," he instructs.

It should be illegal how obscene the sentence sounds coming from him. I scramble back, ass rumpling the sheets in my wake. My shaky arms raise to obediently grasp the wood.

Henry joins me on the mattress, crawling toward me with grace and poise. When he reaches me, he pinches one nipple, then the other, and I moan in delight. I've been waiting for this all day.

His touch is exploratory. Like unsailed oceans waiting to be discovered, he maps out my body, acknowledging every curve, every divot, every line. His fingers skim across the dip of my hip, asking permission for more.

"Tell me what you need," he murmurs into my skin, mouth pressing a hot kiss to my hip bone.

"You. I need to come," I beg, toes curling at his touch.

"You've had a long day," he says, two fingers entering me without any prep. I cry out, hands faltering on the mahogany. "Do not drop them, Emma."

I snap my eyes shut, trying to focus. Trying to listen while also absorbing every curl of his finger and press of his thumb. The feather-light grazes bringing flashes of ecstasy to my vision.

"I'm going to add another finger."

"Okay."

This time, Henry's more controlled and careful as he slides back in, deeper than before, the third digit joining the mix. The stretch is almost too much.

Almost.

Instinctively, I hiss in pain. After a second, though, my legs relax. My thighs open wider, making as much room for him as I can. Five pumps, then a swipe of my clit. Five pumps, then a swipe.

He's been paying attention.

He shifts his position on the bed, left knee near my hip, chest nearly collapsing on mine, tongue flicking my nipple. He's moving faster. More synchronized. Determined and relentless, his fingers sprint in and out of me, ready to help me finish.

"That's it," he praises, the encouragement frying my already electrified nerves. "I can't wait to bury my cock deep inside you, honey."

The endearment is my downfall and I explode around his hand, withering as I crash down to earth. Henry coaxes me through the subsiding pleasure, the pumping changing to lazy circles as I ride the wave to shore, panting and overheated.

"Fuck," I curse, hands falling from the headboard and covering my eyes. I'm exhausted. Invigorated. Still turned on beyond belief and perfectly pleased at the same time. I have no time to recover because now Henry is pulling his briefs off, cock standing proud.

"Knees to your chest," he says, reaching for a condom I didn't know he had on the bedside table. Using his teeth, he rips the wrapper open as I get in position. "God, you're so perfect. Remember your word?"

"Cheesecake." I inhale deeply, preparing myself. He kisses the top of my knee, situating himself between my legs. He grasps my thigh, eyes darting to every corner of my body, unsure of where to focus. "Don't treat me like I'm fragile, Henry. You know what I want."

That snaps him into gear. He expertly rolls the latex over his considerable length and growls as the head of his cock presses against my entrance, almost slipping inside.

"Every time you sit down for the next few days, Emma, you're going to think of me." He pushes inside, the first inches of his thickness breaching me. "Relax, sweetheart. I've got you." His hand pushes down on my stomach, thrusting forward another degree. Little by little, with every kiss to my knee, every rock of his hips, every stroke through my hair, my breathing levels out, becoming more controlled and stable. "There you go."

"Henry," I pant. "More."

"Holy fuck," he exclaims, driving into me with all his might, finally fully seated. He's *everywhere*, going further, deeper than anyone else has before. "How are you this tight?" He withdraws all the way out of me, moisture coating the condom, before slamming inside again. His restraint has snapped, now nonexistent. He tugs hard on my hair as his tongue runs down my throat. Too many actions at the same time. Not enough actions at the same time. "I want to be inside you every goddamn second, Emma. Your pussy is my new favorite spot. I'm never fucking leaving."

"Harder," I whine, clutching his shoulders like a lifeline as my nails dig further into his skin, pink welts forming under the hand of my attack. "I can take more."

"Yes, you can." He pumps into me recklessly, every thrust more aggressive than the one before. It's chaotic. Unrefined. Unscripted and wild. A bead of sweat rolls down my cheek, breasts bouncing in unison with his plundering.

"Close," I let out, the long-forgotten-now-familiar feeling crawling up my legs and settling low in my belly.

So good.

So freaking good.

"Clench around my cock when you come, Emma. I want to feel it."

The orgasm sprints through me, his words having alarmingly immediate effect. Tears spring to my eyes in the aftermath, overjoyed and overcome with stimulation as my body shakes and quakes, plummeting down from its high. There's no time to relax. No time to breathe, because Henry is flipping us, changing our position. My ass raises in the air as I land on my elbows and knees.

"I can't do another one," I whimper, doing my best to cling to the pillows for support.

"If it's too much, say your word. Otherwise, I'm giving you another one."

Then, his hand meets my ass with a firm smack as he thrusts forward, deeper than seconds before, my elevated hips providing a new, bottomless, undiscovered angle. The sound escaping me is half sob, half moan. My brain can't process anything beyond the sting of my skin.

And how much I enjoy it.

"Again." I don't realize I'm saying it until he repeats the smack on the other side, even harder.

Out of body.

It's the only way to describe this sensation. The overwhelming cacophony of desire and lust mixing with something so tender and precious. It's rough, yes. Deliciously so. It's also sweet and caring, evident in the way he rubs over the spots he recently hit, gentle swipes of his palm to calm me down. Whispered soothing words in my ear as he rears back and rails into me again.

Rough. Sweet. Rough. Sweet. Back and forth until I hear his breathing change.

"Emma," he groans, hands dropping to my hips and squeezing tightly. My name is a prayer. A please. An ask. An offering.

I cry out, the last and final orgasm sneaking up stealthily, tackling me quickly. I almost topple to the bed before Henry keeps me vertical. Three more slides in then out and he stills, letting out another moan and silencing.

The only sound left in the room is our panting. He gently spins me around so I'm on my back, looking up at him.

"You're crying." He wipes a tear from my eye. "Why am I always making you cry?"

"You aren't. Your dick is."

He laughs. "Such crass words out of your mouth, Ms. Burns. I'm appalled."

"Then you'd be appalled to know you didn't push my limits. Next time, give me your worst."

His forehead drops to mine. There's moisture accumulating near his hairline and it clings to my skin. "Be careful what you wish for, Sunflower. Keep saying things like that, and you won't be able to get rid of me."

"Maybe I don't want you to go anywhere."

"Ready for a shower and bed?"

"Only if you join me."

"It's safe to assume that from here on out, I always want to shower with you. Come on, I'll fly us there with my imaginary wings."

"Can I ask a question you don't need to answer but I hope you do because I'm a nosy asshole?"

We're cleaned up and back in bed, both forgoing clothes after our shower. It's hard to distinguish where Henry stops and I begin; we fit so well together, like the last missing piece of a puzzle has been found. His words are warm against the back of my neck and I shiver, shoulder blades pressing into his firm chest muscles.

"Of course."

"Why did you start RB's Companions?"

I twist in the sheets so I can face him. "That's what you want to ask right now? Not my deepest, darkest fantasy?"

"Trust me, we'll be coming back to that conversation soon. You mentioned a while ago you use the money to pay for something. If you don't want to share, that's fine. I want you to know you can tell me anything. There's no judgment here." His fingers move up and down my arm in an indistinguishable pattern. I think he's writing out words.

"My debt after college and law school was astronomical. I had seven years of loans to pay off. After graduation, I went to an event with a friend. He mentioned I could do something like this for supplemental income. Hence RB's Companions being born. I don't get paid as much as you do either, so I also have to make up for the discrepancy."

Henry untangles us enough to stare down at me with a furrowed brow and a frown. "Hold on. You're going to have to repeat that last part, because I'm not sure I heard you correctly."

I pause. Discussing the pronounced wage gap after our great sex session sounds like the least hottest thing ever. Recalling earlier in the night, I remember he shared an important and earnest story with me and I want to return the favor. It means he trusts me. And I trust him. Lying with him here, naked without any barriers between us, makes me feel strong enough to tackle this sensitive topic.

"I make 85 cents for every dollar you earn. It's common knowledge in the legal field that despite making up the majority of law school graduates, women are continually underpaid compared to their male counterparts."

"I beg your fucking pardon?" he seethes, rage filling his eyes. "Why have I never heard about this?"

"Because you're part of the problem. Not you, specifically, as Henry Dawson. But you're a guy. You're oblivious to it because you don't know any better. Would you notice if you were missing $200 every paycheck? $300? $400?"

"I sure as shit would."

"But you aren't, so you would never know."

"Do you mean to tell me you make $1,000 less a month than I do, simply because you're a woman?"

"Around that, yeah. It might be more like $1,200."

"This is a big fucking problem, Emma."

"What do you suggest we do? Walk into work on Monday and propose the men in the office, which, might I remind you, make up 99% of the staff, take a pay cut in the name of feminism and equality? That would go over *real* well. Good luck getting misogynistic Brad on board with the idea."

He takes a deep breath and his fists clench. I take his hand in mine, kissing the back of his palm until he relaxes. "For the record, I am livid about this. I want to burn the whole fucking building down. We're going to discuss this further, not when it's 1 a.m. I want to enjoy our time together and not get in my car, drive straight to Wallace's house, and demand he figure this shit out. Immediately."

"Thank you for being so receptive and not accusing me of lying."

"Lying? I would never. I'm going to need websites. Data. Anything that documents this disparity so I can research it further. It's unacceptable, and I refuse to work for a company that doesn't pay its employees the same wage, no matter what gender they identify as."

"What are you going to do, quit?" I joke.

"If this can't be remedied? Yeah. I will."

"Have I told you tonight you're the best?"

Gathering me back in his arms, Henry kisses my cheek. "I used my inheritance money to pay for college and law school and barely put a dent in it. I'm out of touch with how much debt you might have. And that's my own fault."

"It was six figures when I finished my third year of law school."

"Six figures? Fucking hell," he grumbles. "Education in America is a scam. We spend thousands of dollars only to be paid chump change when we enter the professional world. How much do you owe now?"

"$3,800."

"Ah. Explains the exact number you gave me."

"I'm sorry. I hope you don't think I was extorting you. I never thought you'd agree."

"You should have charged more and added interest."

"It doesn't matter. I'm not taking your money. I've already told you that."

"Hey. Look at me." Reluctantly, I raise my eyes to meet his. The anger has subsided, a flame snubbed out. I expect to find pity in its place but something akin to fierceness resides amongst the chocolate brown hue. "A few nights before we met up for the first time, I was hanging out with my buddies, trying to verbalize the mess of feelings and emotions I was experiencing when it came to you. I told them I would find a way to give you the fucking sun if you asked for it. I can't do anything about the difference in our pay. Yet. But I can help you with this. Let me give you the money. It's important to you, which means it's important to me. Please."

"What if someone from the office found out? It could jeopardize my career."

"Forget the people in the office. This is about you. I told you I'd sign an affidavit to protect your identity, and it could include paying off the rest of your debt."

I gnaw on my lip, weighing his proposition. There's a sense of accomplishment in paying off the final number myself. It's a goal I've been chipping away at, and I'd like to see it through.

"Can I think about it? I'm not saying no. I want to table it until we get home and I can look at my spreadsheets."

He kisses my bare shoulder. "I'll accept your motion to table it. It's selfish of me, but I can't imagine you going to events with other men when we get home. I realize that might make me sound possessive and controlling, and please know I would never dictate how you go about your life or expect you to make decisions on my behalf. But I'm in too deep to sit back and watch you touch another man, Emma. Or let them touch you."

"Is someone jealous?"

"Yeah, I guess I am. I never thought I'd see the day."

"There isn't anyone else, Henry. Just you. *Only* you."

"Thank fuck for that," he exclaims, flipping me onto my back and pinning my arms above my head. He spends the next hours giving me all his attention, and I secretly revel in his jealousy as he worships me again and again, the morning light beginning to brighten the room around us until sleep becomes a thing of the past.

THIRTY-SIX

HENRY

GETTING to spend so much time with my family—Emma included—has been bittersweet. I don't get home as much as I should, and this long weekend was a reminder I need to make more of an effort when it comes to seeing my loved ones. During the farewell brunch with a small cluster of close family and friends, I marveled at Emma helping GJ pour a glass of orange juice. Assisting my niece in cutting her pancakes. Laughing with Lizzie and my mom, bright, boisterous chuckles passing over the table as the women giggled over something secretive. When I asked what was so funny, I got three matching eye rolls.

As much as I loved the tight-knit atmosphere of the past few days, I'm eager to get back to the city, and begin to attempt to navigate this new reality between the blonde sleeping peacefully in the passenger seat beside me. My life has changed exponentially in the last few weeks, all thanks to Emma.

No one has challenged me like her. She fights back. She's fiery and passionate. Cute and sweet. Funny and charming while also being dynamic and headstrong. She's shifted my entire world. Altered my reality. Made the world a smidge brighter. As stupid as it sounds, I truly don't know what I was doing before her.

Fucking around and enjoying a different woman each night? Forgetting their name while they were blowing me, confusing them with someone from last week?

Why?

I turn onto Emma's street and shift the car to park, touching her shoulder to wake her up.

"Hey, sleepyhead," I say softly. She blinks, stretching her arms above her head, yawning loudly and wiping a drop of drool away from the corner of her mouth.

Yeah, still cute as hell.

"Wow. Time flies when you're napping."

"Slacker," I joke, handing her a bottle of water. "Hey, before you go inside, I wanted to ask you something."

"Sure. What's up?"

My fingers drum on the steering wheel, buying myself a few moments of time. I didn't think this plan through, and it seemed much easier in my head when I was contemplating it 55 miles ago. Now I think it's going to sound stupid.

Fuck it.

"I was wondering if you wanted to have dinner with me sometime this week."

"Like a date?"

"Exactly like a date. I know we had a conversation a couple of nights ago, so I was assuming you'd be open to the idea. Now that we're home, I can understand why you would f—"

"Of course I want to have dinner with you!"

Lacing my hand through hers, I kiss her knuckles, one by one. "I don't want to pretend none of this happened. I don't want to walk through the halls at work tomorrow and forget what you look like when you sleep, or the way you act first thing in the morning, groggy and relaxed. Those weren't one-night stands to me. They meant something to me. *You* mean something to me."

She puts her palm on my face, running her thumb over my cheek. I lean into the gesture. "I don't want to pretend either. My answer is yes. To dinner. To a title. To anything and everything. Yes to you, Henry, my new boyfriend and other half."

I kiss her, conveying my joy and happiness through affection. I've gone too long without touching her, and I had no idea I could miss her even when she was right next to me until her mouth lands back on mine. This is a new starting line. A new beginning as a real, committed, exclusive couple.

Together.

"I'll check the employee handbook and read up on interdepartmental relationships. The last thing I want is for some dipshit in the office trying to cause issues. You know how those guys are."

"I would prefer if we kept this between us until the partner announcement is made," she admits. "I'm not ashamed of you. I just want that door to be closed and boarded up before we figure out what happens next with us professionally."

"For the record, firing Brad needs to be the first order of business from whoever gets picked. Agreed?"

"Agreed. When do you want to have dinner?"

"Is tomorrow too soon?" I ask, not wanting to come across as too strong. Too avid and enthusiastic. Her answering smile tells me all I need to know.

"Tomorrow is perfect."

The next day at work is excruciating. Between it being Monday, returning to the office after a few days away, and Emma constantly on my mind, I constantly forget about the contracts I have piled on my desk. Instead of focusing on my clients, who usually have my full attention, I'm wondering if she's having a good day. If she slept well. If she's eaten lunch yet and what's on the menu.

While I wish we could have spent last night together, it was

nice to have a little bit of space. I know Emma probably appreciated it after spending multiple days without an escape, needing
some alone time. She took full advantage of our time apart, given
she sent me a picture of her in a bubble bath, face *and* body visible
this time, the suds not hiding any of her feminine features. I
jerked off to the photo in bed, picturing her mouth over my dick
as I came into my hand, much preferring the sticky aftermath
landing down her throat instead of on my stomach.

I can't help it. She's somehow infiltrated every facet of my
brain. Today we've exchanged a collection of secret smiles in the
hallway, and I catalog each one in my memory bank, wanting to
ask her what she was thinking at the exact moment when she
looked so fucking happy.

I'm itching to hold her and kiss her. It didn't help that she
snuck into my office earlier, closed the door and sat on my lap for
two minutes, hands in my hair, mouth on my neck, whispering
about how she always wondered what it would be like to hook up
with me in my office, our colleagues a few feet away.

Cuddling and affection before or after sex has never been my
jam; yeah, I enjoy foreplay and the buildup, but at the end of the
act, I don't want any mindless caressing or lovey-dovey gestures.

Until she came along.

It's different with Emma. I want to hug her. Push her hair out
of her face, kiss her forehead, and nod along while she tells me all
the secrets of the universe. I want to sleep with my face tucked in
her neck, her body wound around mine.

When I park my truck in her driveway that evening, I take a
moment to collect myself. My heart is beating so fast, it rivals a
steel drum. I'm surprised no one can hear it. I'm hopeful. Optimistic. Reckless and bold, because *she* is waiting for me.

And I'm a lucky fucking man.

I walk to the house with jelly legs. It's a damn miracle I don't
trip on the brick. As I knock on the door, I clutch the flowers I
picked up from the market in town on my lunch break, careful to

not damage any of the fragile petals. The door creaks open, revealing a radiant Emma.

My heart seizes at the sight of her. It *burns* as I take in the dark blue dress matching her eyes, contrasting against her pale skin. It hugs her body in the best ways, showing off her soft curves. Her hair is pulled back away from her face, half up half down. She looks like an angel from heaven above, just missing a halo.

"Hi," I rasp, words evaporating from my vocabulary. "You look beautiful."

"Hi yourself."

"These are for you," I say, thrusting the bouquet into her hands.

"Sunflowers! Oh, Henry, they're gorgeous! Thank you so much! Come in so I can put these in some water. I'm ready to go, so it'll only take a second."

I follow her inside, closing the door behind me and taking in the modest living space while she busies herself out of sight. It's not big, and everything is so perfectly her. The throw blankets. The laptop on the coffee table. A stack of books sitting beside the couch.

It feels like a home.

The bright yellow walls radiate sunshine and warmth. The hardwood floors have scratches and dings. The walls are covered in framed photos. There's a bookshelf in the corner, overflowing with spines arranged by color, a rainbow of literature ranging from black to bright pink. There's not enough space on it, and books have started to take over the floor, too.

I have this urge to buy a house with her that's much, much larger. A house that can hold more bookshelves, as well as a white picket fence. A lawn. A porch swing for her to sit on as we watch the sunset.

Domesticity.

Another word that's never presented itself to me before, yet here I am, ready to grab a goddamn hammer and nails and build her floor-to-ceiling shelves so I can stock them with any book her heart desires.

How many books, Emma?

How many books would make you happy?

A hundred?

A thousand?

A million and one?

Say a number, and it's yours, honey.

Let me be the one to give it to you.

Dragging my eyes to the leather couch in the center of the room, I bite back a grin, wondering how many times she sat in that very spot, conversing with me and unaware of what was waiting for us in the future.

"Yes, I have talked to you from those cushions," Emma interjects, reading my mind as she steps next to me. "If you look close enough, you can still see the faint indent I left after not moving for six hours at a time, deeply engrossed with the mystery man on the other side of my phone."

"I'm sure you've also wanted to throw your phone at me from those cushions, too."

"Guilty," she laughs, fixing the strap of her purse. "Should we get going?"

"Not yet." I bend down, enjoying our height difference and how she stands on her tiptoes while I duck my neck to meet her halfway. I kiss her deeply, savoring the lingering spearmint from her toothpaste. "Hi."

"Hey." She beams, wrapping her arms around my waist and resting her head against my shirt. "What was that for?"

"I missed you."

"I missed you, too."

I offer her my hand and she accepts it, leading us outside and into the cool night. I hold the door to my truck open and she smiles as she hoists her small frame inside.

"You're staring at something," she observes from the passenger seat as I pull out of her driveway.

"You," I say simply, eyes drifting back to the road. Her hand finds its way into mine, weaving our fingers together and resting on the center console. "Assume I'm always staring at you."

"What about me is so stare-worthy?" she presses, amusement prevalent in her question.

"I'm just appreciating how pretty you are. And how much you make me smile."

"Did you know you make me smile, too? A lot, actually."

"We're two smiling fools, aren't we?"

"I wouldn't want to be a fool with anybody else," she says, squeezing my hand.

"Are you excited for dinner?"

"You know I have a strong affinity for food. Of course I'm excited!"

We make the short drive toward downtown. When I park in front of Mia Italia, the upscale restaurant Emma mentioned wanting to try weeks ago, I peer over to gauge her reaction.

"Wait, what?! Are you serious? I told you I wanted to go here like, the fourth time we spoke."

"Yup. You did. You then proceeded to tell me you'd break a lot of laws to eat their garlic bread. Tsk tsk, Ms. Attorney."

"How the heck did you make this happen? It's impossible to get reservations! Trust me, I've looked for the hell of it and they book tables three months out."

"I know a few people who were happy to accommodate a first timer."

Once we climb out of the car, I nod my thanks to the valet guy and slip him a ten-dollar bill. My arm slides around Emma's waist as we walk into the building. The lighting is low and it takes a second for my eyes to adjust to the dimness. Soft jazz music filters through the room, hardly audible over the clinking of silverware and buzzed conversations.

The hostess leads us to a small booth, tucked away in a corner. I hold Emma's hand as she sits down, not letting go until she's safely settled on the leather.

"Do you want to get a bottle of wine?"

"That sounds great. Red or white?"

"You pick. Get whatever you want."

She hums, surveying the menu options, looking exactly like she did in high school when she studied—focused and poised. I know she thinks I never noticed her over those four years, but somehow my eyes were always drawn to her.

It's as if they could see something I couldn't, telling my brain *one day.*

Be patient.

It's worth the wait.

I'd see her in the school library, tucked away behind a stack of books, her ponytail barely visible while literature by Faulkner and Fitzgerald sat on her table. In the hallway as she walked to class, I trailed meters behind with my group of buddies, always wanting to say hello and never knowing how. I even noticed her at a baseball game once, high up in the bleachers, wearing a large sweatshirt and hat. She focused on the notebook in her lap more than the game itself, but I once caught her eyeing me with a curious glance.

All those little moments, which, at the time, seemed so unimportant, have somehow led us here. Right now. Me, smiling at her across the table at dinner, two souls that have forged down the same road, eventually intersecting and meeting as one.

Together.

"Let's do the red," she decides. The waiter returns with two glasses and a full bottle. After giving us each a hearty pour, I hold up my drink and she mimics me.

"To the best first date with the most beautiful woman I've ever laid eyes on. I wouldn't want to spend it with anyone else."

Our glasses clink and she blushes before bringing the liquid to her lips. I watch her swallow down the sip, throat bobbing, and all I want to do is kiss down her neck, following its path.

She orders a chicken and pasta dish while I settle on bolognese. Over our meals we exchange stories about our childhoods, favorite memories and best friends. She shows me pictures of her best friend Nicole, and I share the photos I took of my friends during a talent show last year to benefit charity. She tells me about growing up with a single parent. I tell her about my fascination with the postal service. We laugh merrily, still immersed in conversation long after our food disappears.

"Okay, I'm stuffed," Emma announces. "Dessert is a must though, right? The seven-layer chocolate cake was the first thing to catch my eye."

I grin, knowing the decadent option was going to be her choice. "We'd like the chocolate cake and a side of ice cream to go, please," I say to the waiter as he collects the empty plates.

"Ice cream to go?" Emma asks. "Isn't that counterproductive? It'll melt."

"Even better."

"It sounds like you have a plan."

"I always have a plan." I pull out my wallet and take the to-go bag full of dessert items and the check.

"Do you want to split it?"

"Nope. I asked you to dinner. It's my treat. We can split it next time."

"I don't spend money on myself very often, and that includes an expensive meal."

"Hey. I never said I needed to eat at a restaurant like this every night. I wanted to take you somewhere nice for our first date. Drive-thru McDonald's is fine by me."

She wrinkles her nose. "I doubt you've ever eaten a quarter pounder in your life. How about we compromise and settle on tacos instead?"

"Deal," I agree, signing the receipt and leaving a generous tip. "Let's get out of here."

At this point in the evening, I'd be getting ready for a raunchy fuck fest. Slipping my hand up a girl's dress while driving back to my place, fingers slick with arousal and her withering against my leather seats. Do I have visions of Emma crawling over the center console, straddling me in the parking lot, dress bunching at her waist as I pull her tits free and pinch the nipples I really like? Fuck yeah, I do. I'd love to take her in a location where people can see, so they know I'm hers.

I also want to make sure she's even cool with continuing our physical relationship. Technically, this was our first date. Does she usually sleep with guys after their first meetup? Is she pressured because it's *me* and we've already done this?

"Are you doing anything else tonight?" I ask casually.

"Don't you want to stay when we get back to my place?"

"This is new territory for us, and I want to make sure you're okay picking up where we left off the other night."

"Henry, I would very much like you to come inside when we get home."

Home.

Not *her* home.

Just... home.

I think I like how that sounds.

Fifteen minutes later, we park in her driveway, both staring at the facade. I realize for the first time that perhaps she's as nervous as I am.

"We don't have to," I start. "I can head back to my place."

"I want you here." She climbs out of the truck, taking the bag of food with her. As I stand behind her at the front door, I bring my hips to meet hers, her chest flush against my back. She fumbles with the keys and I kiss her shoulder, sliding my hand over hers.

"Need some help?" I undo the lock and push the door open.

"Thank you," she breathes out, walking inside. I close the door behind us, taking off my shoes. I set them to the side, smiling as I see the black leather stacked next to a pile of her sneakers and sandals. I like my stuff mixed with hers.

"No expectations tonight, okay?"

"Henry." Her voice has changed, now silky and sultry, sliding through the air and reaching my ears. "I want you to fuck me.

Hard. I want you to ravish me. I want you to kiss me until I want nothing else to do with you. Which is going to take a long, long time."

"Well," I answer, lip curling in delight. "We better get to work."

THIRTY-SEVEN

EMMA

"MEET me in the bedroom in five minutes," I say, slipping off my wedges.

"Which one is your room?" Henry asks, taking the bag of food from my hold.

"Down the hall, third door on the right. The bathroom is the first door on the left if you need it."

His eyes sweep over me in a parting glance before he turns for the kitchen, humming a melody as he leaves. I hurry down the hall, nearly slipping on the rug. Stumbling into my room, I close the door and pull out a few candles. A glow settles over the space, the dim lighting calming me.

My heart feels like it might fall out of my chest. This is no different than what we've done the last few nights but it *feels* different. There's a heavy realness associated with these next steps. When Henry walks through the door, he's walking in because he wants to. He doesn't want to leave. He wants to stay.

And that empowers me.

I shake out my hair and yank the zipper of my dress down, shimmying out of the material and kicking it to the side. When I look in the full-length mirror hanging on the door to my bathroom, I barely recognize myself.

I bought the black lingerie set I'm wearing on a whim a few weeks ago, purchased with the hopeful, optimistic intent to possibly use it with the mystery man. Wearing it under my dress all night gave me an added confidence and I feel *sexy* for the first time in my life.

Smiling, I take a deep breath and turn toward my bed. Staring at it quizzically, I wonder what position I should take. Do I lie down? Lean on one elbow?

I settle for perching on the edge of the mattress and crossing my legs, hoping I don't look uncoordinated.

A gentle rap on the door causes me to suck in a breath, and my body is alight with nerves and an excited anticipation.

"Come in," I say, squaring my shoulders back. The knob turns and Henry opens the door, standing in the threshold of the room.

His gaze pierces me as it travels from my face down my body, eyes progressively widening the farther south he goes. When he reaches my feet, he exhales and stares at the ceiling. It's silent in the room for an agonizing length of time. He's unspeaking. I'm unmoving, afraid to disturb whatever is happening in his head.

Henry's jaw flexes. He mumbles something to himself. His chest rises and falls before his chin drops, leveling me with a look that knocks the wind out of my chest.

"Stand up," Henry says. It's not a command. It's not a demand. It sounds like… like he's *begging* me to oblige.

I rise from the bed on unsteady feet, happy to do what he asks. He crosses the room in two long strides, reaching out to lightly grip my elbow and steady me before dropping his palm to my stomach, thumb running over my ribs.

"Emma. Is this… Is this for me?" His voice cracks at the end of the question, an awed expression taking over his face.

"I thought you might like it."

It's a two-piece set; the sheer top crisscrosses over the swell of my breasts and enhances my cleavage, nipples on full display. The lace doesn't hide anything. The bottom portion sits high on my waist, attaching across my stomach to flimsy underwear that might as well be nonexistent. The back exposes my ass, covering only a small part of my cheeks. It's the hottest item of clothing I've ever worn, and watching Henry watch *me* makes me want to live in it forever.

"Baby," he starts. He swallows, staring at my chest. His hand skates to my hip, finding a small sliver of bare skin. The pad of his finger brands me, barely a touch but hot enough to scorch every inch he's yet to reach. "I fucking love it. You're so gorgeous."

"Even though I don't wear thigh-high stockings under my work skirts? Present attire excluded."

"Especially because you don't wear thigh-high stockings. You're so unapologetically you. You don't try to be someone else, and it's so refreshing. Jesus, honey. Look at how stunning you are. This fucking waist of yours." He bends down, kissing my stomach before moving lower and lower, dropping to his knees, a man offering up a prayer. "This ass." His hands skate around to my bare backside, squeezing the skin he finds. "And this pussy that makes me never want to come up for air. I want to devour you, Emma." His tongue runs over me through my underwear and I groan.

"Then feast," I say, threading my hand through his hair.

"Do you have a spare sheet?"

The question catches me off guard and I blink down at him. "Yeah?"

"Can you get it for me?" Henry asks, kissing the inside of my thigh before standing.

Nodding, I step toward my closet. I reach up to the top shelf, my ass becoming more visible as I pull the old sheet down, walking it over to him. He watches my every move, cupping my cheek and pressing his lips to my forehead when I hand over the tattered material. He lays the beige cover over my comforter, hiding the familiar white.

"Climb on the bed. I'll be back in a minute. Arms above your head, and don't move."

"Where are you going? Is everything okay?" I don't mean to

sound panicked, but I've never had a guy walk out of the room like this before.

"Everything's perfect. You're perfect. I'll be back in one minute, I promise."

Henry gives me a soft kiss before he leaves, and I follow his instructions, taking residence on the bed and leaning against the pillows. My arms rest above my head, holding onto the headboard. I stretch my legs out in front of me, crossing my ankles, staring at the door and patiently waiting for him to return.

He reemerges holding a bowl and a plate, and I furrow my brows at the objects in his hands.

"Look at you," he breathes out, kicking the door closed behind him. "Such a beautiful sight waiting for me. Are you doing okay?"

I nod. "You brought back food?"

He takes the spot beside me on the bed, mattress dipping under his weight. He's barely out of my reach, and my fingers flex at the desire to touch him and have his skin on mine.

"Dessert. Someone wanted chocolate cake."

"Yes, please!"

"Let me get comfortable, then I'll give you a taste."

"A taste of what?" I joke. Henry removes his pants and socks, tossing them out of the way.

"If you want my cock in your mouth, honey, all you have to do is ask," he fires back, unbuttoning his shirt and sliding it off his sculpted shoulders. He's wearing nothing except briefs that hug his muscular thighs, the bulge he's sporting visible through the fabric.

He grabs the plate of cake, breaking off a small piece and bringing it to my mouth. "Open up."

We've done this dance before, in his kitchen with the cookies. We had more clothes on then, and I almost didn't survive.

Tonight doesn't bode well for me either.

Like last time, I tilt forward a few inches to get closer to the spoon, my mouth wrapping around the utensil. I swallow the delicious bite, blinking up at Henry though my eyelashes.

He hums. "How does it taste?"

"Delicious. Chocolate cake is one of my favorites."

"I'm going to need a full list of your dessert preferences ranked in order, one of these days. How are your arms doing?" he asks, bringing another spoonful to my parted mouth.

I greedily eat the bite, shrugging one shoulder. "They'd be better if I could touch you."

"Bring them down. You did great."

I blush as the praise fills me up. My limbs relax and I shift into Henry's lap, arms wrapping around his waist. "What does it say about me if I missed you the minute you were gone? Before I wouldn't notice if we went three days without speaking or seeing each other. I'm the most independent person in the world. But now? Now… it's like everything gets darker when you're not here." The admission is soft. I'm not afraid to share the truth, but something about saying it *tonight* makes it more profound. Powerful. Lasting.

Henry buries his face into the crook of my neck. "I missed you, too. With you I feel… complete. Whole. Like something has been missing from my life and I just didn't know what it was. Until you. I've never… I don't…"

He's struggling to find the words of a deep confession to me, and I hug him tight, understanding how difficult it is to verbalize a thought like that when you're so used to being alone. "I know."

"As much as I love seeing you in this outfit, I think I'd prefer you naked," he says, playing with the straps of my top.

"Take it off, then," I dare him. In a flash, he has me on my back, pinned under his weight, the tenderness from his admissions evaporating.

His hand travels up my thigh, thumb brushing along the hem of the underwear. "When I get rid of this pathetic piece of clothing, how wet am I going to find you, sweetheart?" he whispers in my ear, thumbs hooking on the side of the material and pushing it down my legs. I lift my hips and he discards the piece completely. "Drenched," he mutters, finger sliding over my pussy. "I fucking knew it." Unhooking the bra, he slides it off my arms and pulls back to stare at me. "How would you feel about playing another game?"

"I didn't do so well last time."

"If you win, you get to come."

I frown, searching for the catch. "That sounds too easy. What happens if I lose?"

"You get spanked, then you come."

I gape at him. How can he already be so in tune with my fantasies? How does he know I've been dreaming about being over his knee, ass red as he strokes my hair and comforts me?

"I-I want to play," I say shakily. My voice might quiver, but I mean every word.

"Good. Get back on the pillows. Arms above your head again. If you drop them, you lose. Okay?"

I nod vigorously, repositioning myself so my head rests on the soft cushions. This is a game I can win. My hands clasp the headboard tightly. Henry reaches for the bowl he brought in with him.

"Ice cream?" he asks, bringing the spoon to my mouth.

"It's cold." I swallow the bite down and shiver.

He scoops out another bite. Instead of bringing it to my lips again, he hovers it over my chest. A drop of sticky goodness dangles on the metal, close to falling off.

"What are you doing?"

"Enjoying dessert." The liquid tips off the spoon and drips onto my body. It's like splatter paint on a canvas, the chocolate dark against my skin. I hiss at the impact. The melted liquid rolls down my breasts toward my stomach. Before it can get too far, Henry licks the mess up with his tongue, starting near my ribs. I moan as my back rises off the mattress. "Oops. I spilled."

Now I understand his game and why I might not stand a chance of victory.

"This isn't fair," I whine, withering on the sheet.

"Do not drop your hands," he says sternly, another spoonful dripping on my hip and running down my shaking thigh.

Another lick up my leg, he purposely avoids the spot he knows would detonate me.

His next scoop ends up on my lower stomach and spills over my waist. He cleans up every drop, and I let out another sound. He's trying to get me to lose. To fail. To give up and admit defeat. Part of me wants to; the thought of being over his knee and at his mercy, sticky ice cream residue fusing us together, is intoxicating.

But I'm not a quitter.

"I could play this game all night," I say through gritted teeth. Even I hear the uncertainty in my voice. Henry smirks, a fresh spoonful of ice cream waiting for me, and I know I just spurred him on.

"Is that so?" He tilts the spoon at a precise angle, the dessert landing right between my thighs. "Better clean that up."

Pushing my legs apart, he looks up at me with a mischievous grin. Then, his tongue parts me, sliding inside, and I almost lose the game right there, ready to forfeit and give in.

THIRTY-EIGHT

HENRY

THE MIX of ice cream and Emma is the sweetest thing I've ever tasted. I lick her skin with long, leisurely strokes, taking all the time in the world. I'm intoxicated, drunk on her, needing more and more to survive. She'd turn a sinner into a saint, asking to worship her existence.

Now that I've tasted her, held her, kissed her, laughed with her, wiped away her tears, watched her chest rise and fall in the early morning hours under the rising sun, and experienced nearly every wonderful piece of herself she has to offer, I know with the utmost certainty nothing, and no one, will ever be good enough again. I've been destroyed and brought to my knees.

It's not torture.

It's pure, unadulterated bliss.

"I need more," she whimpers from above, thighs bracketing my head so I can't escape or pull away. As if I ever would even if I could. I want to start a new life here, between her legs, surviving on her and her alone.

"What do you need, honey?" That term of endearment has become something I crave saying. I want to call her every name under the sky.

Honey.

Sweetheart.

Baby.

Sunflower.

Princess.

Zebra Cakes.

Words that convey a the smallest iota of my affection toward her. They're kind instead of filthy. Sweet instead of degrading. Promising and fulfilling instead of open-ended and lackluster. Domesticated and monogamous instead of uncommitted and wild. All things I want to be with her.

"You. I need to come."

I can tell she's close to pleading, and I don't want to push her too far or be the asshole who doesn't follow through on his promises. My tongue moves away, the teasing ceasing as my pointer finger takes its place, sliding inside her pussy. I'll never get over how tight she is. It's obscene, really, how quickly she consumes me, drawing me in and asking for more.

"Happy to oblige."

Kissing up her thigh, I relish in the way she squirms underneath me. I remember all her missed pleasure, years and years without release or satisfaction. Without being touched. While it's going to be impossible to make up for all the lost time, I'm going to do my damn best to try.

I add a second finger inside her, readying her. Stretching her. Both digits disappear, well past my second knuckle, and I marvel at her beauty. Hair messy. Eyes closed. Lips parted. Nipples pointed.

Absolutely perfect.

I pump into her for several seconds, appreciating the strangled pants she's releasing. The way her hands grip the sheets. How fucking *wet* she is, my fingers covered in her juices, the moisture beginning to coat the back of my hand.

Holy hell.

She's astonishing.

Just as she's on the precipice of her climax, I pull out, slipping the drenched fingers into my mouth, relishing in her delicious taste. Her lips fall into a round O as she watches me, eyes heavy with lust. She moves fast, reaching out and bringing our mouths together. I slide my tongue against hers, letting her savor the taste, too.

"See how delicious you are? It's even better when you come."

"So make me come."

"Ah, I would, but you dropped your hands, Emma. Those were the rules."

She pauses, casting her gaze downward. "I couldn't help it. I needed to touch you."

"Should we stop?"

"No," she says adamantly. "I told you I want to play."

I close my eyes, willing my heart rate to slow down. It's elevated and spiked, rising with every one of her determined nods and concentrated glances.

"Okay. If something hurts, or you don't like it, or you want to stop, promise you'll say your word."

"I promise."

I scoot to the edge of the bed, feet resting on the floor. "Come here. Over my knee." Taking her hand in mine, I shift her so her chest drapes over my right leg and her ass hangs over my left. I trace down her spine, over her vertebrae, then back up. I've dabbled in spanking before and have always enjoyed it; as a guy who likes to be in control, there's not many positions better than this. Plus, her ass is a sight to behold. "Doing okay?"

"Yes," she whispers, squirming on my lap and rubbing against my cock. I don't hold back my groan because I want her to know how well she's doing. How perfect she is. How fucking honored I am to earn her trust again and again, trying new things and learning all the stuff she might like. I rest my hand on her ass, giving it a gentle squeeze before I raise my palm and bring it down, connecting with her sweet, soft skin.

I'm not prepared for the way her breathing hitches and the moan she releases. It's not some stupid sound she's faking so I can feel like I'm doing the right thing. It's authentic. Raw. So enjoyable and wanting *more*.

I'm so unbelievably fucked.

"How many?" she asks, grinding against me. I'm about to toss her onto the bed and fuck her senseless, this game be damned.

"Seven," I randomly spit out.

"I can take it."

I massage the area my hand vacated, rubbing in small, soothing circles. "I know you can."

Another smack.

Another moan. Louder than before.

"That's two. I need five more. I want five more."

I'll give you a hundred million if it keeps you here with me.

"Whatever you want." I smack her twice in a row, on either cheek, meaning the words with a sincere ferocity.

"Give me three more, Henry."

I pause the slaps as I caress my fingers over the marks I've created before dipping between her cheeks, my pinky skimming over the only place of her I haven't been inside yet. Ever so slightly, I push, not close to actually entering her, but letting her know I'm there. And what I want.

She gasps.

Then bucks her hips.

Then *moans*.

Another note I mentally jot down.

"What are you doing?"

"Daydreaming," I reply, dropping my hand, not wanting to do something without permission. "Wondering what it would be like to take your ass."

"Are you going to do that tonight?"

"No. We'll have to work up to it."

"I think I'd enjoy having you come in my ass."

I almost blow a load right there, in my briefs, not a care in the goddamn world. "Is that so?" Two more spanks landing on either cheek, and Emma lifts her ass in the air, presenting it to me. "You're my perfect other half."

"One more, Henry. Please."

The final plea does something to my brain, annihilating my coherent thoughts to shreds. Getting her off is the only thing that will quell my hunger and desire. My hand trembles as I spank her one last time, the hardest yet, my palm stinging in the aftermath. She clenches my calf with her hands and I stroke her back, rubbing between her shoulder blades as her breathing returns to slow and steady.

"Are you okay?" I ask, the need to check on her strong and primal. She nods, peeling herself off me and dropping to her knees, not meeting my gaze.

"I loved every second."

She's embarrassed to admit it. I can understand the hesitation; it's always a little awkward after the first new bedroom experience, unsure of how the other is going to react to the rapture provided or gained. It's clear she enjoyed the last few minutes, and I know we'll be doing that again *very* soon. I'm picturing her in my bed, on her stomach, ass in the air and hands tied together as I kiss every forbidden part of her body. I lick my lips in anticipation.

"So did I," I agree, saving the image for another time. "I owe someone an orgasm."

"Not yet." She skates her hands up my thighs, nails pressing into my veins, and she stops at the waistband of my briefs. "May I?"

"Fuck yes." I rock back onto my elbows, raising my hips so she can move the underwear away. "See something you like?"

"Mhm." The ends of her hair tickling my legs. She licks up the length of my dick, tasting both sides of the shaft before putting the head in her mouth and swirling her tongue.

"Jesus," I groan, twisting the blonde strands blocking her face around my wrist. I want to watch her while she sucks me down. Emma takes me into her mouth fully, not stopping until she's devoured me whole, nose pressed against my body, inhaling deeply.

I shutter my eyes closed, praying I don't explode down her throat within the first six seconds. The plan is almost foiled when she reaches out and fondles my balls, causing me to curse, a string of expletives entering the room.

She chuckles then hums against me, the rival sensations vibrating from her mouth as her teeth graze up from the base back to the head. Releasing me, she begins to pump with her hand, a smooth, purposeful sequence.

"I want you to finish in my mouth," she declares, sinking back down and taking me again.

I yank roughly on her hair, her neck bending back. "Sorry, princess. You can't be over my knee, rubbing that wet pussy against my leg like the needy angel you are, and not expect me to take you how I know we both want."

I stand, scooping her in my arms, and depositing her on the mattress. My words might be aggressive, but I try to move with care.

"Condoms are in the drawer."

I reach over, pulling the drawer open so forcefully, it almost falls to the floor. I take out a packet, rip it open with my teeth, and roll it over my dick.

I've literally never been this hard in my life. I'm throbbing painfully and the pre-cum dripping out of my head doesn't even bother hiding itself.

"How do you want me?"

"Turn around. Hold the wall. Above the headboard."

She listens, back arching as her ass sticks out behind her, proudly on display for my eyes only. I relish in the red shade of her cheeks, the outline of my palm noticeable.

Fucking hell. What an exquisite sight. I nudge her thighs apart with my knees and let my hands rest on her hips, tugging her toward me. A kiss on her neck is the only warning I give her as I push inside her pussy, watching as she takes me inch by excruciating inch, walls clenching around me and welcoming me back home.

"Henry," she moans, golden hair spilling over her slim shoulders. "More. Give me all of you."

All of me?

The command could be construed as a physical or emotional request. Does she want me to pound into her until she can't take anymore, muttering depraved things under my breath while she milks my cock in her bedroom, right here, right now?

Or does she want me to whisper all the promises I intend to keep when it comes to her, well past the hours of tonight and this rendezvous, the time on the clock not signaling anything except another day I get to experience by her side?

Promises like commitment.

The dedication to making her happy.

Vowing to help her smile.

Trying to be the best man I can be. For her.

Both realistic possibilities puncture my lungs. I want her to see all of me. The flaws and insecurities and inexperience. I want her to have all of me. To care for all of me, including the parts she's yet to discover. And I want to offer her the same in return, eager to dive deeper into the pools of her wonder and perfection. I want her so badly it physically *hurts*.

It's overwhelming, the ask. Deliriously empowering. My staunchly non-relationship, anti-monogamy heart crumbles and cracks, disintegrating into a pile of rubble and debris, replaced with fresh-faced *tomorrows* and *forevers* and *yes, baby, anything you want. I adore you.*

I sever the deep thoughts with a forceful thrust. My attention is back to the present. This moment. And the woman I'm buried in.

Two more movements and our hips are fused together. I reach around her body, finding her clit and rubbing in a circle, exactly how she likes.

"This is the first time I've been inside you when you've actually been mine," I whisper in her ear, dropping my mouth and biting her neck. Emma groans, digging her fingers into my thigh and spurring me on. Asking for more.

More what, baby? More hopes and dreams? More roughness and tenderness? How about both?

"We're not pretending, are we? We're not faking," I continue. "When you come on my cock, Sunflower, and I know you will, you better be loud. Because now that I'm inside you, fucking you, *protecting* you, caring for you, and this is finally real? You're never going to get me to leave. There should not be a single doubt in your mind that I'm completely and wholly yours, Emma. For as long as you'll have me."

I shove her hips away, up my length, nearly slipping out, before slamming them back against me. It's almost too much. Too dizzying. Consuming. Yeah, I'm fucking her hard, but beneath all of the rugged motions and filthy words is something more... more devoted. More fulfilling. More impactful.

"I'm yours, too, Henry." She falls onto her elbows, chin turning onto her shoulder as she watches me, mouth agape, silent awe etched on her face.

Yours, Henry.

A poisonous arrow to my heart.

"Do you like watching me fuck you, Emma? Do you like being filled up with my cock?" I pinch her nipple and her eyes flutter closed. "Do you want me to record how you look riding me, so you can see how well you take every inch like the good fucking girl you are?"

She comes first. Always. I can tell she's almost there; she cries out, tightening around me, walls convulsing around my dick, unable to answer my question.

One final swipe over her clit and she's exploding, words muddled as she gasps for air. I bite my lip, wanting to call out her name. Scream it from the rooftops and declare her mine to anyone who will listen. Five more thrusts inside her sweet, tight temple and I'm done, body draping over hers as I finish, my legs shaking as my release continues for several seconds.

Wiping the sweat off my forehead, I take a moment to collect myself. I hear a giggle, and finally open my eyes. Emma's staring at me, and I feel self-conscious under her eye.

"Yes?" I ask, wincing as I retreat out of her, settling back on my shins and waiting for her to speak.

"I like bedroom Henry. Bedroom Henry is hot."

"Is regular Henry not hot?"

"Oh, he is. Very much so." Her arms circle my neck, chest pressing against mine. "But regular Henry would never come up to me in the office and say he wants to... What was it? Take my ass."

"Maybe regular Henry will pin you against your office wall, hike your skirt up, and fuck you right there, using your underwear as a gag since you don't like to be quiet," I retort. "And then he'll make you sit in your chair all day without cleaning up, so you can feel the remnants of what you asked for on your legs for hours after."

"If you're trying to scare me, it's not working."

"I'll add it to the list of Emma Fantasies I'm keeping a thorough record of."

"Speaking of... Yikes, this is kind of awkward to talk about. I'm clean."

"I am, too. I got tested a month ago."

"You haven't been with anyone since?" she asks curiously.

Not since the very first email.

"Nope."

"Really?"

"Really, Emma."

"I... I thought maybe you just weren't bringing people to the office anymore, but you might still be hooking up with people other places."

I cradle her cheek against my palm. "No one. Not a single one. For months," I say fiercely.

She blinks and looks away, sniffing as she breaks our eye contact. "I had no idea."

"Now you do. Are you on birth control?"

"I am, and clearly I'm not sleeping with anyone else if my years-long dry spell isn't enough proof. Maybe next time, it can just be you and me? No condoms?"

"You need to stop saying all the right things. I'm beginning to think you were created just for me," I murmur, kissing her forehead. "Want to shower?"

"Yeah. I'm sticky. There's chocolate in places where it shouldn't be since *someone* can't seem to eat ice cream correctly."

"Allow me to clean up my mess. Then we can discover all the fun things we can do in the shower together."

She squeaks with excitement and jumps off the bed, running toward the bathroom off to the side. I grin as I watch her disappear.

I don't want to sneak out and make an escape. I don't want to hide or cower away, searching for an excuse to leave and never talk to her again. I want to stay here, with Emma, through the night, holding her against me as she falls fast asleep. I want to kiss her forehead when she wakes up, being the first thing to make her smile in the new day.

I hope she knows how serious I am about this.

About *her*.

I never want to let her go.

THIRTY-NINE

HENRY

"HOW ARE YOU AND EMMA DOING?"

My mom's question comes through the phone as I pull the doors to the restaurant open, making my way to the back corner where the group has already assembled. I nod my head in Jack and Noah's direction as I lean against the wood, my back turned toward my friends.

"We're doing great," I say, smiling at the answer and the excitement I feel at knowing I'll see her soon.

"Are you? If something happened, Henry, you can tell us. We wouldn't be mad."

"What are you talking about?"

"I meant with the two of you. The party is over. If you were trying to make us happy by having a girlfriend, you can drop the game now."

"There's no game, Mom. Seriously. We're doing great. We haven't been up to visit in the last couple of weeks because we've been spending our free time together. Work has also been stressful as hell, so finding a professional and personal balance has been kind of difficult."

"Okay. I love you, Hen."

"Love you too, Mom. Can I call you later this weekend?"

"I know that's code for you're out with your friends and rushing me off the phone. Tell everyone I say hi."

"Will do."

Clicking my phone off, I scrub my hand over my face as I slide into the booth.

"You good?" Noah asks.

"Yeah. I'm fine. Just Mom."

"Is Emma coming tonight?"

"Yeah. She should be here any minute."

She's meeting my friends tonight, and I'm nervous as hell.

It's been two weeks since my parents' party, and every day with Emma is like a dream. It sounds stupid, but it's the truth.

We switch off where we have sleepovers a few nights a week while also spending some nights apart, doing things on our own or with our friends. When we're apart, we check in and share how much we miss each other—turns out I miss her a whole fucking lot when she's not around.

We go out to dinner, then hit up dollar bowling night, sharing a slice of pizza and greasy nachos. Sometimes we forgo going out at all, staying in to order delivery and lounging on the couch in our sweatpants, laughing over mindless television shows and critiquing people's baking skills.

Being with her is… effortless.

Easy.

When she's curled up beside me, still fast asleep after I wake up, I search for her, wanting to pull her closer because she's too far away.

In the mornings when we're apart, my phone is in my hands before my eyes open, already typing out a good morning message because I want her to have something to read when she wakes up.

I didn't think a relationship could be like this.

I was expecting eye rolls and arguments over stupid stuff.

Disappointment about missing time with my friends, or feeling forced to do chores and activities I don't enjoy.

Those moments might come, sure. It's early.

But right now, everything is… perfect.

I don't see how it gets much better than this.

At work, we sneak off, desperate for a few moments alone together. I press her into my door, hands pinned above her head while I untuck her shirt, needing to feel her bare skin under mine for even just a second. It's the only way I can get through my day.

She yanks me into the supply closet, asking for help to find paper clips while she kisses me senseless, and I'm left tucking my dick into the waistband of my pants as I leave the enclave, hard as a rock for thirty minutes afterwards.

I bring a plate of food for her and leave it in her office when she's out running errands.

I come back from a meeting to sticky notes hidden on the inside of my desk, grinning like an idiot at her smiley faces and *hope you're having a good day* affirmations, complete with a cute little heart.

My eyes watch every male colleague like a hawk, ready to swoop in and destroy them if they so much as *look* at her the wrong way.

And if they open their mouth and speak to her inappropriately?

I'm going to have a lot of blood on my hands, with absolutely no regrets.

The only looming issue we have is the partner announcement, which should come a week from Monday. We try not to talk about it when we're alone together, preferring to not acknowledge the elephant in the room until the last possible moment.

According to the employee handbook, partner/attorney relationships are explicitly forbidden and grounds for termination. I know we've enjoyed sneaking around and being reckless up to this point, but the threat of losing our jobs isn't a fun addition.

We'll deal with that when it happens.

For now, I'm basking in the bliss that is Emma Burns and enjoying the here and now.

"Finally! I can't wait to meet the girl Henry's been drooling over for weeks. I also can't wait to tell her about the crisis you had in our kitchen. Even the most perfect men can have meltdowns," Jo comments.

"I swear to God, Bowen, if you think about sharing that with her, I will find a piece of your past and blackmail the shit out of you."

My phone buzzes and I yank it from my pocket.

Nothing's changed.

VRG: I just got out of the Uber! I'll be inside in a minute.

HD: Can't wait to see you. I'm starting to think my friends don't believe you're actually real.

HD: Even Noah is pretending like he doesn't know you.

VRG: Maybe I won't come inside.

VRG: Maybe I'll make you squirm for a couple of minutes. An hour, maybe.

I chuckle as I stand from the booth, walking to the door so I can greet her privately. The gang can be intimidating, and I don't want her to think she's jumping into a pile of lava with their jokes and sarcasm.

The door to the restaurant opens, and she's there, looking as beautiful, if not more, as she did when I left her two hours ago at the office. She's traded her skirt for jeans that hug her curves. Her hair is down, framing her smiling face. When her eyes find mine over the sea of people, she lights up, and I grin at the sight of her.

"Hey," I murmur, bending down to kiss her right on the mouth, not giving a fuck who's watching. She giggles against my lips, arms wrapping around my waist.

"Hi, back. You know, I'm not typically a fan of PDA, but I could get used to this kind of greeting."

"Is that so? We'll have to revisit that exhibitionist side. It's Friday, Sunflower. Your place or mine?"

"Needy, are you?" she jokes, poking my stomach before dragging her fingernails over my muscles. "Mine. What games are we going to play tonight?"

My lips drop to her hair, pressing a kiss to her blonde waves and ghosting over to the shell of her ear, my voice hot against her skin. "Whatever games you want to play, sweetheart. You know what? Forget my friends. Let's go home right now. I'm thinking a blindfold. And two of my ties."

Emma giggles, slipping her hand into mine. "Nice try. The blindfolds can wait. It's time to meet the gang. I want to hear all the embarrassing stories about you."

Leading her over to the crowded table, I think my heart is going to fall out of my chest with nerves. "Everyone, this is Emma. Emma, you know Noah. That's Neil and his fiancé, Rebecca. Jack and Jo. And Patrick and Lola."

"Hi!" she says enthusiastically, giving them all a wave. "It's nice to meet everyone."

"I'm so glad you're here. I can't wait to spill all of Henry's deepest, darkest secrets."

"How about the time he didn't realize it was daylight savings time and got to work an hour early?"

"Or when he forgot it months later and got there an hour late?"

"Oh! The time he washed his reds with whites and ruined his new dress shirt."

"See," I whisper in Emma's ear. "They're full of shit. Believe nothing."

"Will you boys get out of the way and act like gentlemen? Let the woman sit down. Where are your manners?" Lola flicks Patrick's ear, and that sets everyone in motion.

My friends tumble out of the booth. Jack dashes off to grab a fresh round of drinks. Noah tracks down some menus. Jo pats the space next to her, offering a friendly smile. Emma's eyes flick to mine, and I raise my eyebrows, checking in, making sure she's okay.

She gives me a nod, taking a seat in the booth and focusing her attention on the women who are welcoming her with open arms. I hear phrases like *"badass attorney"* and *"fuck the patriarchy"* get thrown around.

"She's doing okay," Noah says, nudging my side. Some of the tension deteriorates as the girls all laugh at something Lola says.

"She doesn't seem nervous," Patrick agrees. "This is so exciting, H."

"I feel like I'm on a freaking roller coaster," I grumble, accepting the beer Jack hands me. I take a swig, wiping my mouth clear of foam. "It's only been a few weeks of really knowing each other, but I can already tell she's important to me. Jesus, that sounds cheesy."

"They grow up so fast," Neil sighs.

"They're looking over here and giggling. Why are they giggling?" I ask.

"I hope they're talking about the time you forgot your boxers under your white bathing suit and didn't realize until you were climbing out of the ocean," Jack says, tapping his chin. "Everyone got a glance at that nice dick of yours."

"This is why I keep you around, Lancaster. You really know how to stroke my ego."

The next two hours pass in the blink of an eye. Emma laughs at all the stupid jokes my friends make, indulges in deep conversation with the other women, barely paying attention to me when I kiss her cheek, and holds my hand under the table, fingers squeezing mine every few minutes, reassuring me she's not going anywhere, even after hearing the stories.

Thank fuck for that.

Watching her interact with my friends seems more monumental than watching her interact with my family. These are the people I see every day. The ones I spend my free time with. I want them to all get along, because they are all important to me.

"Next round is one me," I announce, our glasses all empty.

"I'm going to run to the restroom, then I'll help you carry the tray back," Emma says, climbing out of the booth behind me. I swing our hands back and forth until we reach the bar.

"You know I can carry a tray by myself." I press a kiss to her forehead, savoring the smell of lilacs from her shampoo.

"I just wanted an excuse to hold your hand in front of people. I like everyone knowing you're mine."

"You can't say shit like that to me in public, Sunflower. It makes me want to toss you onto the counter and bury my head between your legs. That possessiveness is hot," I mumble, giving her ass a light tap.

"Maybe I'll send you a picture when I'm in there. Add counter tossing to the list," she teases, sauntering away.

I grin while I watch her disappear, teeth biting into my bottom lip as her hips sway and she looks at me over her shoulder, giving me a wink before pulling open the door to the bathroom.

My phone buzzes, and the speed that I pull it out is borderline pathetic.

VRG: Made you look. <3

HD: Taunting me, Emma? Maybe you'd like to revisit being over my knee.

VRG: Yes, please.

I pocket the device before I do something stupid, like barge into the women's bathroom, lift her onto the sink and go to town right there, her jeans at her ankles while I make her come all over my dick.

Or in my mouth.

Or my fingers.

The possibilities are endless.

I'm distracted when I put in our group order, leaning against the counter while I wait and peering over my shoulder every five seconds, waiting for Emma to return.

"Hey, stranger," a familiar voice says. I turn to my left to find Shelby, one of my former flings, standing there.

"Hey! What the heck are you doing here?"

Her job brings her in and out of the city for work, and we've hooked up a dozen times. I haven't seen her in eight months, and there's a clench in my stomach when she leans in for a hug.

Patting her shoulder awkwardly, I pull away, taking a step to my right, creating a distance between us.

"My friend's birthday party. How have you been?"

"Not too bad. Busy with work. What about you? How's the modeling gig going?"

The tray of drinks I'm supposed to deliver back to my table finally arrives, and I want to sigh in relief.

"Great, actually. I just got an ad campaign with a big-time lingerie designer. You know how much I love my bedtime sets."

"Congratulations. That's awesome."

"Thanks. Who are you here with tonight?" she asks, looking over my shoulder and grinning when she finds the space empty. "Alone? I was hoping I'd stumble into you."

"I'm here with my girlfriend, actually. She's meeting my friends tonight."

"Girlfriend? Has hell frozen over? I never thought I'd see the day when Henry Dawson settled down. Where is this mystery woman? I'd love to tell her to get out now. How long have you two been together? A day?"

My eyes narrow. "A couple of weeks. Things are going well, and I enjoy spending time with her. We also work together."

"What a bummer. I wore red specifically for you. Look."

Shelby takes my hand in hers, bringing it to the strap of her dress before I yank it away like I just touched acid.

Wrong.

Wrong.

Wrong.

Wrong.

The quick press of my fingers on Shelby's skin makes me feel slimy and gross.

I want nothing to do with her.

There are no old feelings stirring up, curious about what could happen next.

They lie dormant, paying no attention to the female in front of me, knowing she's not the one I'm head over fucking heels for.

Zero part of me wants to continue down this road, and I back up, doing everything but shove the girl away.

"Did you miss the part where I said I'm here with my girlfriend? I'm not interested in hooking up with you. Those days are long gone," I say through gritted teeth.

"Oh, Henry, it's cute you think one woman can change you."

"Hey, sweetie." Emma joins me at my side, her arm slipping around my waist. "Am I interrupting something?"

Sighing in relief at her arrival, I practically lift her into my arms and spin her around. "There you are, honey. This is Shelby."

"Henry was telling me you two are dating. That's so unusual for him! Congratulations on being the one to wear him down finally enough to commit," Shelby laughs, maliciousness laced through the statement. "You're brave to plunge into a relationship with this stud."

Emma tosses her hair over her shoulder with a placid shrug, her stoic facade showing no hints of cracking. "Maybe. But this stud and so-called playboy is going home with me. He'll say my name when I suck his dick later. He'll kiss my thigh while he calls me princess and the best he's ever had. And after we're finished, hickeys on my neck and his fingerprints on my ass, he'll fall asleep next to me while you go home jealous and alone. Enjoy the rest of your evening."

My jaw drops and my eyes widen at her brazen dismissal. Grabbing the tray of drinks off the counter, I follow behind Emma to our table, my free hand resting on the small of her back as we walk.

"Holy shit, baby," I breathe out, teeth nipping at her neck.

"Did you just tell her about sucking my dick later? Jesus fucking Christ, I'm two seconds away from getting on the ground right now and worshiping you like you deserve. I can definitely get behind possessive Emma."

"Literally or figuratively?"

"Oh, both, sweetheart. Obviously. Fuck the blindfold. Let's try you in charge in the bedroom. I'd fucking crawl if you asked me to."

"I think I'd like to see you on your hands and knees for me," she says, kissing my cheek as we arrive back at the table.

"Your wish is my command."

"Please don't tell me you two banged in the bathroom and that's why the drinks took so long," Noah groans, helping to distribute the fresh beverages.

"We didn't, but it was close. We ran into someone at the bar and Em had a verbal showdown."

"Who?" Patrick asks curiously. "Was it that douchebag you work with?"

My hand lands on Emma's thigh as we take our seats, following the stitching of her jeans toward her hip.

"I hate that guy," Lola seethes. "$100 says he has the smallest dick in the world."

"Are they talking about Brad?" Emma whispers, and I nod.

"Yeah. They're very much Team Not Brad."

"I knew I liked your friends."

Smiling, I pull her closer to me. "It was Shelby, unfortunately."

"Oh, shit. Wait, speaking of banging in the bathroom and Shelby, you two did that once, didn't you?" Neil laughs, and Emma tenses under my arm. "Yeah. At the club that one time. The line got so long someone came and knocked on the door and you—"

"Neil," I hiss, giving him a scathing look. "Shut the fuck up."

"What? It's not my fault it took you 31 years to finally stick to one woman. Emma. Trust me. You're substantially better."

"Thanks for the compliment," she mutters, downing her fresh glass of wine in three gulps.

No one else speaks, and a block of dread settles in my stomach. Emma doesn't pull away from me, but she's stiff and rigid.

There are no more smiles.

No more laughter.

Her eyes have grown dimmer since we sat back down, and when I fumble for her hand under the table, trying to see if she's okay, she keeps her palms folded in her lap out of my reach.

Tell me what I did, baby, so I can fix it.

Let me make it right.

The rest of the night is stilted, conversation feeling forced and my apprehension grows with every minute her frown stays on her lips.

"Do you still want to hang out tonight?" I ask her hesitantly as the rest of my friends disperse at the end of the night, waving their goodbyes and leaving us standing alone outside the restaurant.

"Yeah. We can."

That dread doesn't settle with her agreement. Doesn't abate. Doesn't offer me any reprieve. We sit silently in the car on the way back to her house, only exchanging a handful of meaningless words about how cold it's getting outside.

I can hear the wheels turning in her head from here. She's fidgeting with her hands, fingers intertwining and palms squeezing together. Her foot taps nervously on the floor mat, and I watch her eyes dart to the window, over to me, then back to the glass, no further conversation tumbling from her mouth.

When I pull into her driveway, I shift the car to park and turn my body toward her.

"Hey," I say gently. "You okay, Sunflower?"

Gnawing on her lip, it takes a moment before Emma finally drags her gaze to me, and I reel back when I see her eyes full of tears.

"Sweetheart. What's wrong?" My thumb reaches over the

center console to wipe a tear away, cupping her cheek. Her skin is cold beneath my touch, and I use my free hand to adjust the car heater, doing my best to warm her up. "Talk to me."

"It's… It's so stupid," she whispers, sniffing and peeling my fingers away. "I just…" Pausing, she sighs deeply, shaking her head. "What Neil said got me thinking. It's the same thing Betsy said at the party. And Shelby tonight. A trend people in your life have noticed about you."

"Neil? Don't listen to him. He's an idiot."

I'm going to fucking murder him for the stupid quip he said at the table, reminiscing on my history about bathroom hookups.

"I'm sure he is, but seeing you touch another woman… Henry, it really sucked."

"I didn't touch her because I wanted to, Emma. She made me. I swear."

"And you could've walked away. No one was forcing you to stand there and talk to her."

"What do you mean? Talk to me, baby. Help me understand. I want to understand."

She lets out a huff. "It's hard for me not to compare myself to her. To anyone you've been with. I know I said all those words, and I sounded so smug, but Henry, that woman is freaking stunning. You've snuck off with her when you were with your friends, on a night very much like tonight, and did God knows what with her. It's like… when you put the two of us side by side, why in the world would you *ever* pick me?"

The crack in her voice, the uncertainty in her eyes, the tremble racking her body and the pure fucking sadness ebbing off of her rip my soul in two.

I want to curse. I want to yell. I want to scream and cry and kick my feet into the ground.

"When I saw you touch her," Emma continues, chucking another knife to my chest. A dagger to my heart. "I wondered if you would like touching her more than you like touching me. I realize how… how irrational this all is. How this is a *me* problem.

I'm the one making comparisons. I'm the one harboring self-doubt. It was barely a second of your hand on her. I'm just fearful that I can't make you happy. And I would resent myself for trying to force you to be something you're not."

"The only thing I want to is to be with you. That's it, Em."

"We're out of our bubble and drifting into the real world. And with that drifting comes realizations and recognitions. We dove headfirst into this... this relationship fast. Between you never having dated anyone before and so much time passing since my last partner... Maybe we moved too fast."

Withdrawing from my hold, she opens the car door and stumbles out, closing it firmly shut behind her.

I jump out, hurrying after her, determined to get this right.

"Sweetheart, you aren't being irrational. You're nervous because this is... this is getting serious between us, I think. And I'm fucking terrified, too. Every goddamn day I'm afraid I'm going to mess this up. Look what happened tonight. I did mess up. Because I don't... I didn't understand the boundaries there. But I do now."

"I need some time to think about this. To think about us. All these people are making comments about your past. About who you used to be. You've changed. I see it in the way you look at me. I'm just... overwhelmed."

"Are you..." I stumble on the brick leading to her door, gripping my chest. "Are you breaking up with me?"

"No," she says firmly, shaking her head. "No. I... I like you, Henry. A lot. I just need some space to process all of this. Some time alone. The jokes and comments... They're getting to me. I can't brush them off as easily as you can, I guess."

"Okay." The agreement is like tar in my mouth, but I'll give her whatever she wants. "Okay, baby. Time. It's all yours."

Emma's lip quivers, and she steps toward me, giving me a hug. I put my chin on the top of her head, breathing in her scent. Indulging in her warmth. Trying to stop the tears that are forming in my own eyes, threatening to fall, because I think I did something wrong and there's nothing I can do to help fix it.

"I wish I didn't have a past, Emma, but I do," I say softly, hands reluctant to let her go. Like the second she pulls away, she'll be gone forever. "It's always going to be a part of me, and I'm sorry you have to be subjected to it. I'm sorry for letting Shelby touch me. I'm just..." Sighing heavily, I press a kiss to her forehead, cupping her cheeks in mine and staring at her one final time. "I'm so sorry, Sunflower."

"I know, Henry. It's not forever. Just for a little while. I'll talk to you soon."

She steps away, my hands falling from her skin, and a chill goes through me from the loss.

With a parting glance and a sad smile, she walks to her front door, opens it, and pulls it firmly closed.

Everything hurts in her absence.

My head. My stomach. My chest.

My goddamn heart.

You're who I want, baby.

No one else.

You were made for me.

I'm sorry.

I stare at the space Emma vacated, and I feel empty. Hollow. Broken and incomplete. Resisting the urge to follow her inside, to drop to my knees and apologize from now until eternity, I turn for my car, prepared to drive away from her.

At the snap of a finger, my world has turned upside down. Crashed and burned. And all I want to do is jump into the flames, too.

What have I done?

FORTY

EMMA

PAIN IS A TRICKY, fickle bastard, ebbing and flowing like a gentle stream one minute, then turning into a catastrophic tsunami the next, threatening total devastation.

It's not even full-fledged pain I'm experiencing, but more like a delirious confusion.

You think you have your shit together and then a passing memory, smell, or reminder of what caused the puzzlement and ache you're enduring comes roaring back into view, cascading over you like a waterfall and blocking every breath you're trying to gulp down, struggling to survive and stay afloat.

The most infuriating and agonizing part is when you never thought *you* would be the one to feel the pain, too caught up in a picture-perfect life to consider any different outcomes than the one you dream about.

The hurt catches you off guard, unexpected and unwelcome, not because of what happened, but because of the person who inflicted it.

The hero-turned-villain who caused your fall from grace, flicking a fatal dagger into your heart with a lackadaisical swish of their wrist, releasing emotion and turmoil you never thought possible.

I've spent all my time alone weighing the potential solutions to how I'm feeling, and what happens next.

Where do I go from here?

What should I do?

And who do I do it with?

I scheduled a call with my therapist, discussing that persistent sensation of inadequacy and feeling like I'm the one who might hinder someone's happiness.

Before Henry and I got together, I never pitted myself against other women. I recognized and accepted their beauty, and understood that we all have different physical features that are admired and appreciated by others. Now it's a comparison game, measuring my flaws against their perfections.

I know he has a past. I know he's been with other women. Seeing one in the flesh, talking to him and making him touch her solidified the knowledge that he had a life before me. A life I wasn't a part of, but other women were. A life I know I need to accept because he's not that guy anymore.

My therapist tasked me with jotting down some reasons why Henry is with *me*. What he's told me he likes about *me*. And what I like about myself, too.

It felt egotistical at first, until I filled a whole paper front and back with positive characteristics. It made me realize that I have a lot of good to offer, and Henry's done nothing but reiterate those strengths the last few weeks.

Deep down, I know he did nothing wrong.

I know he didn't willingly walk to the bar, search for someone to chat with, and touch her because he wanted to. When I came back from the bathroom, he looked uncomfortable. Like he would rather be anywhere except in her presence.

I heard the conviction in his voice when he told her he wasn't interested in hooking up.

The relief when he pulled me into his embrace.

The sheer awe and pride when I told her off in an uncharacteristically unkind way.

I also saw the hurt on his face when he recognized what he did was wrong. The way he didn't argue with me or call me a liar or someone who was overreacting.

In the three days since, I've learned I trust him completely. I just carry a lot of self-doubt.

Maybe I always have and always will, a constant emotion that's been prevalent since middle school and in no hurry to leave.

Wondering if I was smart enough to get into my dream college, even though my grades suggested I was.

Wondering if I performed well enough on my LSAT, even though my score reflected I succeeded tremendously.

Wondering if I was better suited for a different career, one where I didn't have to hear remark after remark about my gender.

Remarks that imply I got the position I'm in because I'm a woman.

Because I slept with someone. Because I'm a tick in a box and not valued for my skill set.

Because.

Because.

Because.

Again and again and again, an endless cycle.

Henry has never given me any reason to doubt myself. He never has wandering eyes. He never spends hours on his phone, texting other women or looking at pictures on social media. But with that self doubt comes a niggle of worry. The smallest, tiniest fear that one day he'll wake up and I won't be good enough.

One day, he'll get bored.

One day, he'll want his old life back.

Sighing, I finish an email, scheduling another virtual therapy session for later this week. I already feel better after two conversations, and I hope if I continue down this path, I might finally break free of this lingering, oppressive cloud of *not good enough*, seeing the sun once more.

The knock on my door causes me to look up, checking my phone to see if I have any new messages.

"Em? It's Nic. Open up."

I smile, shutting my laptop and walking toward the door, turning the knob and leaning against the doorjamb.

"A smile?" she asks, raising an eyebrow. "We must be having a good day today."

"Yeah," I nod, gesturing her inside and closing the door behind us. "We are."

"Talk to me. What's going on?"

Nicole and I don't have secrets after being friends for close to twenty years. She knows I've fallen for Henry. She knows about what happened at the bar. She knows I go to therapy. She knows I'm trying to sort through some things, but I think she also knows I'm hurting, missing the man who's absent from my life.

"I spent some time making lists of all my strengths this morning," I say, settling onto the couch. "Turns out, I have quite a few."

She laughs, plopping next to me and tucking a piece of hair behind my ear. "Yeah. You do. Anyone could have told you that, but self-discovery is important. How are you feeling?"

"Better. Almost good. Like I'm nearly there."

"Has Henry reached out to you?"

"No. He said he'd give me time, and he's giving it to me. I... I appreciate him keeping that promise."

She hums, studying my face. "You miss him."

"A lot. Him not being here isn't making this any easier, but it's also showing me how much I do want him in my life. I'm at the point now where I know if I hadn't interrupted their conversation, nothing physical would have happened. I know Henry would have walked away. And I know he would have told me about it afterward, too."

Nicole nods, obviously impressed. "Your doctor is really fucking good."

"And worth the fourth of my paycheck she costs," I laugh, pulling my knees to my chest.

"So. What happens next?"

"I'm not sure. Logically, talking to Henry is going to happen at some point soon. And I should probably get back to the office. I told Wallace I was sick these last two days so I could have some time to decompress. Now that I've taken a step away, I'm ready to dive back in."

"I'm proud of you, Em. You deserve a guy who would run into battle for you without thinking twice and ask questions after. A guy who would sacrifice himself to keep you safe. A guy who cares about your happiness above his own. Do you think Henry is that guy for you?"

I consider her question.

In every scenario I've envisioned the last few days, it always ends with the same conclusion:

Him.

Waiting for me.

And the smile I get when I arrive.

"Yeah," I say. "He is. Without a doubt. I never thought we'd have some cheesy, romantic reconnection, Nic, but I miss him so much. It's never been like this before."

"Why the hell are you sitting here with me when you could be out with your man? What is wrong with you?"

I laugh, kicking her with my foot. "Because I like you and I still need another few days. I'm sure about him. But I also want to be certain I'm sure about me, too."

"I want to go on the record and say that if he ever does anything to hurt you, I will hunt him down and relish in the pain I'll inflict."

"And that right there is why you're my best friend."

"When do you think you'll head back to work?"

"Tomorrow. There's only a few days until the partner announcement anyway, and I need to be there for that."

"Promise you'll keep me posted about what happens next?"

Reaching over to grab her hand, I squeeze her palm against mine. "Duh. Thanks for checking on me. I appreciate it. I promise to reciprocate the generosity when you're having a crisis over a relationship."

Nicole scoffs, rolling her eyes. "Never going to happen. At this rate, I'll be on social security benefits before I find a man."

"Never say never," I sing. She flings a pillow at me, and for the first time in days I laugh, finally feeling like things are falling back into place.

FORTY-ONE

HENRY

TWO DAYS.

Emma hasn't been at work in two days.

Two agonizing, never-ending days.

And I think I'm going insane.

I haven't slept. I haven't eaten. I've done nothing but think about her.

The sad smile on her lips when she shut her front door.

The pain in her voice when she was sharing what was going through her head.

The tension in her shoulders and the worry she's carrying.

I've done nothing but think about how I can make this right.

I haven't found a solution yet. A time machine would be preferred so I could go back and keep my goddamn hands to myself.

Emma's right.

I could've stepped away.

I *should* have stepped away.

I've interacted with Shelby enough times to know the turn the conversation was inevitably going to take, and I let it, standing idly by without throwing up firm boundaries from the get go.

I dug my grave, and now I have to suffer.

Never in my existence on Earth have I had the burning desire to take care of someone before. Now, however, this deep, carnal urge to make sure *she's* okay engulfs my every waking thought.

I caused her to hurt.

I caused her pain.

I caused her to be confused and question what we've built.

While all the bones in my body want to sprint back to her house and take her in my arms, cradling her against my chest and apologizing for my actions... I can't move.

I'm immobile.

No matter how much I want to grovel at her feet and repent for my sins, I won't.

The only thing she asked for is time, and I intend to get it to her, no matter how much it hurts me to do so.

I'll sit idly by, waiting.

For her.

If she needs a week, I'll give her seven days.

If she needs a month, I'll give her four weeks.

If she needs a whole damn year, I'll oblige, counting down every hour until I can be with her again, because she's fucking worth it.

It's Wednesday now, four full days after I last saw her, and I'm panicking. Fuck my feelings; I need to know she's physically okay.

She can be angry at me all she wants, but I need her to still be breathing.

If something happened to her, I would never forgive myself.

Work is the last thing on my mind as I pace my office. My eyes stay trained out my open door. When I stand in just the right place, I can peer into Emma's space across the building. I've never done it before because it feels like a giant breach of privacy and really creepy. Today, I'm out of fucks to give, searching for any sign the universe can give me she's okay. I'll take the hatred and I'll take the blame. I have to know she's all right.

The lights in her office are still off, a darkness staring back at me. Taunting me. Testing me. It's already 9:02. For someone exceedingly early and often behind her desk by 7 a.m., it's safe to say she won't be coming in.

I sigh, shoulders hunching, abandoning all hope and collapsing in my chair.

Not today.

Perhaps tomorrow.

The rest of my day is a wash. Words go in one ear and out the other. I have to ask people to repeat themselves multiple times. Paperwork takes twice as long to read. I fumble my speech on a call with a client and mistakenly add an extra zero to a contract. I had to go back and edit 50 pages. When 4:45 creeps around, I've had enough. I stand, stretching my back, when I notice her office. Illuminated.

I blink twice, making sure I'm not projecting what I want to see. Twenty seconds later, Emma strides out, holding her briefcase and keeping her head down, hair obscuring her face. She's real. Not a hallucination.

I want to cry and roar simultaneously at the sight of her. Even from this distance, I can tell she's paler. Skinnier. More closed in and hunched over. Because of me.

The feeble ball of light in my chest—hope—snuffs out like a candle in the wind, plunging my world into total darkness.

Fury and self-loathing boil in my blood. Pulling out my phone with shaky hands, I click on Noah's name.

"What's up, H?" he asks, answering on the third ring.

I swallow and squeeze my eyes closed. No words convey my duress and turmoil.

"Henry? Are you okay?"

"No," I finally croak out, digging the heel of my palm into my eye. "I'm not okay."

"You're scaring the hell out of me. Where are you? What's going on?"

"I fucked up, man. I fucked up so bad. I've never... I don't... I can't..."

Noah curses and I hear muffled voices on the other side of the phone. "Are you at your office?"

I nod, even though he can't see me.

"Don't move. I'm two blocks up. I'll be there soon."

The line goes dead, and I stand still. Taking a deep breath, I count to five, then exhale slowly. I repeat the exercise three more times, muscles and tension uncoiling. The door to my office swings open, hitting the wall. Noah stands in the doorway, fury on his face.

"Don't you ever fucking scare me like that again," he snarls. "You look like shit."

"I feel worse."

"Good. I texted the guys and they're meeting us in fifteen minutes." He reaches for my blazer hanging on the back of the door and tosses it to me. The buttons hit my nose and I wince.

"You did? They are?"

"For once in your goddamn life you're going to open up to us and tell us what the hell is going on that's making you unable to complete a sentence. You're going to be serious and have an honest conversation with your best friends, because if you're hurting, we want to hurt too, you stupid asshole. You have feelings and emotions and it's time you confront and share them. I'm sick of hearing shit from other people. Let's fucking go."

His orders jostle me awake and I turn off my computer monitors and grab my cell phone and bag as quickly as possible. I flick the light off as we walk down the hall, silence nudging its way between us. Noah doesn't speak, and when I sneak a look at him, his jaw is tense.

"Are you mad at me?" I ask, reluctant to know the answer. He wouldn't lie if I pissed him off. A blessing and a curse to have such a blunt and truthful best friend. The elevator doors open and we file inside.

"Henry, I've known you a long time."

"Okay…"

"And in that time, you've done some questionable things.

Things I haven't commented on because it's your life, and you're free to live it how you want."

"What does that have to do with an—"

"You hurt her, man," he exclaims, glaring at me. I've never heard him this loud before, and I'm afraid he's going to slam me against the wall. "You know I love you, and you know I'm always going to be upfront with you and help you when I can. This isn't a game. Emma isn't another notch in your fucking belt. She's a great girl, and you fucked up."

"Do you think you could do a better job than me? Are you going to jump in and be the hero that mends her broken heart? Here comes Noah, the guy that will give you flowers and forevers instead of quick fucks."

"Oh, drop that shit. She's been yours since high school and I would never. You're just too big of a fucking idiot to notice, but maybe now you'll get your head out of your pretentious ass and do something about it. I think if I was with the woman I waited a long time for, I wouldn't go around touching other people. I don't give a fuck what you think."

"Are you serious?"

"We'll talk about this with the guys." He storms out of the elevator with me hot on his heels, not speaking another word as I trail behind him on the sidewalk and into a crappy bar.

Noah walks to a booth in the back corner, taking one side. I mimic him and fiddle with the paper coaster, wishing I could disappear.

"Can I get you boys something?" The smiling waitress stands with her hand on her hip.

"Shots, please," I mumble, handing her my credit card. "And a beer."

"Could you guys be in a weirder spot? When I left school, I was expecting us to at least be at a place where we could order food without getting food poisoning," Patrick jokes, joining us in the booth and scooting next to me.

"I didn't pick this stupid place," I grumble, crossing my arms over my chest.

"You don't get a lot of say right now," Noah retorts.

"Whoa, what did I miss?" Patrick asks, trying to decide if fists are about to be thrown. Noah ignores the question, gesturing to the door.

"Jack and Neil are here."

The final two join us as the waitress brings a tray of shot glasses back.

"I need to get blackout wasted. Maybe that will help me feel something." I grab a glass, throwing the alcohol back without blinking. It burns down my throat, and I welcome the pain.

"I'm confused. Is that why you gathered all of us here?" Neil asks, frowning. "To drink?"

"Yes," I say, throwing back another shot, ignoring Noah's glare. "And I need to talk to you all, apparently."

"Okay, let's slow down," Patrick says kindly, moving the tray out of my reach. "Why don't you tell us what's going on, H?"

"I messed up," I mumble, staring at the table. A scoff from Noah's side of the table reaches my ears, and I want to kick him in the shins. "I messed up, and I don't think I can fix it."

"How?" Jack asks carefully.

"Everyone remembers Friday night, right? When I introduced you all to Emma?"

"Yeah. We had a great time. Jo thinks she's awesome."

"Rebecca loved her."

"Lola asked for her phone number so they can plan a girls' night."

"Well, I... I went too far with Shelby at the bar when Emma was in the bathroom."

"Henry. You didn't—"

"Kiss her? No. I didn't. But I let her touch me. And Emma saw it happen. Then you," I jerk my chin toward Neil, "couldn't shut the hell up, bringing up my past. It freaked Emma out. She said she wasn't sure if I'm ready to be in a relationship. She told me she needs space and doesn't know what kind of guy I want to be. It… It felt wrong to touch someone else. To be touched by someone else. Her hands weren't soft. She was too tall. I didn't like it. It did nothing for me. There was no urge to pull her into the hallway or take her back to my place. I just… I kept thinking about how lucky I am to have someone like Emma, and I went and did this."

The booth is silent for a moment until I hear someone blow out a breath. The sound makes me smile, just marginally, thinking about Emma's romance books. How she complains about all the breaths people let out, apparently forgetting they were holding them.

She's cute when she gets passionate about a topic.

Emma.

My sweet, sweet girl.

I'm sorry I caused you to wilt, Sunflower. It's all my fault.

"Have you ever thought like that before, Henry? When a woman was touching you, did you ever wish you were somewhere else with someone else?" Noah is the first to speak, and his tone is less hostile than before.

Okay, maybe that's an encouraging sign.

"No."

"You weren't trying to sneak around and do something behind Emma's back?"

"God, no. I was proud to tell Shelby I had a girlfriend. And when Emma told her off, I think my eyes turned into cartoon hearts."

"Thank God this is easy," Neil says, and I frown, raising my chin. "I was wondering how long it was going to take before we intervened."

"Easy?"

"You're in love with her, man," Jack says.

"Emma," Patrick clarifies, grinning at me.

I stare at the table, mouth agape. "Hang on. LOVE?" I declare, knocking over my glass. Half the beer spills onto the table and floor. A passing waiter throws me a dirty look and I smile apologetically, grabbing a napkin to wipe up the mess. "I'm not in love with her," I continue, lowering my voice.

"Jack. You're up," Neil says. "As the most recent member of the 'Oh, there's no way I'm in love with the girl I've thought about for years' club, I'll let you handle this one."

"I'm going to ignore the incredibly sarcastic tone. Let me ask you a few questions, Henry," Jack starts, leaning forward and dropping his elbows on the table. "I want you to answer them honestly. None of us are going to think of you any differently because of what you say, okay?"

I nod, my skin prickling with nerves.

Feelings.

So many goddamn feelings.

Feelings mean something big is happening. Something deep.

"Do you think about Emma when she's not around?"

"Yes, and I—"

"Do you stare at your phone, wondering when she's going to send you a message?"

"All the time, bu—"

"Do you smile when you think about her and miss her when she's gone?"

"Seeing her smi—"

"Do you like spending time with her and wonder when you'll see her next?"

"She's my fav—"

"Despite your recent transgression, do you want to be with anyone else?"

"Fuck, no. That was a horrible mist—"

"Could you imagine yourself being with her forever? Whether that means as husband and wife or life partners? Pick whichever title you want."

"Yes, of course I can. She's fucking amazing and means the world to me. I want to spend the rest of my life with her. I want to walk down the aisle with her while she wears a pretty white dress, my ring and vows on her finger. I want her to be my wife, forever and always, but more importantly, I want to be hers. I want to have kids with her and grow old with her, sitting in our rocking chairs during our last dying days, reminiscing about all the memories we made together." *Holy shit.* "Oh, fuck me," I groan, dropping my head to the table.

"Welcome to the club of lovers, my friend. It's not that scary," Neil adds sympathetically. He grips my shoulder, and the gesture is comforting, like I'm not in this alone.

"How... How is it possible? It's been weeks! You don't fall in love with someone in just a few days, do you?"

"Think about it, man," Noah says, kinder than anything else he's said to me this afternoon. "Has it really only been a few weeks? Or has it been years and years of stealing glances and avoiding thinking about her because it didn't seem logical? Why were you always trying to get her attention? Why did it bug you when she didn't fall for your games?"

"Years? I... I love her. I love Emma. I'm in love with her. Holy shit. Holy fuck. I didn't... It's not..." I chug the rest of my beer and stare into the empty glass, hoping for clarity. "What the hell am I going to do now?"

"First thing is admitting you fucked up," Jack begins.

"I fucked up big time," I agree, rubbing my temples and trying to think. "She was adamant about not breaking up, but taking some time to sort through things. I don't want to rush her or make her feel like there's a deadline, but I also want to fix this. I *need* to fix this. She needs to hear how much she means to me. She needs to know how much I miss her. She needs to hear how incredible she is."

"You gotta talk to her, man. It sounds cliché, I know, but communication is key. You need to own up to your mistakes, tell her what you realized and what you learned, and your plan going forward to ensure this never, ever happens again. And then prepare to apologize over and over and over."

Neil sounds like a natural, a seasoned veteran lecturing on

partner issues many times. It makes me proud. This is a man-to-man conversation, and I'm glad he's here to talk to me. I'm glad they're all here to talk to me.

"You're not proposing to her. You're telling her you want her, *only her*, for as long as she'll have you. Emma deserves the world, and if you aren't going to try to give it to her every day, you need to step aside for someone who will." Noah's voice has changed back to sharp words laced with undertones of protectiveness.

Emma *does* deserve the world.

Would I be content with being the one to give it to her?

I'd give her anything she asked, even if it kills me and destroys my heart. Including walking away.

Is this how you define love? Acting selflessly with the innate desire to make someone happy by any means necessary? Even if that means happiness without you?

"Okay." My exhale is shaky, but I feel my limbs growing lighter. The tension from my shoulders relaxes fractionally. These are my guys. My best friends. If they think I can get through this, I might stand a chance—no matter how fucking terrifying it is. "I want her. Only her. For as long as she'll have me. God. It's only been a few days, but I miss her so much."

I miss her smile when she's elated.

How the corner of her mouth dips down when she's thinking hard. It's not a frown but more of a pensive look.

The way her eyes sparkle brighter when she's talking about something or someone she loves.

Hands that fit so perfectly in mine.

A faint trail of freckles scattered across her nose, more prominent when the sun is setting and she's tangled in my sheets, a halo around her blonde hair.

"You only get one more shot," Jack says. "So you need to do this right. Have you read any of her romance books?"

"Why the hell would I read her books?"

"Jesus," Jack grumbles, shaking his head. "So you know what she likes. In bed. In a grand gesture. Pet names to avoid."

"You're telling me you study Jo's books like you're writing a dissertation on love?"

"Hey. They never fail."

"Stand outside her window with a boombox," Neil proposes.

"No. Too loud. You gotta do it *Love Actually* style. On the porch with signs," Patrick says.

"She might murder me if I do either of those."

Emma isn't a tough woman to understand. She loves to be called *sweetheart* one minute, then told to drop to her knees the next.

She prefers to spend her evenings on the couch, fascinated by both tempered chocolate and historical documentaries.

A strong, independent person who never wears matching socks and likes me, the pathetic, blubbering idiot, a lot.

I sit up straighter.

History.

That's it.

"He has a plan," Noah observes.

"I do," I say excitedly. "And I'm going to need your help."

"All of us?" Jack asks, and I nod.

"Yup. Boys, I'm going to need a shit ton of sunflowers. Some love letters. Zebra Cakes. The most ridiculous coffee order known to man. Noah, I'm going to need you to use your charm to call in a special favor."

"To who?"

I grin conspiratorially. "You'll see."

FORTY-TWO

VRG: Henry?

HD: Hey, Sunflower.
HD: I was just thinking about you.

VRG: I was thinking about you, too.
VRG: I know it's been a few days.

HD: That's okay. How was the rest of your week?
HD: Are you feeling better? Wallace said you were out sick.

VRG: Much.
VRG: My week was pretty good.
VRG: I talked to my therapist a couple times.

HD: Yeah? How did that go?

VRG: Good.
VRG: I was wondering if you were free to meet?

HD: I am. Want to meet at Beans and Brews?

VRG: Sure. Is an hour good?

HD: An hour is perfect, sweetheart.

VRG: I'll let you know when I'm there!

HD: I can't wait to see you.
HD: I'm going to hug the shit out of you.

FORTY-THREE

EMMA

I'D BE LYING if I said I wasn't nervous as I approach Beans and Brews. I'm excited to see Henry, yeah, but I'm also nervous about the next steps. Nervous about sharing these inner thoughts with him. Scared about how receptive he might be.

This is the side I mentioned early in our conversations, before we even know who was on the other side. The dark, ugly parts of me I'm always terrified to reveal. I know he said we could navigate the darkness together back then, a flashlight at the ready.

I hope that's still the case now.

Swallowing away the last bit of worry, I pull open the door to the coffee shop, a smile on my face as I scan the store, ready to launch myself into his arms.

Except there's no Henry.

I'm five minutes behind schedule as it is, the train taking longer than usual to get into the city, and I was sure he would beat me here. My smile slips as I pull out my phone to message him. Before I can hit send, I hear my name.

"Emma?"

I turn around to see Jack standing in the doorway, waving at me.

"Oh, hey! What are you doing here?"

"I'm here on Henry's behalf."

My stomach drops to my feet. "Is he… is he not coming?"

"He's… delayed."

"Delayed? Delayed where?"

"Want to grab a drink? I'll do my best to explain."

He gives me a wry smile and I shrug, relenting to the idea.

"Okay. Sure."

Motioning to the counter, we step toward the register. As we approach, the two baristas grin at each other, then us.

"So, I know we're not quite friends or anything official yet, but I thought you might be interested in a story," Jack starts, ignoring the girls and facing me.

"A story about what?"

"Jo and I used to work together in the same office. Believe it or not, we didn't get along. Every Tuesday we'd have these meetings we both attended. She always brought the small group of us drinks from Beans and Brews, disturbing them after writing our names on the paper. Except for me, of course."

"What do you mean?" I ask, scrunching my nose and trying to figure out where this tale is headed.

A smile tugs at his lips, recalling a fond memory. "I got a whole slew of insults on mine. Arrogant prick. Dimwitted dingus. Grumpy. Those coffee cups were the best part of my week. They were small, wonderful moments I got to share with her. She didn't know it, but those silly scribbles were how I fell in love with her. Slowly. Steadily. It was hard for me to convey those feelings. One day, after we had been together for a while, I brought her here and asked her to order our drinks. When she picked them up, these lovely ladies had written the three words that were so difficult for me to say. 'I love you.' This spot is special to us. And I know it's special to you and Henry, too. It's where you met for the first time outside the secret identities after learning so much about each other."

My pulse spikes and I peer over Jack's shoulder, thinking Henry is going to appear, sitting at a table off to the side.

"He's not here," Jack continues. "Not yet. The girls have a special delivery for you, though, before I whisk you off to your next location. Trust me, be glad you get to deal with me first. I'm the least sociable one."

"Next destination? A special delivery? What the hell is going on, Jack?" I ask, looking at the baristas for guidance. My voice is shaky. My throat is dry. I haven't had a sip of caffeine yet and I'm already jittery and trembling.

My go-to order, the most ridiculous drink on the menu with pounds of whipped cream and extra shots of coffee, slides across the counter.

"Your usual," they say in unison.

"You're not the ones who are normally here in the morning. How in the world do you know what I get?"

"No, we're not," one says, giggling. "Henry remembered your order and called it in."

"What? He only saw me order it one time. Weeks ago."

"Isn't that interesting?" Jack muses.

"Make sure you read the back," the other suggests, waving at us as they disappear down a hallway.

I pick the drink up, spinning the cup around, noticing his scrawly penmanship. The letters take over the entire back side of the plastic, looping and squishing together.

Hi, Sunflower.
I miss you.
I thought you might want some caffeine.
I remember this day vividly. Your overalls. The pink shirt. Your order I unknowingly memorized after hearing it once. The way whipped cream clung to your upper lip, and I wanted to lick it off, even then.
I can't wait to give you a hug.
Are you game for another adventure?

-H

You know my coffee order, Henry.

I miss you too, Henry.

There's a tug in my chest, a yank toward something outside the store. Somewhere other than the safety of my house.

A quiet voice is whispering in my ear:

Jump.

Dive in.

I promise it's safe.

It'll be worth it.

"Another adventure?" I ask Jack, clarifying the message. "Are we going somewhere else?"

"Yeah. But don't feel pressured to answer in a way you think he wants to hear. Don't make a rushed decision. He's willing to wait, Emma, for whenever you're ready to take the next steps."

"I'm ready," I say firmly. "What do I do now?"

"Before you go outside and see, I want to say one more thing. Henry helped save my relationship when I fucked up, and I'm sorry you wonderful women have to put up with us and our shit. I'm not trying to tell you what you should or shouldn't do regarding your situation. I'm not excusing his actions at all. I want to tell you this, though: He's a good man who cares about you a hell of a lot. It always irked him his charming personality didn't affect you. You got under his skin, Emma, and you've stayed there. For years. I know you might think this whole 'Henry with one woman' thing is a recent development, but I think it's more of a 'Henry was passing the time while waiting for his perfect woman who's been there all along' kind of thing. Turns out, the one perfect woman is you. Who would have thought?"

My eyes water. Tears are forming and soaking my cheeks, his words hitting me with a baseball bat of understanding and recognition. I sniff, wiping my nose with the sleeve of my sweatshirt. Jack graciously looks away, giving me a minute to gather myself.

"Thank you," I say when I'm ready, hugging the drink tightly to my chest. "Who's up next?"

"Patrick. Figured you'd need two good guys first so you wouldn't kick Neil in the nuts when you saw him. If the feeling still strikes you, he deserves it."

I laugh, sniffing again. "Fair point."

"Ready when you are." Jack gestures to the door and we walk outside. Patrick is standing on the sidewalk, grinning at us.

"ZC secured? Ready for the handoff to LL?" he asks, nodding in my direction.

"I told you I'm not using stupid code names," Jack grumbles.

"You know the rules, Lancaster. I'm not moving until you say it."

He groans. "Fuck all of you. WD securing handoff to LL."

"I'm so confused," I say and Patrick laughs, leading us away from a still grumbling Jack. "What the hell does WD mean?"

"Do you really want to know?"

"Obviously."

"Window Daddy."

"I beg your pardon?" I sputter, almost tripping over my feet.

"A story for another time. He has to be good and drunk before spilling the beans. But it's so good."

I sip my drink, the sweetened beverage giving me life. Giving me courage. Enabling me to take another step forward, and another, and another, heading toward an unknown destination I'm eager to discover.

"Where are you taking me?"

"The place Henry considers your first date."

"Italian food? I'm hardly dressed for the occasion."

"Nope. Good guess, though. Somewhere different."

We stop at a crosswalk, Patrick checking both ways before allowing us to move forward.

"You're a principal, right? How did you go down that road?"

"I've always loved teaching. I also enjoy managing chaos and little rascals. Being in the classroom was fun, but being in charge of curriculums, testing scores, quality of life, affordable lunch, after school-activities, and hiring the best staff is even more entertaining."

"How cool. I thought about being a teacher when I was younger. It's not an easy job. Good for you."

"Lola's the one who encouraged me to pursue it. You don't see a lot of male educators, and I'd like to change that. It would be nice to live in a world where gender roles and biases didn't matter, wouldn't it?"

"You're telling me," I scoff. "How long have you and Lola been dating? I like her a lot. Spunky. Outgoing. Fun."

The smile Patrick is wearing falters. "We're not."

"Oh, I'm so sorry. I didn't mean to insinuate anything."

"Don't apologize. It's a common question. We're friends. Just friends."

Instead of drawing attention to the sadness behind his statement, I move on. "Right. Of course. So, if it's not Italian food, where in the world are you taking me?"

"Here."

We stop outside a building and my brow furrows when I read the neon lights in the window.

"The escape room? We went here before we were even together."

"Henry has no shame in sharing things he's done. While he's never specific and doesn't use names, I know enough intimate details of his life to write a scathing exposé if he ever became famous."

"And what does that have to do with the escape room?"

"Something happened that night. He hasn't told us what, and he probably never will. All I know is after you two spent the evening together, he was different."

Cookiegate.

The worry on his face when he noticed how cold I was on the walk to his apartment.

His jacket pulled tight around me, keeping me warm.

His confession about the graduation picture sitting on his bedroom wall.

Standing in his kitchen, his tongue on my finger. My teeth almost biting his thumb. The way I hugged him and held on, not wanting to let go.

There was an obvious shift in our time together. A recognition of the charged sexual chemistry between us that had me gasping and short of breath. I wanted him then. On the counter. Against the windows. In his massive bed. The few touches weren't enough. That was the beginning of me needing *more*.

I think I still do.

I don't think I've had enough.

"Different how?"

"He wore this stupid, secret smile, and when we asked what the hell his problem was, he shrugged and told us to fuck off. You've been on his mind a long time, my friend. This night, specifically, he was proud of you. He's always proud of you."

"Are we going to do a room now?"

"Nope. Not this time. I've got to hand you off to the next misfit. Only if you want to, of course."

"It's Neil, isn't it?"

"Sadly," he laughs, sending a quick text. "I'm not one to lecture. And I'm certainly not one to lecture someone as intelligent as you. I have one last thing to say. Some parting wisdom. You're lucky, Emma, to have gotten the chance to care for someone and be cared for in return. Not everyone will be so fortunate. Whatever you decide to do with Henry, cherish those moments. Not only the happy ones; the sad, painful ones, too. Even though they hurt like fuck, it's better to have loved and lost than never loved at all. The suffering reminds you you're alive, and you got to experience one of the greatest gifts of life—being half of a whole."

"You really think being hurt by someone you care about is better than not having anyone and never being tormented?"

"Let me turn your question into a question: Wouldn't you

rather endure a hundred bad days with someone by your side, instead of being alone, just so you can experience one perfect day with them? The lonely days aren't great. Trust me."

I pause, considering. Patrick has a point. How many people would do anything to have the love of their life back, even if it's on a cloudy, stormy afternoon? It might not always be sunshine and rainbows or full of joy, but it would still be a day spent with each other. Stomping in puddles. Laughing in the rain.

What did I tell Henry—JD—early on?

Even if the bad days make little sense right now, they make the happy days appear so much brighter and better.

We can share an umbrella.

My toes wiggle in my shoes, wishing I had on rain boots.

I want to welcome the storm with him by my side.

I want to dash through a field soaping wet, drenched from the storm clouds above, his laughter ringing in my ears as he picks me up and spins me around.

"It appears I've befuddled you," Patrick says.

"You and Jack are great friends. And I'm… happy. Or close to being happy. I'm just waiting on the last piece."

"The good ones are worth the wait, aren't they? Shit, I forgot to give you this." He pulls a small piece of paper out of his pocket. I unfold the note, finding more of Henry's handwriting.

We might have escaped the room that night,
but you haven't escaped my mind.
Speaking of cheesiness, I have something tasty for you.

"Tasty? Is food involved?" I look up, and Patrick is gone. Neil is standing in his place.

"I come in peace," he starts. "Before I start my mission, I want to apologize. My jokes and comments the other night were inappropriate and out of line. I have a tendency to be crass with no filter, and it wasn't intentional. I like you, Emma. You're good for

Henry. I know I had a hand in the confusion you're experiencing, and I'm sorry."

"You know what? I forgive you. You helped me with some soul searching that might not have happened otherwise. You kind of gave me the swift kick I needed."

"Yeah? You don't hate me?"

I laugh, shaking my head. "No. I don't hate you."

"Good. I'm sorry to say my task isn't as cool as the others, though, so I might not be your favorite. Ready for a short walk?"

I slurp the final sip of my coffee down and toss it into the trash can. "I'm running out of places where you could take me."

"It's not far. I brought reinforcements for our journey." He pulls out a family size bag of Flamin' Hot Cheetos and a box of Zebra Cakes from behind his back. "Hungry?"

"Starving," I chuckle. "Lead the way… Wait. What's your code name? And what was Patrick's? LL?"

"LL. Lola Lover."

"He told me they aren't dating!"

"They aren't. My name is BJT."

"Blow Job Taker?"

"Wow. I wish I had thought of that. Bad Joke Teller. They have put me in a timeout. Please accept this cupcake as a peace offering."

"Peace offering granted," I agree, taking the plastic off the treat and biting into it.

We begin our stroll down the sidewalk.

"Can I tell you a story?"

"Only if you hand over the Cheetos."

"Fair enough." He opens the bag and passes it my way. "A couple of weeks ago, Henry and I were out together. I told him I was going to propose to Rebecca."

"That was you!"

"Yup. I couldn't keep his attention. He kept looking at his phone and wouldn't listen. He was distracted."

"Wait." I wipe my cheesy finger on my jeans. "I was talking to him that night."

"Oh, believe me, I put two and two together real quick. He tried to say he was waiting to talk to a client. I saw through the lie pretty easily. He's never stared at his phone so much until you came along. The second it chimes, he's jumping to answer, wanting to hear what you have to say."

"Shoot. I feel terrible. It was your night to celebrate, and I took away from your time. I stole your thunder."

"Don't feel bad at all. I'll admit I was a bit against the idea of him meeting up with a woman he didn't know. In the end, I'm glad he went through with the plan. I like the new Henry better than the old Henry."

"Can I ask you a question?"

"Of course," Neil answers immediately.

"You've known Henry a while, right?"

"We went to college together. So, that's, what, 13 years? I'd say that's a decent length of time."

"Do you honestly think he's able to leave his past behind?"

"Henry's stories aren't mine to tell. I won't deny he's been with a lot of women, because he has. I won't deny he wasn't a shameless flirt. He's also someone who commits 100% to something. Work and his career. Friendships. Sports. He spends time on things and people he wants. He's never spent any time on a woman before. Now look at him. He's created a whole fucking scavenger hunt around the city. Emma, he might have been with Shelby more than once, but that girl owns no piece of his mind. You're the only one he's ever made any sort of effort for."

There's only one friend left. Noah.

I don't know where he's going to take me, or what's next, but I'm excited. Exhilarated. I've come this far, and I want to see what's waiting for me at the end.

"This is where I hand you off," Neil says.

"My office building? Are we going up?"

"Nope. I have your last note, though. Here you go, my friend."

The final piece of paper is the longest one yet. In the distance, I hear a rumble of thunder.

> *Hey, sweetheart.*
> *Having fun?*
> *I hope Neil behaved himself.*
> *If not, I'm going to kick his ass.*
> *I miss you, honey.*
> *The last stop is something we have lots of.*
> *We made a lot of it here at the office, inadvertently.*
> *We made a lot at school, years ago.*
> *And it's something I hope we keep making more of.*
> *There's no one else I want to do it with, either.*
> *When you get there, you'll see two paths.*
> *Whichever one you decide to pick, I hope it'll be easy to find the way.*

"There she is," Noah says, beaming at me.

"Hey!" I give him a quick hug.

"How are you doing?"

"Besides walking all over town blindly with guys I've only met once? I'm great."

"You're a trooper. So, I know you were upset by what happened at the bar. I also know you're an intelligent woman who likes to gather all the facts before she makes a big, monumental decision," he says. "Given everything from today, and what you have learned during your time apart, do you want to follow the note? Or do you want me to take you home?"

"The note," I say before I can think twice. "I have no clue what he means, though. Something we have lots of? Sex?"

Noah bursts out laughing. "God, you've been spending too much time with him. He'll be happy to know that's where your mind went. I'm supposed to blindfold you for this portion. Will that make you uncomfortable?"

"No. I trust you."

"In that case, here's a napkin. Wipe your hands and I'll take the snacks."

I clean off my fingers, ridding them of the frosting residue left behind. "Okay. I'm ready."

The blindfold covers my eyes, hiding the setting sun from view. "Are you comfortable holding my arm?"

"Yes, as long as you don't lead me into a pole or something."

"I would never. Buckle up, buttercup."

FORTY-FOUR

EMMA

"WHERE THE HELL are we going, Noah? We've been walking for twenty minutes!"

"You still trust me, right?" Noah has his hands on my shoulders and I nod as he guides me, nudging me left then right in a gentle and determined manner.

"I wouldn't have let you put the blindfold on if I didn't."

"Not much further," he says.

Wherever we're going, whatever direction we're headed, we're close to reaching the finish line, and Henry's got to be there.

My foot connects with something solid and I grimace at the painful contact, my toes throbbing. "A little warning next time?" I joke, realizing too late I've hit a step.

"Sorry! I was looking at my phone. We have about twenty stairs going up."

"Twenty?!" I slowly raise my foot then lower it, ascending the elevated slabs cautiously. I lift my leg as high as possible to avoid any more injuries, and I hear him chuckle beside me, holding my elbow and making sure I don't fall.

"We made it." Noah loosens the blindfold from the back of my hair. Once it's removed, it takes a minute to figure out where we are.

"The history museum?" I ask. The massive white banner hanging above us billows in the wind. "What are we doing here?"

"You'll see," he says, smiling secretively. He opens the unlocked door despite it being after hours, holding it ajar for me. I step inside carefully, on high alert. The building is empty and silent.

Noah leads me into the atrium, and I gasp. The entire floor is covered in sunflowers, scattered across the black marble and reaching every corner of the space. Everywhere I look, there's vibrant yellow, long stems stacked on top of each other, two or three flowers high.

Spinning around, I take in the contrast of the bright display against the dark columns rising toward the ceiling high above me. A handful of dull lights are turned on, casting a soft, welcoming glow. Upon completion of my turn, I find Noah has disappeared from sight, and I'm alone.

I swallow, nerves on fire.

Two paths. Two paths.

I search for the hidden puzzle.

There.

I walk to my left, finding something different on the ground, unmarked and in a trail heading toward an illuminated exit sign. Squatting down, I pick up the mysterious object.

Chocolate chip cookies.

I laugh, the sound echoing across the silent space. Tucked under one treat is another piece of paper.

Emma,
If you're reading this, you found the first path.
You can see where it leads to. An exit.
Literally and metaphorically.
How we proceed from here up to you, Sunflower.
The choice is yours.
If you want to walk away, there will be no hard feelings. No resentment.

*Out the door, no questions asked, and I'll always remember our
time together.*
It was magical. Spectacular. Special.
*You're special, baby, and I could never, ever hate you, no matter
what you decide. I promise.*
Your other option?
Pick up one of these homemade cookies.
Yeah, I made them myself.
(You're more fun to cook with, though)
Turn around.
And follow the sunflowers.
I'll see you soon.

Henry.

He's what I want.

He's what I need.

I've never moved so quickly in my life.

I spin on my heel, following the flowers. My shoes squeak as I
hurry into the main exhibition hall, another space coated in
yellow.

"Hello?" I call out.

A sound around the corner causes me to jump. I whip around,
the hair on the back of my neck standing up in alarm. On the
other side of the hall stands Henry.

"Hi, honey," he says weakly, voice traveling across the room.
Even with the distance, I can hear him as clear as day. Neither of
us moves toward the other, staying frozen in our positions, the
tension thick and palpable.

"Hey," I answer, a smile growing on my lips.

Henry clears his throat and takes a step toward the center of
the room, the first to attack. My eyes follow his every move. I
think he's waiting for me to stop him. Waiting for me to halt his
advancement.

I don't.

"Hi," I whisper.

He pulls a crumpled piece of paper from his pocket, chin dipping as his hand shakes, starting to speak.

"'I thought I loved you months ago, but since my separation from you, I feel that I love you a thousand-fold more. Each day since I knew you, have I adored you more and more.' Napoleon to Josephine." His foot taps against the old floor, a nervous energy radiating from him before he continues.

"'You don't realize, of course, E.B., how fascinatingly beautiful you have always been, and how strong you have acquired an added and special and dangerous loveliness.' Richard Burton to Elizabeth T—"

"Taylor," I finish for him. He smiles without meeting my gaze, attention firmly glued to the piece of paper.

"'You pierce my soul. I am half agony, half hope. Tell me not that I am too late, that such precious feelings are gone forever.'" He pauses, his thumb swiping under his eyes. "'I offer myself to you again, with a heart even more your own than when you almost broke it. I have none but you. Unjust I may have been, weak and resentful I have been, but never inconstant.'"

"*Persuasion*," I whisper. He nods, folding the paper and tucking it into the pocket of his jeans. He finally raises his chin to stare at me, eyes red. Bloodshot and remorseful.

Something inside me cracks at the sight. Like he's barely been surviving without me.

"Emma." He walks closer, carefully avoiding crunching any flowers and stopping inches away from me. "Do you remember when you asked me about my favorite color?"

"Yeah. I do."

"I told you the story was for a later day. What better time than the present? Green is the color you wore on our first day of high school. I remember the moment we had in the hallway so vividly. It's like no time has passed. Your polo shirt, pink on the bottom, green on top, was a beacon to me. I was drawn to you in the most peculiar, head-scratching way. I noticed you the second you walked into the building, standing out from the crowd. When my eyes landed on you, the rest of the world ceased to exist. There was no noise. No movement. No people. It was only you and me. You stared right back, challenging me, and I thought my heart was going to explode out of my chest. My hands were clammy. I couldn't think. Couldn't speak. I could only stare at you rapturously." He blows out a breath of air, staring at the ceiling.

"It was only seconds, I'm sure, yet it seemed like time slowed to a standstill. You were all I could see. For years after, the green shirt was a constant reminder we would never be friends. I could have tried. I should have tried. Instead, I floated along each day in those damn halls pretending like you didn't exist. Pretending like my heart didn't flutter at the sight of you across the auditorium during pep rallies, because I was fucking terrified. Even the glimmer of your hair as you turned a corner and disappeared caused me pain."

His face is anguished, and I've stopped breathing. Stopped moving, hanging onto his every word.

"You like to say I don't notice you, or I wouldn't give you a second glance. I've always noticed you. I've always known exactly where you are. The second you walk into a room, I sense your presence. I'll admit the night at the bar after learning about the partner position threw me off. That was the first and only time when seeing you surprised me. Still, I felt a familiar tug toward the hot blonde leaning over the counter, waiting for her drinks, ass looking divine, not knowing it was you. For 17 goddamn years, I haven't been able to shake the thought of the very first time I saw you.

"When you wore the green dress in the office the night I zipped you up, I almost died. It was as if I was transported back to the first time I laid eyes on you, the color a stark reminder of how far we've come and how much more we have left to go. When I touched you, I nearly went insane. Never did I think I would be awarded the prestigious honor... the privilege of feeling your skin under mine. You presented yourself to me so freely, unaware and unaffected by the war raging in my head."

"Y-you're telling me you've felt like this for *years*? And you did nothing about it?" I press, dying to know more.

"Yes and no. I couldn't quantify it. I couldn't explain it or verbalize it. It didn't make any sense. I chalked up the feelings to you being around for a while. If you asked me six months ago if I felt anything romantic toward you, I would have adamantly said no.

"Besides my four buddies and my family, you've been the most consistent person in my life. Sure, you vanished for a few years, off to college and law school. In the back of my mind, I always wondered what you were up to. Every time I saw a flash of green, a woman in a coat or a man in a hat, my mind drifted back to you, hoping you were okay."

"What does all of this mean?" I whisper.

Henry exhales. "For so long, I've worn the mask of a man who appears to have it all together. I joke. I laugh. I fuck around. I have a good time. Until a couple months ago, I thought I knew what happiness was. I have money. A great job. Good friends. A loving family. And then along came RB, overturning everything I thought I knew about being with someone. You've opened my eyes, and my heart, to something I used to think was undesirable and unattainable. I wasn't just a night of fun or a dick to ride. You cared about me. I never thought such an emotional and powerful force actually existed. But when I see you standing in front of me, I realize it's *you* that makes all this exist for me. Maybe that's why I've never been interested in anyone else long-term before. Because they weren't you.

"I've never loved anyone the way I love you, honey. And I never will again. It's scary and exhausting and the best and worst thing that's ever happened to me. You've brightened my world and awakened my soul. You deserve the whole fucking universe, Emma, and I want to be the one to give it to you, if you'll let me. I want to spend every day for the rest of my life apologizing for my mistakes and working on making it up to you. Whether that's strictly as colleagues or romantically involved, together as equal halves, it's up to you. I just want you to know I love you so fucking much."

Love.

A nearly inconceivable word.

One I never thought Henry could express.

"Y-you love me?"

"I do. I've loved you for a long, long time, I think. I fell in love with you through every ping on my phone. Every joke and stupid question we exchanged. In the hallway. Across the office. It was a gradual thing. Not skydiving out of an airplane, fast and quick, but more like crossing a long, rocky terrain, building over the last decade and a half and punctuated by the past few weeks we've spent together. It took almost losing you for me to finally define the emotions.

"I'm not asking you to say anything back. I just couldn't live with myself if I didn't fully express to you what you mean to me. If you walk away, it'll be okay, baby. I'll be okay. The only person I resent is myself, for all the time I've wasted. For all the words I haven't spoken. For all the kisses I haven't stolen. For not being there to celebrate your highs and soothe you during your lows. And for letting you slip away. Again. This is who I am, Emma. Completely and utterly committed to you."

The quiver in his tone causes me to ache, the fissure growing deeper and deeper.

"How many sunflowers are there?"

Henry pauses, glancing around the room. "6,205. One for roughly every day I've known you existed. Give or take. God, what I would give to go back and do high school and the past few years again."

I shake my head violently. "I don't want to go back."

"You don't?"

"No. I got to know you in a way no one else does. I got to know you as *Henry*, not Henry."

"And there's a difference, I'm assuming?"

"Mhm. Henry, everyone knows and loves. Henry is recognized out and about, always with friends. I knew bits and pieces of that Henry. But *Henry* is more open. He shares what's on his mind. His hopes and dreams and fears. He's funny and thoughtful. Encouraging. He makes me laugh. He holds me tight, keeping me safe in his arms. He fucks me hard and fast one night and wakes me up by making love to me in the early morning. "

"Which one do you like best? Tell me, and I'll be that version of him for you."

"Both. I love both. I love *you*. Every part of you. And I'm not walking away. Not now. Not ever."

His neck jerks as he stares at me. "You love me?"

I nod, not believing I said the words out loud. How can I not love him?

This man has possessed my entire being and opened my eyes to what a relationship could—and should—look like. He carries Band-Aids in his pockets and fights to defend my honor. He never pushes me past my limits and constantly supports the decisions I make. He's fiercely protective, remorseful about his mistakes, and has been harboring deep feelings toward me for *years*.

Standing in front of him, just out of reach, I know I don't want to be with anyone else. I *can't* be with anyone else. And what's love without forgiveness and growth through the pain and confusion, learning how to do life together?

Walking side by side, hand in hand, cuddled close under an umbrella to keep the rain away?

Using a flashlight to navigate the darkness with another by your side?

"I do. I love you, Henry. So much."

"I might fuck this up. I'm definitely going to fuck this up. Again and again," he says, moving closer.

How have we not touched yet? How have we kept our hands to ourselves? I need to touch him. Feel him. Know that he's real.

"You might. Who's saying I won't fuck this up too? We can fuck up together."

Together.

The constant word we've repeated, anchoring us to each other when we need it the most.

Henry finally takes my hand, fingers running over the knuckles. "Emma. These past few months have been indescribable. I know I did something wrong. It'll never happen again. I also know actions speak louder for words, and I'm going to have to earn your trust back. It won't be overnight. Or tomorrow, or the next day. Or even in the next year. But I want to try harder. For you. Because of you. With you."

I bring my palm to his cheek. He nuzzles into the touch, letting out a content sigh and turning to kiss my hand, the press of his lips igniting my skin.

"We're going to keep messing up. One day, it'll be your turn to be mad at me. We're not going to keep a tally sheet of who's done more wrongs than rights."

"I could never be mad at you, honey."

"When I make you cook your own dinner, you might get pissed off."

"Okay, that's crossing a line."

"You know it's going to be hard to top a rented-out museum and flowers everywhere, right?"

"I'm well aware. I also remember you telling me this would earn me a lot of points."

"How did you even make this happen?"

"Well, you saw the help I had. Not only did they knock some sense into me, but they also sprang into action when I needed help. I'm so sorry, sweetheart." Henry rests his forehead against mine, bending his knees, lowering to my height.

The apology breaks me, dredging up every emotion I've felt the last week. "I'm sorry, too. I have some things I'm working on myself, namely all the self-doubt I've kept inside for years. I should have shared those fears with you sooner, and what happened in the bar brought them all to the surface again. I guess I thought that maybe you wouldn't want to talk about those ugly, dark parts. Maybe you'd only want to focus on the good parts of our relationship. The sex and the fun, carefree moments. Time with our friends and our date nights. Not... not all the serious stuff. The mental health stuff."

"Baby, I want all the moments, okay? I want you to share the good days with me. The bad days, too. Every single one of them is important to me, because they're with *you*. I'm not running away from you either. I love you, perfectly as you are. You are my sole purpose for existing, Em. No one else has beguiled me quite like you have. Everything I have, and everything I am, is yours for eternity."

"What if..." My lip trembles, afraid to voice the thoughts that have plagued my mind as I tossed and turned through sleepless nights, the emptiness of the bed noticeable as the hours shifted from darkness to morning.

"Tell me, sweetheart. Please."

"What if I'm not enough? What if one day you wake up and want nothing to do with me anymore, like the others in the past have done? What if you realize how much you miss your old lifestyle? What if there's someone better out there? You had no problem touching another woman when I was in the same room."

"Not enough?" he repeats, furrowing his brow. His smooth palms cup my cheeks, intense, promising eyes baring into my own. "You're all of it, Emma. You're everything. My everything. And I will pick *you* over anything else, a million times out of a million times, for the rest of my days. There's no me without you anymore. It's always been you. It's always going to be you. From now until forever."

The tears spill out now, falling down my face. Henry wipes them away, whispering soothing words into my ears as he draws me close to his body, arms wrapping around my waist and hugging me tight. The scents I almost forgot come back to memory, cloaking me in comfort and... and love.

"Thank you. Thank you for loving me. Thank you for your apologies. Thank you for being you."

A tear slides down his own, cheek and I wipe it away with my thumb. "It's you and me forever, Sunflower. I'm never letting you go again."

"What about when some hot blonde walks past us down the sidewalk?"

"You're going to use that line on me for the rest of our lives, aren't you?"

"You can count on it." I squeeze his waist. It feels like I never left. "I love you. I love you."

It's a comical cliché to fall in love with someone after pretending to be their girlfriend. Our love didn't originate recently, though. It didn't happen in three weeks. It's been gradually developing, a crescendo in a symphony, waiting to erupt into the final string of notes.

This moment.

"I have to tell you something else. I'm withdrawing my name from the partner consideration."

"What?" I squeak. "Why the hell would you do that?"

"I don't want it. You deserve it."

"Don't want it? Yes, you do! It's the chance of a lifetime. You can't pass up an opportunity like this!"

"I've been thinking about leaving for a while now. Hearing about the pay discrepancies solidified my desire to get out. I love seeing you every day, but I cannot, in good conscience, continue to work for a firm where shit like that happens. Besides, I don't want to sneak around and hide our relationship, which we'd have to do if—when—you get the job. Withdrawing my name will push me to actually get off my ass and make shit happen."

"Where are you going to go?" I ask.

His lips brush over my temple. "I'm not going anywhere without you. I've wanted to start my own firm for a while now. So why not? Even if I didn't want to leave, I would have conceded to you. I'm emailing Wallace tonight. From what he told me, he was going to offer it to you, anyway. Don't think for a goddamn second you're sloppy seconds. You're the grand prize, baby."

I bury my face in his sweater, feeling a mixture of pride and relief. "Thank you."

"This was all you, Em. I'm so fucking proud of you."

FORTY-FIVE

HENRY

"DO you have anything else on your agenda the rest of the evening, or can I kidnap you?" I ask, holding Emma tight to my body. I'm never letting her go again. Seriously. I may have to follow her everywhere like some sort of stalker because I'm terrified to release her even an inch, afraid she might float away if I do.

"Well, I was going to watch *The Devil Wears Prada* and eat a pint of ice cream. Think you have something better in mind?" she challenges, arching an eyebrow.

"While I do adore Anne Hathaway's character development in the movie, I had another idea. Come with me back to my place?"

I'm nervous at the suggestion. The bridge I created might be fixed temporarily, caution tape up while repairs are being made, but I know Emma. It's going to take more than passionate words and a few kisses to win her trust back, no matter what she says. I'm aware that she loves me—cares about me, deeply—but I still hurt her. And hurt takes time to mend. It takes patience and care. All things I intend to give her—and more.

"Okay. We're going to need to grab some dinner first. Spending the evening with your strangely fun friends made me work up an appetite."

"The box of Zebra Cakes wasn't enough?"

"Not nearly. I'm thinking tacos."

"You took the idea right out of my head. Food, then my apartment. Sound good to you?"

"Sounds perfect," she agrees softly.

I want to surprise her with something I've had planned since one of our early conversations.

I remember a lot of what we've talked about, but this one in particular was special to me. It was the first time we acknowledged an *us* outside rigid roles and paid outings. A potential maybe-this-could-be-something-down-the-road comment. It had been an offhanded suggestion, said in jest and without any expectation, and now I intend to follow through with my idea. Especially because she liked it, too.

I check my watch, knowing it's been long enough for the guys to get everything set up. If we divert to get dinner, they'll have plenty of time to evacuate my apartment before we arrive.

"C'mon. Let's get you fed then go home."

"I wasn't aware we lived together."

"Not yet we don't. But you better believe it's going to happen sooner rather than later. I'm not letting you out of my sight again."

Taking her hand in mine, we walk along the trail of yellow back to the atrium of the museum, a complacent, content silence following behind us the whole way.

"Henry."

"Yeah, honey?"

"We need to pick up the flowers. I don't want people cleaning up our—your—mess."

God. This woman. This selfless, caring, thoughtful woman.

After an emotionally charged confessional, what does she do?

Think of other people.

Fuck my heart skipping a beat at her kindness.

It's going to be skipping a beat for the rest of my life, isn't it?

"Which answer do you want to hear? I hired someone to take

care of it? Or that I planned on getting here first thing in the morning to clean it up myself?"

"The second one," she says without hesitation.

I press a kiss to her hair. "The director is letting me in at 6 a.m. sharp. And I'm bringing reinforcements."

Her face relaxes, softening into a small smile. "I love you."

I will never, ever get sick of hearing her say those three words.

Three words I had no clue I was capable of speaking or believing.

Now that I have—and she said them in return, willingly and enthusiastically—I want to scream them from the Empire State Building.

I want to tattoo them across my forehead so everyone can know the woman who has my whole heart.

I'm going to say the declaration so much, she's going to be fucking sick of it.

"I love you, too, Emma."

We take the elevator to the parking garage, climb into my truck, and take off for the closest Chipotle. Emma orders our dinner on the app, and I run in to pick it up, checking out the window every few seconds to make sure she's still sitting in the passenger seat.

She doesn't budge.

After a short drive, we ride up to my apartment where I stop outside the door and turn to face her.

"Close your eyes."

"What? Why?"

"I have a surprise."

"What kind of surprise?" she asks suspiciously. "What the hell can top what you just did?"

"Okay, it's not going to top that. We talked about something very briefly once, and I've been thinking about it ever since. How fun it would be. It's stupid and silly and you don't have to pretend to like it, okay?"

"Henry Dawson, you did not get a sex swing."

I burst out laughing, rubbing her shoulders. "Not this time, no. But good to know where you stand on the matter."

"Fine, I'll close my eyes," she relents. "But hurry up! The tacos are getting cold!"

I unlock the door and push it open, gently guiding Emma into the space and locking the door behind us. Sweeping a glance over the living area, I can tell the boys did good work.

"Okay, open up, honey."

Her eyelashes flutter open and she gasps, nearly dropping the precious cargo she's holding.

"Oh my God," she starts, walking across the hardwood floor.

Fairy lights hang on the wall, twinkling in the moonlight pouring through the curtain-free windows. The couches usually taking up space in the room have been shoved to the side, making way for a large camping tent. It's set up in the middle of the room, with dozens of pillows and blankets stacked inside. A plate of cookies and Zebra Cakes sit on top of the heap of fabric, with a jar of even more sunflowers adjacent to the sweet snacks. I'm pretty sure I've bought all the long-stemmed yellow flowers in the city for this woman, and it still isn't enough. The television is turned on, paused on the opening credits for *The Land Before Time*.

I shift on my feet, nervously tapping my fingers on my thigh. "What do you think?"

Emma steps close to me, the tip of her shoes knocking against mine.

"September 27th," she says.

"Pardon?"

"September 27th. It's when you suggested a movie night. It's when I first... when I first let myself imagine a life with you outside our phones."

I huff out a strangled breath. "It's the same day I imagined a life with *you* outside our phones. What have we been doing all these days and years without each other?"

She throws her arms around my shoulders, dinner dropping to the floor. I kick it away with my foot, picking her up and walking toward the floor-to-ceiling glass. Her legs bracket my hips and when I back her into the window, she gasps.

We've yet to kiss this evening, and as my arms rest on either side of her head, caging her in, I stare into her eyes.

"Henry."

"You with me, Emma?"

She nods, placing her hand on my heart. Can she hear how it syncs up with hers after a simple touch? Can she hear the way it beats for her and her alone?

I love you.

"I'm with you."

I'm never leaving you again.

"I want to fuck you against the window so everyone in the city can know I'm yours. Forever and always."

"Yes," she hisses, fisting the hem of my shirt.

I can't wait anymore. Finally, after too many minutes, too many hours, too many days, my lips find hers, capturing them with a kiss I hope conveys the sincerity of what I've shared tonight.

My everything.

"How do you want it, baby? Do you want me to make love to you, nice and sweet? Or do you want hard and fast?"

"Hard and fast," she whimpers, ripping my shirt over my head. I nearly drop her in the process, and I press her further into the glass so she doesn't tumble to the floor.

I fiddle with the button of her faded jeans, yanking them down just below the curve of her ass and over her knees. I don't bother pulling them all the way off. This isn't going to last long.

"No fucking underwear?" I exclaim, her bare, moist pussy brushing against my hip. I can feel her arousal already. "Are you trying to kill me?"

"I didn't plan for this to happen," she answers, eyes closing, head tilting back. I shove her sweatshirt up, capturing her nipple in my mouth. Hard and pointed. Ready for me. She groans, and I've fucking missed that sound. Music to my ears.

Releasing the pebbled peak, I give attention to the other side, using my teeth this time, enough to make her groan again. I undo my own jeans with one hand, the other rubbing her clit in circles.

So wet.

I can't stop touching her. I *won't* stop touching her. Never, ever. The denim falls to the ground, pooling at my ankles, and I hike her further up my body.

"No fucking underwear from you either?" she asks, reaching her hand between us and stroking my dick.

"Nope," I grunt. I don't use my fingers. I don't use my tongue. There's no prep or caressing or more talking. I simply thrust my cock into her with a single motion, eyes widening as I press deeper and deeper inside, no restrictions between us. "Fuck, Emma," I gasp, taking a moment to gather myself when I become fully seated. Her pussy is so tight around me, walls already clenching.

This angle is perfect. I can drive into her, hips snapping up and meeting hers, while playing with her tits. Her thighs begin to shake around my middle, and I know the second she finishes it's going to be impossible to keep her upright.

"Harder," she pleads, static hair sticking up thanks to the friction against the glass. "Faster. More. All of it, Henry."

"You have all of it, baby. All of me," I grit out. "All the people outside can see. They know I'm yours."

Fuck.

She clenches tighter, and we're definitely going to be revisiting this position and location. Fully naked next time.

Kinky fucking angel.

My left hand finds her clit, giving her exactly what she likes and how she likes it. "You going to come on my cock, Emma?"

"Yes," she pants, fingers gripping my shoulders. I'm out of control. Erratic. A madman possessed. I'm not being gentle. I'm not being kind. I'm being as tough and rough as possible. I'm bruising her thighs. I'm biting her neck, leaving a trail of red marks behind.

"That's what I thought." My thumb circles her clit again and again, greedily licking my lips at the thought of tasting her after we finish. Dessert after the main course. There's nothing better.

"Henry," she moans, clawing the hair at the base of my neck.

She's not being gentle, either.

Good.

Use me, baby. Mark me as yours.

One more combination of quick thrusts and circles and she's detonating, panting and shaking, pussy tightening and fluttering around my dick.

I don't bother trying to last any longer.

She came.

She's satisfied.

I'm a happy man.

I look down, watching in awe at where we're joined, my cock covered in her juices. Rocking my hips forward two more times is all it takes before I'm spilling inside her, grunting as I finish, days of bottled-up emotions releasing themselves free.

We're both breathing hard, and when I raise my chin to look at her, she's grinning.

"Might be a world record," she observes and I snort, pressing a kiss to her mouth.

"Tonight, I don't give a fuck. I'm going to set you down, okay?"

Emma nods, sliding down my body. When I place her feet on the floor, I groan.

"What?" she asks, looking at me worriedly.

"Baby, seeing my cum run down your leg is the hottest thing in the world. Don't bother showering. Wear it forever."

"Okay, fine, if you insist."

"God, I love you."

She beams. "I love you, too. Speaking of love… Has enough time passed where I can say, 'Thanks for the good sex, but can we eat tacos now?' I feel light-headed and dizzy. You have a tendency to fuck me into outer space."

Ten minutes later, after a reluctant shower, we're clean and climbing into the constructed fort. It's comfortable in here. Pillows cushion the hardness of the floor, and the blankets make it cozy. I'm grinning stupidly as we laugh over the low ceiling, my head hitting the top of the nylon.

I bring the Chipotle bag with us, doling out entrees, forks, and napkins. We eat silently, both clearly ravenous, gulping down the meal in a matter of seconds.

"Next time you feel light-headed, you tell me before you almost pass out after sex. Deal?"

"Deal," she agrees, wiping her hands and tossing her garbage into the bag. "This is the best date night we've had."

"And it's just getting started. Ready for the movie?"

We find a comfortable position, me propped up against the pillows, Emma's head on my chest, as I hit play on the remote. Reaching across her stomach, I find the plate of cookies and hand her one.

"How is it that I love you more now than I did 10 minutes ago?" she inquires in between bites. Crumbs fall onto my shirt, and I don't bother wiping them away.

I'm not a religious man. I've never been to church. I've never opened a book of prayer. Heaven isn't something I've imagined or pictured. I realize, sitting here with the angel in my arms, heart beating in time with mine... It's this.

This is heaven.

This is paradise.

Nirvana.

The great beyond.

It's messy. Imperfect. Full of mistakes and forgiveness. Passion and joy. Love. A future. A past. A present. Experiencing it all. Together.

She is my salvation. My one and only.

"Let me love you the way you deserve, Emma. In the early morning under the sunrise, together in our sheets. Late at night when we drift off to sleep, protecting you and keeping you warm.

Here in a tent watching a cartoon movie about dinosaurs that's as old as us. When we argue and fight and then kiss and make up. Over tacos and cookies. All of the above and everything in between."

Her chin tilts up, and I'm met with the smile I unexpectedly fell in love with years and years ago. Soft. Kind. Perfect.

Mine.

EPILOGUE

HENRY

Two years later

I CHECK the time on my watch, cursing under my breath. The meeting I was sitting in ran late, making me even later to my next destination. The vibrating phone in my pocket confirms my tardiness and I curse again, pulling it out and scowling at the onslaught of messages.

JL: I can't believe this is happening.
NR: Me neither. Two years is way too long.
PW: H, Lola told me to let you know she dropped Emma off five minutes ago.
NL: Did anyone else know babies cry an absurd amount? Fuck. Sorry for the delay, I'm here. With spit-up on me.
NL: You ready, Hen?

> **HD:** Speaking of spit-up... I think I'm going to puke.

PW: Thatta boy.

JL: You'll be fine.

NR: Just like we practiced, remember?

NL: Except this time, it's real.

JL: Yeah. Less cursing and use of the words "fucking assholes" would probably be best.

PW: What do you mean, J? Those are words every woman wants to hear.

HD: You aren't helping. I'll text you guys after.

Slipping my phone away, I sidestep a baby carriage, grinning as I approach Emma outside Beans and Brews. She hasn't noticed me yet, and I take five seconds to stare at her. Her head is turned toward the sun, a content smile on her face. Bronzed arms are on display, courtesy of our beach trip last weekend. Her golden hair glows in the light, a beacon that literally draws me closer, feet scurrying across the pavement.

"You're late," she says, bringing her chin down and smiling at me. There's humor behind the chastising, and I'm glad I didn't make her wait too long.

"Sorry," I apologize, hugging her. "Meeting ran long. Hi, Sunflower. I missed you."

"I missed you, too." With a peck to my cheek, she tangles our fingers together, giving my palm a squeeze. "Where's this new restaurant you wanted to try?"

There isn't a restaurant I want to try. It was a lie I fed her to get her out of the office for more than three minutes.

"I'll show you." Leading the way, I hustle her onto the busy sidewalk, merging into the pedestrian traffic. "We need to hurry."

"I don't understand why we're in such a rush and you're acting so secretive. Are we meeting someone?"

I stop in front of a building, reaching our destination. "You trust me, right?"

"Of course," she answers immediately.

The last two years have been blissful and nothing short of

perfect. Other couples tell us the honeymoon phase should be ending soon, and we'll start to grow sick of each other, yet Emma and I are as strong as ever. In fact, our relationship is stronger now than it has been in 24 months. Even with our contrasting personalities and lifestyle enjoyments, we've blended our lives together seamlessly. We work very hard to keep each other happy, but it's never felt like a chore or burden.

Our social calendar is always busy, spending frequent nights out with friends. She gets along great with the guys, and, more importantly, their other halves. The women hang out more than we do, having formed a quick bond they continue to develop with frequent bookstore trips, hikes, and visits to new donut shops and cafes with delicious pastries.

We try to get up to visit my parents at least once a month, making the drive while she sleeps in the passenger seat, holding my hand across the center console. The visits have become less frequent as of late, due in part to Emma's increased workload and the big freaking dreams I've been busting my ass to make happen. I finally spilled the beans and told my parents that what initially started out as a fake dating scheme between the two of us blossomed into something real. Something authentic. Something so fucking wonderful. Every single time I look at Emma, I nearly drown under a new wave of happiness. Again and again, I'm battered by the overwhelming sensation of how goddamn lucky I am to do life by her side.

My mom wasn't fazed by the admission, letting out a laugh and saying it's about time we were honest. Turns out, mothers really do know everything. She picked up pretty early on that we weren't actually together. I guess with Emma, it's been blatantly obvious to everyone but the two of us how I've felt about her all along.

Now? I don't let a day go by where she doesn't know how much I appreciate her.

After five months of dating, she moved into my apartment, saying she only agreed to shack up with me because of the city views. I catch her staring out the window early in the morning, wearing her mismatched socks, a blanket draped over her bare shoulders, smiling at the world below, just like she did the first night she visited my place. Watching her happiness over the little things in life brings me such joy; joy I didn't know existed or could be brought on by another person. While we love the space we've built together in the communal building, I know she's determined to find a stand-alone house for us to live in.

And when she does? I'm buying her every goddamn bookshelf on the surface of this earth. She doesn't know I've already reached out to a local carpenter, tossing around ideas of what kind of built-ins we could construct when we find our permanent residence. I have a ton of things I want to surprise her with.

I'd do anything—and I mean *anything*—to make this woman happy.

"I have an idea," I start, nerves and fear of rejection rearing their ugly heads. I've practiced this dozens of times, but now it's real, and fucking hell, it's terrifying.

"About lunch?" she shields her eyes from the sun and peers up at the steel mammoth of a structure curiously. I could have picked something less gaudy, I suppose. "What does this random building have to do with it?"

"Picture this: Our own law firm. You and me, honey. And whoever else wants to join."

Her neck snaps down and she stares at me, bewildered. "What? What the hell are you talking about?"

Emma got promoted to partner two days after our night at the museum. I left the firm immediately after, taking my time to sort out the next steps professionally and to make sure everything I've been working toward is going to plan. She also stopped her companion services, too; reluctantly letting me pay off the rest of her remaining student loans.

I had a whole speech planned for this moment, but right now words are failing me. I can't remember what I wanted to say. The points I wanted to hit. The plans I wanted to share and the blueprints sitting in my satchel.

"I can't imagine not working next to you. While I've enjoyed the freedom the last couple of years, it's also really freaking lonely, Emma, not having you by my side in an office. Or, more aptly, getting the chance to stand by *your* side. This is step one in world domination."

"Henry Dawson, did you buy me a whole damn building?" she exclaims, and I chuckle.

"Just part of a whole damn building. I'm going to go through this, with or without you, because it's something I've always wanted to do. But sweetheart, you're the best attorney there is. If you want to stay where you are, you know I'll support you. You're doing such a magnificent job and I don't want to take that away. I was entertaining the idea of creating something diverse, inclusive, and revolutionary. Together. Like we talked about years ago."

She gasps, hands flying up to cover her mouth. "Oh my God, how could I say no? Henry, it's amazing! Yes, of course I'll join you!"

I laugh as she wraps her arms around my neck, squealing while I pick her up and spin. "I was so nervous to ask."

"What's step two in world domination? Did you buy a spaceship?"

Settling her back on the concrete, I motion for the door. "I'll show you."

We walk across the quiet lobby. It's a newly developed building, and only a handful of tenants have moved in so far. Filing into the elevator, I press the button for the seventh floor.

"We could bang in here," I suggest.

"Before you even buy the space? I'm sure the future landlords would be thrilled to clean up the mess."

"Mess? Who said anything about a mess? You could just swallow."

She flicks my ear. "I like the mirrors, though. We should do something about that."

"Noted, sweetheart. I'll make our living room look like Versailles."

When the doors open, I grin. I've been to the space dozens of times over the last couple of months, already having plans for desk setups and cubicle areas without putting a deposit down yet.

The room isn't mind-boggling, slightly smaller than where Emma is now but still plenty large to have a decent number of employees. Floor-to-ceiling windows cover the far wall, and beige carpet stretches across the entire space.

"I love the windows," she says, and I beam. I thought of her instantly when I saw them.

"There's something else I want you to see. Go check out what's behind that door." I gesture to a room off to the side. Emma hurries over, pushing open the door and walking inside. I follow leisurely behind, letting her take a minute on her own. A large desk sits in the center, the same windows echoed in here, natural light bathing the room in warmth and brightness. "This is your office."

"Mine?" she breathes out. "It's massive."

"A throne room fit for a queen with plenty of space for your plants. C'mere. Let's talk about names." My arms snake around her waist as we look out the window. "Burns and Dawson."

"No way. Dawson and Burns sounds better."

"I don't care if it sounds better. You're first. Always."

"I'm glad your bedroom practices trickle over to your professional tendencies, too."

I drop my chin to her shoulder. "What if we amended it to something else? Something more dramatic? With more flair?"

"Like what? Dawbu? Buson?"

"Those aren't even words, weirdo. What did you get on your LSAT again?"

"A higher score than you," she retorts, and I give her ass a light smack.

"Touché. What about… Burns-Dawson and Dawson? I like Dawson and Dawson, but I'd be a fool to think you'd surrender your name for anyone. And I'd never ask you to."

Spinning in my hold, she gazes up at me with wide, surprised eyes. "Henry…"

"Look in the desk drawer," I say, jutting my chin toward the lone piece of furniture.

"What? Why?"

"Just do it, baby."

We've talked about the future in great detail. It's obvious we love each other fiercely and know we're going to spend the rest of our lives together. We've been in no rush to commit to the plans, though, enjoying our relationship without a rigid timeline.

I bought the damn ring after only two months together, that's how sure I am about her. Nicole and I spent hours at the mall sifting through diamond options to find the one that was perfectly *Emma*. There was never a doubt in my mind about what eventually happens next.

We've both been so absorbed with our careers, and I know Emma wanted to become completely comfortable in her role before taking on stresses and responsibilities like planning a wedding. The other night we were sitting on the couch, reading our books and enjoying the rainstorm happening outside. I looked over at her when she giggled at her book and *knew* it was time. A flip switched, telling me she was ready. I was ready, too.

Emma gives me a glance before shuffling to the desk. I know what's inside. A ring sitting on a pile of sunflower petals. It's sparkly enough to be dazzling, while not being garish or obnoxious. I drop to my knee, waiting patiently. Her body trembles as she picks up the box and turns to face me.

"Do you remember when you asked me if I believe in marriage?"

"Yes." Her voice is barely above a whisper.

"I said three things: If I ever found a woman who makes me laugh, loves me for my stubbornness, and makes me grin when she walks into a room, I wouldn't be opposed to the idea. You check all the boxes, baby girl. I know you hate clichés. Proposing to you after suggesting we start our own law firm? It's like the epilogue of one of your romance novels, and for that, I apologize. I just couldn't wait any longer."

"I forgive you," she whispers, tears forming in her beautiful blue eyes.

Don't cry, honey.

"Emma." I stare at the carpet, my own eyes filling with tears. "Shit. No one told me it would be this hard. I thought those assholes were exaggerating, but nope. This is painful."

"Hey." She kneels in front of me. "I don't need a speech."

"You deserve a speech. Emma Burns, you are, without a doubt, the greatest joy in my life. I can't sleep without you next to me. I can't get through my day without wondering how you are. I miss you when you're gone, even if it's for only a second. I can't survive without your constant encouragement and faith. You keep my heart beating. You keep my lungs breathing. You keep my ass working toward a better future for us, and you're the most incredible woman I've ever met. Every day I get to spend with you is my favorite day. I could go on and on, but I'm going to end with this: I love you, Emma. I loved you then, years ago, before I knew the depths of my adoration. I loved you in between, falling harder and harder through text messages and unknowing interactions in our office. I love you now, more than words can express, my favorite partner in crime. And I'm going to love you until I depart this earth and haunt you forever. I'm going first, honey, because I can't survive without you. Will you make me the luckiest man in the world and let me be your husband?"

"Yes," she chokes out. I take her hand in mine and slip the ring onto her finger. I knew it would fit. I did a lot of diligent research, wanting to get this exactly right. "It's beautiful."

"I debated putting a tiny Zebra Cake in the center," I murmur.

"Hopefully we can still make some changes," she jokes

through watery sniffs, kissing my palm. "I love you. Then. Now. Forever."

"Maybe I can become Henry Dawson-Burns. Henry Burns-Dawson. Shit, now that I've said it out loud, I like it. I need to make that happen. Let's go to the courthouse tomorrow."

"I like the sound of both of those. And I'd gladly marry you tomorrow. Hell, let's go right now."

"RB. VRG. Zebra Cakes. My sweet, sweet, Emma. Honey. Sunflower. You are my light in the darkness and the warm, sunny good thing on the gloomy, cloudy, chilly days. My forever and always, ultimate dream girl. You never gave up on me, even when I didn't deserve you. Even when I messed up. You came back for me."

"I'm never giving up on you, Henry. You're the best companion project I've ever had."

"The last one too, I hope," I add.

She shrugs, looking down at her new diamond. "I don't know. Someone asked me to go to a banquet with them tonight. I think I might be busy now."

I growl, scooping her into my arms and walking to the desk.

"You're damn right you are."

"I can't wait to spend the rest of my life with you, Henry Burns-Dawson."

"Together forever, honey. You and me."

ALSO BY CHELSEA CURTO

An Unexpected Paradise

***

Stay tuned for a new holiday romance publishing in late 2022, as well as Patrick and Lola's book in early 2023!

ACKNOWLEDGMENTS

Thank you, reader, for giving me a chance. I hope you enjoyed Henry and Emma. If you didn't, that's okay too! I'm thankful you took the time to read something I created. It means the world to me.

Thank you to Brynn, Delaney, Katie, Mel, and Stephanie for offering to beta read for me. I appreciate all your feedback so much!

Thank you to Katie and Sarah for always jumping in and re-reading what I've already written multiple times. You two are fantastic.

Thank you, Kristen, from the bottom of my heart. When I reached out and asked you to beta read the changed version, I didn't think it would make us close friends. I'm so glad it did, though, because you're simply wonderful, and I'm so excited to watch you chase your editing dreams and goals!

To the MFers—y'all keep me going. You make me laugh. You help me find the words I need to finish sentences. You motivate and encourage me. You're wonderful, kind, fantastic people… and I'm so glad I get to call you my friends. I love y'all way too much.

Mom, Dad, Courtney, Grams & little Riley—again, thank you for being the best family in the word. I love you!

Thank you, Brooke, for being such a wonderful proofreader. I appreciate all your hard work and your thoughtful suggestions. You're the best!

To Sam—the cover artist of my dreams. You are INCREDIBLE. You make me want to keep writing books so they can have your beautiful work on the front. Thank you for working me with me and putting up with my unhinged reactions to the drafts you send my way. I can't wait to see what else you come up with, you talented genius!

Mikey and Riley—my favorite guys! I love you. When we're old and eating the same three meals we eat today, I'll still be smiling. Thanks for telling me to keep working hard. One day I'll buy you a jet ski. I promise!

ABOUT THE AUTHOR

Chelsea Curto splits her time between Winter Park, Florida and Boston, Massachusetts, where she's based as a flight attendant. When she's not busy writing, she loves to read, travel, go to theme parks, run, eat tacos, hang out with friends and pet dogs. *The Companion Project* is her second novel, and she has plenty more in the works.

instagram.com/chelseareadsandwrites
tiktok.com/@chelseareadsandwrites
twitter.com/creadsandwrites

Made in the USA
Las Vegas, NV
25 November 2022